EAST RENFREWSHIRE

09453881

KT-167-159

AGENTS of

CL 1/17

Return this item by the last date shown.
Items may be renewed by telephone or at
www.ercultureandleisure.org/libraries

east renfrewshire
CULTURE and **LEISURE**

Barrhead:	0141 577 3518	Mearns:	0141 577 4979
Busby:	0141 577 4971	Neilston:	0141 577 4981
Clarkston:	0141 577 4972	Netherlee:	0141 637 5102
Eaglesham:	0141 577 3932	Thornliebank:	0141 577 4983
Giffnock:	0141 577 4976	Uplawmoor:	01505 850564

BY THE SAME AUTHOR

Power Play
Of Cops & Robbers
The Revenge Trilogy:
Payback
Killer Country
Black Heart

AGENTS of the STATE

Mike NICOL

First published in the United Kingdom in 2017 by Old Street Publishing Ltd,
Yowlestone House, Tiverton, Devon EX16 8LN
www.oldstreetpublishing.co.uk

First published in South Africa by Umuzi, an imprint of Penguin Random House

ISBN 978 1 910400 51 7

Copyright © Mike Nicol, 2016

The right of Mike Nicol to be identified as the author of this work has been asserted
by him in accordance with the Copyright, Designs and Patents Act 1988.

Every effort has been made obtain permission for all illustrations, but in the event of an
omission the publisher should be contacted.

All rights reserved. No part of this publication may be reproduced, stored in or
introduced into a retrieval system, or transmitted, in any form, or by any means
(electronic, mechanical, photocopying, recording or otherwise) without the prior written
permission of the publisher.

10 9 8 7 6 5 4 3 2 1

A CIP catalogue record for this title is available from the British Library.

Printed and bound in Great Britain

For Kate, one day
For Tamzon and Anthony, now

PART ONE

A NECESSARY KILL

1

They met on the parking deck of the tampon towers. As ordered. Out in the open. Late afternoon. Cape Town city sweating below in heat and humidity. Heat coming off the mountain as from a furnace, pulsing.

Three men told the western tower's parking lot, top floor, third bay. Told, today, Sunday, 18:30. Told the car: a Honda Civic. Keys on the visor. Guns in the boot. Told the target. Told wear beach clothes, т-shirts, shorts, nothing fancy. Told the target's locus.

All this conveyed individually in the morning by phone. Told don't introduce yourselves. No names, no recoil. Told afterwards bring the car back. Keys on the visor. Guns in the boot. Go home separately.

Joey Curtains got there first. Joey Curtains was cautious. Being cautious kept you alive.

Had a friend drop him off in the street below, strolled up casually through the complex, went behind the apartment blocks to approach off the mountain in case there was surveillance. Found a place in shade where he could check out the scene. The car was there. Couple of other cars on the deck. During the hours he watched, people coming and going from their apartments in the towers, no one noticing him. People with beach towels, squash rackets, gym bags, shopping carriers. An ordinary Sunday afternoon.

Took him an hour before he noticed another watcher: five floors up at an open window, someone with binoculars. Couldn't tell if it was a man or a woman. The surveillance though, very thorough.

Except from where he sat he reckoned the watcher hadn't spotted him.

Joey Curtains smiled. 'Ja, my bru,' he said to himself, 'you is on the nail without fail.'

Quarter past six a short man arrived, dressed to order. Went straight to the car, checked for the keys, looked in the boot. Went over to the parapet, stood smoking, gazing down on the city. A perspiration sheen to his shaved head. An older man, thick set, maybe in his early fifties, probably a war veteran in the eyes of Joey Curtains.

Joey Curtains watched the watcher. The person up there on the fifth floor taking it all in, the binocs focused on the short man.

Couple of minutes later another man popped out of the stairwell. Jaunty. Springy. This one about Joey's height, tallish, same wiry build. Same age, late twenties. Sort of guy looked like he could run a long way. Joey Curtains could run a long way. This one also dressed to order, sporting a peak cap.

The two men greeted one another, stood now beside the car waiting. Joey Curtains let the clock tick to five minutes after six thirty, watching the watcher at the window, scanning everywhere. Probably starting to worry, probably poeping himself. The men at the car now antsy, the short one checking the time on his cellphone. The two of them deciding, let's go.

Joey Curtains sauntered out.

'My champs,' he said in Xhosa, going through the whole how are you, I am well greeting. Switched to English, 'Sorry for the time, my brothers, Sunday slowness.' He patted the car. 'Nice car. Fast car, hey? Reliable. Not like those Golfs they usually got for us. At last they give us proper tools.' The men grunted at him. Strict protocol: keep the talk to the job, no names.

He glanced from one man to the other. 'Where's the hardware?'

The older one got a bag out of the boot. Said in Xhosa, it was past time they went. Said he would be driving.

'Hey, champ,' said Joey Curtains, 'English or Afrikaans, please, man.'

The driver said, 'You're late, my friend. Where is your discipline?'

Joey Curtains said, 'African time, my bru. So what's a few minutes?'

The other man made a crack in Xhosa about coloureds always being full of shit, called coloureds bushies. Joey Curtains let it go, pretending he didn't understand. Laughed with the men as if he shared the joke.

Bushie, hey, they better be thankful they got a bushie with them. The only brains in the car.

He opened the back door, left-hand side. Before he got in, glanced up at the watcher in the window, waved. The person up there taking a step back out of the line of sight.

The driver noticed, said, 'Who's that?'

'Someone checking we're on the job,' said Joey Curtains. 'You got to watch out, champ. Keep your eyes open. Check your back. You know what they say, mos, man who looks back sees the ghosts. Old Chinese proverb I heard from a Chinaman. One day the Chinks shot him in the heart cos he was looking the wrong way.' Joey Curtains laughed. 'Sometimes you can't win.'

The two men didn't laugh. The driver cursed in his language, the jaunty one half-turned to Joey Curtains said, 'Enough, my brother.'

Joey Curtains shrugged, settled on the back seat, wiped sweat off his face. 'Some air-con, please, man, wind it up.'

The men looked at him.

'What? Hey, what?'

The jaunty one drew two fingers across his lips.

'Ag, my brothers ...' Joey Curtains let it go there, thinking, of all the hitters he could be teamed with, had to be two serious darkies. Serious like Aquarius. Not. Whatta joyride it was going to be.

They drove out of the Disa Towers, down Derry into Mill Street.

Joey Curtains said, 'Some more air-con, come'n man, it's fry city in here.' At the traffic lights with Hatfield, Joey Curtains unzipped the bag with the guns. Whistled. 'Very nice. Very nice. Revolvers, hey. Taurus. Nice little snubnose, The Judge, they call it.' He picked one up. 'Someone doesn't want to risk a pistol jam. Going to make a loud noise without silencers.' He spun the cylinder. 'Probably what they wants, lots of confusion. Close work with this little barrel.' He passed the gun between the seats to the jaunty man. The driver freaked.

'What you doing? What you doing? Everyone can see here. Keep them in the bag. No, no, no.' Smacking the steering wheel with each beat. Going into a string of Xhosa that had the jaunty one sniggering. He took the gun though.

'Better check it,' said Joey. 'Sometimes they put in blanks jus for fun. I've known it. Happened to my chommie. He's got this job, a home job, he pulls off two – pop, pop – but the target's still staring at him. Shit scared. Pissing himself. But sitting there in his comfy chair in his comfy lounge alive and well, staring at my chommie. He has to pull off two more. Okay, they do the job. But, listen, hey, listen, the fifth one's a blank also. Six-shot chamber, they packed in only five, only two for real. My chommie he gets back, he's spitting like a cobra. He can't speak, his words come out in a hiss. Everybody jokes with him, says, don't take it serious, was just for a laugh. Job like that you only need one time. My chommie doesn't see the joke. He smacks this armoury captain, bliksems him right over a counter. Oke has to have two pins put in his jaw. True story. Really. Honest to God. Really. So, you see, what I do now, I check every time, leave nothing to chance, nothing to nobody. Know what I mean?'

'Bullshit,' said the jaunty one. 'That's bullshit.'

'True story, my brother. True story,' said Joey Curtains. Caught the driver's eyes in the rear-view mirror staring at him.

'Enough. Okay, enough.' The driver's eyes bulging with anger. 'We are not to talk.'

'Alright, Chief, just saying, just saying.' Joey Curtains dug an envelope from the bag, slipped out three colour photographs of the target. 'Was wondering how we supposed to pick out the target?' He studied the photographs. 'Mr Handsome. Not someone you can miss.' He tapped the jaunty man on the shoulder. 'Better get an eyeful, champ, don't want to shoot the wrong man. They put that in your file you never get promotion.'

While the jaunty man looked at the photographs, Joey Curtains checked his gun. Everything in place, all the chambers filled with the real deal. Five hollowpoints. He placed the revolver back in the bag. The time now: 18:50. The service would have started.

The driver turned off Orange into Queen Victoria, found a parking space outside the French embassy.

Joey Curtains looked around. Nice part of town, this corner. Reminded him of his childhood. Coming here with his granny to play in the Company's Garden on Sundays. Feed the fish breadcrumbs. Throw peanuts to the squirrels. Sometimes have a Coke float at the café. Coming in on the train, walking up Adderley Street, touching the Slave Lodge like his granny said. Why we got to do that, Granny? Because bad things happened here, Joey. Don't forget. Yeah, bad things still happening.

'Hey, my champs,' said Joey Curtains pushing away the memories, 'how about some music?'

The jaunty man pressed buttons on the radio, up came Cape Talk's golden oldies: Aretha Franklin's 'Say a Little Prayer' playing.

'Every time you listen on a Sunday they play this,' said Joey

Curtains. 'Like the DJ's hot for Aretha. Must be really old he can remember so far back.'

'No talking,' said the driver. He pulled out his cellphone, keyed an SMS.

Joey Curtains sat back. Aretha morphed into Petula Clark into Roberta Flack 'The First Time Ever ...' He picked up the photograph, leant forward to wave it between the two men. Said, 'Champs, the first time ever I saw this face ...'

The jaunty one snorted.

The driver said, 'Where's your respect?'

Joey Curtains wasn't sure if he meant Roberta or the man in the photograph.

'Nice song. Very soulful.'

2

Kaiser Vula placed himself on the aisle in the seventh pew from the holy end. Liked St George's cathedral, the late sun at the stained-glass windows. The organ grinding out some Bachish tune. People coming in for evening service, some in their best, some like they'd nipped off the beach in flip-flops and T-shirts. Everyone shuffling around, heads bowed. Kids whispering. The robed guys tending candles, laying out the communion stuff on the white lace.

Kaiser Vula eased up off his knees. Anglicans had this thing about being on their knees, the cushions as hard as the floor. Something to do with penance. Not a lesson he'd taken on board. Some medieval thing whiteys got hooked into, couldn't let go even in the modern world. As he recalled from his choirboy days.

Sat back, had to reach round to shift the pistol digging into his hip. A little 9mm Ruger centrefire, seven plus one, with a blued finish. Ten-centimetre barrel, a grip that disappeared into his fist. He had it in his fist, Kaiser Vula's finger almost filled the trigger guard. Big man, Kaiser Vula. Big man who liked the little Ruger. You put a load from the Ruger on the money, you could relax. No one was going to tell you I'll be back.

Kaiser Vula laid those big hands in his lap. Hot hands, his palms moist. An evening too hot for a jacket. What could you do? Didn't want to get the worshippers jazzed at the sight of some hardware, no matter the beauty of that hardware. So you had to wear a jacket. He exhaled a stream of air at his hands, felt the cool.

Ah, man, sticky humid February.

The other reason he liked the cathedral was Kaiser Vula remembered those student days of running battles with the cops through the city's streets, ducking into the cathedral to hide from the Boere. Lying among the pews, hardly daring to breathe. Crying from the teargas. Heady stuff, those Struggle days.

Turned his head. To his right, across the aisle, three rows up, the colonel with his family. Wife, two sons, a daughter, the children sitting demure between mom and dad. Young kids, ranged maybe three to ten, well behaved, private-schooled. A perfect family.

Like his own. Many similarities: the military rank, except he was a major, the trappings of wellbeing, the wife, three children, except he had only one son. A penchant for golf on Wednesday afternoons. A taste for whisky. Expensive single-malt whisky. At the thought Kaiser Vula could feel the smoothness of an Islay in his mouth, even smell the fumes, thick, peaty.

He shook his head to dislodge the craving. Looked again at the family, dressed smart-casual, as his would be for church. The colonel in a white open-necked shirt, the two boys in blue golf shirts. Mother and daughter wearing dresses. A pretty picture. Expensive frocks. Not Woolworths. Something designer.

One thing about the colonel, he didn't do brands. Kept his profile down, no bling, no ostentation. His wife too. Unusual trait to Kaiser Vula's way of thinking. Colonels out of uniform, if you could get them out of uniform, more inclined to the stereotype: heavy watches, gold chains, top fashion clothing. Their women too. Young women usually. Not like Colonel Abel Kolingba and his family. Mrs Kolingba in her forties. Good-looking woman, did a lot of gym work and jogging. Kept herself trim. Name of Cynthia. A brainy type, he remembered from the file, degrees from French universities, into gazing at the heavens, not that she'd done much of that in recent years. Kept in touch with other astronomers despite everything. A linguist too, her own language, Sango, French, English, German. Difficult situation for a woman like that.

You looked at them you'd think executive family, maybe riding on black economic empowerment, owned a high-end suv, lived in some gated estate down the peninsula, wife did book clubs, family had holidays at Sun City. You'd be right, according to the file, except for the bit about the executive. Instead you'd read Colonel Kolingba was planning a palace coup. Take his country out of its violent chaos.

Kaiser Vula was up on the file. Had no opinions on the colonel. No opinions on his politics. Kaiser Vula did what he was told. A good soldier. A good major. Only thing, Kaiser Vula never wore a uniform.

In the row behind the Kolingbas two security. Pumped-up steroid types in black suits, had to be overheating. Their shirt armpits soggy. Probably the sweat running down their spines. Those suits the pits. Kaiser Vula knew. He'd done a stint in the goon squads. Two decades back when everyone came home to the new country. He glanced round at another bodyguard standing at the back. Knew there were two more outside on the pavement. All of them wired up. The colonel one cautious man. With good reason.

In his trouser pocket, Kaiser Vula's cellphone vibrated: an SMS. No need to read it. He knew what it said: Everything in place.

Good.

Right on time.

Good.

Out of the vestry came the bishop in his purple vestments, smiling. Raised his hands, the congregation standing. A short beseech for mercy on high, the first hymn. One Kaiser Vula dimly recalled.

> Behold the sun, that seem'd but now
> Enthroned overhead
> Beginneth to decline below
> The globe whereon we tread:
> And he whom yet we look upon
> With comfort and delight
> Will quite depart from hence anon,
> And leave us to the night.

The major sang through to the end of the second verse, closed the hymnal, stepped out of the pew. A man opposite, his mouth filled with song, looked at him. A glance of disinterest that Kaiser Vula didn't acknowledge. Nodded more than bowed quickly towards the altar, then, eyes hooded, shoulders bent, strode down the aisle. Could feel the goons watching him. Made no eye contact, sloped outside into the evening heat, fumbling to bring his cellphone to his ear. Knew the bodyguards posted on the cathedral steps would be tracking him. Wonderful ruse, the cellphone. Paused near them, said loudly, anxiously into the phone. 'I'm coming. I'll see you at the hospital.' Hurried away up Wale Street.

To his car, parked a block higher, other side of the road, a more or less clear line of sight through the palm trees to the cathedral entrance. Kaiser Vula took off his jacket, laid it along the Golf's back seat. Closed the door, opened the driver's, stood looking down at the church. The two security men outside, beneath the trees, beyond them people leaving the Company's Garden, slow Sunday traffic passing the Slave Lodge on the curve into Wale. All fine.

The sun had left the high buildings. Behind them the mountain face would be in shadow. The city quiet, tourists at the pavement cafés, people relieved at the end of the day's heat, relaxing in the twilight. Out on the western rim, the sun would bulge a moment as if it truly sank into the sea.

3

Kaiser Vula slid behind the steering wheel, hitched his slacks where they were tight across his knees. Breathed in the smell of new car: polish, leather, cleanliness warm in his nostrils. From his belt brought out the Ruger, placed it in the cubbyhole. Clipped his cellphone into the hands-free holder. From under the seat pulled a small pair of Bushnell birding binoculars. Adjusted the focus, paid attention to the two guards. They leant against the cathedral wall, smoking, gazing at the drift of pedestrians making for the station. Bored. As Vula'd been as a bodyguard. The sheer tedium. Then the need to be alert. To see everything. To react to what was out of place. To recognise what was wrong.

Nothing was wrong. Everything was as it should be. In the

parking lot beside the cathedral, the colonel's black Fortuner, tinted windows, bulletproof panels in the doors. The driver in place. The support vehicles for the security in Queen Victoria Street: Audi A4s, no stinting on the price tag. By now they would have flat tyres, both front left against the kerb.

Nothing to do but wait.

He waited. Fifteen minutes. Twenty. In the cathedral they'd be full voice with the second hymn. Kaiser Vula put the binoculars on the site: the bodyguards now away from the building, the one talking into his cellphone, the other focused on the crypt notice board. Ah, the job's tedium.

His cellphone vibrated, the name Marc on the screen. Marc, Kaiser Vula's codename for Nandi, the lovely Nandi.

Made him click his tongue.

Kaiser Vula dropped the binoculars in his lap, connected her.

'Darl,' she said. 'When're you getting here? People are chilling already.'

He pictured it. Her chic apartment, the balcony with the view over the Waterfront. Over the whole of Table Bay. Evening like this, the beautiful people'd be looking at a glassy sea, the white scythe of beach, the lights taking hold in the twilight haze. Very Cape Town lifestyle. Glossy, chic, theirs.

He could hear voices. Laughter. The laughter of good times. Music. Adele. Adele was Nandi's soundtrack.

'What're you wearing?' he said.

She laughed. 'The Chanel. The one we bought in Paris.'

That voice of hers, the good-school accent, no sound of the townships.

'Underneath.'

'Kaisy, darl ...' Surprise in there. Playfulness. A pause.

He imagined her lips, pink lipstick, silky. Imagined her turning away from the guests, seeking privacy. Where? On the deck? Facing into the towers of downtown? Smiling to herself.

'What d'you mean … underneath?'

'Tell me.'

'Kaisy!'

'Tell me.'

'Alright.' Drawing out the syllables, teasing him.

'Tell me.' He kept his voice hard. 'Are you wearing a bra?'

'No, my bra,' she said, making a joke of it. 'Not with this dress. Doesn't need one. You know.'

'Touch your nipples.'

'Ah, darl. That's for you.'

'Do it. Make them rise up.' He could see her in the dress, the thin material, the rise of her nipples pressed against the fabric. She had long nipples. Nipples you could get your tongue around. 'Yes, you've got them hard?'

'They're good girls.'

Kaiser Vula shifted on the seat, tugged more room into the crotch of his slacks.

'Run your hand down,' he said.

'I'm doing that, darl,' she came back.

'Now tell me, what's underneath?'

'A thong.'

'Which one?'

'The one you bought. The black one.'

'Take it off.'

A pause.

'Take it off.'

A whispered, 'I can't, babe, not here, I'm on the deck.'

'Take it off.'

Again a pause. He could hear her breathe.

'Wait, I'm doing it.'

Imagining the silk sliding down her thighs, dropped, a pool of material around her high heels. She'd have to step away.

'Pick it up.' She'd have to crouch, the dress was too short for her to bend. 'Have you got it?'

'I'm holding it.'

'Is it warm?'

'Yes.'

'Smell it.'

He heard her draw air through her nostrils.

'What's the smell?'

'Me.'

'Yes, yes. What?'

'Soap. Lotion. Herbs.'

'And?'

'Me.'

'And?'

'Musty me.'

'Throw it over the balcony.'

'I …'

'Do it.' He waited to the count of three. 'Have you done it?'

'I've dropped it.'

'Who's seen you?'

'No one.'

'What're they doing?'

'Drinking. Talking.'

'Touch yourself.'

He heard her gasp.

'Yes.'

'I've got to go,' he said. 'I'll be there soon.' Kaiser Vula disconnected, sat back, sweating, sweaty in the humid air. Closed his eyes: saw Nandi, the lovely Nandi, in her short dress, thongless on the balcony. Breathed out, not a sigh, just a long exhalation.

That girl.

Kaiser Vula brought his attention back to the street, to the knot of people on the steps of the cathedral. The service must have finished. Lifted his binoculars. Saw the family emerging, shaking hands with the bishop. Cynthia Kolingba and the two boys ahead, the colonel and his daughter behind. Behind them three security guards. The goons on the pavement moving through the people, shepherding the family towards the car park. The Fortuner's driver had the doors open, probably the engine running.

Kaiser Vula fired the ignition of his car, kept the binoculars on the dispersing worshippers.

At the Queen Victoria Street traffic lights a white Honda Civic stopped. Two men got out on the left-hand side. Young men in T-shirts, board shorts, trainers. One going round the front, the other round the back of the car. Striding across the street. A lithe hop onto the pavement, four, five paces down the pavement, the men reaching behind, under their T-shirts to pull out revolvers. Raising them. Shooting.

Kaiser Vula counted three shots, a pause, two more shots. Saw the colonel go down, the daughter falling with him. Saw the mother and two boys being forced down by the bodyguards. Saw one of the shooters take a bullet in the face, collapse. The remaining one sprinting for the Civic.

Kaiser Vula eased his car into Burg Street, drove slowly away round Greenmarket Square. Had gone three blocks when he heard the sirens, the cops quick on this one. Almost too quick.

Yes, well. There would be news in due course about the outcome.

4

From a bench on Government Avenue, Mart Velaze phoned in his report. Heard the Voice say, 'Wait, Chief, wait one minute, okay.' Then: 'Now I'm with you. All ears.' In that minute gazed up at the mountain behind the white towers of the Cape Town Synagogue, across at two lovers getting among one another on the lawn. Off to his left, children throwing breadcrumbs into the fish ponds. The mommy doing a record on her cellphone despite the dying light, the daddy looking bored, like he'd rather be watching soccer. No one worrying about the wail of sirens in the city.

The Voice came on: 'Talk to me, Chief. What's happening? Tell me things.'

'It happened,' said Mart Velaze.

A silence. This's what the Voice did. Thoughtful silences. Mart Velaze well used to them, long enough part of the Voice's unit. Over the last year survived witch-hunts, enquiries, debriefs, probes, official warnings. 'Stick with me, Chief, you'll be alright.' He had. Kept his head down, become a Teflon man. For all this, knew nothing about her, though. Nothing about who she reported to. 'Off the books, Chief. Black ops, black, black, black,' she'd said at his recruitment. 'As if we aren't black enough anyhow.' Laughed at her own joke. Her voice slightly husky, always calm.

From her tone Mart Velaze pictured her slim in tailored suits, white blouses. A silver chain necklace. Unmarried. Self-sufficient, self-contained, alone in her office that could be anywhere, handling agents she never met. A lonely job. Just with her secure phones, her internet connections.

'You've got photographs?'

'Of them meeting. Of the operation.'

'Good. They complete the task?'

'Looked like it. The little daughter too.'

'That's bad. That's not nice.'

A silence.

Mart Velaze saw the young family holding hands, moving away. Going home.

'Listen, Chief, a couple of things, okay. One, there's talk, rumours, you know, things I've heard that there's a restless group, mostly communists, could be up to naughty things. Things like what the Yankees call a wet job. You know this term?'

Mart Velaze lied, said he didn't.

'You can Google it. There you can find it means assassination. Like what's just happened to the poor colonel. Only for the restless ones, their target is the president.'

'Serious?'

'Serious. But, Chief, Chief, this's hands off. Ears only. Strictly. Okay, you with me here? If it's happening, if you hear any whispers, ours is not to stop it. A name I've heard mention who could be involved is Henry Davidson. One of our own, one of the old boys. So, like with the colonel's wet job, we're surveillance only. Information only. No action. You got me, Chief? We stay out of it.'

Mart Velaze said he understood.

'Good. Then number two,' she sniggered. 'Be a good idea to help the colonel's wife. Show her we're a democracy. Don't like refugees being shot down after church. Give her some pointers at this sad time. You can do that?'

Mart Velaze said he could.

'Excellent, Chief. That's it for the moment. Go with the ancestors.'

Mart Velaze disconnected. The lovers had disconnected too. Were packing up their picnic. Now in the twilight hour, the face of Table Mountain dark.

5

Three days later, Wednesday: 23:30. Vicki Kahn took KLM 598 out of Cape Town for Schiphol, Amsterdam. Cape Town in the low thirties c all day, Vicki well pleased to be getting out of it. Had laid down two thousand on a pick six for the Saturday races at Kenilworth, expected a tidy homecoming. Right there and then Vicki Kahn revving her life.

During the flight Vicki plugged into Melissa Etheridge on her iPad, '4th Street Feeling', her thoughts drifting below Melissa's voice. Especially the song about being rocked and rolled all night long. Made her think of her own love life. Of Fish Pescado the surfer dude who did her rocking and rolling. Just the thought of him made her smile.

Then sometime in the night, somewhere over the equator, came the realisation: she was on a mission. Her first overseas mission. Full-on cloak and dagger.

'This's what we do, Vicki.' His words.

His words to her about this specific assignment.

Thursday 10:10, Vicki flew in to Schiphol, the plane docking at gate E17. Vicki got off feeling weird, nauseous. Maybe the flight or the food or both. Found her way down the E terminal concourse to the passport control access to B terminal.

The passport officer asked what she did, she told him company lawyer. Meeting other company lawyers in Berlin. He stamped her Schengen, said nothing, looked her square in the face without expression. Vicki stared back, picked up her passport, flicked her hair. The nausea unabated.

Got through the security check no hassle. Walked down the shopping concourse to Bubbles, this seafood and wine bar at the confluence of the spokes for c and B gates. The nausea at the back of her throat.

'You're not there to eat oysters, no no, no sipping a French white, Vicki, you hear me.' Her boss again. The last thing on her mind right now.

Her boss Henry Davidson. How he'd hung in through all the changes was beyond logic. This Tyrannosaurus white from the hated regime. Had to be he had dirt on people. You tracked him, he'd gone from Security Branch to the reformed National Intelligence Agency now State Security Agency. Okay maybe nowhere near the top but still had his finger in. Bewigged Henry with his blazers. A brown wig. She'd seen pictures of Henry in those blazers wearing a cravat. Nowadays favoured a tie in the dark range, green to blue. Sometimes with stripes, mostly without. On Fridays his old boy's tie, stripes of yellow and blue: Rondebosch Boys' High School. The network. The alliance. The syndicate. The gang. One thing about Cape Town there were gangs in every class of society. The high-end gangs hadn't changed much: same schools, same way of working, clubs and pubs, only their skin hue was darker nowadays. Dark rumour too that Henry the Communist had been a mole all those dangerous years. Was still faithful to the cause. He and his comrade relics singing the Internationale in their hi-tech kitchens: 'This is the final struggle ...' The image making her smile.

Vicki bought a bottle of water from the quick food across from Bubbles, drank off a mouthful, the nausea subsiding. But now a tenderness to her breasts.

Some leather couches nearby with a view over a section of the airport. A place people spending hours and hours in transit could relax. Very considerate of the Dutch. Take a seat there, wait, were her instructions. Watch the aeroplanes through the big windows. Wait. Not a bad way to spend the morning. She did. Kept on hearing Melissa being a hundred miles from Kansas City.

This morning snow lay everywhere. Except it'd been cleared from the aprons and runways, ploughed into heaps. The flat expanses glistening in low sunlight. The temperature out there minus six, if you believed the pilot. His way of a landing welcome. The sky a faint blue, hazy. Not a single reason that Vicki could imagine why you'd want to live in a place like this.

6

Half an hour before the meeting time, Vicki stopped watching
the aeroplanes. Saw off an Air France 737 Boeing then swapped
her seat for a couch facing the concourse. Wanted to see her
contact arrive. Didn't want a sudden tap on the shoulder, Are
you Vicki Kahn?

To pass the minutes placed bets on people coming through
the area. Five to two on a woman with a shaved head wheeling
an airport trolley. It wouldn't be her. It wasn't. Vicki collected
from the imaginary bookie. Two to one on a tall classiness with
a sling bag and an elegant coat, pixie-style haircut. The
woman's eyes brushed over her and she thought, oh-oh, you
lost, Vics. But Ms Pixie moved on.

Only things Vicki knew, the person she was to meet was a
woman. A troubled woman. This much she'd been told over
lunch up at the café on top of Table Mountain. Just her and her
boss yesterday, hot windless yesterday, having taken the cable
car up with the tourists, stared down at the city for a while,
then walked over the lumpy ground to the café. Admired the
view way down on Camps Bay beach first. 'Pleased I'm not
there,' Henry Davidson had said. 'Frying my skin into cancer.
Cannot afford to with all the cancer spots I get each year. White
skin is a death certificate, Vicki, consider yourself lucky.' He'd
touched her arm. Vicki'd moved slightly away from him, half a
step to the left, almost imperceptible but there all the same.
And he'd noticed it.

From the buffet they'd helped themselves to pie and chips,
a glass of white wine each. Taken a window table. Henry
Davidson all manners and the lady sits first. Had tucked his
paper serviette into his collar so it stuck there like a small flag.
Said, 'Bon, bon,' hacked into his pie. Vicki suppressed a grin.

Tried to raise the cathedral shooting, still nothing coming up on that yet, but he wasn't biting. 'Not our playing field,' he waved it off. 'They haven't got much evidence yet, as the White Rabbit said to Alice.' Henry Davidson always quick with his Alice quotes. Offered instead office chit-chat, known gossip.

Vicki listened, half-listened. Not a bad pie, she'd thought, for a tourist trap, washing the last mouthful down with a swig of wine. The chips done in fresh oil at least. Not haute cuisine, then again, up on this mountain, looking over this city on a clear day, all the container ships in the bay, who really cared if it wasn't? You were having a great holiday in an exotic destination. The pie filled a spot.

Halfway through the meal, her boss said, 'I want you to meet someone at Schiphol airport tomorrow.' Like he was asking her to meet someone at a Waterfront restaurant, not fly halfway round the world. 'This person's got something for us on a flash drive. Could be very useful.'

'This person? At Schiphol airport?'

Which was when he'd said, 'This is what we do, Vicki. Sometimes it's inconvenient. We have to act fast. If you don't like it, go back to straight law.'

Straight law being a put down.

Boring company merges. Contracts. Litigation. Tax fights. Intellectual property protections.

'I've done that,' Vicki'd said. 'That's why I'm here. That's why I joined.' Joined the State Security Agency. Not that law was a requirement. Some pretty hectic training went with the job: weapons expertise, shooting sessions, unarmed combat, surveillance techniques, anti-surveillance measures. Strange requirements needed for an analyst's position. But interesting. One thing pleased her: her old wound didn't play up during the training. Nobody would've known she'd taken a bullet through the gut.

To her boss she said, 'This person, does he have a name?'

'This person is a she,' Davidson said. 'Linda Nchaba to give her a name. A model. Background bio, cellphone, email details on file. Not much else. Made contact a couple of hours ago by phone about some trafficking organisation. Children mostly. She may or may not be involved. For what it's worth, the hawks in the Aviary believe she is. Now having a crisis of conscience, which is all to the good, is it not?' Hardly expecting an answer, forking pie delicately into his mouth.

'She will ask if you are you, then introduce herself. You just get across there. Have a chat with her in transit. Let her know how friendly we are, let her know that we can be of help. Take possession of the flash drive, but she is the real reward. We need to bring her home. First prize, Vicki. First prize. Easier said than done, of course, especially as she sounds frightened. Scared witless, I would say. My experience, these types, no good rushing them. Got to get their confidence. You know, catchee monkey technique. Talk to her, set up another rendezvous, give her a few days to think things over. Meet her anywhere she wants: Paris, Frankfurt, Zurich, Berlin. Tell her you will be in touch the next day.'

Had raised his head to glance at her, smiled. 'Then something personal. I thought that after your tête-à-tête and while you're trying to get the stricken Linda on side, you might like a short diversion to Germany. Meet someone in Berlin for a chat, an elderly fellow, not the perfect gentleman. Detlef Schroeder is his name. A long-time associate, diagnosed with liver cancer. Such a shame.' Henry Davidson looking out over the Twelve Apostles, pursed his lips the way he did after a pronouncement. 'Terrible thing this cancer. Like a plague really.' Snapped back to her. Vicki noticing his wig shifted slightly. 'So you have a little talk with Detlef, after that you make contact with Linda again. Persuade her to come home to the protection of our bosom.' A dab of the paper serviette at the corner of his mouth. 'Nice little assignment, don't you think? Jetting about the Continent. Dropping in on the old spy capital. Lovely little diversion in your routine. Some of your colleagues going to be jealous. The Queen would want your head.'

Vicki'd ignored the reference. Asked, 'What'm I meeting him for?'

Henry Davidson had put his finger to his lips. 'Shh, this is a secret. A family secret.' Sat there importantly like the March Hare. All she'd get out of him.

A family secret. The only family that'd ever been in Europe was her aunt. Assassinated by a knifeman in the Paris Metro back in the Struggle days. Stories that she'd been in Berlin, too, living on handouts. Been to most of the major cities in the service of the liberation movement. Could only be about that. Typical of Henry to dangle some bait. Like he got some perverse pleasure out of it.

Vicki flicked her attention back to Schiphol's here and now.

The next black woman into the area to the side of Bubbles Seafood and Wine Bar had short pointy dreads, very cute. Nah, Vicki thought. Not this one. She took long odds, and won. Same with another three who circled through the area, went into the toilets or went off elsewhere. Caught in the restless swirl of in-transit.

Right on the dot there was a leggy woman with braids, skinny jeans, boots, roll-neck top, a coat with mock fur edging the hem and cuffs. The coat open showing off a tight figure with a tight waist. Could be, Vicki thought. Figure like that she could be a model. Back home definitely. In Schiphol you could have higher odds. Decided to go three to one this was Linda Nchaba. Could hear the bookie saying, Come'n, sweetheart, where's your money? Vicki reassessed, went for two to one in favour. And won.

7

The woman came up to her, asked if she was who she was.

'I am,' said Vicki Kahn. Left it there, waiting for the woman to take it up.

'My name's Linda Nchaba,' said Linda Nchaba, not offering to shake hands.

Sat down next to Vicki, dug in her leather bag, showed her a flash drive. Silver thing with an orange top. Didn't give it to Vicki, kept it locked in her right fist.

Vicki glanced from the woman's fist to her face. Linda had lovely skin. Expensive skin. Skin with a sheen of health, youth, clean living. Skin that knew beauty treatments, nightly emollients of brand-name care products. Vicki thought, probably we use the same lotions. Could ask her: What moisturiser do you prefer? The two of them going into girl talk about creams, lipsticks even. A way of approaching the reason they were there: the flash drive, the business of Linda Nchaba returning home. A way of getting Linda Nchaba to relax. Because for sure Linda Nchaba was not relaxed.

To look at her, the shape of her, her deportment, Vicki could see Linda Nchaba on the catwalk. Not much of that in the file though. If that was the legal way she earned her bucks, it should've been good money. No need to freelance.

The woman sitting there with the flash drive clutched in her fist. Sat there hesitant, her eyes everywhere but focused on Vicki. Vicki watching her anxiety, waiting, not offering anything. The girl well spooked. Licked her lips, scanned the concourse, the people hurrying through to their connections.

Vicki took a moment to consider the scene. No one hanging around who looked like they were hanging around. Then again, a place like this, could be anyone sitting on the couches, even in Bubbles, eating oysters with a dry white, who could be Linda Nchaba's nemesis.

'Please,' said Linda. And got no further.

Vicki Kahn leant forward, the movement causing a tenderness in her breasts. She said gently, 'You want to give me that flash drive?'

Linda Nchaba didn't take the invitation.

'Maybe I shouldn't be doing this,' she said.

'You're here,' said Vicki. 'I'm here. You said you wanted to tell us something. To give us something.' She looked around. 'This is a good place.'

Linda Nchaba shook her head. 'There are no good places. You don't know him. I thought he didn't know I was here.'

'He? Who's he?'

The woman frowned. 'A high-up. They found me. His people found me.'

'What d'you mean, found you?' Vicki going for perplexed. 'Who're his people?'

'Yesterday they called my cellphone. Told me they knew I was flying to Paris for a modelling contract.' Her face contorted, her eyes filled. 'That cell number only my grandmother knew. She doesn't answer her phone anymore.'

Vicki kept focused on Linda Nchaba's eyes. The woman's face collapsing into grief. Then a resolution coming in hard before the weeping could take hold as Linda Nchaba got her emotions under control. Took some strength to do that, Vicki knew. Linda wiping her eyes with the back of her fists, sucking in a lungful of air.

'We have a protection facility,' said Vicki.

'Ah, sho,' the woman waved it away. No rings on her fingers. 'It is not for me. There are children. Young girls. It would be better for them.'

'Why?' asked Vicki. 'What's happening to them?'

Linda Nchaba didn't look at her, kept staring off at the people crossing to the departure gates. Forced a laugh. 'They are being protected.'

'Yes?' said Vicki. 'By whom? From whom?'

'For whom. For important people.'

Vicki shook her head. 'I'm sorry. I don't understand. I don't know what we're talking about. Why do they need protecting from themselves? That doesn't make sense.' She got no answer from Linda Nchaba. 'Look,' she said, swallowing to keep down a sudden upwelling of nausea, 'I've come a long way to meet you. I am here to receive information from you. Important information. You can give it to me, it will be safe. You will be protected. Nobody will know we have met. Nobody will know we have spoken. We're here, in transit in Schiphol airport. I don't know where you've come from, until you told me I didn't know where you were going to. I know you wanted this meeting. And up above my head, in the high offices, someone said okay let's find out what Linda Nchaba knows. Someone reckons you're that important. This is why I'm here with you.'

Now Linda Nchaba looked at her. Vicki returning the gaze, seeing the fright in Linda's face, the flare at her nostrils, her tight lips, the fear a darkness deep in her eyes. Wanted to reach out, touch the woman's hand. But didn't. Kept her own hands folded in her lap. A tightness gripped her shoulders and neck. She shifted on the couch to ease her tensions, crossed her legs.

'A man answers my grandmother's phone.'

'What? I'm sorry? What're you saying?'

'A man answers my grandmother's phone.'

'A man.'

'He tells me to come home. I can hear my gogo, my grandmother, crying.'

'You said she doesn't answer her phone.'

'She doesn't. The man does.'

'How many times, how many times've you phoned?'

'Five times.'

'You can hear your grandmother crying? You're sure?'

'It's her. It's her voice. Shouting for me to stay away.' Linda Nchaba with her face in her hands, shudders passing through her body.

Vicki eased off. Again had an urge to comfort the woman, touch her, put an arm around her trembling shoulders. But she held back. 'Linda, Linda, listen to me.'

The woman moaned. 'They've got my gogo.'

'We can find her, Linda,' said Vicki. 'We've got people who do this. Good people. They will find her.'

Again Vicki watched Linda Nchaba collect herself. Had to admire the way she suppressed the sobs, the shaking, stopped the waterworks. Like she'd had plenty of practice.

'They won't,' said Linda. 'You don't know these sorts of men. You don't know this man who leads them. These men say they will kill her, if I don't go back.'

'But you haven't gone back. You're here. Now I am here because this is what you wanted. You wanted to give us information. You haven't gone back to them.'

Vicki angled slightly to see Linda Nchaba face-on. Linda turning to look at her, her face bland now, expressionless. 'When I left, the night I ran away, my grandmother said to me, don't come back. Never come back. She made me promise. Never come back. Never ever. Even if …' Linda glanced away.

Vicki waited.

'Even if they have taken her. That's what she said. "Never come back, my child, even if they have taken me."'

'Yes,' said Vicki.

'Do you know what it's like to be told that? "Even if they have me. Never come back, my child."' Her eyes locked on Vicki, Vicki meeting them, seeing the despair. 'Now they will kill my grandmother. Because of me. For ever I have to live with this. That because of me she was killed.'

'She's still alive,' said Vicki. 'You said you could hear her when you phone.' Vicki thinking all her time as a lawyer hadn't prepared her for this. All the Agency training hadn't prepared her for this. How to deal with a situation like this. When your boobs hurt and a nausea hovered at the back of your throat. And in your head Henry Davidson was saying, Get the flash drive. Just get the bloody flash drive, woman. She wanted this. She's got little kids on her conscience. Remember that. It's why we set this up. To get the info. Then to get her to come home.

Linda Nchaba said, 'As long as I phone they won't kill her.'

'Linda,' said Vicki, 'why'm I here?'

The woman opened her hand to reveal the flash drive.

'What d'you want from us?'

'To stop them. To stop him.'

'Who? Stop who? Give me a name.'

A phone rang in Linda Nchaba's bag, the ringtone that of calling hadedas, their kwaak, kwaak, kwaak harsh in the situation. Schiphol airport. Two women on a leather couch. The insistent cry of the ibis passing overhead. Enough to make you laugh. If you were inclined.

Linda scratched in her bag, came out with a phone.

'An sms,' she said. Opened the message. Exclaimed as she read it, raising her head, her head swivelling about, right to left, left to right. 'Where? Where're they?' She stood up. Took a step away from the couch. 'They can't …' She turned to Vicki.

'Can't what?'

Linda Nchaba held out the cellphone. Vicki took it, read the message. 'We see you, sisi.'

'You understand? You understand what I mean?' Linda took the phone back, sat down. 'They know. He knows.'

'They're scaring you,' said Vicki. 'They're trying their luck. Playing a blind hand. They don't know where you are.'

The phone kwaaked again. One word on the screen: 'Schiphol.'

'They do,' said Linda Nchaba. Held up the phone for Vicki to read the word on the screen.

'They're tracking your phone,' said Vicki. 'They've got a reading on it that's all. They don't know anything else.' Sharp moves, though, by whoever was pulling them. Rattling Linda Nchaba no end. Had to have local cooperation. Which meant in-transit wasn't quite as safe as she'd thought. Before she could say anything the hadedas cried once more.

Linda Nchaba opened the message, gasped. Passed the phone to Vicki, Vicki reading: 'The woman you are talking to is called Vicki Kahn.'

'On the money,' said Vicki. Thinking fast, if they knew her name, then someone back at the Aviary was in on it. Didn't mean there was a watcher at the airport, it meant something worse. Someone close in was watching her. Keeping tabs on her phone. Why? Watching for whom? Bloody Henry's need-to-know rule. Not telling her everything. Unless Henry didn't know everything.

Also they were good, these people tracking Linda Nchaba. Sending three smses, that was nasty. Really nasty way to up the paranoia. And it worked. Zipped Linda Nchaba into a state of high anxiety. Her eyes scanning the concourse, left to right, this way, that way, finding no one to pick out. Vicki all the time focused on the woman with the beautiful skin. How to get the flash drive from her.

Linda Nchaba snatched back her phone, stood up. 'This was a mistake.'

'The stick,' said Vicki. 'Give me the stick. Give me a name, names. Tell me what's on it.'

'I'm sorry,' said Linda. 'Goodbye. I'm sorry. I can't. He has my grandmother. He will kill her.' Began walking off.

Vicki called out, 'Here, take this.' She held out a business card.

Linda Nchaba stopped, returned, took the card.

'Phone me,' said Vicki. 'Get a new SIM card first, okay. And shut it off now, your phone. Take out the battery.'

Linda Nchaba frowned. Mumbled something that Vicki didn't catch, might even have been about to release the flash drive. Vicki broke their eyelock, dropped her gaze to Linda's hand, went back to her face. Linda hesitating.

'You've got to give it to me.'

'No. No, I can't. He … He … You don't know what he will do.'

'For the children's sake.' A last throw. Vicki watched a zigger of pain tighten Linda's face. Shifted on the seat, about to reach out, but Linda Nchaba struck at her hand, walked away. Vicki didn't go after her, stayed sitting, waiting to see if anyone made a move towards the woman. No one did. At the Bubbles counter Linda stopped, spoke to the attendant. Then she was gone, hurrying down the C corridor where Vicki had no line of sight.

Shit, Vicki thought, now what? Should she phone home, tell her boss the woman showed but didn't say anything that made sense? Wouldn't give her the stick. Blazered Henry would snort and chort, shift the placement of his wig. Damn it. She could hear him. 'You let her walk away. She has this flash drive for you and you let her walk away. For Christ's sake, Vicki, why?'

To which Vicki would have no answer. Except that she didn't want to make a scene in case they were being watched. How quickly the paranoia transferred. There's no one watching, she thought, grimacing at the pain in her chest. They were tracking Linda Nchaba by remote. Spooking her.

And she'd failed. First foreign mission, she'd failed. Hadn't got the information. Hadn't prepared the woman. Wasn't going to bring her in.

What a stuff-up.

8

Vicki took out her cellphone, was about to key through to Henry Davidson. Glanced up, there was a waiter bending towards her, offering a bottle of mineral water and a glass on a tray. 'Madam, your water,' he said. 'Five euros please.'

Vicki about to say, what? No, I didn't. Saw the flash drive on the napkin.

'Thank you,' she said. Paid the waiter.

She had less than an hour until the Berlin connection. On the info screen the check-in sign flashed next to the flight number. Vicki took out her notebook, slotted in the stick. A couple of folders of photographs of Linda the model. Location shoots: beaches, arty shots in derelict buildings. One file password-protected. Nice one, Linda Nchaba.

She phoned Davidson.

'And so?' he said.

'I've got the flash drive.'

'That's a start. So far so splendid. Have a good girlie chat?'

'She's scared.'

'Umm.'

'On the run.'

'Really now. I had gathered that. And?'

'And her grandmother's being held hostage.'

'This is a complication. What's on the drive?'

'Some photographs, personal stuff. A protected file.'

'Nothing's protected, Vicki. Nothing is hidden.' A Henry Davidson homily.

'I haven't got software to crack it.'

'No matter. It can wait. What story did she unfold?'

'Apart from her granny's kidnapping, no story. Except that her former buddies are powerful and dangerous men.'

'So much we know. She's important to us. Vital. You make a second date?'

'Jesus, Henry, no, there wasn't time.' The churn of failure in her gut.

'What next then?'

'We'll meet. We'll stay in touch.' Vicki not at all sure about this. Staying in touch totally in the hands of Linda Nchaba.

'You had better. I want her back, Vicki. I want her here. Anything else?'

'There is,' said Vicki. Brought in the surprise: 'Someone knows I'm here. Someone in the Aviary.'

A snort. 'I would hardly think so.'

She told him why she thought so. Henry Davidson let a small fortune of airtime tick by before he said, 'Interesting.'

Interesting! Vicki poured water into the glass. Bloody Henry and his say-nothings.

When he next said something, it was, 'Do you not have a flight to catch?'

Vicki said the check-in sign was flashing.

'Off you go then. Give my regards to Detlef. He might be sick, but watch his hands. Enjoy Berlin. Make contact with Linda Nchaba tomorrow. Let me know.'

'And?' she said, resorting to a Henry Davidson-type prompt.

'And what?'

'And who's tracking me?'

He didn't answer. He'd disconnected. Bloody typical.

Vicki shrugged into her coat, picked up her handbag and laptop case. Turned, about to head off down the concourse, stopped at the sight of two security men running, supporting a woman between them. Medics rushing towards them. The woman: Linda Nchaba. Dangling between the men, her head lolling, eyes glazed.

Vicki started towards them, stopped herself. Don't get involved, stay out of it. Henry Davidson's voice shouting in her head. She didn't interfere. Watched as medics arrived, laid Linda Nchaba onto a gurney. The men checking for vital signs, fingers at her throat, running in an IV line. Could have been a cardiac case they were handling. Then the rush away, the security men clearing a path through the ebb and flow of passengers.

Vicki headed for her departure gate. Phoned Henry Davidson once she'd checked in.

'Thought you might like to know, they've got her,' she said.

Henry Davidson responding, 'Who is this her? Who are the they?'

'Linda Nchaba.'

'Got her how?'

'How the hell should I know?' said Vicki. 'Stabbed, pricked, poisoned, doesn't matter. She couldn't stand, her eyes were gone.'

'They? Who are they?'

'Men. Airport security.'

'Get on the plane,' said Henry Davidson. 'Just get on the bloody plane. Phone me from your hotel.'

9

Off Surfer's Corner nothing doing but sloppy wind waves. Okay, given the south-east breeze you couldn't expect anything else. Fish Pescado wasn't expecting anything else. Enough fun on a paddleboard if you liked that sort of thing. When there was no alternative, Fish Pescado liked that sort of thing. Also if there wasn't much else going on in your life, why not be on the water?

There wasn't much else in his life. Some insurance work,

some background stuff on the mining industry for his mother, the whizz-bang business scout. That was about it. Couple of other jobs on retainer. Which was not to say that Fish Pescado was scratching for a living. He wasn't. He was doing okay by his own measures. Life was on the up.

His other business, the herb business, was ticking over nicely too. A few clients wanting to score a bankie of doob, nothing urgent. Nothing that couldn't wait for a Saturday drop. Easy times for Fish Pescado.

Might as well go surfing.

Mostly, though, with Vicki in Germany, what else to do on a Thursday afternoon but go surfing?

Fish spent an hour in the slop having fun. The paddleboard a great alternative when the waves weren't serious. Only problem in choppy water, the shark spotters on the mountain couldn't see the sharks so Fish kept checking the surface. Always lurking at the back of his mind, this imaginary great white. Big pink jaws agape showing sharp teeth. He'd been buzzed by whites a couple of times. Scary fishies cruising through, giving the baleful eye. The eye that saw you as food. No eyes like that this afternoon, hallelujah. When he'd had enough, Fish moved onto a swell, let it take him. With some paddle work he caught broken waves into the shallows.

In the car park the car guard said, 'There's a woman looking for you, Mr Fish.' Nodded towards Knead café, handed Fish his car keys. The good thing about this car guard, he'd actually look after your car, and your keys. 'I tell her have a cup of tea meanwhile. I tell her you going to be some few minutes. Just having fun in the sea.'

'Yeah, thanks,' Fish said. 'How long's she been here?'

'Half an hour.' The car guard's hand rocking in estimation. 'More or less. I tell her, she give me a phone number, I'll pass it on. She say, no, man, it's better to wait. I tell her I can get you called in. She say, it's okay, she can wait.'

'Nice lady?'

'Very nice, Mr Fish. Very quiet voice.'

'Her car?'

'Very nice car.' He pointed at a black Fortuner. 'That one with the dark windows.'

'Tell her I'm just gonna get changed,' said Fish. 'Five minutes.'

Fish headed towards his Isuzu, the car guard coming after him.

'Ah, Mr Fish, man, can you do me a favour, man? The cop fined me again for guarding.'

'What?' Fish stopped. Frowned at the car guard. 'Again? How much this time?'

'Five hundred. The cop doesn't like me.'

'You're not kidding.'

'Can Mr Fish ask Miss Vicki for help with the legal?'

'Sure,' said Fish, 'sure.' Taking the summons the guard held out. 'What's the cop's case anyhow?'

'His sister loves me,' said the guard. 'That's the problem. Foreign Congos not supposed to love coloureds.'

Yeah, thought Fish, you should hear my mother on the subject. Fish's mom a bit edgy about the Indian girlie in his life. Her phrase, as in: 'You still going with the Indian girlie, Bartolomeu?' Fish's mom the only one who called him by his first name, Bartolomeu, after the Portuguese explorer, Bartolomeu Diaz.

'Don't worry, Vicki'll sort it.'

10

Fish changed into a white T-shirt, board shorts, flip-flops, headed for Knead. Noticed a woman gazing at him, serious face, serious eyes watching him. Fish ran his fingers through his hair, surf-blond thatch. Good-looking woman, early forties, striking more than pretty, wearing a black T-shirt, a black scarf around her head. Fish thinking she looked familiar. He came in, she raised a hand.

Fish caught a waiter by the elbow, ordered a double espresso and a Danish, pointed at the woman's table. The woman standing up, waiting for him. He went over, introduced himself.

'Please sit,' she said, sitting herself. A tight, neat lady in designer jeans.

'You?' Fish pointed at her pot of tea, then back at the waiters. 'A refresh?'

'No, no.' The woman fluttering both hands.

A French accent there. Might be Senegal, could be central Africa, Mali even.

'I have heard about you, Mr Pescado,' she said.

'Fish,' said Fish. 'Please call me Fish.'

She smiled. 'Fish? That is a strange name. Is it because you are a surfer boy?'

Fish laughed. Shook his head. 'No. Pescado means fish. At school my friends called me Fish. The name stuck.'

'I like it.' The woman went quiet, Fish watched her hands, fine hands, long-fingered, the tips meeting round the teacup. 'You recognised me,' she said.

Fish nodded. Thinking, but from where: in a magazine, a newspaper, television? On television.

'I am Cynthia Kolingba,' she said. 'Some men killed my daughter. Some men tried to kill my husband. He is in a coma. Probably he will not live.'

Fish remembered: St George's last Sunday. Murder in the Cathedral the newspapers had headlined it, not too bothered about the inaccuracy of the preposition. 'I'm sorry about your daughter,' he said.

'She was four years old. Do you know what it is like to be hugged by someone who is four years old?'

Fish shook his head, watched the tears welling in the woman's eyes.

'I can still feel her arms around my neck. I can still feel her hugging me. I wake in the night from a dream that she is holding me. But she's not there. My bed is empty. Yet I can feel her.' Cynthia Kolingba's voice disappeared in a rush of sobbing. 'That hurt inside,' she said, stabbing a finger at her chest, 'is worse than any pain. They can shoot me, they can cut me, they can whip me, I will feel nothing. There is no pain to compare with this: my dead daughter.'

Cynthia Kolingba wept. Turned away from Fish, her face collapsing in sorrow. Fish let her have her grief, looked into the car park, thought of the anguish of mothers. Relieved he had no children to worry about. Thing was, you looked at the families rocking up at the beach in their suvs, laughing, joking, everyone chilling at the end of the week, and you thought maybe that would be fun. Despite the sloppy surf, moms and dads and sons and daughters pulling on wetsuits, no cares in the world.

Except one family's life was shredded.

Cynthia Kolingba brushed tears from her eyes. Poured another cup of black tea, her hand trembling. Drank it off. Stared at Fish with reddened eyes. 'I want your help.'

'I don't see ...' Fish began, waited for the waiter to place his coffee and pastry on the table.

'You have been recommended,' she said, her hurt now suppressed, a dullness in her eyes.

Fish bit into the Danish. God, they did a good apple Danish. He wiped crumbs from his mouth with the back of his hand. Took another bite.

'I want you to find the people who did this.'

'The police ... Surely?' Fish licked his fingers, took a mouthful of espresso.

'Bah, the police,' she said. 'The police are very nice. Don't worry, Mrs Kolingba, we will catch them. Don't worry, Mrs Kolingba, the investigation is going well. Don't worry, Mrs Kolingba, we have good leads. We will have results soon. Don't worry, Mrs Kolingba. They are saying this. They can do nothing. We are foreigners. They think this is political.'

'You're from?' Fish trying to remember, either Central African Republic or the Democratic Republic of Congo. Not much to choose from. Both of them less than stable. C'est la vie, Africa.

'CAR,' she said. 'The newspapers say it was hitmen from my country. They say my husband is a threat to our government. That he is planning a coup. Everyone is a threat in my country. There are rebels everywhere. Muslim bands. Christian militias. I can promise you, Mr Pescado, Fish, my husband is not a threat. We are here in Cape Town, we are thousands of kilometres away from Bangui. I can promise you he is not planning anything. There is no reason for them to shoot my family. There is no reason to kill my daughter.'

'Why're you here?' Fish asked through a mouthful. Then softened. 'I mean, you're here because you're in exile, right?'

'We are in exile, yes. We have no choice. In Bangui we were in danger, there is anarchy. Sometimes they shoot at our house. Sometimes they shoot at my husband. They try to capture my children, that's how you say it?'

'Kidnap.'

'Kidnap. They try to kidnap my sons, from the school. That was why we leave Bangui. There are people who call it the Republic of Nowhere. They are right. CAR is not a country.'

Fish popped the last of the Danish into his mouth, wondered if he should have another. 'Ah,' he chewed and swallowed, 'when'd you leave? How long ago?'

'Three years.'

He downed the remains of the espresso.

'Three years. Not such a long time.'

'A long time. A long, long time. Every day I want to go home. I want there to be peace in my country. I want to live there in freedom.'

Fish glanced at her, she held his gaze. In her eyes a determination. The same resolution he saw in Vicki when she got on a case. The come-hell-or-high-water attitude.

'While you've been here, it's been alright though?'

She shrugged. The French comme-ci-comme-ça shrug, clearly it was part of the language.

'We live in a nice area. It is quiet.'

'Where's that?'

'Bel Ombre. It is a part of Constantia, near the mountain.'

Fish could picture it: large house, large grounds, high walls, electric fencing, security cameras, buzz-boxes, armed response. Thing about these politicos, they went into exile, there was always money. Most times the host's generosity. Sometimes foreign backers, investors with vested interests: the international mining houses or the Chinese wanting raw materials. Sometimes their own emergency funds in offshore accounts. You could have a good life doing nothing in luxury. Except, you looked at Cynthia Kolingba's face, you saw something else. You saw suffering. Just glimpses, as if the pain came in waves.

'It has not been an easy time for us, Mr Pescado.'

Fish let the formality go. 'You've been threatened?'

'Some problems. There have been some problems.'

'Oh yeah?'

'Yes.'

'Some problems such as?'

'There was graffiti on the garden wall a few times. Once they put a skull on the driveway. Once a puppy was poisoned.'

'You know this, about the poison?'

'The vet said so.'

Slowly, Fish said to himself. What're you doing here, dude? Like you're getting into this thing. He ran a hand up his cheek, realised he hadn't shaved. What must he look like to her? The surfer boykie. One of the Cape Town shoo-wah tribe. He leant back in his chair, rocked it onto its hind legs. Slowly, he thought, first things first. Came forward so suddenly, Cynthia Kolingba gasped.

'Look, Mrs Kolingba,' he said, 'the cops've only been on it four, five days. What can I do better than them?'

'They will do nothing.'

'You can't say that.'

'They will do nothing.' She said it with her face turned away from Fish, looking out at the happy families. Stayed that way, looking out; Fish letting the silence between them roll on. When she faced him again, said, 'You know a man called Mart Velaze?'

'Mart Velaze?'

'He said you would know him.'

'I know him, yeah. Never met him.'

Not exactly someone Fish would call a friend. Fish's only dealing with Mart Velaze being troubling. At the time Fish thought Mart Velaze wanted him killed. Not only him but Vicki too. Then there'd been their last telephone conversation: 'I'm still out here. Yebo yes, I'm still out here. But I'm no hazard. No jeopardy to you or your loved one. Not at the moment. Enjoy the rest of your life, Mr Pescado. Surfing, smoking doob, investigating. Making out with Vicki.'

Since then nada from or about Mart Velaze.

'He said you would help me.'

'Oh yeah?'

'He said you were good at finding people.'

'Mart Velaze said that?'

'Yes.'

Fish thinking, the only time he'd been involved with Mart Velaze and a missing person, he'd not found the missing person. Now here was Mart Velaze giving him the thumbs-up.

'D'you know Mart Velaze?'

Cynthia Kolingba shook her head. 'No. He said he is a friend of my husband's.'

'Is he?'

'I do not know.'

'So why d'you trust him?'

'There is no one I can trust.'

Fish considered this. You're in a foreign country, your family's shot at, your daughter killed, your husband in hospital, what d'you do? You take a chance. A stranger phones you, says speak to this other stranger. Came down to it, desperate people would do anything. 'What'd he say about me? Why'd you think he wasn't lying?'

'He said you are a private investigator. He said you find people who are missing. He said I must talk to you. He said the police will do nothing. He said I will find you here. I find you here. Can you help me, Mr Pescado?'

Fish took a long time looking at her, both of them in the eyeball moment. You had to be crazy getting into something that had Mart Velaze in the wings. He nodded, saw something brighten in her eyes.

'Thank you,' she said.

For the second time Fish realised she was a stunner. The sadness in her face quite beautiful.

'I have money,' she said. 'What do you cost?'

Fish told her. She reached for a bag at her feet, counted out the cash, pushed it across the table. Fish folded the wodge, stuck it into his pocket. He asked for her contact details, said he'd be in touch, probably over the weekend.

As they stood, he said, 'What was your daughter's name?'

Cynthia Kolingba keyed through the menu on her phone, held it out to Fish. An image on the screen of mother and daughter eating ice creams on a boat. 'Calixthe, she was called. My mother's name. We were going to Robben Island with the tourists, the day before the men killed her.'

11

'Who is this person?' Kaiser Vula pointed at the image on the tablet screen. The image that of Fish Pescado and Cynthia Kolingba in Knead. The image slightly blurred, taken through a window. Kaiser Vula's finger tapping on Fish Pescado.

'I don't know, Major,' said Joey Curtains. 'I just got in now-now. I thought, Major wanted to see this urgent.'

Kaiser Vula rolled his chair back, stared up at Joey Curtains. The hotshot Joey Curtains. Bloody hotnot Joey Curtains always quick with the comeback, always a smirk on his lips. A smirk Kaiser Vula believed Joey Curtains was born with.

'What's it that I tell you guys?' Kaiser Vula waiting for Joey Curtains to look at him. 'What's it I tell you? Every briefing, hey, Agent Curtains?' Kaiser Vula liked calling his people Agent. It put them in their place. You are agents of my doing, he told them. Remember it. 'What've I told you?' He paused, stood. 'Look at me, Agent.' Waited until Joey Curtains glanced at him. 'What do I tell you people? Don't come to me with half a story. Half a story's no story. Half a story is a waste of my time.'

They were on the Aviary's top floor, the floor where all the heavies had their offices. Downstairs in the Aviary proper it was open plan. Fieldworkers, agents, don't need offices, the logic went. They need to be out there sniffing around. Give them a desk, a couple of drawers, a typist's chair, nothing too comfortable, don't want them lolling around enjoying the air-conditioning.

'Her phone records? Have you checked her phone records? She must have set this up, this meeting. They must have agreed to meet. Who is he? Her lover?'

'I only got here now-now with the pictures,' said Joey Curtains.

'Her phone records? You've checked them?'

Joey Curtains nodding. 'I checked, Major. Nothing unusual. No strange numbers.'

'Ah, impossible,' said Kaiser Vula. 'They met. Nobody meets like that, by chance. How long did they talk for?'

'Half an hour.'

'Half an hour. Half an hour they were sitting there. Half an hour you didn't think maybe you should go in there and listen? Half an hour. Ah, wena, man.' He tapped his agent on the head. 'You must use this, okay. What else you got?'

Joey Curtains leant forward, flicked at the keyboard, swiping through some more photographs. Fish and Cynthia Kolingba exiting the restaurant. Fish and Cynthia Kolingba shaking hands.

'They are not lovers,' said Kaiser Vula. He stabbed his finger at the screen, at the image of Fish Pescado. 'You find out who this man is. Tomorrow. Tomorrow I want name, address, cellphone number. I want to know what he does, who he is. Okay, you hear me, Agent Curtains? Tomorrow, alright.'

On the screen was an image of Cynthia Kolingba driving off in her Fortuner. The last image that of Fish talking to the car guard.

'You didn't get his car?'

'No, Major. Major said to watch her,' said Joey Curtains. 'She was driving away, Major. Like you said, I didn't want to lose her.'

Major Kaiser Vula rolled his eyes. 'We have a tracker on her car, no one's going to lose her. Another few minutes he would've driven away. One photograph of his number plate and we know everything.' This time he tapped his own head. 'Simple. Don't you think, Agent? Don't you use your mind? Tomorrow, okay, you tell me what he eats for breakfast.'

Kaiser Vula looked at Joey Curtains. 'You know what is happening with the colonel?'

Joey Curtains nodded. 'In a coma still, Major.'

'I know. That is not my question. My question, Agent, my question is: Tell me your plan. Tell me how you will fix this situation? Four days we're waiting. Four days is a long time. In four days what have you done? You bring me the same news all the time. We are waiting. We are waiting. We are waiting. What are we waiting for, Agent?'

'Maybe he will die, Major.'

'Of course. Of course he will die. You will die. I will die. He will die. But he must die now. You understand what is now? Today. Today is now.'

'It's not easy, Major. It's difficult.'

'Difficult?' He frowned at Joey Curtains. 'Difficult. You tell me what is difficult? The colonel is in one place. He can't leave that place. You know where that place is. So where is this difficult?'

'There is security,' said Joey Curtains.

'No, man, no, no, no,' said Kaiser Vula. 'That is nonsense. We are security. You must fix this, Curtains. Fix this properly. Soon. Now. The latest tomorrow. Tomorrow. Finish 'n klaar. Like it should've been.' Kaiser Vula waving Joey Curtains back to the Aviary.

'Talk to Prosper. Prosper can make a plan.'

Prosper Mtethu, the driver, the old man, the Umkhonto we Sizwe veteran.

'Listen to Prosper, Agent Curtains, listen to what he says. You can learn something.' Waving his hand again, dismissing the agent, telling him to close the door.

12

Joey Curtains closed the door with a soft click, his face a mask: hooded eyes, thin mouth, head bowed. Walked slowly down the corridor past closed doors to the stairs thinking, what a prick. What a shitwit. The colonel wasn't coming back. A couple of days they'd switch off the life support. Stupid to get all poeperig. Joey Curtains mouthing the word, smiling at the sound. The sound of the major shitting himself. Had to be a big shit storm coming down the tubes onto the major's head. Arsehole. These army types marching into the Agency like Hitlers. Fuck him.

And Prosper Mtethu again. The man who'd said, as they burnt rubber after the shooting of Colonel Kolingba, who'd said, 'No, my friend, that is not the way. That was a mistake. We have left a man.'

True enough.

But.

But not as if he'd been left for the hyenas. Not as if he was dead on some cassava battlefield in central Africa. No, man, right outside the cathedral. Home ground. Sacred ground. Anyhow the cleaners would pick him up. Make it all nice.

Joey Curtains took the stairs down to the Aviary. Mostly empty, all the birdies flown this late hour of the afternoon. Sat at his desk on his typist's chair, scrolled through his tablet to the photograph of Fish Pescado.

Tomorrow. Tomorrow he'd sort him.

Fish Pescado was the easy part. Kolingba was another story. Joey Curtains phoned Prosper Mtethu.

Got a terse, 'Ja, Prosper here.' No background noise. 'What you want?'

'Hey, my bru, we got to do a job,' said Joey Curtains.

Silence. Then: 'What job?'

'The colonel.'

Silence. Then: 'You got a job,' said Prosper Mtethu. 'I don't fix your problems.'

'Nay, my bru,' said Joey Curtains, 'that's not what the major said. The major said you was the man, you was the man to fix this.'

Silence. Silence so long Joey Curtains thought Prosper Mtethu had disconnected. Was about to reconnect, he heard the man clear his throat, hawk, spit.

'He was a brother that died.'

'Who?' Joey Curtains playing dumb.

'On Sunday. That man we left on the steps was a brother.'

'You mean family?'

'We are all family.'

'Blood family?'

That silence.

'Tonight,' said Joey Curtains. 'We gotta do it tonight. Or there's kak from the major.'

'It was a problem.'

'What? What's this problem.'

'That he was shot.'

'Hey, man, what's this? There was more of them. It could of been me they shot, just as easily. Couple of turns the other way it was me would've gone down. It's luck, my bru. Easy as that, luck of the draw.'

'You are senior. You got experience. That man was a boy in this job.'

Joey Curtains counted slowly in his head, one crocodile, two crocodile, three crocodile to ten crocodile. At ten said, 'My brother, we have orders. We must make a plan.'

Again the hawk and spit. 'You know the One&Only?'

'Waterfront, of course.'

'There's a bar in the foyer. Six o'clock.'

Joey Curtains left listening to dead air. Joey Curtains with a couple of hours to kill.

13

Berlin, the Hackescher Markt Hotel. Vicki Kahn, topless, stripped down to jeans, stood looking at her breasts in the bathroom mirror. Relaxed her shoulders. Her breasts felt different to yesterday. Same size, same shape. But her bra had seemed too tight. Like between today and yesterday there'd been a seismic change. Not just period sensitivity. A change way up the sore barometer. You touched them they screamed. Sensitivity like heat. Out of the bra wasn't much relief either. Covered her breasts lightly with her hands. Fine delicate hands with long fingers that hid them. She applied pressure. And there was the tenderness. Excruciating. She grimaced, dropped her hands onto the basin. Leant forward until her head touched the mirror. Why now? Why on this trip? With so much happening off-script.

Which was as far as she was going with those thoughts. Two days, three max, she would be through it. Back home the problem could be sorted. Enough.

Her thoughts shifted, turned to a scotch and soda. Wasn't every day you were on an expense account in a hotel with a minibar. She pulled a t-shirt over her head, gently over her chest. Washed her face, ran fingers through the black bob of her hair. Shook her head at herself. Wished it was that time of the month. Like a really radical time of the month. Like a time of the month never experienced before. But odds on she knew what it was. And it didn't fill Vicki Kahn with joy.

She went over to the minibar, upended a glass, took out the miniature Bells. Twisted the cap off, caught a whiff of whisky and gagged. Couldn't even pour it into the glass. Went for a straight soda water.

Then sat on the sofa looking round the room. A room at the top of the Hackescher Markt Hotel. Henry Davidson's recommendation. Not so much a recommendation as a directive.

'You'll like it there, Vicki. In the centre of things. Very historic. Very chic these days.' His wet-lipped grin. 'It's your sort of place. A wonderland.'

Whatever he'd meant by that. However he saw her.

Here she was in a big room, very nice, Swedish furniture, straight neat lines, blond wood. White linen on the bed, the duvet folded in the German way. A sexy standing lamp. Snake-eye reading lamps over the double bed. A little desk with a black anglepoise light. Very stylish.

Vicki glanced at the skylight, the sky that dark blue before it went black. Could see the Alexanderplatz tower reaching up. Iconic. That new word everybody used. Historic. Not a city she knew although she'd heard stories of her aunt being here in the Honecker days: days of grim streets, dull streetlights, shot-up buildings, Checkpoint Charlie, people machine-gunned trying to jump the Wall, trying to swim the Spree. Spy days. John le Carré was about as close as she'd got to that Berlin.

Now here she was due to meet an old spy – a lecherous old spy if you went by Henry Davidson's brief – from those days. From the Struggle days when her aunt had lived on East German stipends before she got the posting to Paris.

What was she doing here, really?

Why the meeting with Detlef Schroeder?

What chance now of bringing in Linda Nchaba? No chance.

She sighed, reached across for her cellphone, put a call through to Henry Davidson. Might have rung once before he answered.

'You like the hotel?'

'It's lovely.'

'I told you. You have a nice room?'

She laughed. 'I do.'

'With a view?'

'Sort of.'

'You can see the tower?'

'The top part.'

'Good.'

Where'd Henry be this time of the evening? In his office still? At the Cape Town Club? She guessed the club. That weird hushed place of leather armchairs. You sat there, you couldn't hear the city, as if you weren't part of it any longer. She could see him, wig, blazer, gin and tonic, cigar. A scattering of whites among the new elites. Rich black men settling into the club.

'A good flight?'

People always asked that. Vicki could never understand why.

'Yes. A bit bumpy.'

'Ah,' said Henry Davidson, 'it can be in winter.'

She waited, her expenses paying for silence while Henry used up airtime. Doing what? Taking a puff? Taking a swig? Oiling his voice? She waited.

'Look, Vicki, I made a few calls. Got some help from the embassy. From a young man there, very efficient young man I have to say. He got onto Schiphol, seems Linda Nchaba had a panic attack. Something like that. She is fine. They let her rest. Booked her onto another flight. All is well, no cause for alarm.'

Vicki looked at her watch: quarter to eight. All that in three hours. Said, 'I'm pleased to hear that.' Wondering if she was being told a story.

'You should contact her, first thing tomorrow. Set up that rendezvous. Keep on her. Let her know we are serious, that we can help her. You are okay? Not jittery?'

'I'm fine.'

'Good. Good. Ah, one other thing,' said Henry Davidson. 'The flash drive. Keep it with you all the time. Just to be on the safe side.'

'The safe side? Only you know where I am.'

Henry Davidson chuckled. 'An expression, Vicki. Only an expression. Nothing sinister. Now, watch out for Detlef's hands tomorrow. They'll be all over you otherwise.' Again the chuckle. 'An unreconstructed lech. Give him my best. And enjoy Saturday, drink a glühwein for me. At one of those markets, in the snow. Good girl.'

And he disconnected.

Patronising bastard, thought Vicki. Threw her cellphone onto the bed. What was all that about anyhow? What sort of line was he spinning?

Like Linda Nchaba had a panic attack?

Really?

14

Vicki Kahn connected her notebook to the hotel's wi-fi, Skyped Fish Pescado, needing some reality.

And there he was, pixelated, but no mistaking that wild blond surfer hair. Like he'd just come in from a surf. Which he probably had.

Lover. Beach bum. Hardarse. And what'd he call it on his business cards these days? Investigative Consultant.

'Vics,' he said, his image coming clear. His image taking a pull from a bottle of Butcher Block pale ale: 'Where're you?'

She shook her head. Said, 'No, Fish, how can you? Use a glass with a beer like that.'

'Tastes the same,' he said, wiping the back of his hand over his mouth. 'Cheers.'

She'd been the one weaned him from the milk stout onto ales. 'Artisan beers, craft beers, that's where it's at, Fish, when're you going to grow up?' Immediately, it turned out. She bought him a four-pack of Butcher Blocks, hooked the surfer dude with the first slug. 'Cool,' he'd said, 'where's this been all my life?' No place for stout in the fridge after that. Figuring she was on a roll, Vicki managed to get him grooving on red wine at meal times. Shiraz mostly. No pinotage. Definitely no pinotage. Cab sav merlot blends at a push. Thing was, she turned her back, she knew Fish hit the ale. Mother's milk he called it. Though the thought of Fish's mother Estelle expressing milk wasn't a thought Vicki wanted to hold for long, or at all.

'Cheers,' he said again. 'Let's see what you're drinking.'

She raised hers.

'What's that? Looks like water?'

'J&B light,' she lied. No good telling Fish she wasn't drinking, he'd want to know why not.

'So?'

'So what?'

'So show me. Your room. Out the window. Tell me about Berlin.'

'Shoo, Fish, I just got here.' But she unplugged the notebook, gave him a tour of the room, the bathroom, a close-up of the snake-eye lamps, a view of the buildings over the street, the tower and ball in the distance.

'Bloody hell,' said Fish. 'Amazing what my tax buys government workers.'

'You don't pay tax, Fish,' said Vicki.

'If I did.'

She looked at him grinning at her in his kitchen, late sunlight filling the room. For a moment thought: Wouldn't that be better? Sitting there with him in the summer warmth. Eating seafood. Drinking a crisp sauvignon blanc. Better. In one way. But what about this? She wanted to like this. This idea of herself. The agent at Schiphol receiving information. The Berlin tourist. Would like it better if she weren't sore.

Said, 'Fish, can you do something?'

'Depends.' Fish sitting back, his hands linked behind his head. 'Official or unofficial? Money or spec?' His head tilted, quizzical.

She said nothing. Shrugged, leant forward, her face filling the screen. Winked.

Fish smiled. 'Okay. So what's this something?'

This something. Three thoughts in Vicki's head: Why get Fish into this? Why not wait till she was back, do her own legwork? Why not get boss Davidson to assign the help? Because she didn't trust the help. Maybe didn't even trust bewigged Davidson. Because she wanted to know more about Linda Nchaba. The file had been too skimpy. Or there was another file she wasn't shown. Henry's secrecy rules.

'Unofficial, no money,' she typed, watched Fish's smile turn into a grin.

'Hey, hey, what's this? Berlin rules?' Fish saying it aloud. 'You've only been there a couple of hours, you're already George Smiley.'

Fish went blurry. Skype told her it was a slow connection, drop the video feed. She clicked away the message. Said, 'See what happens when you make jokes. Now keep still, you're moving around too much.'

He did. His image cleared, his fingers on the keyboard, typing: 'Unofficial, no money. Spooky.'

'I said don't joke, Fish.' Read his message: 'No money, really?'

'I can't,' Vicki said. 'Not straight away. Maybe later.'

'Ah, something you don't want anyone to know about,' said Fish. 'Nice place you work for.'

She let that go.

'Please.' Vicki watching surfer-dude Fish mulling it over, staring straight out the screen at her. Watching him take another slug of the pale ale.

'Alright. I got a job this afternoon. How urgent's yours?'

'Very.' Decided to allow him some slack, show interest in his new job. 'What sort of job?'

'A scary one.'

She smiled, thinking he was taking the piss.

'No, strues. You know that Congolese got nailed outside the cathedral? Him. Well, not him. Mrs Congolese actually.'

Vicki typed: 'Colonel Kolingba?'

'Ja, him.'

'Central African Republic. Not the Congo.'

'Doesn't matter. Darkest Africa.' Fish got up, disappeared off screen. Still talking though, telling her the pasta was ready, telling her about meeting Cynthia Kolingba after surfing in blown-out waves, telling her the Kolingba story. He came back on screen with a bowl of linguini, mixing in tomatoes and basil pesto, strips of Parma ham and black olives. Sprinkled Parmesan over it. Forked up a mouthful. 'My supper, I'm starving.'

'Looks good,' Vicki said, feeling her stomach lurch. She sipped water. Waiting for Fish to deliver the pay-off line. Dreading it. She got it between his mouthfuls.

A typed response: 'Wants me to find the shooter.'

Remembered what Henry Davidson had said, 'Not our playing field.' The way he'd brushed her query aside. 'Not our playing field.' Not even wanting to get into it. Despite all the corridor rumours, all the coffee gossip, Davidson wasn't interested. Davidson who was interested in everything. Who collected information constantly. This time he didn't want to know. Why? Because it was an inside job? Like wonderful, here was her man on the trail of a secret-service hitter. One of her colleagues, in a manner of speaking. Vicki closed her eyes, shook her head.

'She came to you?'

Fish frowning. Looking hurt. 'Don't sound so surprised. I have a rep about town.'

'All the private dicks in the city, she comes to you? You, rather than the big boys?'

'Yeah.'

'You don't think that's strange?'

'No.' Fish slurping up a long noodle.

Vicki messaged: 'You don't think she knows about us, me?'

She watched Fish twirl his fork in the pasta, his eyes intent on the effort. They flicked back to her. 'That's paranoid.'

Vicki typing: 'You've heard the rumours that we did the job?'

'Sure.'

Said, 'You don't think maybe ...'

'No.' Fish lifted the forkful, bent forward to pop it into his mouth. 'Why do that? Kill him. Kill his daughter.'

'Diamonds? Gold? Wood? Coal?'

'We got all that stuff here.'

'As a favour?'

'I could go with that, a favour.' He grinned at her. 'Here's what'll really make you paranoid.' Keyed in the name: 'Mart Velaze.' Said, 'He gave me the nod. Remember him?'

Not a name she was going to forget in a hurry. A name that'd caused them both grief. Maybe even Mart Velaze who'd sent the shooter to kill them, the day she got shot. The sinister Mart Velaze who'd vanished at a finger click. She'd mentioned his name to the birds in the Aviary, come up with a blank. Not even Henry Davidson'd reacted to the name. Then again, Davidson didn't react to anything. Henry Davidson was not the sort of player Vicki would want at a poker table.

'Really?'

'None other, apparently. Told her, get hold of Fish Pescado. Told her I was the man for the job. Kind of him, hey?'

'And you took it, knowing that?'

'I like mysteries.'

Vicki drank water. Her mouth dry, the nausea for the moment suppressed by the pulse of her heart.

'Jesus, Fish.'

'Jesus Fish nothing. You can talk, with the job you do.'

She had to accept that. Didn't need to work where she did except it gave her a kick. Same as the gambling. You got that kick, you wanted it again and again.

'Probably he's one of your colleagues.' He was shaking his fork at her. Smiling. Like he could read her mind.

Vicki typed: 'Could be. Though no one's heard of Mr Velaze.'

'Mr Shadow Man.'

Said, 'Don't joke, Fish.' Entered: 'Get hold of him first, ask your client for his number. Find out why.'

Fish went blurry. Skype repeated its bad connection message. Fish saying behind the pop-up, 'You wanting to run me now? Give me the moves. Handle me. I'd like that.'

She filled her glass with water from the bottle. Swallowed a mouthful. 'Just a suggestion.'

'Thanks.'

The two of them staring at one another. Vicki deciding no sense in backing off on her request. The more information she had, the better. Take the mystery out of Linda Nchaba.

'So,' said Fish, 'what's this favour you want?'

Trust Fish not to let anything drop.

She waved a hand dismissively. 'A small thing.'

'Tell me.'

Hesitated. Building up Fish's curiosity.

'Tell me.'

This time did so. Typed a brief. Leaving out that there might be a leak at the Aviary. Leaving out the trafficking angle.

To which Fish said, 'Bloody hell, Vicki, what's to work on?'

'A name. You've got her name,' Vicki said. Keyed in: 'It's probably Zulu. She's done some modelling. Must be good enough to land a contract in Paris. Which means she's got a reputation, she's going to be on an agency's books. Try Durban. How many agencies can there be? A couple only. Joburg. A couple more. Five? Ten? Two hours you'll—'

'Isn't this something—'

She typed: 'I know what you're going to say, the answer's no, I can't. I told you, unofficial.'

'Why?'

'I'm not talking about it.'

This time Fish messaged: 'There's a problem at the Aviary?'

'I'm not talking about it.'

She saw Fish's mouth pucker, heard him whistle. Saw a new light pop on in his eyes, like she'd pressed a switch. Saw him lean back, his gaze now to his right, probably through the open back door at the boat in the yard. The *Maryjane*.

He came back to her.

'Okay, no problem.'

'Asap.'

'Asap only happens tomorrow morning.'

Vicki nodded. They sat looking at one another. 'Talk tomorrow,' she said, knowing in Fish's mind there'd be the worry: girl walks into a casino. Girl in a wild city would go out looking for a poker game. Satisfy that itch for cards in her fingertips.

'I'm not going to do it, Fish,' she said. 'I'm staying in. I don't do that anymore.'

He smiled. Said, 'Cool.'

'Trust me.' She watched the smile broaden, expose his teeth. Pretty Fish. Gorgeous when he smiled.

'Sweet dreams, princess.'

They went through their ritual air-kiss goodbye. Disconnected.

Vicki stared at the screen, thought, one last look at the flash drive. Brought up professional shots of Linda Nchaba on the ramp: she had attitude, she had style. You could see Linda Nchaba making it on the European circuit. In another folder, couple of party-party snapshots: group round a table downing shots. A man with his arm over Linda's shoulder, possessive. Showing off his trophy. Attractive dude, laughing. Confident. A face Vicki didn't recognise, not someone with a news profile. Could be the man Linda Nchaba feared. The granny-stealer, the trafficker. She clicked through more pictures: no other boyfriends, no more pictures of the dude.

Ended up at the protected file. Guessed some passwords: gogo, model, adnil. Told herself she could be at it all night guessing blind. No point when the techies would crack it in seconds.

Vicki pulled out the stick, went online, clicked through to 888poker. She'd been off the gambling addiction programme, been on the cards for months. Keeping it real. Within financial bounds. Her lapse unknown to Fish. Fish would blow a fuse. The last thing she needed was Fish on her case. What she needed now was distraction. Something to get her mind off how her body felt.

15

Joey Curtains parked beneath the One&Only, took a lift to the foyer. Walked into grandeur. His first time in the hotel. Like flash, bru. Gold statues. Gold vases. Everything big and golden. Was surely a hit with the brothers and sisters swanning about as if they owned the place.

Joey scanned the tables, the crowd round the bar. Saw Prosper Mtethu at a window table. Prosper scrubbed up: white open-necked shirt, black leather jacket. Even in close to thirty degrees heat, he's wearing his black leather jacket. Sitting there quietly gazing at the people on the patio. Impressive playground, big view of Table Mountain rising behind as the backdrop. Nice this hour of the evening. Soft twilight, warm air. Prosper sitting with a blue cocktail.

Joey Curtains slid into the opposite chair. 'A draft,' he said to the hovering waiter. The waiter rattled off a list of brands. 'No, wait,' said Joey Curtains. He pointed at Prosper's drink. 'What's that?'

'Blue Lagoon,' said the waiter.

'No shit. Like what's a Blue Lagoon?'

'A cocktail. Vodka, Blue Curaçao, lemonade. Orange or lemon slice, whichever you want.'

'Sounds alright,' said Joey Curtains. 'Cool on a hot day.' He looked at Prosper Mtethu. 'He's drinking it, has to be alright. Don't worry about the fruit though. Fruit's for breakfast.' To Prosper said, 'Howzit, my bru.' Got a nod for his trouble.

He settled into the chair, feeling a little underdressed in his white shirt open over a grey tee. Jeans, Lonsdale slip-ons that'd cost a bomb on a London trip, no socks. The way he'd been dressed all day. Joey Curtains not giving it a moment's thought that he should freshen up to meet Prosper Mtethu. He looked around. 'Fancy place. I heard about it, heard about it being a top-class joint. Never been here before, myself. But now I can change that. Tick it off.' He paused, brought his eyes back to Prosper Mtethu. 'You like coming here?'

Again got a nod for his trouble.

'All the beautiful people. Who're they? Advertising? Government? Private banking?'

Prosper Mtethu shrugged. Swirled the ice in his glass. Since Joey had sat down, he'd kept his eyes averted, his gaze focused on those outside. The brush-off starting to irritate Joey Curtains big time. Went for one last breaker with a comment about the weather. The weather a big talker in this city. Heat and wind in summer. Slashing rain and gales in winter. Always a subject there to get the bounce going.

Got a grunt out of Prosper Mtethu as he lifted his drink, took a sip.

Enough, thought Joey Curtains. Came forward in his chair. 'My brother,' he said, 'listen, okay, listen to me. Doesn't matter what your problem is with me, the major put us together. We gotta sort this one. Me' – Joey Curtains stabbing his forefinger into his chest – 'and you.' Pointing that forefinger at Prosper Mtethu. 'Both of us, my brother, together. Tonight.'

Prosper Mtethu sipped at his Blue Lagoon. Said nothing.

'So what we gonna do, my brother?'

Prosper Mtethu put down his drink. 'What did the major tell you?'

'We must fix it. Fix it properly. Tonight.' Joey Curtains sat back, relieved the man had come out of his funk. Nothing worse than a darkie with attitude. Thought they were bloody owed everything. Thought they bloody should own everything.

'You know this colonel?'

'Kolingba?'

'Him.'

'I heard of him,' said Joey Curtains.

'He is a good man.'

The waiter came up all cheery, bearing the drink on a silver platter: 'Your cocktail, sir.' Placing the highball glass on a coaster in front of Joey Curtains. 'One Blue Lagoon.' Stepping back, smiling. 'Enjoy, gentlemen, enjoy.' The gentlemen nodding at him. Joey Curtains distracted, saying thanks. Coming back to Prosper Mtethu.

'Yissus, my brother, what's this? Philosophy? Every man is a good man to somebody. Know what I'm saying? Doesn't mean anything. Good is good like it's relative.'

'He is a good man for his people. For his own country.'

Joey Curtains waved a hand, irritated. 'Ah, man, you can say that about anybody. Priests, presidents, princes. They still get up to shit. You take Barack, he says he'll close Guantanamo. Like five, six years later, has that happened? Everyone's still there.' He tasted his drink. 'Tjee, that's sweet. You sure they throw in vodka, it's not all lemonade?' He drank again. Set the glass down. 'You was there Sunday, my brother, don't come with this good man nonsense to me. You didn't have to be the driver.'

'I didn't know it was him.'

'That would've made a difference?'

'Of course.'

'You wouldn't have driven.'

Prosper Mtethu shook his head.

Joey Curtains eased himself back. 'You were MK?'

Prosper Mtethu stared at him.

'Part of a icing team?'

The man nodded.

'Let me ask you.' Joey Curtains clasping his hands behind his head. 'Let me ask you, my brother. You killed people in the townships? Shot them? Used bombs at bus stops where there's women, children?'

'It was the Struggle.'

'Ja, it was the Struggle, okay. In the Struggle bad things happened. Good people died. Not so, my brother? In those times good people died. Everybody that died was a good man to somebody, like I said. So now what you saying?'

Joey Curtains wishing the man would look at him. Make eye contact so he could read something there. Instead followed Prosper Mtethu's gaze to the outside scene: people lounging back, making whoopee in the summertime.

'You see that man there?' said Prosper Mtethu, pointing at a man and woman sitting at a small table. The man, wearing sunglasses, facing towards them.

'Sure,' said Joey Curtains.

'They've been here since before I got here.'

Joey Curtains laughed. 'Probably lots of people been here before you pitched, my brother. Looking at them, some have been here all afternoon.' He took another pull at his Blue Lagoon. 'You know the dude?'

'Don't you?'

Joey Curtains took another squint. Thought, yeah, now he looked closely he might've seen the guy lurking around back at the Aviary. 'Could be I've seen him in the corridors. So what?'

'I don't like him,' said Prosper Mtethu.

Joey Curtains spluttered a laugh. 'Saying nothing, Prosper. Saying nothing. You don't like me. Only person you like is the colonel we supposed to switch off.'

Prosper ignored him. Said, 'That man is a problem. So is his girlfriend. She is a killer. We must finish and go.'

'He's having a drink, my brother, with his chick. What's the problem? It's nice here. He's relaxing. Relax, man, we got to talk about our job. That's what the major wants. That's what he tells me, talk to Prosper. We got an order, bro.'

'Not now,' said Prosper. 'Tomorrow afternoon at the hospital.'

'We gotta do it tonight.'

Joey Curtains getting no leeway on Prosper's face. 'Tomorrow. You tell them tomorrow.'

'Alright. Alright. Tomorrow.' Joey Curtains wondering how he'd run that one past the major. Have to come up with some serious story. But getting Prosper into this was the first score.

Prosper telling him, 'No cars this time. You go there by taxi. Understand?'

'Sure.' Joey Curtains amused at Prosper the Planner organising a hit, using public transport for the getaway. Like minibus taxis were a good option. Crap idea, he thought.

Prosper frowning at him. 'After the visiting hours: five o'clock, we meet.' The man finished his drink. 'You wait for me outside.'

'No problem.'

'Now I am going.' Prosper stood. 'I have a granddaughter to cook for.' Before he moved off, made a call, said, 'I am leaving town now, Litha.' A chuckle. 'You do your homework. No more television.' Joey Curtains hearing lightness in the man's tone. Then serious Prosper Mtethu bent towards him to say, 'You must finish your drink slowly. Watch our friends outside.'

'What's his name?'

'Mart Velaze,' said Prosper Mtethu heading off across the foyer for the steps.

Joey Curtains thought, paranoid arsehole. Took ten minutes over his drink wondering what plan Prosper would have for the good colonel. With each sip the Blue Lagoon more cloying in his mouth. He finished it though. Joey Curtains finished things. Part of his upbringing: If you can't do it, don't start it, Joey. The words of his pa.

When he got up there were Mart Velaze and his dolly bird passing through the foyer. Couldn't see her as dangerous. Good-looking girlie. Young too. Another coloured throwing herself at the darkies. Joey Curtains waited but Mart Velaze didn't glance his way.

Thing about Prosper Mtethu, thought Joey Curtains, was he didn't know what was the real world anymore. Sad shit. Time they gave him the ticket, game over.

16

Kaiser Vula, on his cellphone, told his wife he would be working late.

'Again,' she said.

'Yes. Again,' he came back. Angry at the weariness in her voice. He was driving down Bree Street in the dusk, shuttling between the traffic lights. Pulled into a parking bay at Heritage Square, kept the engine running.

Heard her saying, 'Every night this week. Since Sunday. You have to be late every night.'

'It is my job,' he said. 'You know that.'

'Not like this.'

'We have a problem. These people we are dealing with do not stick to business hours.'

'Ai, Kaiser, we have a problem. We have a problem between us.'

'What problem? What's this problem?'

'You don't know?' She laughed. A harsh, forced laugh that Kaiser Vula hadn't heard from her before. 'You come home, we don't speak. We don't touch. We don't make love. You are a stranger. In the morning you do not even kiss me goodbye.'

She broke into her mother tongue, the language beating at him like hail.

'What're you saying? Talk English.'

'You want me to talk English? I will talk English. You are a bastard. That is what I said. A bastard.' Her voice rising. 'A bastard. Like all men you are a bastard.'

Now Kaiser Vula railed at her in his language. Swore at her and her family. He heard her gasp at the rawness of it. Went back to English. 'We will talk about this later. You wait for me. Tonight we will talk about this. When I get home we will talk about this.' He was shouting, the roar of blood and language loud in his head. Disconnected, threw the phone onto the passenger seat.

Sat, gripping the steering wheel, staring down the street until his breathing calmed.

At his side window a bergie grinned, tapped on the glass. Saying, 'Mister Meneer, you got some money for a poor gentleman?' The vagrant offering a cupped hand.

Kaiser Vula waved him away.

'Ag, please, Meneer, just a two rand.'

Kaiser Vula opened the glovebox, drew out a pistol, pointed it at the bergie. The man stepped back, ran off on shamble legs. Kaiser Vula watched him disappear into the dusk. Dropped the gun back into the glovebox. Drove off, his mind seething. For a moment thought of confronting her. Going home to confront her. Now. Immediately. While the fight was in him. But he did not turn back. Continued towards the woman who pleased him. Drove into the parking below her apartment block, stopped beside her Audi coupé.

Sat in his car thinking, what was her case, his wife? There'd been other women before. He suspected she'd known that. She'd said nothing. But those women hadn't been Nandi. Those women had been different. Flings. Nothing serious.

Wham-bams. That'd been good for them. Brought mojo to their bedroom. He'd screw a stranger, rush home to screw his wife.

Except not with Nandi.

She changed that. As if she'd cast a spell. Sprinkled muti on his parts. Nandi and her muti. This modern girl with her witchdoctor powders. Where'd she get that from? Going off somewhere in the townships to buy her packets of magic. To see a witchdoctor, some sangoma from some backlands village.

He'd teased her about it. Told her it was deep rural. That she was superstitious. All this nonsense about bones, herbs, powders, contact with the ancestors. Traditional bullshit.

She'd look at him smiling, run a hand across his chest, stop over his heart. Enough to get him randy as a rabbit.

In the street one day he'd been handed a flyer: Prof Habi Mama Zuhra, the king of herbalists, consultation fee R50. Do you need more rounds for Sex. Do you want to control your Lover? Payment is done after problem is solved. Treatment 100% guaranteed.

'Your sangoma's got competition,' he'd said.

'Bah. Prof crook.' She'd dismissed his teasing.

'It's the same thing.'

She'd glanced at him. Suddenly serious. 'No. It is not the same. Not the same thing, Kaiser. Not at all. You must come with me. You'll see.'

His turn to dismiss the topic.

She'd given him that faint smile, that smile that hinted at something he didn't know.

He walked up the stairs to the foyer, greeted the security guards. Both of them snapping mock salutes. He waved, took the lift to Nandi's floor, let himself into the apartment.

Kaiser Vula found Nandi on a lounger on her balcony. Paused in the doorway to look at her. Her lean body stretched out in the warmth of the night. Elsewhere on the peninsula the wind howled, but the city was hot, breathless. A heat close as cotton wool.

She wore a long nightdress, white spaghetti straps over her shoulders. Buds in her ears, white wires linked to her iPad. Beside her a bottle of water in an ice bucket, some magazines, her phone. Away in her own world.

Her strange world with its mesh of new and old.

She raised a hand in greeting.

Kaiser Vula shook his head. How did she do that? How did she know he was behind her? With that noise in her head how'd she know he was there?

This uncanny thing about her. Her sixth sense. Her female sense. This weird foretelling women had.

He leant over her, ran a hand from her knee down her thigh, her dress folding back as his hand slipped between her legs. She clenched her thighs, trapped his hand. Opened her eyes. Her smile giving a glint of teeth.

'Kaisy,' she said.

He felt the prickle of her pubic hair.

'Now?' she said.

He wanted to say yes but his voice was husky. He nodded.

She moved his hand away, pulled the buds from her ears. 'Here or inside?'

'Here.'

'Okay.' Kept her gaze on him. 'Undress.' Propped herself up on her elbows.

Kaiser Vula found himself doing what she'd ordered. He pulled his shirt free, undid the buttons, his fingers fumbling. Dropped the shirt over a chair. All the time she watched him. A serious expression. Her gown rucked up as he'd left it.

He'd not undressed while a woman watched him before. It was troubling, unsettling. It was wrong. But he couldn't stop.

Unbuckled his belt, unzipped, his pants sliding down his legs, pooling at his ankles. He had strong thighs, thin calves, his limbs scattered with sprigs of hair. He stepped away from his clothing, closer to her.

Kaiser Vula wore boxer shorts patterned with red spots.

'Off,' she said. Pointed at the glass panelling that walled the balcony. 'Throw them over.'

Again he obeyed. Watched his underwear zigzag down to get stuck in a tree.

Kaiser Vula turned to see his Nandi beckoning him.

17

Major Kaiser Vula woke with his phone ringing. He was in her bed. She was asleep beside him. He frowned trying to remember how they'd got there. Could remember throwing his boxers away, but nothing after that.

He answered the phone.

'Major,' said the voice. A man's voice. 'You have a call from the president.'

'The president? Who's this?' Believing it was a joke. Some random troll.

'You heard me,' said the man.

The president.

Kaiser Vula hesitated. Slipped off the bed, walked into the lounge. The doors to the balcony still open. Stood naked looking out at the lights of the Waterfront. Cast about for something to wear. His trousers flung across a chair. Keeping the phone hard against his ear, pulled on his pants using one hand, balancing first on his left, then his right leg. Once, in that other life, that dangerous time fighting the Boere, once, before the president was the president, when he was the spymaster, then, for a short while, he'd been his boot boy. Run his messages. Driven his car. Been his protection.

'I am not fooling,' the man said in Zulu.

'How do I know?'

'We do not joke.'

'You can say that. You can be anybody.' Kaiser Vula tucked in his genitals, zipped up. Next shook out his shirt, fought his way into it.

'Major, we do not joke.'

'How did you know my cellphone?'

'We asked your director.'

That made sense. Kaiser Vula noticed smudges on his shirt, inspected his fingers to see they were covered in a grey dusting. He rubbed thumb against forefinger, couldn't feel the powder's granules.

Nandi's muti. When? When had she done that?

Said, 'At midnight? You phone at midnight?'

'The president is awake. He is working. This is serious, Major. Serious.'

In the background Kaiser Vula heard another voice demanding the phone.

'You are going through to him,' said the man.

'Major Vula,' said this voice. A voice Kaiser Vula recognised, from the past, more recently from press interviews. The clear incisive voice of the head of state. 'Major Vula, it has been a long time, my friend. My friend Kaiser.'

'Mr President,' said Kaiser Vula.

The president going into a run of greetings in Zulu. Kaiser Vula responded.

Then in English: 'Major, my friend, can you come to this place tomorrow? Bambatha Palace.' A pause. 'I should say today. It is today already, I see. There are some things … Some things to discuss. We can meet. In the evening I am having a party, you will stay for that. Is this fine?'

'Of course,' said Kaiser Vula.

'Good. I am pleased. I am pleased.' The president sounding distracted. 'You must bring your wife, if you want to. Or whoever. At your discretion. Come for the whole weekend. I remember you, my friend. Like an elephant remembers, I remember you. I am pleased. I am pleased. Sobonana futhi.'

Kaiser Vula disconnected. Yes, he thought, we will see one another again soon. But why?

He went back to the bedroom, finished dressing in the dark. Leant over Nandi, slid a hand over her breast to tweak her nipple. Heard her mumble at his leaving.

Later he would phone her. Tell her the arrangements.

18

Not long after eleven thirty Vicki told herself last game. She was up five hundred US. Time to quit. She was finished. Had drunk two pots of chamomile tea ordered up from room service, eaten four slices of toast. The toast had killed the nausea. There was an ache in her boobs still but not as bad.

Last game, then nighty-night.

Clicked through to a new game, chose pot limit. Why not give it a thrash for the final? Five hundred dollars to play with, like playing for nothing.

Vicki poured more tea, no milk, no sugar. Took another piece of toast from the covered basket. The toast cold. Didn't matter. Dry toast was what she wanted. Crunched into the slice.

Selected a table of three, bought in with the maximum ten

dollars. Came out of that game seventy dollars up; a two pair, Jacks and twos. Bloody lucky.

The whole play less than ten minutes.

One more.

One more quick one.

This time on a table of five. She went down eighty. Thought of ducking out but didn't.

Last game.

Came up a hundred and fifty in the two games following. The cards good there, kings and queens favouring her.

Vicki did more cold tea and toast.

Clicked back in. Got through five games on the up, even winning the pot with a king high. Amazing. The good Lady Luck sitting right beside her.

Gone one a.m. she logged out. The tiredness coming over her. Stretched, rose stiffly out of the chair, walked to the window: no one moving in the windows opposite. Standing on tiptoes, could just see the street. Empty, wet. A figure with an umbrella walking quickly away, a glint of high heels beneath a coat.

Made her think of Linda Nchaba. Same size, same grace, even briefly glimpsed. A sudden guilt that she'd done nothing. That she'd let the medics take her off. But what could she do? Could she have done? Except made a mess of the whole operation.

She closed the blinds. Walked through to the bathroom.

Thank all the gods of fortune her training had kicked in. Let alone Henry Davidson's voice in her head, shouting to stay the hell out of it. All the same, what had happened? What was going on inside Linda Nchaba's head?

Five minutes later Vicki curled up beneath the duvet. Too tired to read, switched off the light.

As if that was a signal, as if someone was watching her

window, waiting for it to go dark, her cellphone rang. She groped for it, came up on an elbow, saw restricted number on the screen. Considered not answering. Except this time of the night it could be an emergency. Answered. Saying hello, hello, hello. Nothing. Dead air. She flipped the phone onto the bedside table, collapsed back on the pillow.

The phone rang again.

Again the same screen display. Again she said hello three times. The same dead air.

No sooner disconnected than it rang once more.

Vicki switched the phone off, clicked on the bedside light. Took out the battery, laid the pieces on the table. Fully awake now. Sitting up in bed, hugging her knees. The thoughts occurring: Someone was getting at her, or hoping to. Someone who knew she'd met Linda Nchaba. The most likely scenario. Maybe knew she had the flash drive. In that case had to be someone from the Aviary trying to knock her off her perch. Why? Why put the frights on? Wasn't going to put her off the job. Hardly. Was going to make her more careful. More suspicious. More paranoid. Thing was, with the amalgamation of the agencies there were old rivalries, old hostilities. The Aviary not home to a happy flock.

She thought about putting her phone together again, ringing Henry Davidson. Imagined he'd give his famous snort at her theories. 'I wouldn't think so.' Still he'd tell her to do what she'd done: take the phone apart. Tell her to keep the flash drive safe, go back to sleep. Enjoy her meeting with Detlef in the morning. He might be sick but watch his hands.

The last thing she felt like right now. A meeting with some German has-been.

Vicki wondered if maybe she should call Fish. Let him know that digging around in Linda Nchaba territory might have consequences. Except he'd be well out of it, apart from fast asleep. Probably smoked a portion of herb, drunk a Butcher Block four-pack listening to his music up too loud. Raising Fish in the hours before dawn was not a good idea.

Vicki sighed, switched off the sidelight. She wouldn't disturb him. Fish was a practiced operator. He could handle whatever fell out of the tree. She settled herself under the duvet, turned away from the city lights, an orange glow at the window.

She would wake to a grey morning.

19

Fish woke to the wind, the thrum of it in the overhead wires, the flap and knock of a fascia board. For weeks he'd been meaning to fix it. Every time the wind blew he'd been meaning to fix it. Then the wind would go down, he'd forget about it. Until the next blow.

Like now the clatter brought him up from a far place, a distant apprehension nagging. Nothing specific. Just a shadow outside a window, a hand raised, tapping. The stuff of dreams.

Fish lay in the sheet tangle, unmoving, eyes open, staring at the ceiling, trying to place the shadow. The shadow of a man. A man he'd never seen.

A name came to him: Mart Velaze.

'You know a man called Mart Velaze. He said you would help me.'

That got Fish out of bed.

The name going over and over. Mart Velaze. Mart Velaze.

In the bathroom pissed out a long stream of last night's doob and ale straight into the water in the bowl, creating froth. A noise Vicki hated. Would shout at him to shut the door. Stop being a barbarian. He was a lid-closer though. Thanks to his mother. She'd taken no nonsense there. No crystalised drops on the seat. No coming into the loo to face a gaping bowl.

He flushed, catching a whiff of ammonia.

The name still there: Mart Velaze.

How to get hold of Mart Velaze?

Showered. Dressed.

The question still with him while he made coffee, checked his email (nothing of consequence), surfed the surf sites (nothing of consequence). Stood looking at the *Maryjane* in the back yard while he drank his coffee. Thought, the scene he'd been through before with Mart Velaze put Velaze in some sort of agency, some sort of government agency. Like the secret services. Could be Marty was a spy? Why not? Fish tapped his teeth with the coffee mug. Worth a try. Thought: Google State Security.

There it was: Welcome to our new website. Buttons to Facebook, Twitter. One hundred and fifty-seven likes on Facebook. No comments. The Twitter feed something else. Something lively. A cheeky comeback tweet telling a journalist: 'Ah please, don't flatter yourself.' Another having a go at one Maggs: 'Really Maggs? We still look forward to your serious and engaging comment, surely this can't be it.' The ominous thrown in among the banter: 'We have headed President's call to restore the authority of the state.' Okay headed should've been heeded but kinda amusing. Fish clicked follow.

Then clicked back to the website: background colours dark green above shading down to earthy reds. Caused Fish to ponder. Like what was the meaning here? Blood on the ground? Secrets in the shadows? Scrolled through the menu, came up with a Cape Town post box, no phone numbers.

Another option: the telephone directory. That great source of info. Under some magazines found a directory, flipped through the government pages. Behold, a listing for the National Intelligence Agency. According to the website the NIA was supposed to have been collapsed into the State Security Agency. Seemed to be one of the few things government hadn't collapsed.

Fish dialled it.

Got through.

Asked for Mart Velaze.

Was told one moment.

Heard Mart Velaze say, 'Velaze speaking.'

'We haven't met,' said Fish. 'We've talked before.' He gave his name.

'What d'you want, Fish Pescado?' said Mart Velaze.

'It's time we had coffee,' said Fish.

'You reckon?'

'I do.'

A pause. Then: 'I'll get back to you.'

'I'm supposed to go with that?'

'Yes.'

End of conversation. Dead air. Fish snorted. The cocky bastard disconnected. You had to give it to Mart Velaze, he played hardcore. Fish was about to ring back when he thought, no, there'd be surveillance on the line. One call was random, two calls weren't. Sometimes you had to have faith.

He'd give Mart Velaze a couple of hours, then hassle him again. Meanwhile there was Vicki's request about Linda Nchaba. Google again: Durban modelling agencies. About to start the slogwork when his landline rang. International call, a number he didn't recognise.

A voice speaking at him, 'Bartolomeu, this is Estelle. I'm in your city as it happens, flying out tonight to Beijing. Would've been nice to have seen you but the world is demanding, as you know. Next time, I hope. Meantime, Barto, a favour please. I

81

wonder if you could do some research for me? I'm with my principals Mr Yan and Mr Lijan.'

'Hey, Mom,' said Fish.

'Estelle, Barto, Estelle. Remember my suggestion. You're too old to call me mom. Time to grow up Bartolomeu.'

Fish ignored the suggestion. 'Nice to hear from you. Cape Town, hey. Wow. Getting out and about. Thought you were still in London?'

Estelle into some NGO called Invest South Africa. To Fish's way of thinking, a front for government.

'I travel, Barto. Hence China because China's the future. That's why I'm on the move. I do things. If I had a law degree to finish, I'd finish it. Not let my girlfriend show me up. How's your Indian girlie by the way? Victoria.'

'Vicki.'

'Vicki. How's she?'

'In Berlin.'

'You see. Lawyers travel. They get around. They're needed in all jurisdictions. They don't waste their lives surfing.'

'She's a spy these days.' Fish dropping the detail in for the hell of it. 'On her first international operation. Code named Caterpillar.'

'Oh don't talk nonsense, Bartolomeu. Honestly. Lawyers may be many things but I very much doubt she's a secret agent.'

Fish heard Mr Yan or Mr Lijan say something in the background. His mother responding, 'Yes, yes, of course.' Coming back to him, 'Now listen, Barto, we're about to go into a quick meeting. Can you do some research?'

'Free or paid?'

'This is professional, you can invoice as per your normal rate. Not over the top.'

'Five hundred's not over the top.'

'It's higher than last time.'

'Inflation. Five hundred plus expenses.'

'Itemised expenses.'

Fish grinned. His mother. These days you couldn't tell what would come next.

'Here's the thing, as hip people say: could you find out about a man called Rings Saturen? Coloured businessman. Politician. My principals met him a year ago, now they might be firming up a deal so they need a due diligence as it were. There was some issue last year, a friend of his was shot. And there were rumours the friend had once been a gangster. I don't know, sounds a little messy to me. So some discreet background. Family. Connections. Standing in the community. You know the sort of thing.'

Fish knew the sort of thing. The alternative cv. Meant Rings Saturen probably had sidelines. Common enough these days. Wrote down the name, circled it twice. Said, 'You going to tell me what sort of business deal?'

'No, I'm not.' Mother Estelle in forceful mode. 'Don't ask silly questions. You should know not to do that by now.'

'It helps,' said Fish, 'knowing what's going on.'

'Oh, for goodness sake, Bartolomeu. Just let us have whatever comes up. We're talking about investment. We're talking about partnerships. We're talking Brics. You've heard of the Brics group of countries?'

Fish tempted to say no. Went with, 'That third world thing: Brazil, Russia, India, China, us.'

Heard his mother sigh. 'Never mind. I've got to go. Just get me what you can, Bartolomeu, dear. As soon as you can.'

Fish thought, what was it with his mother? No contact from one week to the next, not even time for a quick coffee when she's in town, then a business request. Mind you, he wasn't the best of sons for keeping in touch. Wasn't for Vicki's insistence they'd talk even less often.

He disconnected, keyed into his landline the number of the first agency on the Google page. Asked the receptionist for Linda Nchaba. Was told he'd be put through to Angie.

Angie came on, said, 'You're looking for Linda? She's with SupaGals. Or I think she was. I wanted her to come to us but Linda likes money. I couldn't offer her enough.' Angie laughed. A nice laugh, Fish thought, that conjured a picture of a woman in her fifties, short hair, lots of white cotton, a rich laugh as if Angie had smoked a few too many from a young age. 'Fair enough, I suppose. Looks don't last forever. You got to cash in on them while you can. Good luck, doll.'

SupaGals was three down the list. Fish Googled the agency, brought up pictures of their models. There was Linda Nchaba named in their gallery. Range of photos of her doing a summer fashion number. Hot piece. Fish dialled. This receptionist said, 'I don't know anybody like that.'

Fish said he'd been referred by Angie of Double M Models.

The receptionist said, 'Wait.'

Fish waited. One minute, two minutes, was beginning to think he'd been dumped. The reception came back, wanting his details. Fish gave more or less the truth except he said he was a movie gofer, doing the dog work for a casting agency.

Another long wait. A man came on, said, 'You're looking for Linda Nchaba?'

Fish said he was.

'Why?' The voice officious. Challenging. A suit, Fish reckoned, but not a collar and tie. A pale blue open-necked shirt. Probably once upon a time a lawyer. 'We haven't seen her for a year. She's overseas somewhere.'

'Yeah,' said Fish, 'that's what Angie told me.'

'Angie at Double M?'

'Mm-hmm.'

'Thinks she knows everything. Mrs On-Top-Of-It.'

'us, Angie said.'

'As far as we're concerned, and we're her agency, Europe. Holland. Amsterdam, to be precise. I'll email her your details.'

'Please,' said Fish, hesitated. 'Listen, a favour, you couldn't let me have her contact numbers?'

'We don't do that.'

'Sure. It's just …' He let it hang there for a moment. 'It's just they asked for her especially. You know. Like they really want …' Left that hanging too.

'Who wants her?' said the man.

Fish gave him the story he'd told the receptionist adding two details: the name of a casting agency taken off a Google scan; the fact that it was in Los Angeles. A scan he'd done while they were talking. Chances were the dude with the blue open-necked shirt would Google a check too. Chances were though he wouldn't bother phoning. The sort of gamble Vicki would put odds on.

A silence, Fish staring at Linda Nchaba on his laptop screen, waiting, wondering if he'd get lucky. His cellphone rang. Unknown number.

Fish answered.

Mart Velaze said, 'Two p.m. Truth. You know Truth?'

'The coffee shop,' said Fish. 'With all the bones.'

'Exactly.'

'How'll I know you?'

'You won't. I know you.'

Fish heard the agency man say, 'We're her agents. Any contracts have to come through us.' Fish keyed off his cellphone.

'Yeah, sure. I'm just trying to find her. You know these movie types, they like the hype, like talking things up. That personal contact. When I was talking to …'

'You tell them we're her agents.'

'No problem.'

'I've got an address. Edendale. That's a township.' He read off the street name and number. 'Got that?'

Fish said he had.

'Anything in Amsterdam?'

'Can't help you there. Only a cell number.'

'That'd be good.'

He got that too, keyed off the phone. Not surprised that it'd been this easy. Most people'd give you a break if they thought it was legit. Or there might be money in it.

He grinned. Half an hour's work was all it'd taken. The man on the top of his game. Thought he'd take himself down to Knead for breakfast.

20

The president emerged from the swimming pool, a neat man for his age. No flab, no potbelly, the rigid carriage of a controlled man. Towelled his face, his shaven head. Drank from a glass of fruit juice. Real squeezed oranges, mangoes thickening the juice. Ice cubes clinking. Condensation on the glass, leaving wet rings on the table top where he'd placed it.

His secretary held out a cellphone. 'The minister for you, Mr President.'

The president took the phone, turned to look back at the glittering water.

Said, 'Comrade Minister.' Drank his juice, listened to the nervous run of the minister's explanation. Said, 'Comrade Minister, you know what the cabinet instructions were. You understand the situation. There is no use in telling me these things. The cabinet has decided.' A pause. 'No. No. I cannot do that. I cannot override the cabinet. Of course I have done so when it is necessary, but on this occasion that is not the situation. You know what your fellow ministers expect from you and you know what I expect from you.' The president pausing for a quick swallow of juice, saying, 'No, Comrade Minister, we, I, have outlined how you will proceed. Yes, there will be unhappy people – important unhappy people, and this cannot be helped. You are minister of defence. We have a problem, and that problem must be finalised. Now. You have the file, you have the documents, everything is set out for you to cause this action. You will not follow any other course. You have work to do, Comrade Minister. I will not keep you from it.'

The president thumbed off the call. Handed the phone to his secretary, a man in a grey suit, pink tie, shined shoes. Immaculate.

Said, 'You will need to chase him.'

The secretary nodded.

'Some comrades forget too quickly. They forget the life before. They forget what I know.' The president finished the orange juice. Held out the glass. 'Some more, I think.' Stood there, the water drying rapidly on his body in the early heat.

The secretary took the glass to the breakfast table under an umbrella. A jug there of the president's morning blend. Refilled the glass. 'Coach is ready, Mr President,' he said.

'At the tennis court?'

'As you instructed.'

'Good, good.' He waved away the glass of juice. Set off across the slasto paving. After a couple of paces, stopped, called back, 'Where's Zama?'

'Running, sir.'

'He is always running. Does he never stop this running? It is bad for the joints, does he not realise this? When he is my age he will suffer. He will need operations.'

'He has told me he is training, sir, for the Comrades Marathon.'

'Ah, my son the athlete, always drawn to these marathons: the London Marathon, the New York Marathon, the Two Oceans Marathon. Good, it shows his stamina and dedication. Phone him. Tell him we need to talk this morning after my session. He has an hour to finish his training schedule.'

At the tennis pavilion the president changed into whites, bounced onto the court, brandishing his racket. 'You are ready to be beaten, Coach?' he shouted at the man retrieving balls from the further reaches.

The man came quickly towards him. At the net, they touched rackets. 'Prepare to meet your match, Coach. Or have you been taking lessons?'

The coach sniggered. 'We'll see, Mr President.' Handed over a bucket of balls.

The president walked to the backline, bounced a ball, once, twice, three times, preparing to serve. Threw it up, smashed an ace down the centre. Stepped to his left, waving the coach out of the way. 'You do not want to get hurt, Coach.' Cracked another hard one. Had it returned to his backhand, lobbed, the coach running left, getting behind it. The president at the net for a soft stopper. Triumphant, continued from side to side until the bucket was empty.

Said, 'Okay, Coach, now let us see what the white man can do.'

'You do not want to warm up, Mr President, sir?'

'The match will warm us up, Coach. There is no time for messing around. Best of three. My serve.' Put down two strong balls: thirty love. The coach returning the next hard down the line on his backhand: thirty fifteen.

'So. There is some spark left in the white man.' The president smiling. 'It is good to see, Coach.'

From outside the court the secretary said, 'Mr President, the minister is on the line.'

'The minister of defence?'

'Yes, sir.'

The president prepared to serve. 'You must tell him to wait. I have business here.' Powered a drive that the coach smacked back, to the president's surprise.

Thirty all.

On the next serve a sharp exchange.

'Forty thirty, Coach. Maybe I should take on the Yankee John Isner, give him some competition with my service. What do you think?' Jiggered about from foot to foot. 'You are ready for this?'

The coach raised his racket, bent forward, balancing on the balls of his feet.

The president served. The ball too low, grazing the top of the net, deflecting wide. Undaunted, cannoned the second ball, the coach taking it on the forehand for a stinging return. The president backhanding down the tramlines, getting a cross-court high bouncer. Took it at the peak, smashed. The coach on the backline jumping, getting his racket to it, the stroke awkward, the ball too long.

A shout from the president.

'That is the lesson, Coach. Never be caught on the wrong foot. Anticipate and position. The lessons of tennis, the lessons of politics. When you have a second chance it must be strong like the first. Otherwise what is the point?' He held up his hand. 'Wait a minute. I must talk to this mampara. Sometimes I think we are a country of stupid men. Stupid women as well.' Beckoned for his secretary to bring the phone.

Said, 'Comrade Minister, you are interrupting my day. You are making it unpleasant. When it is beautiful like this with blue sky I do not want storm clouds on the horizon. I want you to fix what has happened. You are the minister of defence. What happened, taking care of what happened, is within your portfolio. If you cannot fix it, then you must tell me, and I will fix it. This is simple, Comrade Minister, all you have to do is say you need my help.' A pause, the president listening, tapping his racket against the toe of his tennis shoe. 'Good, Comrade Minister, good. You have my cooperation. You will find that I have already taken action, Comrade Minister. It is as I said to Coach: The second serve must be as strong as the first. Take care, Comrade Minister. Hamba kahle.'

Without disconnecting handed the phone to the secretary. 'Write his letter of resignation. Tell him he must sign it this morning.' To the coach called out, 'No need to change sides. Your serve.' As he wheeled away said to the secretary, 'Have you got hold of Zama?'

'He will meet you at the hives.'

'Good. Now let me show Coach how we Zulus sort out the wizards. Just call me Dingaan.'

21

They got to the hives in a golf cart, the secretary driving. The president sipping another fruit juice. Dapper now in a grey suit, white shirt, skinny blue tie with thin stripes. There was Zama waiting, looking at the hives: a cluster of eight in a stand of bluegums. Old trees that'd been there when Bambatha was part of a large cattle farm. Zama standing with a bottle of power drink in his hand. A tall man, light skinned, sleek with sweat. Two bodyguards waiting to the side.

'You see them, Zama?' said the president, approaching his son, pointing at the hives, at the active bees. Drawing Zama closer to the swarms. 'Hear them. They are our lifesavers.'

The hives, his father's pride. How often hadn't he heard the old man trot out the notion that without bees human beings wouldn't last a week. That being the start of the sermon, the rest about how commercial honey was a mixture, a cocktail of import and local from who knew what source. But his honey was pure. The best in the country. His mission to have hives built at every village. Real African honey from African bees would ease the hard lives of his people. It was the medicine of the Zulu, the muti of their ancestors.

'A golden sweetness that is both energy and health,' said the president. 'You should have a spoonful of honey every day. My people sing its praises. They thank me for showing them the wisdom of our culture.'

Zama shrugged, took a drink from his bottle, pushed closed the lid. Called out to his guards that they could go.

'Zama.' The president reaching up to touch him on the shoulder. 'It is time. Time we talked of some matters.'

Zama looking at him, frowning. For years his father had kept him out of the family businesses, the imports and exports, the mining interests, the Chinese deals. Probably the old man didn't realise he knew about these dealings, believing his son had his own matters. True, Zama had gone his own way. First the military. Then something with fashion models that kept him busy, earned him money. What Zama did was never his father's concern, but now he was saying it was time to talk of family matters. This puzzled Zama, made him wary.

'My son, there is family business for your attention.' The president finding Zama's eyes behind the sunglasses, holding them until they both glanced away.

'I have a full plate.' Zama gazing again at the hives.

That was the problem with his father. His expectations. That no one else had a life. That he could click his fingers to command. Build them hives. Give them the lives of bees, their legacy. What did he know about his children, the children from his other wives? What did he know about him, his eldest? Nothing. They were strangers. Mysterious beings that could be seen and heard but whose lives happened elsewhere.

'You must find time. This is important, a big business that supports our family.' The president waved an arm at the palace buildings, the amphitheatre, the guest cottages, the tennis courts, the swimming pool, the clinic. 'You think only government money can build this? No, no, it needs more than government money to build this. This has family money. From our investments, my son. Investments you must now control.'

'Under your eyes.' Zama defiant, taking off his sunglasses. Saw the president smile, no doubt pleased to see the insolence. The spark. He would need the spark to stand up to his father. 'No. I have other matters.' Zama keeping his lips tight, his eyes squinting against the glare. 'Why do you bring me here to say this? Why can't we talk inside?' Zama feeling the sun on his skin, too hot. 'Inside, out of the sun.'

'You do not like the sun. You are like white people. Worried about your skin.' The president raised his hand, called to the secretary for one of the big golf umbrellas, said, as it was opened above them, 'There are ears in the palace. It is better to talk here.'

'Pah!' Zama shook his head. 'That is nonsense. You have been president too long, my father.'

'I am president-for-life. Is that too long? Perhaps it is too long. But this is what the people want. It is the people who asked me to stay. I am the people's vote. I must listen to the people, Zama. I am their servant.' The president indicating that they should walk. 'Maybe one day you will find out about being a leader. Then you will understand what it is to be alone.'

They walked closer to the hives, Zama waving bees away from his face. 'We are too near.'

'They sense your fear,' said the president. 'Those who are afraid can be attacked, subjugated. It is a law of the universe.'

Zama stepped back. Said, 'About what? What are we to talk about?'

The president turned to face him. 'I will tell you. It has been on my mind. You see, for five years we have had major mining interests elsewhere in Africa. Gold. Diamonds. We are serious players.'

'For five years, you kept it secret.' Zama unsurprised. 'For five years you have never told me.' Looked at his father. There had always been unease between them. He was too much like his mother, the other mothers told him: the shape of his nose, his thin lips, his caramel skin. There had always been this between them.

'There is lots you don't know, Zama. You were not ready. I am telling you now.'

Zama thinking, they were right those who talk about patience: for everything there comes a time. A man. Now it is my time.

'Where are these mines?'

'You will see. There are men coming later who will talk to us.'

'What men?'

'You will meet them.' The president touched his son's elbow. 'These mines are very productive. Major investments. I think it is time for you to manage them. This is your portfolio now.'

'Why?' Zama, edged off. The bees still an irritant.

The president followed him. 'Why do you ask that? Why do you question me?'

'I know you. You are my father.'

The president laughed. 'You are my son. Are you worried when something good happens? You are sharp. You question, why does he do this now? It is a good question. We must be sharp because there are many knives hidden in the smart suits. Come, we must prepare.'

'Is that all you'll tell me? Not where these mines are? What they produce? How much they produce? What we earn? Nothing?'

'You will learn everything from the men.'

'I know.' Zama walked out of the shade, put on his sunglasses. Contempt curled his lips. 'I know where these mines are. In a war zone? Yes?' Stepping towards his father. 'Yes? DRC? Central African Republic? Eritrea? Maybe even Rwanda? The Lord's Resistance Army? The naughty children taking our money. Yes? This is right, yes?' He sucked at his power drink, spat a mouthful on the red earth. 'Ha! I'm right. When my father is in trouble, he calls for his sons.'

'One son, Zama. You.' The president looking up at the tall man.

'The son he can throw away.'

'The eldest son.'

'The motherless son.'

'No.' The president angry, his fists knotted. His face hardened. 'No. You cannot say that. You cannot raise this matter.'

'It's the truth,' said Zama, low, calm-voiced. Standing defiant, his arms crossed, the drinking bottle tight against his hip.

The president brought up his hands, flexed them to release the tension. 'I could have given this to any one of your brothers. I chose you.'

'And I must be grateful?'

'You. Zama. I came to you. You have the army training. You are the best one. Your brothers are playboys, and this is a problem for a man. I am not begging, Zama, I ask you do this thing for me, as a man to a man.'

'My father asking politely? What's the angle?'

'There is no angle, my son.' The president indicating for the secretary to close the umbrella. 'I have enough to manage, affairs of state. One day you will understand that fathers come to rely on their sons.'

22

Vicki Kahn woke to the grey morning, let the room coalesce. Wanted to go back to sleep. Felt as tired as she'd been six hours before. Wanted to curl up, forget about the world.

But she couldn't.

There were issues.

Vicki thought of calling Fish. Groaned again at the sight of her cellphone in three pieces. Sat up, placed the battery back in the phone, clipped on the cover. Connected. One missed call. Number restricted. Either they'd realised what she'd done or they'd got bored.

About to make the call to Fish when the nausea swept through her. Vicki closed her eyes, bunched duvet in her fist. Remembered. A thought deeply troubling. She felt hellish. Another groan. Pushed back her hair, staggered through to the bathroom to pee. Her pee rank, smelling of mushrooms. While she sat on the loo, her phone rang in the bedroom. No way she was rushing for it.

Vicki Kahn did not like how her morning had begun.

She flushed away the stench. It was now all she could smell. Stared at her face in the mirror. Small lines at the corners of her eyes. A puffiness under them. Nothing that cold water wouldn't sort out. She should have got more sleep.

Still there was the poker win, a small triumph amidst the drek.

She put the call through to Fish.

'I've found her,' he said. 'About to celebrate with a Knead breakfast.'

'Who?' said Vicki, opening the blinds, rain pattering the window. Rain was really the last thing she needed this morning. Except for her jaunt to Detlef Schroeder, she didn't need that either.

'Well, not found her, you know, got an address. And a cell number. Only thing the address is fifteen hundred kays away in KwaZulu. You going to stump for that? You want me to check it out?'

'No.' Vicki coming in quickly. 'Leave it.'

'Whokaai. Don't have to bite.'

Vicki eased onto a chair at the desk, pulled over the hotel stationery. 'Sorry, babes, I didn't sleep well. Listen, this Linda Nchaba causes vibes. I don't know why. You might get calls.'

'Calls? What sort of calls?'

'No-number calls. Back-off calls.'

'Not a big deal.'

'Just back off, okay? No heavy stuff.'

'Cool,' said Fish.

'You can give me the cell number. Type it.' He did.

'So you got calls?'

'I did. Last night, late. They woke me.'

'That's weird.'

'Everything's weird in this world.'

'You're worried?'

Vicki typed: 'A bit. Only people supposed to know where I am are you and Henry Davidson.'

'I don't know where you are. Not exactly. I mean I know it's Berlin. You just never told me which hotel.'

'Good then, they can't torture it out of you.'

'Seriously, Vics.'

'Seriously, what?'

'Should I be worrying about you?'

Vicki sighed. 'I don't know. We'll talk when I'm back.'

'Sure, sure.'

A pause from Fish, Vicki about to say she'd be in touch later when Fish messaged: 'I talked to Velaze.'

'You what?'

'What I wrote.'

'Just like that you found him?'

'Yeah, in the phonebook. Don't know why I didn't think of it before. National Intelligence Agency.'

'They don't exist anymore.'

'Says who? A lady answered.' Entered: 'I asked for Mart Velaze, she put me through.'

'We're State Security now,' Vicki staying with text. 'NIA's called Domestic Branch. Like a cleaning service.'

'Ha, ha. That's what you keep saying about State Security.' Fish pulled a face. Said, 'Have to admit my phonebook's a couple of years old.'

Vicki laughed. 'Incredible.'

'I thought so too. Just goes to show what archive research can do.'

'An old phonebook!'

'Don't they teach you that in spook 101? Check out the phonebook first?'

Vicki thinking, strange Mart Velaze doing this. Pushing Cynthia Kolingba to Fish. Being prepared to talk to him. Exposing himself. He'd know she was in the Aviary. All this time he'd kept out of the way. Like once wanting to have them killed wasn't anything personal. Like at the time they'd been an inconvenience. Suddenly, now, why was he surfacing?

'When're you meeting him?' she said.

Fish typed: 'This afternoon at the coffee shop in that mausoleum.'

No telling what drove Mart Velaze. Fish was right, Mr Shadow Man, lurking somewhere in the dark reaches. One thing for sure, he wasn't doing Fish a favour. Had to have his own agenda to bring him out into the daylight. If he planned to go that far.

'He won't pitch,' she said.

'Wanna bet?' A pause. Fish coming in fast, 'No scratch that. Scratch it. Sorry I said it. No bets. Bets are off.'

'A bet's okay,' said Vicki.

'No, no. Sorry I said it.'

'Loser pays for dinner at the Foodbarn.' She waited. Could hear Fish sucking on his lip. 'It's hardly a bet, babes, he's not going to pitch.'

'He will. I've got a feeling about this.'

23

Vicki Kahn checked the time on her watch. Seven forty-five. Three and a bit hours before meeting Detlef Schroeder. She needed to shower, eat some sort of breakfast, get to his apartment. Told Fish she had to go. Like fast. 'Talk to you later,' she said, disconnecting. Poor Fish thinking that Mart Velaze would be there.

She showered, letting the hot water sluice onto her shoulders, run down, the warmth giving some relief. Dressed casually: black jeans, burgundy cowl-neck jumper, the feel of the cashmere soft against her skin, boots. Went down to a meagre breakfast: an apple, half a bowl of muesli and yoghurt, dry toast, coffee. The coffee tasted foul. She had to go with chamomile tea. Sat there gazing at the breakfast buffet: croissants, cheeses, cold meats, bacon, eggs, enough to make you weep.

Back in her room she phoned Detlef Schroeder on the hotel line.

'Ah, Miss Kahn,' he said. 'So you are a real living person. Sometimes with Henry I cannot tell his seriousness from his joking. This is very good that we are talking. Very good. Now, we are still meeting this morning?'

Vicki assured him yes.

'Good, very good. Wilkommen im spy city. Now tell me where are you?'

Vicki told him Hackescher Markt.

'That is my old side of the city,' he said. 'But these days I do not go there anymore. I do not go anywhere anymore.'

Vicki thought, not self-pity in his voice but a sadness which he quickly brightened.

'So, this is your first time in Berlin?'

Vicki said it was.

'Then we will give you some tourist sightseeing when you come to me. You do not mind a little walking? There is not so much snow anymore although there is ice. You have shoes for ice?'

Vicki assured him walking was fine.

'Good, very good. Now, Miss Kahn, you can walk to the Karl-Liebknecht-Strasse, a short walk from where you are. This is Berlin's famous street. There you can take a bus 100 down the Unter den Linden to the famous Brandenburger Tor. The Brandenburg Gate. This bus route goes into the Tiergarten. If you like you must get out there at a stop. In this weather nobody will get out in the Tiergarten. So if maybe someone is following you, they now have a problem. They cannot get off, they must stay on the bus.'

Vicki wondered why he thought someone would be following her. Worried her that first there should be the calls in the night, then surveillance. Who even knew where she was apart from Fish and Henry Davidson? And Detlef Schroeder? Perhaps his warning was just the precaution of an old hand in spy city. A relic who couldn't believe he'd left the world of upturned collars, figures smoking in doorways. Vicki smiled at herself in the room mirror.

Caught Detlef Schroeder saying, 'In ten minutes, sometimes not so long as that, there will be another bus 100. You can take it and sit upstairs for a nice view although maybe the windows are, how do you say it, condensed? From the cold.'

'Condensation,' said Vicki.

'That would be a pity,' said Detlef Schroeder, 'if there is too much condensation.' He paused, his breathing laboured. 'Sorry, I am talking too fast.' Another pause, then: 'So now you go round the Golden Angel to the terminal at Zoo. There you can find the 149 bus up Kantstrasse to Savignyplatz. Then I am not far, half a block in the hinterhaus. You know this sort of building?'

Vicki said she didn't.

Detlef Schroeder explained that she went through the first building, across a courtyard to the rear building. There she would find his name next to a buzzer. 'It is no problem to find me,' he said. 'You will be here in one hour's time?'

Vicki said she would.

She hung up, wondered what the little talk was that Henry Davidson thought she and Detlef Schroeder would have? Sometimes the mysterious, everything-will-be-revealed-in-due-course world of the old spies was irritating. As if no one was to be trusted. As if only a select few should see the full picture.

She could hear Henry: 'It is best you only know what you need to know. Keeps you focused. Your mind uncluttered. Something I envy. Like Alice at the tea party.'

Bullshit.

What irritated the hell out of Henry Davidson was the thought that someone knew more than he did. For Henry Davidson there was always something else. Something that needed to be discovered. Some secret that others possessed.

She shrugged into her coat, buttoned it, slipped a grey snood over her head, twisted and triple-looped it. Fluffed the material round her neck, shook her hair. Looked the image of a smart European girl. What she needed was one of those furry Russian hats. She'd Googled them: ushankas, very stylish.

Glanced round the room: a model of tidiness, except for the unmade bed, though that seemed hardly slept in. Her netbook locked in the safe, Linda Nchaba's flash drive in her jeans pocket. Swallowed to suppress a rise of nausea, then left the room.

24

The bunker's war room: cool, air-conditioned. Neon-lit. A long table with twenty chairs down the length of the room. Maps on the walls. Under a spotlight the president's portrait: the president in doctoral gown.

Zama stared at the portrait. Could be only one reason his father wanted a handover. The enterprise was in the shit. Mr Teflon making an exit. He'd hear him out, do the due diligence. Play it casual. Casual worked in most situations.

The president pacing the room. On his phone to a comrade minister, his voice low, sibilant.

Working the room, three agency techies, gadgets out, doing a clean. The soft buzz of their magic wands like bees to Zama. Bees at a hive, bringing in the honey. The bunker like a hive: the president its queen bee. The thought made him smile.

Zama perched on a chair arm to watch the techies. Hiked up his jacket sleeves. Zama in a white shirt, open collar. Slacks, loafers, no socks. The jacket waxed cotton, black.

The president in uptight mode, in jacket and tie, laced black shoes. The president saying into his cellphone: 'Minister, Comrade Minister, your report must come to me. I appointed the commission. I must get the report. We must follow protocol. There must be transparency.'

Zama raised his eyebrows. Yes, transparency. Of course. Presidential commissions. Presidential investigations. The old man's way of keeping everything in-house. Everything under control.

Always amused Zama how his father ruled. Got the dirt on someone, then had a quiet word. Worked all the time. Everyone in his cabinet stitched up.

Zama shifted from his father's soft menace with the comrade minister to the flat-screen television. Sixty-five-inch screen, wall-mounted. Showing a black Mercedes-Benz, always it had to be a black Mercedes-Benz, coming through the security boom. The car tracked from camera to camera to the palace side door. Interesting entrance, not through the normal formalities. Two men getting out, both military, both settling their caps. Generals.

At the door the secretary said, 'Mr President, the generals are here.'

'Ah.' The president keyed off the comrade minister with his thumb. 'And you?' he said to the techies.

'All clean,' one replied. The men packing up their gadgets.

As far as Zama knew, they'd never found a bug. But every morning the president wanted a clean sweep. Maybe the techs lied. They were secret service. Spies were spies. Maybe they told him what he wanted to hear. Maybe they were listening to the bunker's secrets all the time.

'Can I bring them down?' The secretary hovering at the door, standing aside as the techies squeezed past.

'Of course. And tea. With those chocolate cupcakes. A great temptation.' The president picked up a remote, clicked off the relay from the outside cameras. Said to Zama, 'You have had the cupcakes?'

Zama shook his head.

'This thing,' said the president, 'what you are going to see now ...' He put his finger to his lips, made eye contact. 'You keep this quiet.' Coming towards Zama, laying a hand on his arm. 'Okay? Yes. Okay?'

'Okay.'

'You stay shut up. You hear me.'

Zama felt the weight of the hand, the heat coming off his father's palm. Pulled back. 'I said okay.'

The two men locked in the measuring gaze. The president smiled, sat down at the long table. 'Good. I am pleased for you, my son. This is your time.' Again the smile. 'You will like the cupcakes. Not even the fancy bakeries in the fancy malls can make them like ours. We have the best.'

The president stayed seated when the generals arrived. The two men saluting. Said, 'This is my son, Zama. From today he is the man you talk to. Now you will report to him.' The generals shaking Zama's hand. 'Please, Generals, we don't have much time for this meeting.'

The generals set up a laptop, plugged into the flat-screen. Brought up the video footage.

'You will see at first it is sharp,' said the younger general. 'Afterwards it becomes blurred. Very jumpy.'

An image on the screen of men and boys wearing bands of bullets, carrying automatic rifles. Dressed ragtag, necklaces, vests, camouflage pants, headbands, sunglasses. The camera focusing on laughing faces. A group of thirty, forty males in a forest clearing.

'This is taken by our intelligence?' The president pointing towards the screen with his cellphone.

'No, Mr President,' the generals said together. The older one saying, 'The recording was left for us.'

'Left for us? You did not tell me this. Explain. Who are these people?'

'Rebel forces. Fighting against their government.'

The video cut to the armed band walking single file along a forest track. The general paused the image. 'It was found at the site, Mr President. We will address this issue.'

Zama glanced at his father, the old man hesitating: his face closed, his eyes on the screen, letting the silence extend. A trick Zama'd seen his father use before. Usually the victims burbled forth. The generals didn't. After long minutes they were told to continue.

On the screen Zama saw the forest edge, the men dispersing left and right. One thing he'd been on the money about: this was central Africa somewhere. Had to be with vegetation like that, with an armed group wandering around like that. Beyond the rebels, a stretch of veld grass in the light, bordering the waste piles of an opencast mine. The camera panning right to a cluster of buildings behind a security fence: the compound.

'You see that?' The president up, his finger tapping at the image of the buildings, a zoom enlarging them. 'You see that, Zama? This is our big mine in the CAR. Highly productive. The best gold. We have many, many people working here.'

The camera picked out a military guard, sitting on a box outside one of the buildings, smoking. His weapon resting against his knee. People behind him hanging washing on a line: camouflage fatigues, brown vests, underwear, socks. A man on a chair cleaning his gun, iPod buds in his ears.

'That is the barracks, the camp,' said the general. 'Fifteen soldiers present, the others on duty.'

The camera moving onto three soldiers walking along the fence, rifles cradled in their arms.

'This was the only security? To me this could be a holiday camp.'

'There was good security,' said the general. 'Patrols. Sentries. Two squads. Twenty-four soldiers.'

'But for a whole night you tell me these attackers were there, waiting. Nobody saw them. Nobody heard them. They are like a ghost army. No, my generals, this is impossible.' The president striding about the bunker. 'How can this happen? How can they be there all night but no one knows? You tell me we have patrols. You tell me we have sentries watching the bush. But still this happens.'

In the silence, the president breathing loudly. The generals with bowed heads.

'What happened?' Zama's question breaking the tension.

'Show him. Show him what you told me.' The president moving back to his chair.

'This is what happened, sir.' The general aiming the remote at the screen.

The images vague in the dawn light. Men moving about.

Zama said, 'There's no soundtrack?'

'No, sir. Not yet.'

'What am I looking at?'

'The rebels crossing the open space towards the compound fencing, sir.'

'Electric fencing?'

'No, sir. Only razor wire.'

The president coming in, 'You see, Generals, with Zama you can't hide behind technicalities.'

The image on the screen suddenly brighter, the direction now back to the forest. There in the gloom men kneeling, steadying grenade launchers.

'RPGS.'

'Correct, sir. We believe at least three, maybe five.'

The camera coming back to the compound, focusing, zooming closer. Buildings in the compound exploding.

The soundtrack came on. Men yelling. The clustered smash of automatic fire, rapid pops, then the boom and tear of explosions, silences in between.

'Fuck,' said Zama.

The image now blurred, wavering as the cameraman ran over the open ground. In front of him boys with AKs, screaming as they ran, firing as they ran.

Then clarity: the image steady. The rebels pulling down the fences, pushing through the razor wire, running into the compound.

'How'd they do that?' said Zama. 'How'd they get through the fences so quickly?'

'We think they cut them in the night.'

'You see, Zama. This is the sort of army we have.' The president on his feet again. Up and down the bunker. 'This is the rubbish we have for soldiers. They cannot hear people cutting fences at night.'

'No spotlights on the fences?' asked Zama.

'There are spotlights. But that night there was a power failure.'

'No back-up generators?'

'Yes, sir.'

'But they weren't deployed.'

'No, sir.'

'Why not?'

'This is subject to our enquiry, sir.'

'Listen to my son, Generals. This is a man you cannot feed nonsense stories.'

The camera on the move again, the video blurred, jumpy.

Clear enough to see people gunned down. The soundtrack constant gunfire, people screaming.

Into this the secretary entered with tea and cupcakes. Shouted above the noise, 'Here you are, Mr President, sir.' Put the tray down on the long table. 'Enjoy.'

The general paused the clip: the image on screen a woman in shorts, vest, automatic rifle in her hands, her head bursting.

'Generals,' said the president, 'you are privileged. Bambatha specials. The best cupcakes in the country.' The president peeling back a paper cup, delicately lifting off a tiny forkful of the mousse coating. 'You taste them.'

Zama watched the generals oblige. The three men standing round the tea tray with chocolate moustaches. Who were these men? The one probably an MK veteran. The other too young. His own age. A fast-tracker.

'Generals,' he said, 'when was this attack?'

The younger one swallowed quickly, wiped his mouth with a paper serviette. 'Last Friday, sir. Exactly.'

Zama poured tea, drank it black, unsweetened, watched the president quarter a cupcake, eat only a segment. Push the remainder to the side of his plate.

'Zama,' said the president, 'you must have one. Truly delicious. But I must have no more. Weakness is to be resisted.'

'We only get to see this now?' Zama sipped the tea, relishing the deep flavour. 'A week later.' Another thing his father cherished: good tea. The Indian connection flying in the best Darjeeling second flush. A strong amber tea with the muscatel flavour. Superb. Zama let the taste linger in his mouth. Refrained from taking a cupcake.

'There has been confusion,' said the older general. 'The mine is difficult to reach. The operation to secure it has taken time to get the troops there.' He gestured at the screen. 'This video was only flown to us yesterday. We reported to the president when we had information.'

'Last Friday night, Zama,' said the president. 'That was when I heard for the first time.'

'There has been nothing on the news.'

'No. There will be time for that when we are ready.'

Zama drank more of his tea, again held the liquid in his mouth, before swallowing. 'Tell me how many were killed?' Wondering how this one had been kept secret. The old goat up to his tricks.

'Look at the movie, Zama. See for yourself.'

The general activated the video. A slaughter. Soldiers stumbling into the killing zone, going down. The rattle of automatic fire, constant, unrelenting. A lone gunman in a window of the barracks shooting back.

'Complete wipe-out,' said Zama.

The generals didn't respond.

'Twenty-four troops dead,' said the president. 'Eighteen workers. Even the manager.'

On screen the firing had stopped. Occasionally the pop of a single shot, the spurt of an AK. The camera moving over the dead soldiers, panning onto the other buildings in the compound, bodies splayed at the doorways.

'Most of the workers escaped into the forest,' said the older general. 'That is our intelligence.'

'And the rebels?' Zama put down his teacup on the tray.

'You must have a cupcake.' The president held out the plate of cakes.

Zama shook his head, saw his father smile. 'Willpower, my son, willpower.'

'What about the rebels?' Zama met the eyes of both generals. Both glanced away.

The older one replied, 'The rebels are gone, sir. They are back in the forests. No one knows where.'

'You know this?'

'We have intelligence on the ground.'

'The mine is secure?'

'No, sir, not at this time.'

'Your intelligence?' said Zama. 'What is this intelligence?'

'From the government army. They have been there.'

'There's an offensive against the rebels?'

'No, sir.'

'They could be waiting to attack again?'

'It is possible, sir. No one knows, sir.'

'The army patrol found the video?'

The generals nodding, their mouths full of cake.

'Tell him where, General. Tell him where.' The president up close to the screen, his hand over his mouth as if he could smell the horror, the putrefaction.

Zama waited. Watched the generals swallow quickly. The younger one saying, 'It was left for us between the teeth of our commanding officer.'

'No respect, Zama. No respect.' The president swinging round. Zama glanced at him, thinking, this was the moment. The moment the old goat had been aiming for. His father standing there at the long table, hands on the back of a chair, skin tight over his knuckles. 'You must go there, Zama. Clean up this … this mess. Secure the mine. Get it working again. You will do that, yes?'

Zama feeling the generals looking at him. Seeing his own reflection in the president's eyes. Knowing it wasn't a request.

25

Joey Curtains couldn't believe his luck. Hadn't been parked at Surfer's Corner more than fifteen minutes, here comes a rust-bucket Isuzu bakkie, pulls into a space in front of Knead. Jaunty dude pops out: tanned, wild surfer-blond hair, baggies. Slops on his feet. The way he walked you'd think he'd won the Lotto. Hop, skip kinda guy.

Yeah, well, maybe he'd not be hoppety skippety in a couple of days. All depended what the great Kaiser Vula had in mind.

Joey Curtains had his camera up, clicked off a few frames of the surfer boy. Got one of his car reg this time. Phoned it through to the help.

Not a lot of customers at the café this windy morn. With the southeaster blasting, the place was a wipe-out.

Joey Curtains saw Fish Pescado slip onto a high chair at a window counter. Just visible through the salty glass.

Ten minutes Joey Curtains sat there wishing he could be inside chowing down on bacon and eggs. Thick slices of white bread. Then thought, probably a place like that didn't do real food. Probably only did eggs Benedict, crispy bacon, fancy-pancy portions for the body beautifuls. Joey Curtains favoured his bacon rashers thick. Chewy.

The notion of bacon churned a growl from his stomach. He considered he might as well walk in there himself. Could sit down next to the surfer boy, catch the vibe. Except his cellphone rang, the help with an address.

Joey Curtains sighed, switched on the car. Breakfast coming off his menu. Best to check out the dude's possie while the man was stuffing his face. He drove away down Sidmouth, Clarendon, swung into the main road at the railway bridge. Cruised slowly past the millionaires' beach houses, crossed the bridge over the vlei. At the robots went left, pulled over to thumb through his map book. Found the street. Two turns he was there. Real poor-white house: patchy lawn more sand than grass. Curtains drawn at the street windows, like there was no one living there.

Joey Curtains killed the engine, took some snaps. Got out, let himself in the gate. A notice on the gate read: Dogs Beware. Joey Curtains couldn't see any evidence of dogs in the property, walked up the driveway. There in the back yard a boat. Sleeping in a chair a person with a blanket pulled over their head. Joey Curtains deciding by the shoe size and type it was a woman. A bergie. Strong stench of smoke, piss, sweat coming off the blanket. Beside the chair a mug half-filled with coffee. A plate of buttered toast. Some nibbled crusts. Like Fish Pescado had made this bergie a quick breakfast.

Joey Curtains shook his head, backed out fast. Thinking some strange stuff happened close to the sea. All that wind got into people's brains. He drove off. Up to Kaiser Vula now.

What Joey Curtains didn't see in his rear-view was the woman in the blanket peeping at him from the corner of the house.

26

Linda Nchaba recognised the room. The Ikea chest of drawers. The Ikea chair. The blue mat with the animal image discreet in a corner. It was the bedroom she'd slept in for the past ten days. In the apartment she'd rented. The apartment she'd left in her need to keep moving. To keep one step ahead.

She lay in the bed. The curtains closed but grey light infusing the room. There was her suitcase, unzipped, in the middle of the floor. The clothes she'd been wearing draped over a chair. She rubbed a hand down her body, naked. No bra, no underwear.

They'd stripped her. Had a good look. Probably taken photographs.

She curled on herself. Her head hurt. Her mouth was dry. For long moments she lay, burning with anger. Then sat up, pushed the duvet aside. Moaned as the movement stabbed a pain behind her eyes. Steadied the dizziness. Sat on the edge of the bed, staring at her feet, her painted toenails. Trying to remember.

She'd left the apartment. Given the keys to the letting agent. Wheeled her suitcase to the bus stop. Taken a train to Schiphol. For an afternoon flight to France. To Paris. A modelling agency had signed her up. There were prospects, money. She could do something about her grandmother.

But before the flight …

Before that she'd met the agent. Vicki Kahn. They'd talked. Then there'd been a problem. SMSes. The flash drive. What had she done with the flash drive? She remembered. Had left it with the waiter. Asked him to give it to the woman, Vicki Kahn. A nice woman. A sympathetic woman. Someone she could trust. Someone she felt she could trust.

Then what?

She'd rushed off. Gone down the terminal corridor to catch her flight. Her flight to France. There were people, lots of people. People going to planes; people coming from planes. People on the moveable walkways. People rushing.

Then nothing.

She raised her head, looked about the room. There was a jug of water on the chest of drawers. She needed to drink. To rid her mouth of the harsh taste. Stood. Groaned again. Leant over the bed, supporting herself on her arms.

There'd been two men asking about a flight. They'd stopped her. She'd tried to brush past. Had said, 'I can't. I'm sorry.' The one had her arm. Then … A swirl of faces. Medics. A woman telling her she'd be alright.

After that, nothing.

Nothing until she'd woken back where she should not be.

Linda Nchaba closed her eyes, tried to slow her breathing, tried to still the soft yelps that surged from her chest.

She'd felt this panic before.

On her fifth run with the traffickers, they'd been stopped by soldiers, held captive for most of a day. Locked up in the truck with the girls while the driver tried to work a deal. There'd been shouting. Shots fired. She'd got the soft yelps then from the heat in the truck, the crying girls, the fear. Fear the soldiers would rape her. She'd known rape, she didn't want to know it again. At nightfall they were told to go. Why she'd never found out. But it scared her, the blank faces of the soldiers standing with their guns.

She shuffled to the chest of drawers, poured a glass of water, her hand trembling. They'd brought her here. Undressed her. Put her to bed. She scratched at her arm, her fingers coming away red-tinged. A needle-stick wound oozing a tear of blood.

But no memory of an injection. Of the stab of the needle.

She shifted aside the curtain, looked down on the street. A woman and a small boy walking towards the canal. Parked cars. There were always parked cars. Further down the street men at a delivery truck shifted out a fridge. She could hear their voices. Their laughter.

She drank the water. Drank a second glass. Moved away from the window to the bedroom door. Listened with her ear hard against the door. Nothing. No radio, television, no snuffles and snorts of someone, a man, waiting. She tried the door handle, felt the door open.

Again she paused, listening. Across the passageway, the bathroom: the door ajar to the shower, the loo, the basin. Down the passage the open-plan living room and kitchen.

On bare feet, backed against the wall, she slipped towards the lounge. Took a breath, stepped into the room. Empty. Tidy as she'd left it. Except: on the kitchen counter, a bowl of fruit. A plate with two croissants. On the bread board a ciabatta. In the fridge four instant pasta meals, milk, yoghurt, cheese, a selection of salami.

She tried the front door. Locked.

The landlord was two floors below: he wouldn't hear her scream, he wouldn't hear if she banged on the floor. The apartment below was vacant. From a window she could call into the street for help. She could do that. She would do that.

Then she saw her cellphone.

Plugged into a charger on the kitchen counter. Its display flashing a message notification. Opened the SMS. It read: 'Hello, sisi.'

Zama? It could only be. The thought of him cramped her stomach. Zama the reason she was here. The reason she was on the run. She dry-retched, swallowed acid. That'd become the taste of him in her mouth. Bitter, vile. At the back of her tongue.

The phone rang.

'Hello sisi,' said the voice. A man's voice. In Zulu, he said, 'We will be there later in the morning. You must be ready.'

She disconnected. Stood staring at the phone in her hand. This was a new voice. Not harsh, but not polite. Soft, friendly yet commanding. Who was this now? How many people were tracking her? Linda Nchaba knew fear as a tremble in her hands that she couldn't control.

The phone rang again. Shaking, she put it to her ear.

The man said, 'You must be ready, sisi.'

'No.' Her voice was faint. 'No.' She cleared her throat. 'The police are coming.' Her voice stronger, the resolution in her voice surprising. 'I have phoned them.'

'You must be ready, sisi,' said the man. 'Don't worry about the police. On this phone you can only talk to me.'

27

'I told you last night,' said Major Kaiser Vula on his cell to Joey Curtains. 'It was supposed to be urgent.' Hissing out the words. 'When I give the order, I mean the order. You understand me, Agent? You don't make your own arrangements.'

Major Vula on his way to the airport. Sitting beside him the lovely Nandi in her ripped jeans, leopard-skin pattern to her T-shirt. Like they were on safari.

Little things irritating Major Kaiser Vula on this bright blue summer morning.

When he'd picked up Nandi there she was in leggings, also a leopard-skin print. A short tulle skirt with camouflage pattern. Plus the T-shirt. Seriously on safari. To meet the president. Major Vula didn't think so.

Thing about Nandi, she could read situations. She read his face. Changed into the jeans. Was not going to lose the T-shirt. It was Aeropostale. Told him so.

Kaiser Vula grateful there wouldn't be a scene, backed down said, okay, keep the T-shirt. But come, my honey, come. The major not relaxed about catching aeroplanes.

On the hands-free now to Joey Curtains. Listening to the agent tell him he'd met with Prosper Mtethu, the operation was scheduled for this evening.

Kaiser Vula thinking, if Prosper was on this, then, no problem. Prosper was old school. Proper GDR training. Years in the Angolan camps. Time doing hits in the townships. Prosper would sort it.

'You listen to him,' he said to Joey Curtains. 'He's the agent on this one. You do everything he says.'

'Ja, Majoor.' Joey Curtains saying it in Afrikaans. Kaiser Vula hearing the sarcastic inflection. Jumped-up Joey Curtains.

The new breed, pissed off because they weren't dark enough. Well, Agent – the major pronouncing it to himself the Afrikaans way with a long A, guttural G – Well, Agent Joey Curtains would have to come to the party. Prove himself. Prove he wasn't some hip-hop gangster.

'Just do this right this time, Curtains. No bugger-ups.'

'Nee, Majoor.'

Kaiser Vula about to disconnect, remembered what else he'd asked of Joey Curtains.

'You traced that investigator yet?'

'Ja, Majoor. I know where he lives. What's the major want me to do about it?'

'Nothing,' said Kaiser Vula, amazed that Agent Joey Curtains had got something right.

'I got pictures.'

'Good.' Kaiser Vula unable to say good work. Said, 'Send them to me.'

'Ja, Majoor.'

The major disconnected before Joey Curtains lifted his blood pressure another notch. Glanced across at the lovely Nandi. Her face so young. So perfect the profile.

She turned to smile at him. 'Who was that?'

'One of my men.'

'Is he on an operation?'

'Something like that.' Major Kaiser Vula alert to the smile in her voice.

'What's it called?'

'What? What d'you mean what's it called?' Smiling back at her.

'You always give them names, your operations.'

Kaiser Vula reached across, squeezed her thigh. 'It's a secret.'

'Does the president know?'

'The president has his mind on many things.'

'You know,' said Nandi. 'No one would believe me if I told them about you. Even when I tell them I've been to the palace. They'll all think I'm joking.'

Kaiser Vula shook his head, took his eyes off the road to give her the stern look. 'Not a good idea. Better if you don't say a word.'

'What?' Nandi pulling back. Raised eyebrows, mouth open. That pretty tongue lying pink behind her perfect teeth. Their whiteness that so dazzled him. 'You're kidding.'

'I'm not.'

'No ways. No ways, mister. I go to the president's palace for a weekend I want to be able to say so.'

'Look.' Kaiser Vula leaning towards her. 'You can't, alright? For my sake, you can't. You know what I do. How many times've I said it.' Holding a finger to his lips. 'Secret. Okay. Secret.'

Nandi turned away from him. 'Why, darl, why can't I tell anyone?'

'Those're our rules. Between you and me.'

Nandi doing a pout. She did it well. Sometimes enough to make Kaiser Vula relent. Not this time. He focused on the road. Spinning down the fast lane, a Merc behind him wanting to overtake. Kaiser Vula ignored the guy's flashing lights.

Put through a call to Prosper Mtethu. The old man greeting him in Zulu.

'You have everything arranged?'

'Yes, Major.' Respect in the voice. None of Joey Curtains' nonsense.

'There must be no problems.'

'No problems, Major.'

'And tonight,' said Kaiser Vula. 'This must happen tonight.'

'It is planned, Major. Major must not worry.'

'You get him to do it.'

'Yes, Major.'

Kaiser Vula glanced in the rear-view mirror at the agitated Merc driver. A white man, grey hair, his mouth working, a hand waving to clear the lane. Kaiser Vula smiled. Slowed down to the speed limit.

'You phone me when it's done.'

'Yes, Major.'

'Whatever happens. You phone me.'

'Yes, Major.'

'I must know.'

'That is understood, Major.'

Kaiser Vula disconnected. Took another look at the Merc man, now bluster-faced. Moved left into the middle lane. The Merc accelerated past, the man gesticulating his fury.

Kaiser Vula stared at him: impervious with dark glasses.

'Another one of your men on the operation?' said Nandi.

'Uh-huh.'

'Your operation without a name.'

'That's right.'

Nandi leaning towards him. 'You don't mind if I tell just one person.' Her hand sliding over his thigh into his crotch. 'Please.'

'I do,' said Kaiser Vula. 'You will never get to the palace again.'

28

Vicki Kahn went right from the hotel past a small park, the snow still thick there under the shrubbery, turned left towards the Karl-Liebknecht-Strasse. No footsteps echoing behind her.

The cold bit her nose, made it run. Why people handled this sort of winter was crazy when elsewhere in the world there was sun. She dug her hands into her coat pockets, hurried on.

Vicki found the bus stop, waited there with four other people: three oldies, a metalled teenager jigging to her tunes. Watched a young man approach, on his phone, carrying a take-away coffee. All of them wrapped up in their lives, the way any good spook would be.

When the bus came, Vicki took a seat three rows from the rear door. The pensioners sat in the section behind the driver; the jigger stood beside the middle doors; the man on the phone headed upstairs. In Detlef Schroeder's spy city the youth would be the agent. Maybe.

Before the bus pulled away, she heard someone bang through the rear door, plonk into the seat behind her. Someone panting. A woman by the waft of scent. Vicki tensed, decided, okay, she'd take Detlef Schroeder's advice. Kept her senses riveted to any movement the woman made.

The bus ground its slow passage down the Unter den Linden through a chaos of roadworks, building sites, traffic snarled in the disruptions. Vicki stared at buildings she couldn't name, wondering what would be the best here. Move to another seat? Get out?

The bus was almost at the Brandenburg Gate. Tourists everywhere taking photographs with iPads, cellphones, even cameras. She could get out here, mix with the tourists. That would give the follower some excitement. Or do as Detlef Schroeder had suggested and hop off in the Tiergarten.

Vicki got up, stood near the middle doors, waiting for the bus to stop. Glanced back. The seat behind hers empty. A knot of people at the rear also about to get off. A young woman among them, elegant in coat, gloves, a black ushanka, the earmuffs hanging loose. She carried a briefcase.

Nice hat, thought Vicki. Perfect for this weather.

The young woman paid her no attention, alighted, heading across the street towards Hotel Adlon. Not her then. Vicki sat down again. Decided to take a chance. Detlef Schroeder might like his constant tradecraft but the Cold War was over. The old spies needed to move on. Far as she could see, she was clean.

At Zoo recognised one of the pensioners with a wheelie shopping bag, and the far-away teenager. Didn't notice the young man until she stepped onto the 148. He was standing in the middle section, his coat open, his scarf hanging loose. Still talking on his phone. She walked past, sat again three rows from him. He kept on chatting, leaning into a corner.

Not many passengers but he chose to stand, absorbed in his phone. When he wasn't talking, was checking email, SMSing, scrolling his screen. Vicki kept him in the corner of her vision, wondering what were the chances of coincidence. Her training telling her, it's him. He's your tracker.

Imagined Henry Davidson sniffing, doing one of his mini-lectures during a meeting. Striding up and down the room. 'There are no coincidences, ladies and gentlemen. Well, not true, there are, there are coincidences all the time. Except. Except when you see a coincidence your first thought is?' He'd stop, stick out his chin, look down at them through his glasses. 'Your first thought is?' None of them would say a word. 'Your first thought is' – Henry hamming up his idea of a London cockney copper – "'Allo, 'allo, 'allo, what's going on here, then?'

At Savignyplatz, Vicki brushed past the young man on her way out. Met his eyes briefly, a surprise there that she'd bumped him. He frowned, followed her off the bus. On the pavement keyed in a number.

Jesus, thought Vicki, now what?

Heard him say, 'Ja, ja, alles gut,' then head off across the road.

'Allo, 'allo, 'allo, what's going on here, then?

Best to pretend ignorance. Not let her followers know she knew. A need, though, to up her game.

Vicki turned to face the buildings, found the one where Detlef Schroeder lived. Buzzed her way through the first door into the courtyard. At the hinterhaus buzzed again at Detlef Schroeder's number. The intercom crackled. 'Come up to the second floor,' he said.

29

Detlef Schroeder was waiting for her.

Older than Henry Davidson, she reckoned. Henry was mid-sixties, this man had ten years on that at least. Unless the cancer had taken its toll, aged him. He stood there in a patterned jersey, suit pants, slippers. A tall, bald man wearing thick-rimmed spectacles. His lips a damp blue. Patches of white stubble under his chin, on his neck. Haphazard shaving.

'So,' he said, drawing out the sound, 'like a vision from the past. You remind me of a most striking woman.'

Vicki shook his hand, the grip firm, but he held too long while he stared at her.

'Come inside, nur herein, bitte,' he said, standing back. 'I will make some coffee.' As she squeezed past him he leant forward, sniffing. 'You see, you awake my memories.'

Vicki scuttled into the overheated apartment, suddenly uncomfortably warm.

'You even smell like someone I knew. Do you know that? We all have a smell. This doesn't matter if you wash, this doesn't matter if you have perfume, underneath is always your smell.' He closed the door.

Vicki unwrapped the snood, left it hanging in two loops. Unbuttoned her coat.

'Let me take your coat,' said Detlef Schroeder, his hand held out to receive it. 'Sometimes some of us have a family smell. Maybe this lingers in your family. After all these years to find that smell again. How wonderful. How strange this is.' He took her coat, hung it on a rack beside the door. 'We do not use this sense we have enough, I think. Animals sniff about the world all the time. Dogs want to smell you, and cats too. Sharks they tell us can smell blood in water, one part per million. That is, I think, something in the proximity of more than one hundred metres away. Fantastic, yes? In our world we have forgotten to use this sense we have.' He reached out to rub her arm.

'Watch his hands,' Henry Davidson had said. 'They're all over the place.'

Vicki drew back. 'I'm sorry,' she said. 'I don't know what you're talking about. I don't know why I'm here. I don't know who you are, except one of Henry's old contacts. Can you please tell me what this's about?'

She watched his blue lips draw into a smile, not far off a sneer, his hand still lightly on her arm. A lecherous man. What was she doing here? What was behind this Davidson/ Schroeder conspiracy?

The room was not only stuffy, it smelt of old newspaper, old carpets, old dust, cigarette smoke, gas. Piles of newspapers rose behind the settees. On every surface files, documents, notes. Old Persians covered most of the wooden floors. Vicki sneezed.

'It is the change of temperature,' said Detlef Schroeder. 'We are snug in here, do you not think so?' He let go of her arm.

'I like your jersey,' he said, admiring her. 'They make a woman so …' – he paused – 'how shall I say it, so desirable. The soft wool against the skin. You have the same shine to your skin as the woman of my memory. Very lovely, yes, very lovely.'

Creepy. Very creepy. Vicki folded her arms across her tender chest. What the hell had Henry got her into? What the hell was she doing here? She should go.

'You would like some coffee?' Detlef Schroeder was asking.

'Why'm I here?' said Vicki. 'What's going on?'

He shrugged. 'I have something to tell you.'

'What?'

She watched him assessing her, hesitating. 'It is important. But, please, I cannot tell you like this. We must be civilised.'

She kept her eyes on him, forcing him to break the stare.

'Okay.' He laughed. Teeth were missing at the back of his mouth, some of the grinders. 'So? Coffee?'

'Tea,' said Vicki.

He frowned at her. 'You don't drink coffee?'

'I do. Just not this early.'

'For me it is the only time to drink coffee.' His gaze dropping from her face to her breasts to her crotch. 'You are married?'

'What? What's that got to do with anything?'

'A friendly question, that is all.'

She shook her head, told herself, calm down, don't let him creep you out.

'A boyfriend?'

Nosey old bastard. 'Yes.'

Again the damp smile. 'Good, good.' He beckoned. 'Come with me into the kitchen for the tea-making.'

A grey light infused the kitchen as did the sweet tang of gas. Vicki stopped in the doorway. Noticed the breadcrumbs on the sideboard, showered like ash around the toaster. An open carton of milk on the centre table. A dish of soft butter, a knife upright in a pot of jam. Chunks of cheese, slices of salami.

'How would you like a German herbal tea? Some ginger tea?' he said. 'This is my favourite.' Searching among an array of tea packets until he found the right one. 'Also a biscuit to nibble?'

'I've had breakfast,' said Vicki.

Detlef Schroeder ignored her, opened a cupboard of tinned food, packets, bottles of condiments. 'Yes, here.' He brought out an unopened packet of Maria biscuits. 'The same as Marie biscuits in South Africa. Please.' He tore open the packet, held it out. 'Go on. They were a favourite.'

Vicki obliged, thought it the best option, stop the old man's fussing. Finished the biscuit in two bites. Helped herself to another.

'You see. You also like them.' He'd taken mugs from the wash-up stand, rinsed them, dropped teabags into both. 'Now you must tell me why you didn't get off in the Tiergarten.' He set the electric kettle to boil.

Vicki frowned at him, shook her head. 'You! It was you? That guy phoned you?' She laughed. 'I don't believe it.' He sets up this meeting, then has her followed. Jesus!

'What do you not believe?'

'That you would do that. Have me followed. Why, for heaven's sake?'

Detlef Schroeder tapped his right index finger against his lips, staring back at her. Then held out his hands like a supplicant. 'You want to know? Alright. There are quite some reasons. The first one is to make sure you are safe. For number two to see if you are of interest to someone else. For number three to observe your skills. Also I want to know if you will listen to me.'

'And will I?'

'I think so, yes, even though you disobeyed.'

Vicki kept her eyes on him. Unsure how to react. Henry had sent her here to learn a family secret. Henry Davidson did nothing unnecessarily.

'What you must understand,' said Detlef Schroeder, 'is that there are people who still want to kill me.'

Vicki saw no humour in his eyes. He was serious. No twist to his lips, no half-smile. He meant it. He was living the Cold War still. A paranoid, or maybe he had good reason. Maybe this wasn't a fantasy of spy vs spy. Maybe he wasn't lost in dreams of the Cold War.

'Who is going to kill you?'

'There are some wanting their revenge. Some people in this city even.'

The kettle boiled, clicked off. Detlef Schroeder poured water into the mugs.

'You must take this work seriously, Ms Vicki Kahn. It is not a game we are playing.' He chuckled. 'Doch, it is a game of course but it is a dangerous game. Too many people I have seen get hurt. Too many people killed. So when I say you should get off the bus in the Tiergarten, I mean this.'

He offered milk, sugar.

Vicki waved them away. Stretched for her mug of tea.

'You must be more careful.'

Vicki snorted. There were the midnight phone calls but they had nothing to do with Detlef Schroeder. 'There is no reason anyone here should be interested in me. My only purpose is to see you.'

'Genau. Exactly. This is why you must be careful. An appointment with me is enough to make people interested.'

Vicki lifted the bag from the liquid, dumped it on a saucer.

'You don't believe me?'

'Why would you endanger me?'

'It is a good question you ask. I do not bring you here lightly. I have something you must know.' He got to his feet, steadying himself against the table. 'Let us go in the sitting room, it is more comfortable.' Detlef Schroeder guiding her with a hand on her back, letting his hand drop down the softness of her cowl to brush her bum.

Vicki took a quick step forward beyond his reach, sat in a sagging armchair, wasn't going to have him dropping down on the couch next to her. He lowered himself, letting out a sigh as he sat, tea slopping from the mug onto his trousers. He was unconcerned.

'Ja, this old-age business is not easy,' he said. 'Now, we must begin at the beginning.' Smiled at her, gulped his tea. His blue lips taking on a shine. 'Henry did not give you a clue why you are here?'

'Not really. Except to say it was a family secret.' Vicki sipped the tea, a strong metallic taste. Looked at the old man looking at her.

'You are, what do the English say? Yes, you are her spitting image. A strange phrase, this spitting image. In *Brewer's*, do you know *Brewer's*? Once I looked it up. It means, I recall, the exact likeness, as if you were spat out of her mouth.'

'I'm sorry, what are you talking about?'

'Your aunt, Amina.'

'My aunt?'

'Yes, your aunt that was murdered in Paris.'

'You knew her?'

'When I look at you I can see her. In the shape of your mouth, you have the same eyes, in the way you are when you stand up, in your movements even.' Detlef Schroeder laughed. 'As if you were spat out of her mouth. This strange saying but it is true.'

Vicki drank more of the tea, at least it was warm. Where was he going with this? How could he have known of her assassinated aunt?

'Now let me tell you my story with Amina so that the truth does not die with me. This is very fortunate you are in Germany for me to tell this story of Amina.' He nodded. 'Very lucky Henry could arrange this. You know about Amina, something of her story?'

Vicki sipped at the tea, kept her hands around the mug for its warmth. 'I didn't know her. Or if I met her I was too young to remember. All I know is the family story, what I've been told by relatives over the years in bits and pieces. I know she had to leave South Africa because the security police were after her. I know she came to Europe. I know that she was stabbed to death in the Paris Metro. That is all I know.'

'Ah so. Then that is very little.' Detlef Schroeder settled himself further into the couch. 'You believe it was apartheid agents that killed her? A useful assassination.'

'Yes.'

'There are some other people that didn't want her alive.'

'Other people? What other people?'

'That is my story,' said Detlef Schroeder. 'So let me tell you.'

With the back of his hand scratched at the bristles beneath his chin. A rasping loud enough for Vicki to hear.

'When Amina escaped she came to East Berlin for some months before I met her. She was here with the African National Congress working for them in their office. But this you must know. So my story is one day in the Russian Embassy in East Berlin there is a cocktail party and there is Amina, like you, most striking, talking to some of my colleagues. I think, she is a lovely woman, I must find out her name.'

Vicki wondering what it was Amina had had to do with this man. The old version gave no hint of the younger man.

'Slowly,' Detlef Schroeder was saying, 'over the next months we would meet at such receptions. By then she was a student at the university in West Berlin, Freie Universität, so she would go there to that side of the city three or four times in the week. She had a special pass that I am not sure how she got it. Maybe the British helped her.

'This was very good for me. Very fortunate. One day I asked her to take a letter to a friend over the Wall in the West. She did this some more times but by now we are more friendly. We meet to go for walks. We like each other. Never does she ask me about the letters.'

'What were they?'

Detlef Schroeder chuckled. 'She doesn't ask me but you do? That is where you are different. Different generations. Different times.' He paused. 'They were intelligence for the British, MI6.'

'You were a double agent?'

He nodded. 'Ja, this is not so shocking. This was a way of life on both sides.'

'But Amina knew?'

'I suppose, yes, I suppose. She would not ask, I would not say. We lived secret lives in those days. You must understand this.'

'We all do.' He kept his eyes on her, Vicki seeing in them the dull grey sky of Europe. Cold War eyes.

'This is true, but in those days, in that time, we had to be careful. We had to keep secrets. This is what it meant for us. How it was for us to be alive in that time. Today it seems like a bad movie with everyone lying. As if there was no truth.'

He put down his mug on the arm of the sofa.

'But we must go back to the story of your aunt. So then I say to her, we must have a weekend in Rugen and I can show her what it is like by the sea. I remember she says to me that no sea can be the same as the Cape sea. The sea of Cape Town. She is so homesick for Cape Town it is like a pain she has in her chest. But yes we have this weekend, and we become lovers.'

'You what?' said Vicki.

'This is a surprise for you?' He was smiling at her. 'You see, in a better world I would be your uncle.'

Jesus, thought Vicki. Talk about family secrets! 'When?' she said. 'When was this? Why didn't anybody know?'

'The year of 1986. Some few months before she went to

Paris.' He scratched his bristles again. 'There is a reason no one knew because we did not broadcast the information. We did not live together in East Berlin, we had separate apartments. The same in Paris. Sometimes I would stay overnight or for a weekend but it was never for long. That was difficult for us, the Paris months. It was difficult for me to be there. I could not travel so freely all the time because it would have looked bad. People would have asked questions. Most times she would come to East Berlin which was okay, she could do it to meet her comrades. There was always a good reason for her to go to the GDR. So my times in Paris were, how do the English say, far and few between. But we had many good times in that city, Paris was the place we felt a freedom.'

He stopped. Vicki waited. His hands were clasped in his lap, long bony fingers knotted together. He sat with bowed head. Punctuating the silence the sound of a dripping tap. From outside voices, someone calling a child, farther off a small dog yapping. Detlef Schroeder lost in his memories. Vicki wondering how this musty old man had attracted her aunt.

Eventually he pointed at an envelope on the small table beside her chair. 'There are photographs in there for you.'

She reached over, drew out of the envelope a colour photograph of a woman in her mid-thirties on a beach, carefree, laughing into the wind. Another of her wearing a cheeky red beret, sunglasses, a long black coat. A cigarette stuck between the fingers of her right hand. You glanced at it quickly, you could see Vicki's posture, her stance, mirrored in this woman. Uncanny. The one or two pictures she'd ever seen of Amina looked nothing like this. Those versions of Amina were demure. Formal.

Next to the woman in this photograph stood a man in his early forties, athletic, tall, his face lean. He, too, wore a coat, unbuttoned to show off a dark suit, a roll neck instead of a shirt. Detlef Schroeder as James Bond. He had his right arm around the woman, in his left hand a cigarette. They looked happy. They looked at ease.

'In the one we are at the Baltic. There, in the one you are holding, we are in the Tuileries, December 1986. We asked someone to take the photograph,' he said. 'We were very happy for that weekend and then something, I don't know what, happened. Or I should maybe say I did not know then what it was but many years later I was told.' He reached over for the photograph. 'Yesterday was the first time for many years I looked at this. Now when I look at you, I see Amina. You must keep the photographs, please.' He looked at her.

'What happened?'

'It was a month before we met again. This time in East Berlin. Maybe she was quieter. I thought maybe she was worried. She had a big job in Paris and there was all the time the threat of assassination. A letter bomb, a bullet, even poison like anthrax. Always there was this worry. But still we enjoyed a few days together.'

Vicki watched him closely for any twitch, any tic that he was making this up. Nothing. His face relaxed, a moisture in the corners of his mouth, his eyes flicking between her and a spot on the wall as if the past spooled out there like a movie. He cleared his throat, once, twice.

'Then she tells me by telephone about some six weeks, maybe it is two months later that she has to go to Botswana. Okay, I understand, in these jobs of ours we are deployed everywhere at sudden notice.'

He sniffed, pinched at his nose. Cleared his throat again.

'Because we have been apart for two months I say what about a weekend holiday in Rugen? No, she is going the next day to Gaborone. So that is that. For half a year we are apart.

Then suddenly she is back in Paris. No reason. A redeployment. For me I don't need a reason, there is nothing strange in these movements.

'When I see her she is my Amina. The same quickness. The same life. Yes, of course we would go to Rugen to enjoy the weekend we missed. Of course we did the same things. Ate smoked fish on the beach. Stayed in the same small hotel. Again it was wonderful. Except that when I wanted to know about Botswana, Amina would say something then talk about the new things that were happening: the sanctions against the apartheid government, the protests. The trained MK guerrillas going from Botswana into South Africa to fight for freedom.

'Because she will not talk about Botswana I think it was not a happy time. This puzzled me but what could I do? What could I say? Here she was. We were together. We spoke instead about the new things. And also there were talks with Afrikaner businessmen. Even Afrikaner priests were coming to see her. She said the days of white government were finished. Over. There was going to be a new country. Not even two months later she was killed.'

He stopped there. Took off his glasses, wiped the lenses.

Vicki waited, reflux at the back of her throat unsettling her. 'A government hitman,' she said, swallowing hard to keep down the acid rise.

'That is what we all thought.' Detlef Schroeder glanced at her. His eyes lost their force without the spectacles, Vicki thought. They were small, piggy. Yet Amina had gazed into those eyes, as her face came up to meet this man's in a kiss. Vicki shivered. Detlef Schroeder, the spectacles in both hands, slipped them back onto his face, blinked.

'You know something different?' she said.

'I do not know anything for certain. I hear stories. This is all. I put things together from the stories to make my own story.'

'Which is?'

'Ja. Which is a strange story. You see at that time Amina was talking to a South African man called by the nickname Dr Gold. He was in Switzerland, a most important person in the apartheid government. There was millions and millions the South African government had stolen from the taxpayers which Dr Gold had brought to Switzerland. Gold bullion too. He was what is called in thriller books the bagman. The story is that Dr Gold shared these millions with the ANC top men. They made a deal. How do you say, they came to this arrangement. Long before there were proper talks of a settlement in South Africa these men helped themselves to the money.'

Vicki shrugged. 'This story's been around.' She'd heard it before in relation to Amina, just didn't want Detlef Schroeder to know she knew.

'But the thing I heard was Amina didn't like her comrades taking this stolen money. She told them it was wrong. The money should go back to South Africa. Then in the future they could use it for building hospitals, schools, houses.' He paused, Vicki going into the pause.

'You're saying her comrades had her killed? That's pretty serious stuff.'

'I am saying many things, many interpretations. Maybe her comrades did not protect her. They knew she was a target. Maybe they wanted a hitman to kill her. Or maybe they even connived. That is the right word, yes?'

Vicki nodded.

'This was convenient for them. For both parties this was convenient to get rid of Amina Kahn. She was becoming a troublesome woman. Writing letters to the ANC president in London telling of the wrongdoing, she was making these waves in the movement that some people did not like. Then she was trouble for the apartheid people because she knew about the gold. So if she is killed there is no stain on the comrades. She is a martyr. For both sides this is what you call the win-win situation.' He rubbed his hands together, the skin rasping. 'But there is more, something else. Something I found out from my old friends in MI6.'

His cellphone rang, the classic ringtone. He fumbled it up from a pocket. Said, 'Was?' The German clipped, harsh, hard. He listened, didn't speak again except to say danke before he disconnected. The phone went back into a pocket, he smiled at Vicki.

'I am afraid we cannot continue now.' He pushed himself up off the couch. 'This other bit of the story must wait. Maybe this afternoon we can talk again?'

'Can't you tell me quickly?' said Vicki, rising, fighting the nausea that rose with her. It would be a damn nuisance having to come back.

'It is not a short story. But it is important for you. For your family.'

Vicki nodded, thinking what the hell could be so important that it couldn't be trotted out in five minutes? The old man just wanted her back in his flat again, to project his fantasies of Amina onto her. Touch up her bum again.

'Good. Shall we make a time at five o'clock? If you give me your cellphone number that would be handy.' He laughed. 'I make a pun. In Germany we call them handies.'

'I'll phone you,' said Vicki, 'to confirm the time.'

He made a face. 'You do not trust me with your number?'

'No.'

He laughed again. 'Now you are like your aunt. I look forward to our next meeting, Vicki Kahn.'

30

Fish Pescado parked his bakkie in Bree Street. A miracle to find street parking, in tree shade as well. Tree shade a bonus under a hard sun pushing the temperature north of thirty-two degrees centigrade.

'You want thirty minutes? Five rand fifty,' said the parking attendant.

Fish gave her twenty rand, told her make the chit for an hour, keep the change. 'Buy a Coke.'

'Coke's twelve rand,' she said.

Whokaai, wena! Fish stared at her. Plump, short woman sweating in her uniform. Writing his parking slip. Not looking at him.

'It's a contribution,' he said. 'A sponsorship.'

She put the slip under his windscreen wiper. 'Sometimes people steal it,' she said. 'The slip. Just for fun.'

'I get a fine,' said Fish, 'I'll hunt you down.'

The woman still not looking at him, shrugged. Walked off to nail another citizen.

Fish pulled out the parking receipt from under the blade, put it on the dashboard. Locked the cab. No trusting anybody.

He took the Fan Walk bridge over Buitengracht. Shit, chided himself, not the Fan Walk any longer. Nowadays the Walk of Remembrance. City packaged its fun with the shame of the past. Fish remembering the winter afternoon he'd done the Fan Walk to watch a World Cup match: Uruguay against the Netherlands. About a hundred thousand people streaming across the city. Bloody wonderful time that'd been. The Dutch winning. You did the history, that was one for Jan van Riebeeck.

Stood for a moment on the bridge, scanning the Prestwich Memorial, wondering would Mart Velaze pitch. Perhaps the guy'd had a change of heart. Anyone had a change of heart, there had to be a reason. His gaze shifting up along the ridge of Signal Hill to the grey mountain. Amazing sight this city, this mountain behind it.

Fish trotted down the bridge's steps, jaunty, hyped up to meet the spy. Found a seat outside, under a sun umbrella, ordered a cappuccino. Thinking great place this, a coffee joint next to an ossuary. Boxes and boxes of the jumbled bones of ancestors on the shelves of the memorial. Had caused a ruckus, the digging up of those bones. Thing about the city, there were skeletons everywhere.

His coffee came, lovely design in the foam. Clever that, the way they did it. Fish doing his appreciation: 'Hectic design, man.' The waiter smiling, giving him a note.

Fish cocked his head. 'And this?'

'Dude left it for you.'

'Dude? What dude?'

'Fris guy. You know, sharp.' The waiter doing a jig. 'Cool oke. Well built.'

'Black? Coloured? Indian? White?'

'Black.'

'Where's he?'

'Gone.'

Fish standing. 'Gone which way? Come'n, which way?'

The waiter backing off. 'Dunno. Sorry, hey. I just work here.' Hands raised. 'Dunno which way.'

Fish picked up the note: Athens lookout. Fifteen minutes.

Athens lookout. What the hell was Athens lookout? Where the hell was Athens lookout?

Took a hot mouthful of coffee, wiped off a foam moustache. Bloody Mart Velaze playing his spy games. Athens lookout had to be nearby.

Fish dialled the professor. Professor Summers. Political

science expert, history buff, never without food stains on his jerseys. Jerseys he called cardigans. One of Fish's top dagga clients, bought a consistent baggie each week.

'Yes, Fish,' Summers came on. 'When will you be delivering?'

'Whenever you like,' said Fish. 'And a hello howzit to you too.'

The professor ignoring the retort. 'How about this afternoon? Unless you're surfing, of course. Wouldn't want to interrupt your worship of the waves. Your chance of getting eaten by a great white.'

'Sure,' said Fish. 'No problem.' Clearing his throat. 'Ah …'

'Ah, what, Fish? I hear that sound I know you're after dope.' The professor chuckling. 'You get that, Fish. You like my pun?'

Fish wanting to say no, asking instead, 'What's Athens lookout? Or where's Athens lookout?'

A silence. Then: 'Sometimes, Mr Pescado, your ignorance truly astounds me. Your complete and utter lack of knowledge about the city you live in. How long have you lived here? No, don't answer. I suspect it's all your life. And short as that has been, you've managed to remain blissfully unaware of your surroundings. Of your history. Amazing, really. Probably it's all that water you get in your ears, washes out your brain.'

'Prof, it's urgent.'

'Of course it is. With you it would only ever be urgent. Google it on your phone.'

'It's quicker to call you.'

'You think I'm a walking history book?'

'Sort of.'

'Ah, your flattery. So cheap.' A pause. 'Athens lookout, my ill-educated friend, is near the Mouille Point lighthouse. In the great gale of May 1865 the RMS *Athens* ran onto the rocks, losing all thirty crewmen. You can still see the engine block sticking out of the water. Is this a help?'

'It is. Got to go.'

'Remember my delivery.'

Fish thumbed him off. Took another dash of coffee. Left thirty bucks on the table.

31

Ten minutes later, Fish Pescado drove onto the gravel parking area above the rocks, the remains of the wreck sticking out of a low tide. The sea calm, the kelp glistening. Three other cars parked there. Fish wondering, what now?

Drove to the right, away from the other cars: people taking a break, enjoying the view. A couple, a lone man on a phone, three men in a black Benz.

Waited, lamenting the summer sea. Flat, flat, flat. Not a surfable ripple around the peninsula. Two minutes. Five minutes. After ten minutes decided Mart Velaze had chickened out.

Couple of minutes later saw in the rear-view a white Audi swing towards him, stop alongside. The dude gesturing for him to hop in.

Oh, yeah, thought Fish. Here we go. All the same did as requested.

Got into the air-conned Audi.

'You're Mart Velaze?'

The man not answering the question, starting with, 'You got the balls for this, Fish Pescado? This's big league. Like surfing Dungeons bonecrushers.'

'You sent her to me.'

'Maybe it wasn't a clever idea.'

'Look,' said Fish, 'what's your problem?'

Mart Velaze didn't answer that either. Sat looking at the sea. Fish half-turned in the seat, getting him in profile. Smart-looking boykie, good profile, snappy threads.

Fish went for another tack. 'Why'd you send her to me? Cynthia Kolingba. This such a big wave, why didn't you take it?'

Mart Velaze tapping a finger on the steering wheel. 'Don't you want work?'

'Not the issue, china. Why'd you send her to me? If you got the inside story, why'n't you handling it? You're right there.'

Mart Velaze turning his head, smiling at him. Big white smile. 'Personal reasons.'

'What's that supposed to mean?'

'What it says.' Mart Velaze's smile shutting off.

'Personal reasons means you're having a fling with her?'

A snort from Mart Velaze.

'So what's it?' Fish waiting him out.

A silence. Fish seeing the rigid lips, the set of the face. Turned to look at the sea. Waited.

Eventually Mart Velaze saying, 'Why I'm here's to say I'm serious. I'm running a risk meeting you. Could be watchers. In the other cars, somewhere behind. I don't think so, but could be. We're not a happy agency. That's what this's about. There's shit going on. Shit that'll be buried. I can't do this one. Got to be someone outside.'

'Kolingba was an Agency job?'

'Let's say this, could've been us. Could've been us on contract for his own. Might be someone else who didn't like his face.'

'But you don't think so?'

The tap tap of Mart Velaze's finger. Then: 'I'm giving you a name: Joey Curtains.' Gave him a cell number too.

'Who's he?'

'A field agent.'

'AKA a wet worker.'

'Your words.'

'Agency?'

'Maybe. These days it's a big place. Domestic Branch. External Branch. All the services lumped together. I don't know everybody. Most likely neither. Most likely freelance.'

'You got staff records. You could search them.'

'I have. No Joey Curtains.'

'So where'd you get the name? The phone number.'

'I got them, okay. Be happy.'

'And this Joey Curtains is involved how?'

'Could be the driver. Could be one of the shooters.'

'Whokaai, man, wait, wait, wait. You're secret service. You supposed to keep us safe 'n sound. You're supposed to know what's going on. You're telling me you know bugger all? A major oke gets done coming out of church, you didn't know zilch about it?'

'No.'

'Chrissakes.'

Mart Velaze coming round on him. Fish pulling back. The man's finger in his face. 'You're the PI. I've given you the client. I've told you there's shit happening. I've given you a name and number. As of now I'm out of this. No more phone calls. No more contact. Think of your Vicki Kahn.' Mart Velaze lowering his hand.

'That's a threat?'

'Advice. Consider it advice.'

'You leave her out of it.'

'I want to. I will. Your Vicki Kahn's on a fast-track. But things happen. You got to remember that.' Mart Velaze reached forward, started the Audi.

'One more thing,' said Fish. 'Daro Attaline.' Fish bringing

up the past. A case where a surfing buddy had gone missing, Mart Velaze somehow in the mix of that one.

Mart Velaze shook his head. 'No idea.'

Fish stared at him. Mart Velaze staring back. Fish seeing nothing in his eyes. Shark eyes, not a glint in them.

'That's it,' said Mart Velaze. 'We're done.'

'You know,' said Fish. 'You know what happened to him.'

'Out,' said Mart Velaze.

'One day. One day you'll tell me.' Fish saying it with meaning.

'Yeah, yeah,' said Mart Velaze. 'Goodbye, Fish Pescado.'

Fish slid out of the car into the heat, pushed closed the door. Watched Mart Velaze drive off. Bloody spies in their bloody secret world. Like there wasn't enough smoke and haze hiding what was going on.

32

Vicki had no urge for sightseeing. Five o'clock was four and a half hours away. Four free hours in Berlin, all she wanted was to lie in the quiet of her hotel bedroom, not feel so nauseous.

She could hear Henry Davidson. 'You what? You went back to your room! Are you mad? All that time on your hands. You went back to your room?'

All the things a tourist could do in Berlin. See the Memorial to the Murdered Jews of Europe or the Jewish Museum, or hitch onto a tour of the Old Jewish Quarter?

'If you've got to do the Jews,' Henry Davidson had said, 'take a wander through the old quarter. It's not so in-your-face. There's a memorial there by a chap called Will Lammert: these standing figures. Emaciated. Waiting. A little group of them.

Quite disturbing, really. If you must see anything of the city's horror, take a walk there. Forget about the concrete blocks, look at some real art.' He'd patted his hair. 'Of course there is always the Topography of Terror if you prefer that to Jewish.'

Right then, as she came away from Detlef Schroeder, Vicki wasn't in the mood for doing Jewish or anything else. Right then Vicki wanted nothing other than to get back to her hotel. To stop feeling shitty. To think about Amina, about what Amina had seen in the creepy Detlef Schroeder.

She reversed the journey of earlier in the day. Took a bus down Kant to the Zoo terminus, the 100 across the Tiergarten up the Unter den Linden. Couldn't give a monkey's if she was being followed or not. If she was, give them something to do. Sat in the bus, wiped condensation from the window to stare at the busy city. In this cold, the city going on uncaring.

She thought about Amina in such weather. Wrapped in a coat, hurrying through the icy streets, her breath visible, the snow squeaking beneath her boots. Amina heading for a liaison with Detlef Schroeder. Her lover. Was she followed too? By the spies spying on the spy? Or by her own, keeping tabs on her? What did Vicki know about her? Nothing. Just family lore about an aunt who'd been in the Struggle. Been called a terrorist. Would have been locked up if caught in Cape Town, gone through the terrors of a Security Branch interrogation. Instead she'd been assassinated by an icing unit. This much was known.

Detlef Schroeder was saying there was more. That maybe her own had wanted her gone. Maybe she was a nuisance because of her knowledge of this Dr Gold. Maybe there was something else other than Dr Gold?

And what else was he on about? 'It is not a short story. But it is important for you. For your family.' What could be important to her family? What was left of her family. Both parents deceased. No siblings. Some relations still in Athlone, others in Johannesburg. Not exactly what you'd call close-knit. The family had fallen apart even before the deaths of her parents; everyone too into their own lives.

So what could Detlef Schroeder tell her that would get family tongues wagging? There weren't any busybody aunts left anymore.

She got off the bus at the Marienkirche, the landmark she'd remembered, crossed Karl-Liebknecht, working her way back through the small streets to the hotel. Stopped at a café, thinking maybe ginger tea or chamomile might be an option. Smelt the coffee and walked out. Had to. Her once-upon-a-time must-have drug was going cold turkey on her. Next thing she'd have a withdrawal headache.

In a small supermarket Vicki bought two packets of Maria biscuits. Wondered if two packets would be enough. Then again, the shop was just around the corner.

She tore open the packet outside the shop, crunched down on a biscuit, swallowed, the mush taking off the nausea's edge. She could rest for two hours then trek back to Schroeder's place. What a drag.

Vicki stepped into her hotel room, thought, strange, the cupboard door wasn't closed, a fraction ajar. Hotel like this, house staff would get it perfect. Her bed was made, everything freshened up smelling faintly of roses. One of the first things they'd taught her, look for disturbance. Caught her eye instantly, the cupboard door. Glanced in the bathroom: nothing out of place. Her box of goodies – toothpaste, floss, deodorant, moisturiser, headache pills, contraceptive pills, pads, tampons, clippers, scissors, tweezers – as she'd left it. New bottles of gel and shampoo in the shower. Went back to the cupboard.

Stood staring at the door, preparing herself. Expecting the safe unlocked, her netbook gone. Her visitors intent on leaving a message as much as theft. Thought, hell, not twenty-four hours in the city, you've caught the paranoia. Or Schroeder's version: eyes watching everything, ears always listening, scare-tactic phone calls. Aside from the flash drive, no reason she'd be on anyone's surveillance list. No reason for anyone to toss her room. The cliché popping up. Vicki shook her head, smiled. Henry Davidson would be amused. She wasn't. Something on the flash drive causing ripples even here.

Vicki Kahn took a breath, opened the door. Her clothing as she'd unpacked: underwear on the right of the shelf, T-shirts on the left. At the back, the safe shut. She exhaled. Reached forward, pressed her code into the keypad, the door buzzed open. Her netbook there, her passport, her wallet of credit cards.

Except they were on top of the netbook. The way she remembered it, she'd put them in first, to the side. The nausea came up again, sent her scurrying for more Maria biscuits.

Went back to the safe, took out the netbook. Sat on the couch, flipped up the screen. Thinking, here goes: switched on, watched everything opening as per. Okay, what'd they done?

They?

Could've been a man alone. A woman alone.

A man alone she decided. Neatly dressed, jacket and tie, black slacks, a coat over his arm. Came into her room, shut the door, dropped his coat on the bed, pulled on latex gloves. Went straight to the safe. Had an override key. Got out the netbook, maybe sat where she was sitting. Copied her files, maybe left some spyware inside. Some little sting that'd come alive when she connected.

Job done. Pocketed his memory stick, returned everything as he'd found it. Well, almost. Had flipped through her passport, checked her credit cards, put them back on top of the computer. Not very professional. Again, maybe that was deliberate. We've been here. We can do this. The man locking the safe. Not quite closing the cupboard door. Giving a short psst of air-freshener to hide his scent. Pulling off the gloves, picking up his coat. Took the lift as if he was checked in. Quietly walking out of the hotel foyer behind a group of Americans on a sightseeing tour.

What'd he got for his expedition? A bunch of useless files: legal case histories, spreadsheets of statistics, internal memos about holiday protocols, iTunes with her music, a file of photographs, mostly of surfer-boy Fish, downloads from news websites. Big deal. No state secrets because she didn't know any state secrets. Nothing there worth anything.

'Always keep a lot of useless stuff on your computer,' was the wisdom of Henry Davidson. 'Just in case someone thinks they should copy your hard drive. Give them a sizeable haul.' Henry snickering at the ruse. 'Give them Alice's evidence.'

'Alice's evidence?'

'Nothing whatever.'

What Henry couldn't snicker away was how it spooked her. Harassment calls were one thing. A faceless man with latex gloves another. A man unfazed, knowing she was out. Having easy access. Going through her stuff.

Had to have inserted spyware. Some key-logging system. Left the little clues to make her life uncomfortable for a few hours? Seemed so completely pointless, the whole exercise.

She pulled her boots off, lay back on the bed. Crashed out on the bed more like it. Closed her eyes. One minute lying there imagining the man with the gloves in her room, the next it was two hours later. The room gone grey in the winter light.

She woke spluttering, a well of saliva pooled in her mouth. Propped herself up on her elbows, groaned at the rise of bile in her throat. The digital clock on the television read 15:32.

Time to go back to Detlef Schroeder. She sighed. The bus rides were the last thing she needed. The hard cold stinging her face. But she wanted Amina's story.

Vicki eased off the bed, wondering if she should change. Decided against it. Put through a call to Detlef Schroeder. Always best to check ahead.

'My dear, my dear,' he said, 'where are you at this time?'

At this time she was staring at herself in the bathroom mirror. Finding it hard to motivate herself. 'I'm sorry. What?'

'Where are you? Nearby perhaps?'

'At my hotel.'

'So, good. Good. Then I will not inconvenience you. My apologies for this, but you see I must make new arrangements with you. Now it is not possible to meet again today. My apologies.'

'No?' Vicki frowned. Thought, what was he playing at? What could possibly have come up in the old man's life? What could possibly happen in his world these days? Very little.

'You must understand, please. I am sorry, there are sometimes complications in my life when other matters interfere. This is something out of my control. You have something in your life like this, where you are not in control? I'm sure. It is the human condition. We are at the whims of fate, you will agree? Please, my apologies for these whims. So we make a new arrangement. We meet tomorrow instead. In the morning at eleven o'clock, would be perfect for you perhaps?'

She wanted to say, no, you ancient bastard, what is so bloody important you can't give me half an hour? Instead, she said, 'Alright.'

'Thank you. This is very important to me that we meet. I have important things to tell you, Vicki Kahn, about your aunt. One other important thing I must tell you is that you are like an apparition for me.'

She heard him chuckle. 'Like a visitor from the past. Auf wiedersehen, Vicki Kahn, until tomorrow.'

Then disconnected, leaving Vicki wondering what was more important – their second meeting or whatever had caused him to cancel. Probably he just wanted to seem important: a long-forgotten spy still pretending he was in the game.

Which left her now with empty hours.

Vicki wiped the lipstick from her lips, stared into the mirror. Something tired in her eyes. A dullness to their brown. No glint. Her cheeks waxy. Her mouth slack. She bowed her head. Decided a long bath first, then a couple of hours at 888poker.

If she started early, she could get an early night. Play through to nine, that'd give her watchers a thrill. Phone Fish, be lights out by ten. All bright-eyed for Detlef Schroeder's tales of love and intrigue in the morning.

Yes. She ran a bath. Lay for a good while wondering about Amina. What had happened in Botswana? Who had killed her in Paris? Her own or an icing unit? And what was the more Detlef Schroeder had to tell? Assuming he even intended telling her more. Assuming he wasn't behind whoever had gone through her stuff.

33

They sat in the bunker at the long table, Zama and the president. The generals were gone. The president distracted, drumming his fingers against the teapot. Zama flicking through emails on his phone. The sound of gunfire from the television, the volume down.

Zama shut his phone, said, 'This is impossible for me. Ask my brothers to do it. They do nothing.'

'No.' The president again fascinated by the video footage of the massacre: the soldiers dropping beneath the gunfire. The man in the window firing out. 'He was brave shooting like that. A brave warrior.' The president breaking into a run of Zulu praise for the soldier. Until incoming blew out the building. 'Such cowards, cowards to fight like that. You must go there, Zama, sort them out.'

'I don't think so.'

'You are afraid?'

'No.'

'My son is afraid.'

Zama watched his father open the jar of honey on the tea tray. Dip a teaspoon into the honey, bring the spoon to his mouth. The tinkle of the teaspoon placed back on a saucer. Then the president wiped his fingers with a napkin. His movements fastidious, almost delicate. His fingers not those of an old man, the skin hardly folding at the knuckles.

'No. That is not my reason.'

'You are afraid. That is why you left the army. Yes? Because you are afraid of this fighting.' The president folded the napkin, laid it on the tray. Lifted the remote, brought up the sound. 'All those bullets.'

'Ask my brothers to do this,' said Zama. 'Mining is no business for me.'

'What is your business? Models. Fashion. What sort of business is this for a president's son? That is women's work. For gay boys. Maybe that is your problem.'

Zama stood, looked down at his father. 'My life is my life.'

The president smiled. 'Sometimes it is not always like that, my son. Sometimes others become interested. They want to know what is happening in our lives. Mr President, they say to me, why is your son with all these fashion boys? Once he was a captain. Now he is …' The president flapped his wrist.

Zama laughed. Forced, hard. No mirth in the sound. 'No,' he said. Turned towards the door. 'No, you must find one of my brothers.'

'I have found you. I have found Linda Nchaba.'

Zama paused. Coming round slowly to face his father.

'You see, you know this name?'

Zama too exposed to deny it. 'Where is she?'

'She is safe.'

'Where is she?'

'You do this thing, then we will bring her back to you. You cannot let a woman like that run around. She is pretty, this Linda Nchaba.'

Zama came down at his father, fast. Angry. Got in the old man's face, could smell his honeyed breath.

'You leave her for me, you hear. You leave that girl for me.' The spray from his outburst flecking the president's face. 'Where is she?' Zama thinking, how? How had his father's spies found her first?

'You must have no worries, my son.' The president rising from his chair. 'When you are finished this job, she will be waiting.'

'Where is she?' Slow, separate words.

'That doesn't matter for the moment.'

'Where is she?' Zama bunched his fists into his father's jacket. 'Tell me!'

The president put his hand against his son's chest, pushed him away. 'Let me go.'

Zama kept his hold. The two men taut, rigid.

'Let me go.'

Zama released his grip, stepped back. Watched his taut-faced father straighten his jacket.

'This Linda Nchaba has caused trouble. Trouble for us all, my son. Not only here, in other countries, too. I am told she has a lot on her conscience to clear away. You must be more careful with your fashion girls. You must keep a stronger grip. We cannot have them talking to whoever they want.'

Zama ignored the taunting, said, 'Tell me where she is.'

'First you make the mine safe.' The president nodding at the television screen.

'That will take weeks. Months maybe.'

'There is no problem. Linda Nchaba can wait. Why not? She has everything, all that a young woman can want.'

'How …?'

'How what?'

'Nothing. Forget it.' Zama sat, looking up at his father: bastard. The bastard. It was him all along.

His father saying, 'The sooner you begin, the less time she must wait. When everything is working, then you can have Linda Nchaba.' Chuckling. 'We have a deal? I think so. I think this is a good deal, my son. We will show the rebels they cannot make trouble for us.'

Zama didn't hear him, shifted his eyes away from his. How had he even known about her? The questions circling like vultures. Zama only half-aware of other people entering the room, his father making introductions. He glanced up.

A tall man held out his hand. A woman to his side wearing ripped jeans, a T-shirt in leopard print. Pretty woman. Angular as a model. The way she held herself, she'd be no stranger to the camera.

The man said, 'Major Vula.'

Zama stood, shook hands. A strong quick grip. The major releasing, making no eye contact.

The woman likewise, eyes down. Her hand warm in his. A smile on her lips. 'I am Nandi,' she said.

Zama flicking from the woman to the major, thinking, not his wife. Unless the major was another of the dinosaur polygamists. Unlikely though, the way she was dressed. The major was uptight. Rigid. Severe. A man with worries. He would not have a household of wives.

'He is my son,' said the president, putting a hand on Zama's shoulder. 'Once he was a captain, Major. Like you, a military man.' He took the woman Nandi's hand, held it in both of his. 'My dear, you are welcome to my palace. This is a place where we are all friends. You know what I mean? A place we can relax with everyone.'

Behind them, scenes of killing spooled across the flat-screen. The soundtrack now muted. Major Vula's eye drawn there.

'That is a rebel attack,' said the president. 'A massacre of miners. You can see, a very bad scene. Lots of casualties. Heavy casualties. Even all our soldiers. These rebels are a problem, Major. A big problem. Even for us here, they are a problem.' The president shook his head. 'But you know this. I cannot tell you this news.' He ushered them towards the door. 'We cannot stay down here all day. We have sunshine. We have lunch to eat. Come, my dear.' The president ushering Nandi before him. 'You are like one of these model women.' His glance sliding to Zama, Zama not rising to it. 'All the young ones have the bodies of models. It is good to see such health. Remind me to give you a jar of my delicious African honey. It is good for the skin and the digestion.'

Nandi giggled.

Zama liked the sound. Perhaps Nandi was a party girl. Another of the flock that swirled through Bambatha. She would find her weekend here demanding. Then so would the major. Zama stood aside at the door.

'After you.' His eyes on her round backside in the tight jeans.

The smile she flashed him, demure. Zama liked demure. Demure often hid the wild ones.

As he closed the door to the bunker, the president said, 'Zama is going into the rebel territory, Major. You must talk to him about this Kolingba. This colonel who has taken refuge among us.'

34

The men didn't introduce themselves. Let themselves into the apartment, greeted her with smiley faces. They weren't the men from the airport. They'd been white. Or whitish. Coloured. These were young men, the jeans and leather jacket brigade. Now bundled into anoraks like Michelin men. One with spectacles, the other holding a box of pastries.

Linda Nchaba sat on a couch. Showered, wearing black tights, a thigh-length dress. Self-possessed. Looking stronger than she felt.

'Who are you?' Stared at them, arms folded across her chest. Heart racing.

'Nobody, sisi,' said the one with the box. 'Doesn't matter. We are your friends. We are the ones who phoned.' He moved to put it down on the kitchen counter.

The one with glasses said, 'We have fresh croissants, sisi. You can make coffee.'

The men shrugged out of their anoraks. Linda Nchaba watched them, these two guys waltzing around unconcerned. Like they knew her.

'Make your own coffee. I'm not your Zulu girl.'

'Hey, my brother, what'd we hear about her?' The men laughing. The one who'd said they were nobody, saying in Zulu, 'They tell us you have a wild tongue.'

'Crazy as a mamba.' The man with glasses filling the kettle.

'We can make the coffee, sisi, we are your friends. Zulu boys make good coffee.' The men doing a high five. Young men playing the fool.

'Who undressed me?'

That brought a stop to the banter. The one sighed. The other busied himself finding mugs in a cupboard.

Linda Nchaba relaxed her arms, raised a hand, waved it. 'Hey, hey, look at me.' Neither man meeting her gaze. 'You! You with the glasses? What's your name?' Not waiting for a response. 'Look at me. Your friends kidnapped me. Your friends abused me.'

The men shuffling, fidgeting with kitchenware.

'It is bad. We are sorry.' This from the coffee-maker.

'We have made a complaint.'

'You have made a complaint.' Linda Nchaba snorted, raised both arms, her eyes to the ceiling. 'Oh, that is fine. That's okay. Nothing to worry about. All sorted.' Dropped her hands. Groaned. 'My God! My God! Who are you from?'

The men still not looking at her, nodding.

'You were there.' Linda Nchaba sat forward, put her head in her hands. Zama. This was Zama's punishment for her. 'You were there. You bastards were there. You did nothing. You let them do it. You watched. You also …'

'No, no,' said the one with glasses. 'We were not there. We came afterwards.'

'We did not know. They told us you are fine, you are sleeping. Everything is okay. But still we came to check.'

'You touched me?'

The men standing silent, heads bowed.

'We put you in the bed, covered you.'

'I was naked. You took pictures?'

'No. Never. We covered you. That is all, sisi. We are sorry. This is a very bad thing.'

A very bad thing, Linda Nchaba hearing the words, their echo loud in her head.

'A very bad thing. A very bad thing.' Standing now, shouting. 'I've been kidnapped. I'm sore and bruised. I have men undressing me while I'm drugged. This is a very, very bad thing. Why am I here? Today I should be in France. I have a job in Paris. Who are you? You bring croissants and you want coffee like I am your sister. You think kidnapping me is nothing.' In two paces she was at the counter, picked up the box of croissants, hurled it into the sitting room. Swept the mugs onto the floor. 'You chase me. You capture my gogo. You abuse me. Why? Why? Tell me why? What have we done to you?' Linda Nchaba wiping tears from her face, staring at the men. Quiet now. 'You say you are my friends. Why? Tell me why?'

'We are not those chasing you,' said the one who had brought the croissants. He went over to pick up the box, the croissants scattered on the floor. 'We had to save you.'

'In France,' said the man with glasses, 'they were waiting for you.'

'Of course they were.' Linda Nchaba seeing herself reflected in the man's glasses. Her chin jutting out, challenging. 'You can say that.' She sniffed, blew her nose. 'You can say that. It is easy. You can say anything you like. What do I know? You could be talking rubbish. All of it, rubbish. How can I believe you?' Coughed to clear her throat, cover the crack in her voice.

The shorter one, the one who had picked up the box, said, 'We know that, sisi. We ask you, believe us.'

'Pah! Who was waiting for me in France?'

'Some from the DGSE.'

'I'm supposed to know what that is?'

'The old French intelligence service.'

'From before.' The man with the glasses taking a packet of

coffee from a cupboard of groceries. 'From the Struggle days, they have contacts with some of us. Some bad comrades.' Spooned three helpings into a cafetière. 'You don't want to know about them.' He poured water over the coffee.

'Who are these people?'

'They would have killed you.'

Linda Nchaba rubbed at her eyes. 'You save me from the French so that your friends can leave me naked? Photograph my body to put on the internet? Hey? Yes? Is that what they have done?' Another of Zama's little tricks. She turned away. Went to the window. A woman in a long coat and boots, under a red umbrella, walking down the street. A woman cycling with a dog in the front basket. Ordinary life going on. 'Tscha! You are men. You are the problem.' Aware suddenly of her trembling. Clasped one hand over the other. Don't let them know your fear. Stay angry. She spun towards them. Knew they could see only her outline against the grey light. 'What do you want with me? Hey, butis? My saviours. My heroes. What happens now, can you tell me? Maybe you are the messenger boys? So, my messenger boys, tell me. Tell me the message from your boss.'

'Ai, sisi, we come to protect you, you mustn't blame us.' The shorter one, biting into a croissant. Chewing. Crumbs fluttering from his mouth.

'Now. Now you come to protect me. After the Dutchmen have attacked me. Sho, what protection is this?'

'Here is coffee,' said the one with glasses, pouring from the plunge pot. 'We'll tell you.'

Linda Nchaba took the offered mug and a croissant too. Hunger roiled in her stomach. Bit, chewed, taking a sip of coffee to swallow the mouthful. She sat perched on the couch, the muscles in her shoulders tight, her long neck stiff with tension. Eyes flicking from one man to the other.

They sat on the couch facing her: also on edge, sitting forward. The shorter one now dunked his croissant before each mouthful. The one with glasses didn't eat, held his coffee mug with both hands. He spoke.

'Our mission …'

'Your mission? Your mission for who?'

'We are Foreign Branch.'

'Before, we were called the SA Secret Service.' The shorter urgent between mouthfuls. 'Now we are all together, the new State Security Agency.'

Linda Nchaba closed her eyes, in the darkness conjured an image of her grandmother on a mat on a concrete floor. Head bowed, shoulders slumped. 'You belong to the president.'

'We belong to the country.' The one with glasses coming in quickly.

Linda blinked to get focus, looked at him. 'It is the same thing.'

Both men shook their heads. 'No.'

'Our mission is to be with you. Keep you safe.'

'Safe from kidnappers? You are kidnappers.'

'We are here now.'

'You were there then.'

'No, we told you. We weren't there when they caught you.'

Again Linda Nchaba closed her eyes, massaged her forehead with the fingers of her left hand. 'Ai. You guys. What, what?' She gazed at them again, defeated. Both of them staring at her. Two men on a mission, foreign agents in a strange land. First the woman, Vicki Kahn, now these two. Everyone supposed to be friendly. Everyone wanting something from her. Wait till they saw the video on the flash drive. That would make them grateful.

She let the tension out of her shoulders. Rolled her head. 'Tell me,' she said, 'tell me what happens now.'

'Now we wait,' said the one with glasses. 'Today, tomorrow, soon there will be someone to see you. They will explain.' He smiled at her. 'Until they come, we are your protection. We will keep you safe.'

Linda Nchaba drank her coffee. A bitter, thin liquid.

35

Joey Curtains' attitude was to hell with Prosper Mtethu. What was his case? Don't drive! Take a taxi to the hospital. No ways, my bru. Not on a Friday night. This sort of job, you needed wheels. You needed to leave the scene asap. How're you supposed to do that on foot? Run? Wait for a taxi? A running man's got to be a thief, mugger, rapist. A passing cop sees a running man, he chases after him. Shoots him most likely.

The other option, take a taxi. Joey Curtains could see himself waiting for a taxi. Rush hour. Cleaners, nurses, shelf-packers standing on the kerb, wanting a taxi. Everybody in the taxis squeezed tight already. Like going home among the workers is the way to leave the Kolingba job.

Not a blerry chance.

Joey Curtains parked his BM in a side street. This white 2009-model 3 Series with 110,000 on the clock he'd picked up for forty grand at an auction. A giveaway. He couldn't believe his luck. The leather interior still smelt new, a sunroof for those brilliant days. Manual transmission, air-con, sound system to rock the chicks. Sixteen-inch mag wheels that spoke to his heart. His heart that'd gone apeshit during the bidding. Taken a couple of minutes to get his voice back afterwards.

Zapped the lock as he walked away. Five paces, looked back to give it a check. Very nice. Three weeks he'd had it.

Three weeks of driving with the angels. He'd get into the car afterwards, drift into the highway traffic, he'd be home safe. Let Prosper take a taxi. Sit in the crush for an hour. All that sweat and cabbage breath.

Joey Curtains, dapper in light jacket, brown slacks, walked into the hospital foyer, there was Prosper Mtethu reading a newspaper on a bench. Right underneath a camera. CCTV cameras everywhere. Bored security guard chatting up a nurse near the doorway. Guy'd probably been on duty all day, his shift about to end.

Joey Curtains took a look at the board giving floor designations. No clue on which floor Kolingba'd be. Decided to go outside and have a smoke, wait for Prosper to make the moves.

Been there most of his cigarette admiring the view. Some view: the roofs of Observatory, distant cranes in the harbour. Wondering, what's with Prosper? When's he going to start the show? Then out drifts the man himself, newspaper folded under his arm. Comes over, asks for a cigarette. Joey Curtains goes through the act, takes out a packet, taps up a stick. Prosper lifting out the offering. Asks for a light. Joey Curtains flicks his Bic, the two men standing there like they'd come to visit ailing loved ones.

Prosper said, 'ICU is fourth floor. Out of the lift turn left. Kolingba is the third unit, left-hand side.'

Joey Curtains not sure what to do with this.

'So, my brother, we gonna just walk in there? Like, howzit, can we have a moment with the colonel?'

'You. Not we. You.'

Joey Curtains laughed. 'Uh, uh, uh. No play today.'

Prosper flicked ash. 'Fifteen years ago I stopped cigarettes. Twenty-three years I smoked. From age thirteen. Always, I liked the first time you pull in the smoke from a new cigarette.

It is still good.' He stubbed the cigarette, bending it on itself. 'You go to the colonel. I will make a distraction.'

'Simple, hey.'

'Yes. Up there in ICU it is chaos. Like wartime. I've seen it before, that sort of situation. People rushing about.'

'So it's hectic. So I can slide in. How'm I supposed to do it?'

Joey Curtains wishing Prosper would look at him. The man gazing off like he wasn't part of this.

'Since he was shot, the colonel is in a coma. It will be no problem for you. Nothing that is difficult. He has the oxygen mask. You lift it, pinch his nose closed with your fingers.' Prosper pinching his own nose, now turning to meet Joey Curtains' eyes. 'A minute maybe, that is all it takes.' A pause. 'You can do it this way? Kill a man this way? With your fingers.'

Joey Curtains couldn't hold those eyes. Their blackness too solid. No compromise there. Only judgement. He looked away at the traffic clogging Main Road.

Heard Prosper saying, 'It is not the same as with a gun. With a gun you don't feel the man's life dying. If you want, you can watch it. But you are separate. You are not connected. With this job you can feel the life go. Even the unconscious colonel will jerk when he cannot breathe. I ask you again, you are okay with that, my friend?'

Those black eyes searching his face. Joey Curtains thinking he couldn't trust Prosper Mtethu. 'Why don't you do it?'

'I can do it. No problem.'

'So?'

'The order was for you. I am the officer. I have made the plan.'

'That's the plan, my brother? I walk in there, pinch his nose closed. You reckon that's gonna happen? The security'll be on me long before.'

'There is one police.'

'One is enough.'

'I will make a distraction. It will be easy for you. Afterwards you go down the corridor, there is a door to stairs at the end. No problem. You can walk away.'

'Stairs to where?'

'They take you into another building. You can go home.'

Oh, ja, thought Joey Curtains, simple like a pimple. He tapped a finger on Prosper Mtethu's chest. 'You better not be shitting me, my brother.'

Prosper Mtethu reached up, put a grip on his hand. Joey Curtains pushed back, feeling the strength of the older man. Realised they were being watched. An ambulance man, leaning against the building, smoking, grinning at their antics. Joey Curtains laughed, broke the moment. Clapped Prosper on the back. Whispered, 'We are being watched, my brother.'

'Then you must stop the nonsense.' Prosper Mtethu saying loudly, 'Come, time to see family.' The two of them going past the smirking ambulance man into the foyer.

Inside, Prosper said to Joey Curtains, 'I go in the first lift. You take the next one.'

Joey Curtains thinking, all this on CCTV. Blerry wonderful. Kept his face averted. No ways they'd get a clear visual.

The lift pinged, the doors opened, he was in it. Two nurses with him, who got off at the third floor.

Fourth floor Joey Curtains came out of the lift seeing what Prosper meant. Commotion. People on gurneys, people on crutches, nurses, doctors. Like this was some casualty ward. There's Prosper at the nurse's station, into his distraction, waving his newspaper. His voice high-pitched.

Joey Curtains went left down the corridor. Units either side, people in them dead to the world. Wired up, bags of gunk dripping into their arms, heads, hearts, any place the medicos could hook a feed.

Sitting on a chair opposite the colonel's door, the cop, standing up now, intent on the scene of Prosper rampant. Joey Curtains hearing Prosper's voice, loud, demanding, the slap of the newspaper on the counter top, the cop brushed past him to sort out the fracas.

Joey Curtains entered the colonel's unit, there was a white guy lying on the bed. Guy had most of his head in bandages, most of his torso too, a blood leak crimson on his shoulder. Only his one arm showing. A hairy arm. Freckles. Sun spots on the hand. The guy's eyes open, staring at him. Blue eyes.

'Long live,' said Joey Curtains, waving.

Shit, thought Joey Curtains, turning on the spot. So much for Prosper and his plan. Went across the corridor to the opposite unit, the one the cop'd been sitting outside. Maybe Prosper couldn't tell left from right.

Inside what looked like a woman. Not much visible but the bumps on her chest, the giveaway in Joey's assessment. Also too short to be Colonel Kolingba.

Fok!

In the corridor Joey Curtains made a decision. Bugger this. Abort. Get out. At the nurses' station Prosper still in full anguish, the cop restraining him, moving him towards the lifts.

Joey Curtains reckoned probably ten units along the corridor. No ways he could pop in and out of every one until he found the colonel. If he found the colonel. No telling if the colonel was still here. Might have been transferred to a private hospital. Anyone with any sense'd do that.

What a balls-up. The thought occurring that the whole safari was a con. Could be tacked down to Prosper's not being committed to the operation from the get-go. Or worse, a set-up. Not something Joey Curtains wanted to contemplate. Except the more he looked at it, the more he got the rittles. A cold skin creep. He looked down the corridor, those rittles brought up the hairs on his arm.

There was Prosper Mtethu pointing his way, the cop taking out his gun. Shouting, 'Hey! Hey!' Prosper shouting, 'Stop him. Stop him.' Prosper no longer doing a distraction, now Prosper on some other mission: mission take down Joey Curtains.

The cop yelling, waving his pistol. Joey Curtains couldn't see him shooting. Too many pop-up targets might take the lead.

All the same, Joey Curtains ran. Headed down the corridor remembering what Prosper had said, stairs at the end, no problem, you can walk away. Oh, ja, nice one, my brother. Had to be Prosper had back-up at the bottom of the stairs.

Hello, Joey boykie, we got a car round the corner. This way, bru. Quick. Quick.

Ja, like that was gonna happen.

36

Joey Curtains ducked into the stairwell, went up not down. Two storeys higher he stopped. Could hear the cop and Prosper going down. The clatter of the cop's boots. The cop still shouting. 'Hey, hey, stop, man, stop. Police.'

Made Joey Curtains smile. He pushed through double doors into an empty ward. Checked for CCTV cameras. Nothing. Some beds up against the walls. Drip stands. Stainless-steel food trolleys. Gurneys. Stack of blankets on a couch. A table down the far end, cups, an urn, kettles, tea packets, coffee tins stacked on it. Filtering from somewhere a television golf commentary the only sound in the quiet. No voices. Joey Curtains went through this ward into a corridor. The commentary coming from an open door to his left. He went right along a passage with milky windows giving him a vague outline of Devil's Peak. Meant he was headed away from the hospital entrance. There'd be police out there soon enough. Wouldn't take Prosper long to work out which way he'd gone. He slowed. Facing him, a bank of lifts. Corridors to the left and right. No CCTV.

Keep right, boykie, he thought. His trainers squeaky on the lino, Joey Curtains walking fast, not running. Locked rooms both sides. No telling where he was.

He tried doors as he went, one opening into an empty room. Through a barred window saw tree tops, what looked like gravestones in the distance. Joey Curtains relaxed. Had his bearings now. If he could make it to the graveyard, he'd be away.

Came out of the room, there was a cleaner staring at him. Big woman with a mop, bucket of soapy water. Hadn't heard her coming.

Joey Curtains went into his broken Xhosa, asked how he got out of the place.

The woman clicked her tongue. Told him there were stairs.

'Where? Where's the stairs?' Using English now.

The woman waved her mop, pointed farther down the passage. There was another cleaner beckoning to him. The two mocking him in their language. The stupid couldn't find his way out.

Down a flight, at an open door, more cleaners unloading from a van. Joey Curtains hurried past them, going down the road. Out of sight, vaulted the wall into the graveyard.

Could hear sirens as he took a well-worn path across the grounds. Old gravestones scattered about. Names you couldn't read. Dates worn away. Most of the graves untended. Joey Curtains walked fast, not glancing back. Plenty of tree cover to keep him hidden. No sound of pursuit. At the far end, came out on a concrete parking area, passed between municipal buildings, walked downhill to Main Road. Ten minutes later was in his car thinking about Prosper Mtethu. Sat there in the side street, thinking about Prosper Mtethu. The Struggle hero. The grandfather who looked after a granddaughter.

Prosper Mtethu who'd done the planning. Who'd arranged the set-up. Who must've known Kolingba had been transferred, who'd pushed him into it anyhow.

Joey Curtains wondered what to do about Prosper Mtethu. Wondered what Prosper Mtethu would do about him. Thought maybe it wisest not to sleep at home. Wondered, too, should he phone the major? Major Vula going to throw a major shitstorm. The major going to tell him find the colonel, sort it. Joey Curtains thinking, enough with the fun and games. He needed a drink.

Decided Vusi's on NY43 would be the place. Big noisy tavern. Lots of honeys on a Friday night. Blow a couple of Blackie bugles, scheme out a way to put this right.

His cellphone rang: unknown number. Joey Curtains connected, heard Prosper Mtethu saying. 'Where're you, my brother? Where're you? There's still cops here. Stay hiding.'

Joey Curtains said nothing, disconnected. Opened the back of the phone, took out the battery.

Ja, Prosper, ja, ja, ja.

Joey Curtains swung the ignition, headed for Vusi's shebeen.

37

Vicki Kahn sat upright on the bed, pillows in the small of her back, netbook on her lap. Relaxed now after a long soak.

Thinking, okay guys, you want to log my keystrokes, enjoy. Powered on the netbook.

Vicki wearing the hotel's towelling bathrobe. On the side table, a cup of ginger tea, a peanut-butter sandwich from room service.

The woman who'd taken her order astounded. 'You don't want anything on the menu? Some club sandwich perhaps? You want a bread with peanut butter? This is all?'

The waiter who'd delivered it deadpan. Backing out the room with a 'Guten appetit'.

Vicki smiled at her reflection on the screen. Big-time Friday night in Berlin.

She'd hardly got her system running, Skype popped its tune: Fish calling. Vicki thinking better now than later. Keyed him on. The two of them going through the hello babe routine. Fish's blond hair wild.

'Had a good surf?' she said.

'Blown out,' said Fish, raised a Butcher's to toast her. A gloss of condensation on the bottle. 'Prost.'

Vicki lifted her cup of tea.

'You're not drinking! A whole minibar. Agency account, you're not drinking?'

'Not yet.'

Fish asked about the weather, the snow, said he'd taken a swim, a southeaster mushing up the bay.

Said, 'How'd it go with the Kraut?'

She gave him the story. Ended: 'What I can't get my head around's this old man having a thing with my aunt. Alright, he was younger, she must've seen something in him. But people don't change their habits. The man's still suspicious of everything. Reckons there's a watcher in every shadow. Even had someone track me on the bus. Would you believe? And his place's a mess. Smells like old food, you know, musty.'

Telling him then about the interrupted meeting in the morning, the cancelled arrangement in the afternoon. 'Like what was the guy's case? He's got this busy life? At seventy whatever the hell age he is?'

Not telling him about the phone calls, the intruder, that probably there was a spy in her netbook, not telling him her boobs were sore, that she was nauseous all the time. Not telling him what she didn't want to admit.

She told him that last bit, he'd be positive. Would be acceptable for Fish. Not that they'd talked about it. Never. Like getting together. Marriage. Children. It wasn't an issue. But she knew. Vicki knew Fish would go for it. She'd seen him with kids. Grommets learning to surf. All the patience in the world had Fish. She told him her condition, it'd be another complication in her life. No ways Fish would see this as a difficulty.

Fish right there on her computer screen, riding his chair, clutching a bottle. Fish relaxed. Heading into his Friday night, would sink a few ales, blow a reefer, mellow with one of his muso chicks on the player: Laurie Levine, or that other one, Wendy Oldfield.

'What're you doing for supper?' she asked.

Fish coming forward on the chair. 'Fettuccini. Some fried courgettes and onions. A chocolate brownie from Knead to finish.'

'More pasta.' Vicki swallowed hard. The thought of fried onions enough to make her gag.

'And you?'

'Room service.'

'All those restaurants you could choose from?'

'Thanks very much. Go out in the frozen cold. Sit alone in some place with everyone else enjoying themselves. Battle with my non-existent German. Really enticing.'

'Be adventurous. A spy in the spy capital.'

'My name's not Amina Kahn.'

Fish inclining his head. 'I don't know. Where's it you work these days? Why're you where you are?'

'Point taken.'

Both of them smiling, Vicki wondering if anyone was listening this time? The thing about Skype was that it took some doing to break into. Quick conversations you could get away with. This one would be a sitting target. Not a problem. Fish understood the need for caution. Anyone listening would assume she knew her room'd been picked over. That she didn't trust her netbook any longer. Anyone listening would get the message: she was a player, could handle the double game as well as any Berlin spy. Vicki shifted the conversation to Fish's day. 'You met …?'

'I did.' Fish tilting his chair. Keyed in: 'The perfect spy.'

'Yeah? Really?'

'Mm-hmm. Very mysterious. Lots of smoke and mirrors.'

'You believe any of it?'

'Wouldn't doubt it for a moment, as they say. Thing is' – Fish breaking off for a quick guzzle – 'thing is what's his case?'

'You asked him?'

'I did.'

'And?'

'Personal, he says.'

'Personal? That's handy.'

'Exactly what I said.'

'Of course you did.' Vicki desperately wanting another bite into her peanut-butter sandwich. But not wanting Fish to know. Fish saw her eating a sandwich he'd ask why, what, how much it cost? She keyed off the video. Pressed the microphone mute button.

Fish protesting. 'Where've you gone? What's up with the video? I can't hear you?'

Vicki took a quick bite of the sandwich, chewed fast, swallowed. Wiped her mouth with the serviette, threw it aside, out of the camera angle. Got the video back, the sound with it.

'Bloody wonderful connection,' said Fish.

'Modern technology.' Vicki pulled a face. 'You know? You were saying, he said it was personal?'

'Right. Then I asked how come? He said he wouldn't say. It was too close to home. What he did say was the – what shall I call it?' Saw Vicki was entering text. Read, 'The event.' Typed: 'Exactly, the event could've been rogue, black ops, whatever you guys call it. Extracurricular.'

Vicki said, 'He told you this?'

'Not in so many words.'

'And you don't think it's weird he tells you this?'

'I think it's very weird.'

Vicki back on instant message: 'He's using you. He could do his own dirty work.'

Fish read it, said, 'He could. Instead he's sent a client to me. Even given me the name of a person of interest. Very generous.'

Another message in caps: 'HE'S BEING MANIPULATIVE.'

Fish tapped out: 'I got my eyes open. It's okay. Seems we're on the same side.'

'Seems is the word you've got to remember.' Vicki saying it aloud, shaking her head.

Fish typed: 'He's your colleague.'

Got in response: 'Except I don't know him. I've never met him. I don't even know who he works for. What's the name he gave you?'

'Joey Curtains. Mean anything?'

Vicki read the name on her screen, lifted her shoulders, her hands.

Fish wrote: 'A field agent?'

'I don't know, Fish,' Vicki said. Entered: 'I can't help you.

It's too new for me. There're lots of field agents. Most of them off the books. Seriously strange how he's contacted you.'

'It's a job,' said Fish. 'A paying client. Bit of intrigue on top. What more could you ask for?'

'Just watch it.'

'I will. Chill, Vics. I surf with sharks.'

Typed: 'Not these sort of sharks.' Heard Fish say, 'Oh shit, the onions.' Disappeared from her screen. Left her looking at a sink with unwashed dishes, banana skins.

Bananas. Bananas were something she could fancy. Get room service to bring up a couple, maybe another peanut-butter sandwich for emergencies.

Fish returned. 'No harm done. They're okay, crispy.'

'Burnt.'

They both laughed. Fish saying, 'Depends how you look at it.'

Vicki said, 'You'd better go. Finish cooking your supper.' Hesitated. Doubting Fish would have missed the opportunity to bring up Daro Attaline's disappearance. Typed: 'You ask him about Daro Attaline?'

Fish grinned. 'Of course.'

'And he said no idea.'

'His exact words.'

'You left it there.'

'For the time being.' Fish took a pull from the bottle of ale. 'When're you seeing Schroeder, tomorrow?'

Vicki told him.

'Can't wait to hear the great secret. Same time tomorrow?'

After they'd disconnected, Vicki wondered if he'd done anything more about Linda Nchaba. Was like Fish not to listen to a word she said. She finished the sandwich. No, Fish would've hinted if he'd been digging. Also there'd have been his Friday-afternoon dagga run to supply the ad guys, the academics, the bankers, lawyers, chartered accountants wanting a stoned weekend. Linda Nchaba would have to wait.

Right now Vicki's thoughts were about maybe asking reception if she could move to another room. Or was that too paranoid? What did Henry always lecture: pretend. Pretend everything was fine. She decided, okay, she'd go with that. If there were listeners on her phone, listeners trying to hack into her Skype calls, so be it. Only to be expected. Pretend you're cool. Nerves of steel. Shifted her thoughts to bananas, to peanut butter smeared thickly on ciabatta. Followed by 888 poker. She switched off her cellphone, took out the battery. On the bedside phone, dialled room service.

38

Fish filled the pasta pot with water, set it on the burner. Turned up the heat. The image of Vicki sitting on the bed still vivid. Yo, she was pretty. That black hair. Those Indian eyes, deep, enigmatic. That sharp nose. The perfect lips like they were out of a catalogue. Fish sighed. Okay, only one more day. Sunday she'd be back.

He finished a Butcher Block, uncapped another one. What the heck? Live large. Only topic on his agenda was Joey Curtains.

His phone rang, the landline, an international number. Had to be mother Estelle. Fish hesitated. Not now, ma. Not now. Saw the name Rings Saturen circled on the pad. Tomorrow, he'd do it tomorrow, track down the politician's unofficial cv. Let the call ring until voicemail picked it up. The thing about Estelle was her insistence. Her nagging. Fish drank off a mouthful of beer, turned his attention to matters food.

With the water at the boil, dropped in the fettuccini. Switched off the flame beneath a pan of courgettes. Dialled Joey Curtains from his second cell. Even a spook wouldn't get a street address from this number.

The call went through. Sounded like Joey Curtains was partying. Major background noise: loud music, loud voices. Shebeen. Had to be.

Joey Curtains shouting, 'Who's this?'

Fish said, 'I got to speak to you.'

'What? What, man, speak up.'

Joey Curtains sounding to Fish like maybe he'd sunk a few. Fair enough. Was Friday night. He'd also sunk a few. But a good few less than Joey Curtains, he reckoned.

'I want to speak to you.'

'No, man, I can't hear a thing. Phone back later. Like tomorrow.'

'Got to do it now,' said Fish. 'Can you go outside? Somewhere quiet.'

'Who you, man? What's this you want?'

'To talk.'

'Ja, to talk about what?'

Fish not prepared to tell him right off. The next thing, Joey Curtains would hang up.

'Where're you?' said Fish. 'I can meet you there.'

'You sound like a whitey,' said Joey Curtains. 'Aren't any whiteys I can see here.'

'Where're you?'

'Vusi's. You know Vusi's?'

'I know Vusi's. Vusi on NY43. I can meet you there.'

He heard Joey Curtains laugh. Joey Curtains saying to someone, 'This whitey wanna come here.' The other person saying, 'Let him come.' A cackling laughter. 'Whiteys got to learn to live. No fun being a whitey.'

Joey Curtains saying, 'No, my whitey. You don't want to come here.'

'Give me an hour,' said Fish. 'I can come there.'

Joey Curtains telling him in fast Afrikaans to fuck off out of his face. Who the hell was he? What'd he want? 'Fokof, jay.' The run of the words making Fish smile.

Fish deciding the dude was so stoked, may as well go for broke. Said, 'Joey—' Got no further.

'Who's your Joey? Hey, my bru, whose your Joey? Naai weg, ek sê. You speak to me you call me Mr Curtains.'

Fish catching most of this above the racket. Joey Curtains shouting into his phone.

'What's your name?'

Fish told him. 'Go somewhere we can talk, Joey. You'll want to hear this.'

'Hear what? What you got to tell me?'

'About something you did, Joey, last Sunday.' Fish knowing he dropped the name Kolingba now there'd be no more Joey Curtains. Rather dangle something.

A silence from Joey Curtains. Vusi's pumping in Fish's ear. Music he didn't recognise.

'What you talking about?'

'I think you know. We need to meet, Joey.'

The noise diminishing, Fish heard a door bang closed, the music dulled.

'My friend,' said Joey Curtains, 'what you saying to me?'

'I'm saying I know what you did last Sunday,' said Fish.

'What's that?'

'Don't play games, Joey. Just meet me.' Fish fishing up a strip of fettuccini, tasting it. Al dente. Positioned the phone between his shoulder and ear, took the pot to the sink.

'Alright.'

Fish surprised, almost dropping the pot into the sink. 'In an hour.'

'No, my friend. Not here. Tomorrow.'

Fish thought about this, what options? Rather let Joey Curtains call the tune. 'Where?'

'I've got your number. I'll phone you. Tell you where.'

Fish drained off the water. 'Not good enough.' Realised he was talking to dead air. Anyhow. He had the man's number. He could try him again.

Heaped fettuccine into a bowl, smothered it with the courgettes and onions. Sprinkled Parmesan. Forked up a mouthful. Not bad. Washed it down with a mouthful of ale. Raised the bottle to meeting Joey Curtains.

39

Kaiser Vula hated parties. Enforced good times. Everyone laughing, smiling, kissing, hugging, loud with make-believe. Getting their jollies. More champagne, more whisky, more beer. Chasing lines. Falling about. Making out.

Kaiser Vula drank sparkling mineral water at parties. Stayed sober. You learnt things that way. Could watch everyone getting drunk, getting stupid. Saying things they shouldn't. Doing things they shouldn't. Men pawing other men's women. Women dancing like prostitutes. People vomiting in the flowerbeds.

Party fall-out. Some parties you wanted the fall-out. The fall-out could be useful. Other parties there was no gain.

The reason Kaiser Vula hated Nandi's parties. No gain. No revelations. No confidences. No secrets. Nothing. The people too obvious. Too shallow. Models, advertising execs, radio jocks, TV hosts, actors, artists, trust babies. Only reason he stepped into Nandi's parties was because of Nandi.

Kaiser Vula knew women, you couldn't trust them. Nandi

likewise. Nothing she'd ever done. Nothing she'd ever said. But Nandi had those muti powders, you didn't know what was in them. Why Kaiser Vula wouldn't miss one of Nandi's happy-happies.

Other hand, a party at the president's palace, that could be useful. Kaiser Vula could put on his ooze and smooze, be Mr Charming. Except here now he was anxious, irritated, on edge. The scene overflowing with cabinet ministers, the new oligarchs, bishops, kings, princes, princesses, generals, mining magnates, Russian moneymen, slick Romanians, Indians in Gandhi tunics, Italian bagmen, ambassadors, robed Arabs, all the fawning minions. And he was uneasy. His stomach tight with worry.

Worry that there was no word from Prosper Mtethu.

Worry that there was another cock-up.

The apprehension all-consuming. Not even Nandi getting onto the worry meter.

He could see her. With the president, attentive to his every word. Letting him take her into a nightclub two-step shuffle. His shiny head. His thin smile. Kaiser Vula clucked his tongue. Of all the pretty girls, the president chooses her. Sending a message: Everything is mine. Everyone is mine. What could you do? There were only his rules.

Kaiser Vula took his flute of mineral water through the happy groups. Through the jiving bodies. Out onto the terrace. A band played here. Dressed like a band from another time, the men in bow ties, penguin suits, the singer showing remarkable cleavage. Had a raspy voice. Smoker's voice. Sexy voice. A Miriam Makeba voice. Voice he could've listened to in another mood.

But Kaiser Vula was agitated. Couldn't relax. Couldn't stand still. He wanted to be out of the light. Away from the careless noise.

From the swimming pool came insistent chatter, young bodies floated there, appealing. Kaiser Vula saw breasts, bums, wet flesh, once he would've been there. Not now. Not anymore. Too risky. Too many ever-ready cellphone cameras.

Skirting the wet slasto, headed for darker patches of garden, beyond the lights. Passed the earnest groups in chairs on the lawns, the serious dealers, murmuring together. Where he should have been, listening to secrets, releasing select titbits of intel.

At the flowerbeds edging the grass he stopped, turned to look back: the palace ablaze with light. People crowded in the reception rooms, dancing on the patios, the music swinging, the singer's voice ripe with seduction. Good times at Bambatha.

Major Kaiser Vula set his glass on a bench, fished out his cellphone. Tried Prosper Mtethu. Voicemail again. 'What's happening, Agent?' he said. 'You must call me. First thing.' Tried Joey Curtains. Also voicemail. But Kaiser Vula left no message.

Sat on the bench thinking, what to tell the president? The important thing was, what did the president know about Kolingba? Had to know about the hit. The botched hit. Yet hadn't said anything. Had made as if he didn't know. As if a week later the gatekeepers still had the president outside the loop. Hadn't briefed him on the whole fiasco. Maybe. It was possible. No telling for sure. No telling who knew what.

Moments like this, Kaiser Vula wished he smoked. Wished he hadn't given up, after all his wife's nagging. Thought maybe he'd break his rule, have a drink. Was about to head for the bar, a voice said, 'Major.'

40

Zama hated parties. Or rather, palace parties. He worked the rooms, did what was expected, loathed the people. Usually he was away after an hour. Intended to be soon. Had gone into the garden to make a call. Have a private chat. Unheard by listening ears.

Afterwards stood waiting for the return call in the deep shadows, watching the revellers. All here for his father's pleasure. The old man's sense of power. Few the president didn't have the drop on. Few who didn't want to praise him.

The fawning hordes.

Zama despised them all. Yet knew he was among their number. He needed his father. Needed the name that opened doors. Didn't make it any better. Made it all much worse.

Turned his head, spat the thought into the red KwaZulu earth. The earth of his ancestors.

Yeah, that was another story.

Then saw the guy, the major, come onto the terrace. Vula. Interesting first name, Kaiser, its German allusions. What was Major Kaiser Vula? Who was Major Kaiser Vula? Military? Police? The Security Cluster? Some faction of the secret service?

What had his father said they must talk about? Some refugee colonel from the CAR. The one who'd taken the hit.

Zama watched Kaiser Vula pause, uncertain, glancing about, then amble past the swimming pool, cross the lawns towards him. As if he knew he was there. Zama kept still, waited.

Saw the major put down his glass on the bench. Make the two phone calls. Heard an urgency in the message he left. His soft cursing.

As the major turned back towards the party, Zama said, 'Major.' Stepped out of the tree shadows onto the grass.

Heard Kaiser Vula's, 'Wena, you! What's this?'

'We meet again.' Zama took two paces towards the man, holding up his hands, showing his cellphone. 'Like you, I needed to make a phone call.'

'You heard what I said?'

'Only that you had to leave a message.' He shrugged. 'On a Friday night everyone is somewhere else. We must expect this.'

Zama waiting for a response from the major. Getting none. The man uneasy, gesturing towards the party.

'I must get back.'

Zama switched to Zulu. 'I have not seen you here before, Major. This is your first time?'

Major Kaiser Vula nodded.

'A place for all the chiefs to meet.'

'I don't know.'

Zama swept his arm across the breadth of the party. 'You can believe me. There is business being done tonight. Deals. Arrangements. Handshakes. Contracts, even. Understandings. You know what I mean?' He laughed. 'Some of it you will read about in the newspapers. They will call it corruption. But we know the other side, hey, Major. It is how the world works.'

His phone vibrated, the ringtone muted.

'Ah, my people are on the ball.' He held up his phone, the screen flashing. 'Next time we must talk about Colonel Kolingba. I need to know about this man. About what happened.'

'There was an assassination attempt.'

'That much I know, Major. What I don't know is did they do it? Or did we?' Zama held out his hand. Again Major Vula took it, they shook. Zama putting strength into his grasp, feeling it returned. Smiled. The major would not be an easy one. 'Until next time. Please.' He stood aside. 'I must answer this.'

Major Kaiser Vula nodded. Walked off towards the party-goers. Zama waited until he was ten paces away, pressed connect. Said, 'Yes, Mr Davidson, what can you tell me?'

41

The president enjoyed parties. Enjoyed the obeisance, the deference, the fear that could be glimpsed in his guests. Enjoyed too the lovely girls. The shine on their skins, their smell, the way they walked, their giggling.

Nandi was one of these. From the feet up. Silver shoes, long legs, some shape to the calves, firm thighs. When she moved, a muscle tightened there, tempting. Asking to be caressed. For a hand to glide up beneath the short skirt. The president stopped himself.

Lifted his eyes to her camisole, spaghetti straps. An interesting term, spaghetti straps. You hooked your finger underneath one you couldn't even feel its softness. Same with the cami, the silky way it swirled over the swell of breasts.

The president focused on the woman dancing in front of him. This woman telling him things. Speaking with her body. Moving up to him, moving away. Smiling. Enjoying herself. Making out with the president.

The band powered on the tempo. Nandi taking the president by the hand. Swirling round him. The president feeling he must indulge this woman. But not with dancing. Dancing was for young people.

'Come,' he said. 'Let me show you the palace.' Feeling no resistance as he drew her away from the dancers. People parting with smiles as they saw him coming through. People reaching out to touch him, casting down their eyes.

His people, his adoring people.

Led her through a doorway, closed off the noise. Said, 'Come, come.' Nodding at her. 'We can have a moment of quiet.' Leading her upstairs, following her now, his eyes on the bulge of her backside, the movement of her buttocks beneath her skirt. What underwear would she have on?

'Where are we going?'

Her voice soft, her head tilted upwards. The long curve of her neck. Could imagine his hand against her neck. The flutter of her pulse on his palm.

'My special place,' he said, guiding her into a long lounge: earth-colour walls, pale curtains, coir wall-to-wall, leather couches. Standing lamps with skin shades, subdued. 'My African room.' Yet no trophies, no spears, no shields, no knobkerries. No zebra skins. No porcupine quills. No cluster of calabashes.

Only one painting centred on the end wall behind a white screen.

She walked towards it, delicate as a klipspringer on her high heels. The snick of them across the carpet, her calves moulding, relaxing. Her thighs tight, a long muscle stretching there.

The president took from a cabinet a bottle of cognac. Poured into two snifters, tasted from the one.

'A drink,' he said, coming up to her, holding out the glass. Seeing hesitation in her eyes, sipped at his again. 'Vintage cognac.' She took the glass. 'You will not taste better outside of France. This is very fine.'

She sipped.

'You agree.'

She smiled. 'I don't know cognac. It is the first time I have tasted it.'

'My dear, for a city girl, you have not drunk cognac? What is your drink? Champagne? There is champagne: Lanson, Moët, Veuve Clicquot, if you would rather. You like the bubbles.' He drew a Lanson from the fridge, uncorked it and brought her a flute. 'For you.'

She took the glass, sipped.

'You think that is better than my cognac?'

Again her quick bright smile. Her lips moist. She didn't answer his question, instead pointed at the screen. 'Can I see the picture?'

'Of course.' With a remote dimmed the lamps, brightened a spotlight, the screen rolling up.

There revealed a presidential portrait: himself in dinner jacket, dark glasses, head turned slightly to the right in triumph. Gazing towards distant people looking up at him.

Nandi stepped back, said, 'Oh, wow.'

'You like it,' he said. 'I do. It is not finished yet.' Took her hand, led her towards a couch. 'But tell me, my dear, about you and Major Vula.'

42

'Chief,' said the Voice. 'What's happening? Tell me things. Things I want to hear. How's the colonel's wife?'

Mart Velaze stood at a Weber, cooking ostrich steaks, his aspect the city by night. A dazzle of lights below him. The hot face of the mountain above. In the house a woman preparing salads.

Said to his boss: 'I had to meet with the investigator.'

A silence.

Mart Velaze glanced at the woman, one sexy piece. So young. So stunning. Could outgun him on a shooting range. Had a mouth on her too.

'That's not something I want to hear. Was it wise?'

'I took precautions.'

'I'm sure you did. But yours is not a face we want exposed, Chief. We want you in the shadows. Understand?'

Mart Velaze said he did. Opened the Weber lid, used tongs

to turn the steaks. The trick with ostrich steaks, sear the outside, have them bleed when you cut into the medallion. For this you needed a hot braai. A white-hot bed of coals. Earlier he'd thrown on woodchips soaked in beer for that smoky flavour, closed the lid.

'Got some bits and pieces you'll find interesting, Chief. Seems our friend Henry's well connected. Can buzz the president. Also on speaks with the son, Zama. Seems he let both of them know he's tracked down a woman called Linda Nchaba. Know anything about her, Chief?'

Mart Velaze said he didn't.

'A name to keep in mind. And now, hear me, our Henry's been busy with his commie chommies. No transcriptions available, but some out and abouts, would you believe? Meetings in parks, libraries, at the restaurant on Table Mountain. Lovely view, I'm told. Trouble with the commies, you can never tell if they're serious. Never know when one of them's going to swing at you with an ice-pick.'

Mart Velaze watched the woman come out of the house carrying a bowl of salad, a French loaf balanced across it, the neck of a wine bottle caught between her fingers. On her face a quizzical expression: like who the hell're you talking to now? Always the attitude. She came up to him, blew gently in his ear. Whispered, 'Oh, baby.' Got Mart Velaze ducking away, almost going into the swimming pool.

The Voice saying, 'Where are you, Chief? You cavorting, might I ask?'

'Braaiing,' said Mart Velaze.

'A barbie! Doesn't have you down as a barbie man in your file, Chief. There's a thing. You learn one every day. Okay, I'm going to let you go back to your burnt offerings with this little morsel: the brother who got the Kolingba hit together's now being pulled in by the president. Old comrade from the military secret service called Major Vula. Major Kaiser Vula. A name Mrs Kolingba might like to know.'

Mart Velaze turned round to look at the woman picking steaks off the grill with her fingers. When she stood against the light he could see through her dress. Brought the Afrikaans word woes to mind. Hectic, wild. One woes chickie this one.

Heard the Voice say, 'There's a little present I want you to give the major. Usual place, tomorrow afternoon. Go with the ancestors, Chief. Enjoy.'

43

Fish woke to the wind. The endless bloody southeaster. Its rattle of the loose fascia board. Once more. Irritating. Relentless. This blow now into its third day. Soon it'd start wearing on the nerves. Another day of thrum and howl. Another day of blown-out surf. Sometimes winter couldn't come soon enough in Fish's scheme of things. Those days of glassy seas. Big-walled sets pushing in from some storm in the southern oceans. Oh, for the cold fronts.

He reached for his phone, checked the time: 07:43. Got up for a piss, his bladder aching. Relieved, wandered through to the kitchen for a glass of water. In the open doorway, stood naked to the wind looking at his boat, the *Maryjane*.

The boat he'd inherited. The boat he seldom took out. Wasn't for his neighbour bugging him to go fishing, he'd never take it out.

One thing facing a two-metre outrider wave feathering along the top, another thing being on the back of the ocean. The cop neighbour Flip loved it. Didn't find the swells unsettling, the instability alarming. Called the motion rocking.

Would go on about the peace of being out in the middle of False Bay with a cold beer. Only place Fish couldn't hold his drink. Every time they went out – the three times they'd been out – Fish hurled a cat. A pale, amber cat.

Great bloody way to spend a Saturday afternoon.

Thing was, Flip could be useful. Had access to criminal files and dockets. Information. Fish had to keep in there, build some credit. You never knew when you needed a withdrawal.

Heard a voice saying to him, 'Mornings, Mister Fish.' A toothless woman in a long jersey-knit dress down to her knees, coming round the house towards him. 'Mister Fish doesn't want to put on some trousers perhaps.' The woman pointing at his genitals. 'I can't talk to Mister Fish with that thing dingle dangle. Please, Mister Fish, man.'

'What you want, Janet?' said Fish. Janet probably his own age. Looked twice that. Too much blue train, cheap wine. Too long sleeping rough. Janet one of the bergies slept on his back stoep sometimes. Fish kept a chair for them. His own social responsibility programme.

'Some toast please, Mister Fish.' Janet not looking at him, keeping her eyes on the *Maryjane*.

'Yussis, Janet,' he said, 'what time is this?' Shaking his head. 'You're making a habit of it. You know my rules.'

'I know, Mister Fish,' she said. 'I know it's mos early. I know only once a week. But Mister Fish, please man, please. One or two pieces. You knows I don't ask in the normal course.'

Fish finished his water. 'Wait.' Turned to go inside.

Janet whistled. 'Remember your trousers, Mister Fish.' Called after him, 'Where's Miss Vicki, Mister Fish? Maybe Miss Vicki wants me to vacuum. I can do some quick cleaning for her.'

'It's my house,' Fish shouted from the kitchen. 'I do the cleaning.' Janet's ideas about gender roles related only to money.

In the bedroom his cellphone rang. The name Cynthia Kolingba on the screen. He thumbed her on, didn't even get to say hello.

She went straight in, 'Last night they tried to kill my husband again.'

'What?' Fish, fishing among discarded clothes on a chair. 'Who did what?'

She repeated herself. 'Now he is moved to a private hospital, the Constantiaberg. Perhaps it will be safer there.'

'Did they hurt him?'

Fish sticking with the plural they for the moment. Heard what sounded like a sob. 'No. He was safe. According to the policewoman, the assassin went into the wrong room. My husband was lucky.' A pause. 'Please, Mr Pescado, you must find out who is doing this.'

'Yes,' said Fish, trying to dress while he talked to her. 'Did anyone see this person? Get a description.'

'They say it was a man. A metis. A brown man. What you call a coloured man.'

'Height? Size?'

'No, they can't tell me exactly. They say he is tall. Not so big in the shoulders.'

Fish found jeans, boxers. Thought, take this back a step or two. Mart Velaze still bothering him. Said, 'Tell me again how Mart Velaze contacted you?'

'I told you that he telephoned me.'

'You've never met him?'

'No. He phoned me. He said he is my husband's friend. That you will find who has killed our daughter. Who has tried to kill my husband.'

'And since then nothing from him?'

'Nothing.'

'Did you try to phone him back?'

'There was no number.'

Fish struggled into his boxers. Pulled on jeans. Thinking, what was the SSA connection? Mart Velaze was SSA. But Joey Curtains? Not on the SSA payroll, Velaze had said. Had also said maybe Joey Curtains was a field agent. A hired gun. Except if Joey Curtains was freelance, he could be acting for anyone. Didn't have to be on a SSA job. Could've been contracted by Kolingba's opponents. Why not? Made sense. More sense than a SSA tender. Which was why the SSA wanted it handled off the books. Let Cynthia Kolingba pay the investigation fee. Handy solution. Always assuming Joey Curtains was involved somehow. Fish zipped his jeans.

'Okay, Mrs Kolingba,' he said. 'If you can afford it, put private security on your husband.'

'Yes. This is done.'

'Let me see what I can do. Maybe I'll contact you later.'

'Please, Mr Pescado. If you can find these people, then they can be stopped. I fear for my husband. If men can get into a hospital so easily, they can do anything.'

'It's more difficult in the private ones.' Fish hoping there was truth in his reassurance. 'He should be fine.'

'He is still in a coma, Mr Pescado. That is not fine.'

Fish disconnected, went to the kitchen. There was Janet in the doorway, her odour reaching him.

'Where was you, Mister Fish? I thought you had forgotten me.'

'How'm I going to do that, Janet? You're standing right there. I can see you. I can smell you.'

'Ag, sorry for you, Mister Fish. You know mos on the mountain there's no showers 'n Badedas for a lady.'

Fish cut slices of bread, dropped two in the toaster. Boiled up water to make her tea. When he was done, handed her the plate and mug.

'Mister Fish maybe got a spoon of jam for me, please, man, Mister Fish.'

Fish gave her a jar of marmalade. Janet bent into a half-curtsy. 'You's too kind, my gentleman.' About to retreat to her chair outside, she stopped.

'There was a coloured man come here yesterday, Mister Fish.'

'Oh yeah, what'd he want?'

'I dunno. Man, I just sleeping here, Mister Fish, under the blanket to keep the wind out. But you know the blanket's thin so I see him standing there peeping round the corner. First I think it's another bergie, maybe Jonnie or Suzie or someone, also come for a bit of toast. Then I can see this is not a bergie. This man got a nice haircut, a nice jacket. Even Nike shoes. I stay still like I'm fast asleep. He sees me, he gets a fright. Even jumps a little bit backwards. Next thing, he goes down the drive to his car. A white car. Before he goes he takes some pictures with this big camera. He don't see me.' Janet frowning. 'Mister Fish not going to sell, is you, Mister Fish? Was the coloured from estate agents?'

'Uh-uh.' Fish shook his head. 'I'm not selling.' Wiped toast crumbs from his fingers. 'What sort of car?'

Janet sniggered. 'It's white, Mister Fish, man, I don't know cars.'

'You try and remember the number?'

'Mister Fish always wants the numbers, hey? Last time I give you numbers, you help me with a little cash.'

'You got the number?'

Janet told him off the top of her head. Fish wrote it down. 'That cost you one hundred, Mister Fish.'

'Okay, I owe you.'

'You in my debt.' Janet walked off to her chair. Called out, 'You must tell Miss Vicki I think she a lucky girl. From what I seen.'

44

Kaiser Vula woke with a sense of dread. As if someone had been in the room. As if he had heard the snick of the door being closed. Lay unmoving, listened to silence. Distant lawnmowers, the sudden quark of hadedas in the garden. Listened to Nandi's breathing: shallow, rhythmic. What had happened to her last night? The stupid woman getting so drunk. He refocused. Kept his eyes closed, kept absolutely still. In his temple the hammer of too much whisky. Even he had weakened beneath the president's insistence.

He put out an arm, found his cellphone: no missed calls, no message from Prosper Mtethu. No message from Joey Curtains. This did not sit well with Kaiser Vula's pounding temples.

In the bathroom, swallowed two headache tablets. Drank one of the mineral waters from the minibar, these chalets stocked like hotel rooms. Craved greasy food, a Coke.

But first he needed to sweat out the Johnnie Walker Black.

Kaiser Vula yanked on Lycra running shorts, moulded a neat bulge in his crotch, tight, macho. Reached in, adjusted his balls. Pulled on a T-shirt, laced up his trainers. Took one look at Nandi sprawled under the sheet.

The president saying to him, 'She is a young one. Young ones do these things.' The president making light. 'Have another Johnnie, Major.' Calling for women to sort out the lovely Nandi. The lovely Nandi sprawled on a couch, flashing her thong. He'd accepted the Johnnie, turned away from the sight of the stupid, stupid girl's dry-retching. What had she done to him? Forever now the sniggers of the major's drunk girlfriend. Yo, yo, yo, remember that party where …

Shit.

The girl had been out of it. Crying, vomiting. The stink of

her mess acrid in the room. What had she drunk? In front of the president. Never seen her behave like that before. The Nandi he knew was together. In control. Loving.

He let himself out of the room through the French doors, went into the bright morning. Heat already pushing down. The sky a white glare of light. From somewhere came the laughter of people splashing in a pool. Kaiser Vula sucked his teeth, hardened his face, hid his eyes behind sunglasses. Set off across a lawn towards the security point.

The guards saw him approaching, straightened up, snapped salutes as he passed through. Both guards grinning. The mad major running in this heat. Too much of the president's good stock. They knew. They'd seen it all before.

Kaiser Vula ignored them, ran onto the road, turned uphill, running easily, bottle of water in one hand, cellphone in the other. Didn't take long for the sweat to start. For his chest to tighten. Ran against the pain, against the heat, up the long rise of the hill. Near the crest, a gravel road fed off towards woodlands. He took it: a red strip leading into shade, patchy shade, but shade out of the relentless sun.

As he jogged, checked his cellphone signal: two bars. He stopped beneath a jacket plum, an old tree, tall, thick-leaved. The sort of tree the elders would gather under to discuss village affairs. A good place to hear what his men had to say. A place of wise counsel. Keyed through to Prosper Mtethu.

Heard ringing, until the call went to voicemail.

Kaiser Vula cursed. Wiped sweat from his brow, flicked it from his fingers, swore again. The throb of the headache behind his eyes relentless. Stale whisky thick on his tongue. He spat into the dirt. Where was Prosper Mtethu? Why had he not phoned? The major about to call Joey Curtains when his phone rang. Prosper Mtethu.

'Major,' he heard Prosper Mtethu say. 'It is early.'

'Not so early,' said Kaiser Vula, heaving, still short of breath after his pull up the long hill. 'You should have reported.'

'It has not been easy,' said Prosper Mtethu.

Kaiser Vula stopped his breathing, squinted against the ache of his hangover. 'Tell me.' Keeping his voice low. 'Tell me, Agent, tell me.'

'The operation was not good.'

Kaiser Vula hearing the words, the confirmation he dreaded.

'You cannot say that to me, Agent Mtethu,' he said. 'That is not what you should report. You had strict orders to make this operation good. There could be no failure.' He paused, rubbed his hand over the tree's smooth bark, reassuring, dry. This bark he knew had protective charms. Maybe he should tell Nandi, have her make medicine from its magic. Shook his head to clear the thought. 'Is that what you are telling me, that you have failed? This is your report?'

'Yes, Major.'

'You know there can be no failure.' Kaiser Vula waited. 'Where is Agent Curtains?'

'I do not know what has happened to the agent,' said Prosper Mtethu. 'He does not answer his phone.'

'Since how long?'

'From yesterday.'

'After the operation?'

'Correct, Major.'

'And this morning?'

'Correct, Major.'

'Is he alive?'

'I do not know, Major.'

'He has not been detailed?'

'No, Major.'

'You know this for certain.'

'I have checked, Major.'

Kaiser Vula closed his eyes against his hangover. 'You briefed him?'

'Yes, Major.'

'Then what, Agent? Explain it to me. What happened?'

'Agent Curtains did not complete the operation.'

Why did this not surprise him? Why was he expecting to hear that Joey Curtains had made this operation fuck up?

'Why not?'

'There was a problem, Major.'

'From last Sunday there have been problems, Agent. Nothing but problems. Big problems. This was a simple task with three trained men for the operation. Nothing should go wrong. But everything has gone wrong. Both times. I have to explain this, Agent Mtethu. I have to explain this to important people, why we could not perform a simple operation. Why we are so useless. What happened?'

Kaiser Vula leant against the tree, looked back the way he had come, the roofs of the palace buildings just visible in the valley. Waited for Prosper Mtethu's explanation. Imagined the veteran, probably standing to attention in his shorts and white vest, a sheen of perspiration on his forehead. Uncomfortable, resenting the conversation, the operation's outcome.

'I went to the target's location and told Agent Curtains everything that I found out.' Kaiser Vula nodding at the efficient language. Good. The young ones could learn from a man like this. 'Then we went to the target. I told Agent Curtains he must go first, then I would come behind. He must go down the corridor to where the target is. While Agent Curtains was walking I made a disruption at the nurses' station. During this time the policeman on guard came to find out what was causing my problem. He moved me back to the lifts. During this time I did not know what happened to Agent Curtains. At some moment the guard saw Agent Curtains and chased him. When this happened, I went down in the lift.'

'At what moment, Agent Mtethu? How long before he was alerted to Agent Curtains?'

'It was about three or four minutes.'

'Long enough for Agent Curtains to perform his task?'

'It was long enough.'

'And then what?' Kaiser Vula catching an acid rise at the back of his throat. Swallowed the reflux.

'I left the scene.'

'You don't know what happened to Agent Curtains?'

'No, Major.'

Kaiser Vula walked out into the sun thinking, this was not good, this was not good, this was not good. This was not what he wanted to report. This was going to cause major shit.

'Find him,' he said to Prosper Mtethu. 'Find him. Complete the operation. Report to me every two hours. You understand, Agent? I must have this information.' He disconnected before Prosper Mtethu could reply.

On Monday, back in the Agency, he would be called to account. Have to wait under the eyes of the secretary, her red lips pursed. The woman not smiling at him, sitting behind her desk, poised for the light to flash on her telephone. The call from the big room. 'Go in now, Major.' Her eyes shifting to the door, coming back to him, softening with pity. He could imagine it clearly. The long walk across the wooden floor. Being watched every step of the way. To account for the reason he was here.

Here beneath the elders' tree, sweating in the early heat. Sweating not just from the sun. Kaiser Vula glanced down the slope to where the road curved into a ravine. There would be shade in the cut, maybe even river pools. He could think more clearly in the coolness. As he started forward, he heard voices greeting him. Turned. Three runners heading towards him. Zama with two bodyguards.

'Major,' Zama said, 'come run with us.'

Kaiser Vula trapped: needing to be alone, unable to refuse. Said. 'You are too fit for me.'

The men laughed, jogging on the spot. 'Not for you, Major. We know your running. Come, we are good for ten kays.' Zama with his hand in the major's back, pushing. 'Come, come.'

Kaiser Vula with no option. Phoning Joey Curtains would have to wait.

45

Vicki woke in darkness. Switched on the bedside light, assembled her phone. Four missed calls: no numbers displayed. One an hour from midnight. Jesus! The nerve game. Yet they hadn't escalated the harassment. Kept the pressure to a message of unease: We are watching. Who was we? One thing, they didn't know about the flash drive. They wanted it, they'd be more proactive.

Vicki sighed. Lay back against the pillows, trained her breathing into a steady rhythm. Brought her thoughts to the night's play. Her triumphs: a pair of kings; four straight diamonds; three aces; a pair of black twos.

Oh, she'd gone down in the beginning, come off a hundred and twenty dollars. Game after game in the losing streak. Weaker hearts might have folded. Not Vicki Kahn. Vicki Kahn stayed with it until the pair of kings changed her luck. What lovely boys.

She smiled.

Brought her back, those kings did. Focused her. Helped her regain the loss until she was two hundred and thirty up. And rising.

Wonderful.

Wonderful too lying here without the nausea. She kept motionless, her body didn't exist. No pain in her breasts, no pain on their skin. None of that queasiness in her throat. She lay still, she felt normal. Seemed such a long time since she'd felt normal.

A pair of kings. Four straight diamonds. Three aces, a pair of black twos. The sort of luck you'd put money on. The sort of luck that opened a winning streak.

What she needed. A winning streak that'd pay her gambling debts. Help her bring home Linda Nchaba and the intel to Henry Davidson. Prove her worth. With two nights up on the cards, maybe she was on a roll.

Wondered if those logging her keystrokes had enjoyed her run. Maybe they'd scored too. Whoever they were. The telephone callers.

Her thoughts drifted to the coming day. Detlef Schroeder. Amina's story. With that, the nausea returned. Forced her out of bed, hand over mouth, her stomach convulsing. She knelt at the toilet bowl, dry-retching.

She went through the motions, washing, dressing, eating toast with peanut butter for breakfast. This sudden urge for peanut butter. A little after nine thirty phoned Detlef Schroeder. Just checking.

The old man coming on, 'Of course, of course, eleven o'clock is fine. It is what we agreed. I am up for many hours already. I have pastries from the delicatessen, I have fresh coffee. If you prefer, I have bought Maria biscuits. Herr Schroeder is a thoughtful man, no? He has even been to the post office. Completed his morning chores. What do you call them? My little tasks. So I see you soon to tell you the rest about Amina. Remember, change buses in the Tiergarten. Be watching for the people in the shadows. Tschüss.'

Vicki disconnected. The people in the shadows. The guy didn't let up. Except there were people in the shadows. The telephone creeps for one, and maybe others.

This time she changed buses in the Tiergarten. Six others had boarded with her; if the shadow people lurked among them, no one got off when she did. Vicki waited ten minutes alone in the white cold, wondering to what purpose. Neither the snood nor her coat enough protection against the fierce bite of below zero. In the next bus sat where she could see all the passengers. At each stop checked no one she recognised from the first bus got on. Didn't ease her anxiety. Those watching her would know where she was headed, wouldn't need visuals.

At Zoo changed buses, got off at Savignyplatz. This time no young man muttering 'Ja, ja, alles gut' into his cellphone as she headed for Schroeder's block. No one else she recognised on the street. For all she knew could be someone higher up the street in a parked car watching through binoculars. Could even be the passing pensioner with the wheelie shopping basket had a mic wired into her scarf. Her rheumy eyes not missing a moment. Vicki smiled. You wanted spooks, there were spooks everywhere.

Buzzed Detlef Schroeder. Before he could answer, the door opened, a mother coming out, kiddie in tow. The kiddie whining, the mother in full outrage. Or so it sounded. Vicki stood back to let them pass. The joy of children.

Crossed the courtyard to the hinterhaus, found the door unlocked. Went into the warmth of the building. How had Amina managed in this cold? Cold that hurt. Day after day under a low sky, no warmth from the sun, no sun. Like living in an ice age.

All very depressing.

She took the stairs slowly, wondering at her shortness of breath. Had to be the cold. Couldn't be her condition. Not already. Not so soon. Then again, maybe she needed to phone today. Make an appointment next week with her gynae. Get the matter sorted asap.

On the second floor, went left down the corridor. Expected to see Detlef Schroeder waiting for her. Would he be wearing the same jersey, the same shirt, the same suit pants? Undoubtedly. The way he smelt, he didn't change clothes often.

His apartment door ajar, a strip of light falling into the corridor.

She knocked. Called out, 'Detlef. Detlef. It's Vicki Kahn.' As if it would be anyone else.

No response.

Hesitated. Listened for the shuffling of his slippers. The clink of crockery. The snick of a kettle switched on. Could hear a television somewhere, the presenter's insistent voice. But no sounds in Detlef Schroeder's apartment.

She pushed at the door. That smell of old newspapers, the dust in carpets, furniture, cigarette smoke, burnt toast raising her nausea. Swallowed.

'Detlef? Mr Schroeder?'

Expecting the papery rasp of his voice.

'Detlef, can I come in?' Stepping into the apartment, closing the door with a gloved hand. In his sitting room, the morning's *Berliner Zeitung* on a chair. Next to it a mug of tea, half-finished. A stubbed cigarette in an ashtray. He'd been sitting there reading, waiting for her.

'Detlef?' Moving sideways towards the kitchen. Thinking, what if he'd had a heart attack, a stroke, pegged on the spot? All she needed. She edged round the kitchen door. Again that whiff of gas, sweet, lingering.

Saw the kitchen as she'd first seen it: the pot of jam with the knife, the dish of soft butter. Breadcrumbs on the sideboard. Then the Maria biscuits on a plate. The tag of a teabag in the teapot. The heap of saucepans in the sink, two plates in the wash-up rack. A teaspoon with a squashed teabag on the draining board.

Then the blood. Not much. A smear on a cupboard door, low down.

Below it the body of Detlef Schroeder.

'Chances are you're going to see bodies, corpses.' The nonchalance of Henry Davidson on an outing to the morgue. 'Victims. The murdered. The human debris of car accidents. You'll never get used to it. Mostly because you won't see enough. Something disconcerting about a corpse.' Henry Davidson, rolling back a plastic sheet, revealing a corpse on a gurney. Standing aside, smiling, like a magician. 'Take a decko, chaps. Acquaint yourselves.'

Acquainted herself now with the corpse of Detlef Schroeder. A small hole in his temple. Seemed he'd twisted away from the shooter. Kept his eyes open. Kept hold of a pen in his right hand. Had gone down against the cupboard, dislodged his teeth.

Jesus.

Vicki straightened, fighting the urge to vomit. Backed slowly away. Knew she should feel for a pulse, wasn't going anywhere near him. The way he was lying, the awkward angle of his head, he had to be dead. She kept backing off.

In the sitting room paused, took in again the newspaper, the mug. Instinct telling her, get out. Get out now. Training telling her, he was writing. What was he writing?

Meant she had to return to the kitchen. She did. Forced herself down the short passageway between the rooms. Glimpsed through an open door his bedroom. A television screen flickering blue light in the dimness, revealing his unmade bed, a heap of clothing on a chair.

On the table in the kitchen, a pad, nothing written on it. She tore off the top page anyhow, might be something visible there.

Then got out. Pulled the apartment door closed behind her, the lock clicking fast.

Went down the stairs, crossed the courtyard. Not hurrying. Anyone looking out would see a woman in a long coat walking purposefully. Nothing untoward.

At the street door, raised the snood to cover her chin. Took a breath, opened the door going left down Kantstrasse. Still unhurried, the tremble of adrenalin starting in her hands.

At the first bus stop, she waited. Three other people there: two elderly men, a young woman connected to her own world. They'd been there ahead of her. No one coming behind. Vicki stood aside, vigilant.

In her mind, Henry's injunction, 'Anything untoward, you phone me. I am your handler, Vicki, I need to know. In the field you will not have the full perspective. You won't know what's going on.'

Bloody right there. But how to phone Henry? Skype from the hotel room? They'd pick it up on their bugs. Call by cellphone, they'd have an intercept. Find a public phone. But where?

Get out of Berlin, her first priority. Change her flights. Catch the next KLM out of Tegel. Doing that, they'd log her keystrokes, know exactly her plans. Jesus, they had her, every which way. Except the hotel would have a business room, a computer she could use. That problem solved. Get her through to Henry, too, on instant message.

A bus came. She sat downstairs, behind the two men. The young woman strap-hanging. No one leaping on at the last moment.

At Zoo changed to a 100. No one on the bus she recognised. Stayed that way until she got off at the Marienkirche. Her mind a confusion of Detlef Schroeder's corpse, the smear of blood down the cupboard door. The smell of burnt toast. Henry

Davidson's 'Anything strange you phone me.' No, Henry, not this time. Too risky.

Then all the whys. Why'd he been killed? Why just before her visit? Why was her hotel room searched? Why was her netbook copied, assuming it had been? Why was she being watched? Why the harassing phone calls? Had to be because of Linda Nchaba, because of the flash drive. That was a home matter. Unless it wasn't. Unless there were international connections. Something on the stick that implicated powerful people in Europe.

If that was so, not even Henry Davidson had guessed it.

Crossing Karl-Liebknecht she glimpsed a man taking photographs, had a lens like a small cannon pointed at the church behind her. Angled quickly away from him.

At the hotel, her cellphone beeped: message after message. Photographs of her entering Schroeder's building, leaving Schroeder's building, catching the buses, crossing the street with the church behind her. The last one: entering the hotel.

Her phone rang, Henry Davidson's name on the screen.

46

Saturday morning, Fish wondered, what point in trying the licensing authorities? His contact strictly a working-week man. Saturdays he'd be driving his wife to the supermarket. Fish tried the man's cellphone anyhow.

The guy came on. 'What you want, Fish Pescado? This's Saturday morning! Can't you give a man a break?' The man cheerful, relaxed.

Fish stammered a 'Sorry, but can you still do a find for me?'

The man giving an exaggerated sigh. 'Always the can you, can you, can you? Gonna cost you. Big time, big baggie.'

Fish squatted in the shadow of the *Maryjane*, watched Janet scoffing her toast and jam. Told the man no problem. SMSed the number through.

Janet said, 'You a connected man, hey, Mister Fish. With all your contacts. Like a network through the city. That's what I say. Mister Fish's in the information business. You want to wheel and deal with Mister Fish, you got to have the dope. That's the truth. Hey, Mister Fish, you maybe got a little stop to see me through the day?'

Fish stood. 'You never let up, Janet. Toast. Tea. A little stop. You want to move in?'

'Ney, man.' Janet released a toothless grin. 'What Miss Vicki going to say about that? Find another girl in your bed. Ag, sis, Mister Fish, how can you think like that?' Janet going off into a cackle.

Fish's phone rang, number withheld. He raised a hand to quieten Janet, connected, said a tentative hello.

'I said I would phone.' A voice Fish couldn't place. 'You going to meet me, surfer boy?'

Joey Curtains.

Bloody amazing. 'We can meet. Sure, sure. Where you want to do that?' Fish heading inside out of the wind.

'You didn't expect I would phone, hey?'

'Best not to expect things.'

'Best not to, my bru. That way there's no disappointments. But now you not disappointed. I keep my word, surfer boy. So where you wanna meet? In a parking garage? Maybe on a highway? In a bioscope? Maybe on a beach?' Joey Curtains finding this amusing. 'How about there by you? Surfer's Corner, we can look at the sea. That nice little café there. Where you were with the colonel's wife.'

Interesting. So Joey Curtains had been watching Cynthia Kolingba. Was probably the very same dude came snooping with a long lens, that's how he knew he was a surfer.

'You mean Knead?'

'Ja, my friend, Knead. Where all the larnies drink their lattes.'

'When?'

Fish thinking, what was the angle here? What option was Joey Curtains working? Had to be something he was after.

'Make it thirty minutes.'

'How'll I recognise you?'

'You don't have to. I know what you look like, surfer boy.'

A shadow darkened the doorway, Janet holding out her mug and plate. 'That was a short call, Mister Fish. You going for coffee there by Knead. Nice for you.'

'You want to come?' Fish distracted, searching through a cupboard drawer for his Astra. Small gun with a powerful bullet.

Janet blushed. 'No, man, Mister Fish, I'm not wearing my smart dress.' Put the plate into the sink, kept hold of the mug.

Fish took the Astra from the drawer, checked the clip, the breech, stuck the pistol into his belt.

'Hey, Mister Fish, that's a smart gun? You like a boy scout. Always prepared.' Janet giggling. 'That's what I say, Mister Fish's always one up. You know. Ready to fire.' She held out the mug. 'Before you go, one more cup for a poor woman.'

'Bloody hell,' said Fish, 'enough now. I've got to go, Janet. I'm going to be late.'

'Quickly.'

Fish dropped a teabag in her mug, filled it with kettle water. Got her out of the house, the door latching behind him. 'You satisfied now?'

'I'm going to sit here, drink my tea while you in Knead, Mister Fish. Enjoy.'

Fish tried to start the Isuzu, the engine reluctant. Hunnah, hunnah, hunnah. Gave it a rest. Saw Janet grinning at him. 'Give petrol, Mister Fish, give petrol.'

He gave petrol, fired the ignition again, this time it caught. Heard Janet call out, 'Don't be scared. Be prepared.' Mad Janet, a pain in the butt, still she'd been useful.

Going over the bridge, his cell rang. Fish pressed it to loudspeaker, got a background of Carly Simon, 'You're So Vain'. Long time since he'd heard the song. Talk about clouds in your coffee. Talk about being with some underworld spy.

'Got all you want here, Fish Pescado,' said his contact. 'Like I said, gonna cost you plenty.'

'When doesn't it with you guys?'

'Hey, you want this? Treat me nice, polite. Saturday morning, bru. I'm out here with the wife doing together things, shopping, you know. You should try it.'

Fish pulled into a parking bay, kept the engine running. 'What you got for me?'

'Big baggie, we talking?'

'I said.'

'Just want to hear it again.'

Fish catching a sniff. Imagined the guy in some hyperstore among the TV displays staring at a wide flat-screen. Back-pocket cash payment, no doubt. These guys coined it. But who's complaining?

'So, what you've got is your three-series BMW. Oldish model: 2009. Manual. White, very nice. No accidents. Bought at an auction.'

'Good to know,' said Fish. 'How about the owner? His address?'

'How d'you know he's a he?'

'A guess.'

'Very pee-eye. Nice one. You got a paper 'n pencil handy like a good investigator?'

Fish let it go. Told him sure, jotted down the name, Joseph Curtains, an address in Parklands among the up-and-coming. Said, 'I owe you.'

'A big baggie.' Then: 'What'd you get, Fish, a 50-inch screen? This's one of those with wi-fi. Pricey, but it's only money.'

'Someone pays you too much,' said Fish.

'Not you,' the guy cut back. 'For you I do charity work.'

Fish keyed him off, thought, Joey Curtains might dis the larnies, but he was aspiring. One of the new bourgeoisie.

47

'Change of plan, Vicki,' said Henry Davidson into Vicki Kahn's ear. Vicki slipping her phone under the snood. Walking into the warmth of the hotel. Thinking, what now? Keeping her cool about the killing of Detlef Schroeder. Being the professional, listening, engaged.

Henry Davidson speaking fast, 'Want you out of there, chop-chop. Can do? Where are you, anyhow? In some museum admiring the ancient artefacts? In a gallery before a modern marvel? Sorry to spoil your cultural safari. Another time, eh? Bound to be another time. Always another time. So where are you? What sort of timeline are we talking to have you out of there?'

'I'm going to ring you back,' said Vicki, pleased to hear her voice so calm. Like she had this whole number nailed down: dead bodies, nausea, the tremblies, dealing with it all like a pro. Except that was the front. Behind was a little girl terrified.

'No, uh-uh, we have to talk now,' said Henry Davidson. 'No time like the present. Doesn't matter if you're standing there in front of a Kienholz installation or wandering through a Modigliani retrospective. Now, Vicki.' Henry Davidson paused. 'So how long are we talking? Two hours? Three hours?

Four hours max? Got to have you away this afternoon. This evening. Now the thing is this, Vicki …'

'I'll ring you back. I'm going to ring you back. Give me a minute.'

A pause. Henry wising up. 'I see. Alright.'

Vicki pressed off the call. Made her way between tourists in the lobby to the business alcove, her phone ringing. Answered, 'I'm going to Skype you, Henry.' Disconnected before he could say a word. Her phone buzzed again, she keyed it to voicemail.

Henry'd be puce above his cravat, his blood pressure in the red band, his toupee flipped sideways, couldn't be helped.

At a computer brought up Skype, logged through to her account, her contacts, typed a message to Henry Davidson: 'Detlef Schroeder shot dead.' Waited. One, two, three minutes. When was he going to answer?

Then: 'Get out now. Phone me from Schiphol. Go.'

So encouraging to be in the hands of a decisive handler. So to the point.

Wanted to type: What's going on?

Saw that Henry Davidson had logged out.

Vicki clicked off her account, shut down Skype. Cleaned her links from the history. Went through to reception. About to tell the woman on the desk: Unexpected change of plans, have to check out. I'll be down in half an hour, please call a taxi. Was about to. Then had second thoughts. Why give the watchers the heads-up?

In her room packed in twenty minutes. Methodical, focused: clothes first, bathroom items, netbook, chargers, passport, credit cards from the safe. The flash drive in her jacket pocket. Stood at the door, gazing round the room: nice room, weird time. Like being in someone else's story. Swallowed to clear the dryness in her mouth. Wheeled her suitcase to the lift.

At reception the woman said, 'Such a pity you cannot stay

in Berlin for longer, Ms Kahn. Maybe you will come again one day.' Smiled at her.

'Maybe.' Vicki returned the smile. 'You live in an interesting city.' A city of ghosts.

48

In the taxi Vicki Kahn wondered if the receptionist would be phoning the Berlin spooks. Standing at the foyer door watching the taxi pull away. Saying quietly into her cell, 'The woman you want to know about has checked out. She is going to Tegel in a great hurry.'

That's where they'd be waiting for her. The men in black leather coats, fedoras. Two of them. If this was a movie. 'You must come with us, Ms Kahn. For a little chat, ja.' The men who'd killed Detlef Schroeder.

Nausea rose in her throat. Vicki clapped a hand to her mouth, shut her eyes. Don't hurl in the taxi. The wave passed, left a hot prickle of sweat across her chest.

An hour later at the KLM desk, Tegel, Vicki had her seat on the next flight out. Watched her luggage bump onto the conveyor belt. Looked round. No men in black leather coats had been waiting at the drop-off point. Weren't hovering on the concourse reading newspapers, drinking takeaway coffees.

Was a man in a brown anorak reading a magazine. Wore jeans, black Converse sneakers. No backpack, no laptop bag. Standing twenty metres off against a pillar. Farther down the concourse, a woman also in jeans, low-heeled ankle boots, duffel coat. Standing there. No hand luggage. Gazing up at the departure board. Waiting.

Were they secret service?

'Excuse me, excuse me,' the booking clerk tapping the boarding pass on the counter. 'Excuse me, Ms Kahn, the gate will close in half an hour. You must hurry please, Ms Kahn.' Sliding a diagram of the airport towards her, indicating the route with a shiny red fingernail. 'This is terminal C where you must go. It is a long walk. Please.'

'Yes,' said Vicki, swivelling back. 'Yes, of course. Thank you. Where?'

'Over there.' The clerk, pointing. 'You see the C on the board? You will be in time.' Telling Vicki to have a nice flight.

Vicki hitching her bag onto her shoulder, starting towards the man in the anorak. Noticing the length of his hair, how it curled over the collar. As she passed, licked his finger to turn a page. Didn't look at her.

The woman about her own age, fiddling with her phone. Keying numbers. Talking softly as Vicki approached. Head down, hair falling forward over her face. Vicki noticing the boots, scuffed, creased, in need of polish. The woman turning away, shielding her conversation.

Vicki passed, walking briskly. Headed down the corridor towards terminal C. Midway, at a coffee shop, stopped. Dug a purse from her bag. Checked her watch.

You've got to hurry. The gate's going to close.

Glanced back: the woman was gone, the man too.

Paranoia, Vicki told herself. You get into this thing, you see menace in everyone. Guy can't even stand reading a newspaper. Woman can't take a phone call. You get into this thing, you become like Detlef Schroeder. Except you didn't want to be like Detlef Schroeder.

Talked herself away from the image of Detlef Schroeder crumpled on the floor, the red flower in his forehead. Talked herself out of the paranoia all the clip to terminal C.

Went through security: laptop out the bag, belt off, boots

off, coat folded into the tray. Still rang the buzzer on the walk-through detector. Vicki taking a breath, calming herself. Woman with a wand scanned her. Didn't once make eye contact.

Thirty minutes she sat in the lounge, watching the passengers. People sitting down, getting up, moving around. The restlessness of travellers. Expected at any moment someone to bend over her, whisper: You are Vicki Kahn. Come with me please.

At the boarding call checked through, walked down the corridor to the plane. The quick smile of the hostess, glancing at her pass, directing her. Vicki found her seat. Tense, expectant. Telling herself: Relax, think of Fish. Fish probably surfing. Sea and sun. Wild-haired Fish with his firm flesh. Bronzed Fish. Walking out of the water, surfboard under his arm. Keep with Fish, you'll get through this.

49

They ran down the slope into the ravine. From the light into a shadowed cut, dense vegetation on the rock face, a high canopy. Ran along a narrow path, not much used, ferns, creepers snagging at their shins. Branches whipped back to strike their faces. The running difficult on the uneven ground.

Kaiser Vula kept the pace Zama set. Each breath damp, heavy. The heat oppressive. Sweat trickling down his back. But his legs were strong. Behind him, the security men panted.

They ran for half an hour until Zama stopped.

'Listen,' he said. The word faint between his gasping breath. 'Smell.'

Kaiser Vula could hear nothing but blood-throb, his heaving

lungs. Slowly his pulse subsided. No sound. Not birdsong. Not the whisper of leaves.

He sniffed the pungency of sweet rot, damp fur. 'What is it? This awful smell.'

'It is memory.' Zama pushed through bushes. 'Come, come.' Led them into an amphitheatre.

Here no vegetation grew. A sandy floor, sheer rock walls to a jagged sky.

'It is a grave of white people. That is their smell. You have heard of the Bambatha uprising, a hundred years ago. Here our warriors had a victory. We killed the white wizards. This is why nothing will grow to remember our triumph. Many, many are here gone under the earth. Settlers. Boers. Farmers. Men, their children and women as well.' Zama walked round the clearing. Scraped with the toe of his trainer at the dirt, a fine dust rising. 'It is a memory in this dark wood. There are memories everywhere in Africa.' He pointed at the exit. 'Enough. We must go.' Went quickly, calling, 'Follow, follow.'

Kaiser Vula took a last look: something had happened here. The ground was soft. Weeds starting in the soil. It was not that nothing grew here. It was that the earth had been dug, turned over. Something buried.

The security men crowded him. 'We must go. We must go.' Patted at his shoulder. Held aside the bushes. Bumped against him.

Kaiser Vula shook himself free, went through the bush to the path. Zama there, jogging on the spot. He said nothing, headed along the path.

The route was up, a short, sharp climb. At the top Kaiser Vula bent over, hands on knees, gasping for breath. His legs wobbly. Below them lay the Bambatha compound. Distant figures moving about the gardens, shifting hosepipes. Before them, the road that led to the palace gates.

'From here it is downhill,' said Zama. 'Five kays. Let's go.'
He set off. Again the security men hustling Kaiser Vula to follow.

Now the pace was easy. Kaiser Vula matching his stride to Zama's, letting the gradient propel him. Inside the palace gate, Zama stopped. Waved on the bodyguards.

'Wait, Major,' he said. 'One moment. Let me get my breath.'

Kaiser Vula stopped, his chest heaving, a taste of iron in his mouth.

'You are a marathon man,' said Zama. 'A fit man.'

Kaiser Vula shrugged. 'I can do it.' Felt his cellphone vibrating against his thigh. Maybe Joey Curtains. Moved off a few steps, withdrew the phone, saw the name Marc on the screen. Nandi. She was a matter for later. An embarrassing matter for later.

'You don't want to answer?' said Zama.

'It can wait.' He let the call go to voicemail.

'Come,' said Zama. 'Walk with me.' Guiding Kaiser Vula towards the lower cattle kraal.

They walked in silence, Kaiser Vula preparing a question. Wondering if he should ask it. He spat out a glob of saliva, said, 'What happened at that place?'

Zama slowed. Glanced at him. 'What place?'

'That place you showed me.'

'I told you. It is where the corpses of white people were buried. The ones who stole our land.'

'Even today?'

'Perhaps. Who can tell what happens in our secret country? You can find bones everywhere.' He smiled at the major. 'I thought it would interest you, that strange place. But now I have something to ask. You don't mind?'

Kaiser Vula shook his head. 'I am your guest.'

'My father's guest.' Zama laughed. 'You are the guest of the president.' Grinned. 'Not the same thing as being my guest.

But enough.' Waved his hand, changing the topic. 'I must go to the Central African Republic, I want you to come with me.'

'I have …'

'You work for the state, Major. This work is for the state. I will sort your secondment. What I want is a military man. I am a military man, you are a military man but also in intelligence. That is an important combination. Together we can sort this matter in the CAR. We are talking to the rebels. You have heard this, in the Agency? Our breakthrough.'

Kaiser Vula frowned. 'I thought …'

'The situation has changed, Major. It has changed very quickly. You know, I know, nothing stays the same. There are always new details coming up. New things to think about. What is the situation today, is not the situation tomorrow. We must test the wind all the time.'

'Yes,' said Kaiser Vula. 'Yes. I understand. Then with Colonel Kolingba …'

'We must be vigilant. Concerned for his welfare. That was terrible what happened. Agents of another country fighting their battles on our streets. We cannot condone this, Major. We are not a go-to zone for assassinations. Not at all. We must see the colonel is safe. That he gets the best medical attention. These are the wishes of my father.'

They stopped at the kraal fence: cattle grazing in the farther paddocks. Kaiser Vula confused, wondering who to obey: his standing orders, or this new information from Zama. He needed clarity. He needed time. First contact Prosper Mtethu. Stop him. Get him to stop Joey Curtains. Do this urgently.

Zama pointed at the cattle. 'Those are my father's.' He turned, leant back against the fence. 'Everything is my father's. My father makes things happen. What do you think, Major?'

Kaiser Vula unsure how to answer. 'I think everything is possible.'

'Of course. The diplomatic answer. Good. Then we will proceed. You will join my staff.' Zama pushed away from the fence, held out his hand. 'We have an arrangement.' They shook. 'And now we must become sociable, Major. I have kept you from your lady.'

50

Fish got to Knead with ten minutes in hand. Parked the bakkie in a back street, walked round to the café. No need to advertise his arrival. Hellish southeaster coming off the sea, he had to lean into it along Sidmouth Road.

The parking area empty except for an old kombi, farther off a dad and two boys sheltered by a double-cab, struggling into wetsuits. Good luck to them in a blown-out sea. Have to be desperate.

As he entered the café, a gust wrenched at the door, ushered him in. The Nigerian waitress grinning at him from the counter. Her pixie smile irresistible. Something Vicki didn't let up on. Always kidding him the waitress was after his bod.

'Welcome,' she said. 'To the place of howling wind.'

'Becoming a pain.' Fish glanced round the café. Couple of tables with people breakfasting. Lone man with a croissant and coffee reading a newspaper. Fish'd seen him about. Teenagers drinking milkshakes, two women in conversation. Nobody out of place.

'You want a pain aux raisins with your cappuccino?' The waitress leading him to his usual table at the window.

'Somewhere different today,' said Fish. Chose a table away from the windows. Anybody out there pitched up to take photographs, wasn't going to get him in the frame with Joey Curtains. Not a chance.

'That'll be good,' said Fish. No need to let her know he was waiting for anyone.

Sat down, toyed with his phone. Wondered should he SMS Vicki a good morning, tell her she wasn't the only one with an interesting life? She'd be off to finish with the old German spy. Probably eating breakfast. All hyper about her new status: the international spook in spook city. Strange thing Vicki'd got herself into. Like after she'd been shot, law wasn't enough. She wanted in on the action. Wanted to know what was happening behind the scenes.

Her bag. Her career.

Fish decided, no, let her be. Leant back in his chair, stretched out his legs. From where he sat, had a view of the parking lot through the salty panes. The boys and their dad heading towards the sea, fighting their boards in the wind. Along towards the toilet block, the kombi still parked. Real old surfer's kombi with ratty curtains.

Fish checked the time on his cellphone. If Joey Curtains was going to appear, he had less than five minutes to make good. The waitress coming towards him with the pain aux raisins on a plate.

'Coffee's on its way,' she said. Fish smiling up at her, his gaze flicking off to the two women. Caught the eye of one, the woman quick to look down, to keep on listening to her friend.

'Quiet,' he said to the waitress.

'It's the wind. Who'll come here when the southeaster's pumping?'

'Me.'

She laughed. 'You live here. You don't count. I only wish it'd give us a break.'

'No kidding,' said Fish, noticing a white BM crawling down the road, pull into a bay outside the café. The reg number belonged to Joey Curtains.

A wiry man in a T-shirt, broadies, flip-flops, sunglasses got out. Remote-locked the car. Started towards the café entrance.

The barista called out one cappuccino. The waitress told Fish, hang on she'd be right back.

Fish watched the man glance round at his car, slip his keys into a pocket. A man coming in for his morning coffee, no troubles in the world visible on his face. Might even be a small smile to the shape of his lips.

What've you got to tell me, Mr Curtains, Fish wondered.

Heard then the rumble of a bike. Saw Joey Curtains look up the street towards the railway line. Joey Curtains hesitating, turning towards his car.

Fish saw the motorbike then, approaching fast. Two riders, black helmets, black leather gear. The bike slowing, coming level with Joey Curtains. The guy on the back, his arm extended, nasty-sized revolver in his grip. A .45. The muzzle flash. The explosion.

A woman in the café shrieking.

Fish taking in the waitress with the cup of coffee in her hand, the teenagers looking up from their phones. The man with the newspaper risen half out of his seat.

On the pavement, Joey Curtains going down.

The motorbike stopped. Two more shots hitting Joey Curtains, knocking him back across the pavement. A spray of blood patterning the window, blurring into the salt haze.

The bike took off fast. Fish realising, the kombi's gone. When did the kombi go?

Coming out of his chair to see about Joey Curtains. The café suddenly quiet, people rising from their tables, bewildered. Fish dodged his way through. Shouted at the waitress to get the medics, call the cops.

He got to Joey Curtains: one gut shot, one heart, one head. A pro hitman, wasn't taking any chances. Take the target down with the stomach wound, whack him with the mortal zingers. Wasn't anything Joey Curtains would be telling anyone now.

Fish searched through his shorts pockets, found the guy's cellphone. Had it away. No reason anyone needed to know who'd been on Joey Curtains' morning call roster. When the waitress came up, moved him aside, said she'd been a nurse in Nigeria. Thought she was done with seeing people shot up in drive-bys.

'Nothing you can do,' said Fish.

'You know this man?' The two of them standing, looking down at the body.

Fish shook his head. 'Never seen him before.'

'Too many gangs round here,' said the waitress. 'Too many drugs.'

Fish waited inside the café when the cops came. Told them he'd been in for a morning coffee. Told them what he'd seen. Gave them a statement then and there.

'You want counselling?' asked one of the cops when he was done.

Fish said, no, he could manage.

'You can come to the station any time you want,' she said. 'This stuff can get to you.'

It did. Hours later Fish still had a line running round his brain: Curtains for Joey Curtains. Thing was, who dunnit?

51

'Now what?' said Vicki Kahn to Henry Davidson. Vicki talking while she walked. Moving at a fast clip down the corridor, people still brushing past her. 'I'm in bloody Schiphol.'

'Relieved to hear that,' said Henry Davidson. 'Pleasant flight?'

Pleasant flight. Typical Henry, as if she was on some holiday. Not a care in the world.

'You going to tell me what's going on?'

'In a minute. No one at Tegel then? I would be surprised if there wasn't.'

'I don't know. Maybe. Maybe not. A man and a woman.'

'Yes, it gets like that, doesn't it? You start imagining things. Things about people standing around, I mean. Curious things. They look normal, like they're waiting for someone, but you just cannot tell if they are going to disappear. Of course once you have been through the training, nothing is ever the same. Pity, that, is it not? Losing our virginity.' He sniggered. 'Pity, too, about poor Detlef.'

'Henry,' she broke in. 'This line …'

'Oh, don't worry about that. Nothing I intend saying is of any interest to our … your … listeners. Nothing they do not know already, if you get my drift. They are probably as baffled as you.' Again the little snigger. 'Germans always seem to be a bit on the back foot, I feel. But then what do you do with a name that long? Bundesnachrichtendienst, BND for short. Rather a mouthful for the poor intelligence chaps. Where are you now, Vicki? I mean specifically.'

Vicki looked round, recognised the champagne bar, Bubbles.

'In the shopping mall.'

'Dreadful place.'

'My phone …'

'Don't worry about the listeners. BND types. Our business does not interest them. Just did not want their stopping by for a chat with you in Berlin. Oh dear, oh dear. No time for that.' Heard Henry snort. 'Right, now. Time for our chat. Find somewhere comfy, Vicki. Funny thing, you know, Detlef loved Schiphol. Said it was designed by spies. All those little snuggeries where you can have a quiet chat. Find a little snuggery, Vicki, so we can have a quiet chat. That was the thing about Detlef, never got past the secret agent phase. Never outgrew it. Guy gets to be seventy-something and keeps on playing spy vs spy. Loved the cloak and dagger, he did. Not my forte. But Detlef mainlined adrenalin. Could not get enough of sneaking around, felt right at home in the shadows. What I would not want to know about Detlef is how many people he killed. A fair number, I would wager. Even some children among them. And one or two elderly citizens. Bad as those CIA tourists. The black book missionaries. How are you doing there, Vicki, settled yet?'

Vicki slipping onto a three-seater couch. A businessman up the other end, tapping away at his iPad. Said, 'I'm sitting.'

'Good, good. Take the weight off your feet. Poor old Detlef. Always thought it might come to this. What goes around comes around, does it not? Just thought it would happen a lot earlier. Trust he refrained from touching you up? Women colleagues were always on about dirty Detlef. Cannot imagine how your aunt managed. So, Vicki. How are you? Not too flustered by this little inconvenience?'

Vicki wanted to tell him corpses didn't turn her on. Corpses made her really nervous. So did getting out of cities with the hounds at her heels. Wanted to say, I'm tired, Henry, can you let me get to a hotel? Instead said, 'What's happening?' A resignation in her question.

Which Henry Davidson picked up. 'Now, now Vicki, no flagging. Got to keep up with this. Cannot have you fading on us. Eat some chocolate. Lindt. The one with orange or ginger. Good for a boost. That and a strong black coffee. Double espresso. Macchiato. Whatever your poison. In no time have you twinkling in our firmament. Work to be done, Vicki. Need to be on point, on message, sharp-sharp as they say in the streets of Soweto. Alright, Vicki. A for away are we?'

Vicki thinking, get on with it. Henry always exhaling words like smoke. Could imagine him in his flat wherever it was, somewhere under Devil's Peak. One of those old blocks: parquet floors, pressed-metal ceilings, teak windows. Faint smell of drain cleaner. Dust motes in the sunlight. Henry in his faux-leather recliner. Big-band swing twitching his foot. Newspapers on the floor. Schooner of sherry to hand.

'What's happening is this. Our friend Linda Nchaba ...' Henry paused.

Last seen drugged, being wheeled away by medics, Vicki filled in silently. Right here. Right over there next to the tie shop. At the time Henry Davidson's voice in her head telling her, move on, don't get involved.

'Well, she is in our care. A tad obstreperous. Your job to bring her home.'

Vicki stared out the window, the dark closing in. Snow still in mounds on the aprons, piled against the terminal buildings. Remembered a frightened Linda Nchaba sitting right here on these couches. Scared shitless.

'You told me she was on another flight to Paris.'

'Admittedly.'

'Now you're telling me we've got her?'

'Yes.'

Realising, this was an Agency operation. What Henry Davidson had in mind all along. Said, 'You planned this?'

'In a manner of speaking, yes.'

'Jesus, Henry, thanks for letting me know.' Vicki thinking maybe this wasn't her scene, this shadow work. At least the law was codes, procedures, protocols. This was duplicity. Everybody running hidden agendas. Maybe she should go back. Law had a kind of honesty.

Recalled Henry Davidson saying once in another world: 'Out there in the field, you are down a rabbit hole, you do not want to know everything, you do not want to know what is going on. Better you do not. Better you let your handler work the bigger picture.'

Heard Henry Davidson, 'Vicki, listen. Listen to me.'

Broke in, 'She's okay?'

'Fine. Fine. She's fine. Been a rough couple of days for her but she's fine. As I said, as I was told, quite lippy.'

'And she wants to go home? She has changed her mind?'

'Ummm. Now this is the crux, you see.'

Vicki waited. Sitting there on the couch next to the guy poking at his iPad. Beyond them the world and their business rushing from terminal to terminal. At Bubbles people drinking champagne. Lovers waiting for connections to sea and sun. To the promise of paradise.

'We need you to convince her coming home is the right way to handle this. Get her on board. On side. That kind of thing.'

'She's not going to do that. She's frightened.'

'I know. I know.'

'You drugged her. Kidnapped her.'

'We. I prefer the first-person plural. More precise, more inclusive, would you not agree? Allows us to include the help. And no need to get all uppity, Vicki. The world is what it is.'

'So what do I give her?'

'Protection. Promises. Possibilities.'

'Oh, that'll do it. She'll love that. Protection from what? From who? What promises? What possibilities?'

'That pigs have wings. I cannot say, Vicki. Let us talk when you get there. More I cannot say. Don't need to bore our listeners with domestic matters.'

'That's it?'

'Yes, yes, I think so. Word of advice: sell yourself, Vicki. Sell yourself. Convince her. She comes home with you, her whole world changes. For the better. Now. Quick Skype so I can give you an address. Then it's up to you. All in your hands. No pressure of course.'

Vicki getting his snicker, snicker. Disconnected. Gave a long sigh.

The iPad tapper glanced over, smiled. 'You are waiting for a connection?'

'Always,' said Vicki, opening her netbook. Thought, if she was a gambling girl, how much'd she wager on Linda Nchaba going home? Not a helluva lot.

'We could have a drink while we wait, perhaps?'

Vicki glanced from the address Henry had sent, to the man in transit. 'Love to. Next time.'

Decided two to one against.

52

Fish was thinking, amazing things, bullets. Tapped one on his kitchen table: 9×19mm parabellum, size of his first thumb joint. Life-changers, these little bits of lead.

He'd seen people shot. And die. People he didn't know. People he did. His one-time partner Mullet Mendes, for instance, shot in a car park at night. He'd been made to watch from a distance. Some gangster bastard sitting beside him with a gun in his ear. Titus somebody. The anger of just sitting there. The helplessness. Seeing the muzzle flashes.

Then there'd been Vicki's shooting. He hadn't seen that. Had heard when she'd opened the front door, the retort, her scream. The after silence.

Now Joey Curtains. The shooters waiting for him to pitch. Fully in the know about where Joey Curtains was going to be when. Riding up to him. Pop. Pop, pop. Riding off.

Shootings didn't distress Fish. They upset him. Riled him. Especially when they came with a message. As Mullet's had done.

As did the killing of Joey Curtains.

If Joey Curtains knew about the Kolingba hit, maybe was involved in the Kolingba hit, then …

Either a retaliation.

Or a silencing.

Maybe something Cynthia Kolingba wasn't telling him. Maybe why she wasn't returning his calls.

Fish at his kitchen table with a bullet and a cold Butcher Block tried her cell again, got voicemail. Stared through the open door at the *Maryjane*. His yard in shadow, the sun on the rim of the mountain. Could drive to the hospital, wait for her there. But why? She'd have got his messages. Her problem if she didn't get back to him. Wasn't his job to chase clients. They didn't want his info, that was their problem. Better to sit here. Chill. Crack some more ales. Have a toke. Listen to Shawn Colvin. Skype Vicki.

He did. Nada. Vicki still offline. Tried her cellphone, also went to voicemail.

Wasn't anybody out there?

Except Estelle. His mother. Came through on the landline from whatever Beijing hotel she was holed up in. He pressed her on. Held the phone away from his ear.

'Bartolomeu, I expected to have heard from you already. I expected an email. What have you got? Bartolomeu, tell me you've been on the case, as they say.'

'Yeah,' said Fish, 'sort of. Watched my contact get gunned down earlier in a drive-by.'

Heard his mother snort. 'Oh, please. Where do you get that stuff? Where do you think you're living? In some cheap thriller? Get real with me, Barto.'

Not entirely untrue about Joey Curtains being his contact.

He'd thought if Joey Curtains was Agency, he'd probably have something on the politician, Rings Saturen. Some information he could feed his mother. Keep her smiling.

'That's as real as it gets,' said Fish.

His mother speaking over him. 'We're talking thirty-two hours since I commissioned you. Thirty-two hours. To make a couple of enquiries. One or two phone calls. That's all it takes. Do I have to teach you to suck eggs?'

'There've been things.' Fish taking a swallow of pale ale, wondering why he always felt he had to explain himself to his mother.

'Look, please, Barto, please. Do this for me. It's urgent. I'm leaving Beijing day after tomorrow. I'd like to give this to them before I go.'

His mother changing tack, become more expansive. Clearly not in the company of Mr Yan and Mr Lijan. Her tone almost wheedling.

'They're going to be back there in April on a tight schedule. First the mines on the Reef. Then to Cape Town. To meet again with Mr Rings Saturen. I'm not coming, of course. I've got to be in London for a trade fair. But they need to be prepared. It's my job to keep them fully briefed. I need to know about Mr Saturen. Please, Barto, don't let me down. These are important clients. I need to stay in their good books. More than that, you could say it's in the national interest.'

Fish thinking, wow, here's a different Estelle. Saying, 'I'll do what I can, Ma, I told you.'

'Please, Barto. Please. With some alacrity, given my deadline. I know what you're thinking, April's six weeks away, what's her problem? My problem is that I know you, you procrastinate. And I'm not even going to mention your surfing addiction.'

Thought of his mother in her hotel room, nipping herself. Nipping. The word made him laugh. Vicki would've told him very funny except wasn't a pun. Wrong nation. Vicki not into racial jokes.

Where was Vicki? Should have been footloose in Berlin after her meeting with Detlef. Kicking back with some free time. Except Vicki'd gone off the radar. Again he tried her number. Again got voicemail. Didn't leave a message. You could only say 'me again' so many times.

Fish sat staring at the old boat, the ghost of Mullet Mendes leaning against the gunwale. Time he got rid of it. Maybe sold it to Flip the cop in the house behind. Fish's thoughts drifting.

Drifted back to Joey Curtains. To Cynthia Kolingba. To Mart Velaze. Maybe he'd be worth another contact. Despite the guy's attitude.

'You're the PI. I've given you the client. I've told you there's shit happening. I've given you a name and number. As of now I'm out of this. No more phone calls. No more contact. Think of your Vicki Kahn.'

There it was, the threat. Enough to get you riled.

Fish rolled a joint. A little early in the evening but what the hell. Chill, dude, chill. Rocked back on the chair, feet on the table edge. Put fire to the carrot, took a long, slow inhale. Decided the problem was Cynthia Kolingba, why she wasn't getting back to him. Held his breath. Feeling the smoke rub around his lungs. Maybe the colonel had died, maybe she was in mourning. Exhaled. Pictured Joey Curtains sprawled on the pavement. Lifeless Joey Curtains. Tapped the bullet. Amazing things, bullets. Could take you where you didn't want to go.

53

Late afternoon Mart Velaze pressed the buzzer on the bookshop grille. Lights off inside. Could see someone moving about.

Kept pressing. A short man wearing a bow tie came from behind the counter, stepping briskly towards the door.

Said, 'We're closed. Can't you read the sign?' His lips purple beneath a pencil moustache.

'I've got to pick something up,' said Mart Velaze. 'A birthday present.' Half-turned, gestured at his car ramped on the kerb with a pretty young woman in the passenger seat. 'It's for my girlfriend.'

The man pointed at the sign. Mouthed: 'Closed.'

Mart Velaze stuck his finger on the buzzer. Kept it there till the man opened the door.

'You're being very rude,' said Mr Bow Tie, pursed his lips. 'I've told you we're closed, I can't help you today.'

'You the manager?' said Mart Velaze.

'You could call me that. You could also call me the owner.' The neat little man folded his arms across his chest. 'This is my bookshop.'

'Nice bookshop.' Mart Velaze kept his grip on the metal security gate. 'You can let me in. I've bought books here before.'

'We're closed. We've been open all day and now we're closed. I've got another life, you know.'

Mart Velaze put his hands together, beseeching. 'Look, please. Do me a favour, please, man. I've just got to collect it. Help me out here. I'm not going to browse or anything. I'm in and outta here in thirty seconds.' Wondering why the Voice thought this funny little mlungu was a good cut-out. Her sense of humour kicking in. The poor man had no clue what his shop was used for. Would snap a wrist if told. 'It's paid for, and the gift wrap. In the name of Izwi. Mrs Izwi.'

'Oh, why didn't you say so?' Mr Bow Tie shaking his head. 'In that case, wait there I'll get it.' Disappeared into the dim depths, returned with the present. Asked: 'What is it? If you don't mind my enquiring?'

'A book,' said Mart Velaze.

In the car tore off the wrapping, took out an envelope stuck between the opening pages, handed the book to his companion. Said, 'You're a reader, it's all yours.'

'Oh wow,' said the woman, mock serious. Read the title: *The Hidden Hand*. Intriguing. You trying to tell me something, Martie?'

54

'You?' said Linda Nchaba.

The man with glasses had opened the door. Said, 'Welcome. We were waiting since yesterday.'

'Good,' said Vicki, stepping into the apartment, trailing her suitcase. Glad of the warmth, the prospect of tea and biscuits to settle the insistence at the back of her throat. To Linda Nchaba, 'Me, indeed. We meet again, I'm pleased to say.'

The two men greeted her, didn't introduce themselves.

'All very cosy.' Vicki glanced round the room. 'Nice place.' Saw relief on Linda Nchaba's face. Linda looking elegant but uptight, her hands knitted, her mouth slightly open. Sitting on the edge of her seat.

'Some tea, please, gents?' Vicki rubbed her gloved hands, slipped out of her coat. 'This's a cold place, this Europe. No wonder they all want to live somewhere else.'

The man with the glasses took her coat, hung it on a rack beside the door. 'You said it, sisi. Me, myself, I need to go home. I'm—'

She held up a hand, smiled at him, said, 'No names. Don't want to know your names, okay? Best we keep it like that.' Dug in her travel bag. Came out with a handful of chamomile teabags, a packet of Maria biscuits. 'All I can bring to the tea party, and you can't eat my biscuits.'

The men grinned at her. Linda Nchaba on the couch tight-faced, not giving anything away. Going to be a hard one, Vicki thought. Hours before she'd get some sleep. Hours and hours.

Worked off her gloves. 'You alright, Linda?'

The woman nodding at her. Except there'd been a hesitation. A hooding of the eyes. Quick. Brief. Then a quiet, 'I'm good.' And the nodding.

Two days back she'd been fraught enough. Haunted. Whatever'd happened since, she was holding in.

Vicki turned to the men. 'So, guys, I need to make a phone call. Which of you is going to lend me his cell?'

The short one in the galley held up his phone. Likewise the one with glasses. His was closest. Some whizgig Samsung she had to ask how to dial. In the end let the man tap in the number. Flicked back her hair, raised it to her ear. Felt like holding a calculator.

Heard Henry Davidson answer, 'I would imagine this is Vicki Kahn?'

Always the funny man. Vicki didn't rise to it. 'You imagine right, Henry. Good guess.'

'Sixth sense. Never fails. It didn't take you long to get there. Such are the marvels of transport in the European city.'

'I took a taxi, Henry. Last I looked, we've got them too.'

'Oh dear, a little testy are we? Never mind, as the White Queen said to Alice, "First the fish must be caught."'

'What?' said Vicki.

'Never mind. Everyone there present and correct, I assume? Yes.' Not waiting for an answer. 'Now just listen. You do not have to say anything, just listen to me.'

Vicki listened through a five-minute biog spiel about the dubious life and times of Linda Nchaba. Said, 'You could have told me this before I left.'

'Need-to-know, Vicki. Need-to-know. No forecasting how the world is going to work, is there? Best-laid plans and all that.' He sniffed. 'Up to speed?'

'Yes,' said Vicki. She'd crossed the apartment to the window. Gazed down on a quiet street. The occasional car swishing past. No one out in the cold darkness. This wouldn't go easily. In fact, she couldn't see it going at all. Moved the odds to five to two against. Turned into the room. The two men, Linda Nchaba, focused on her.

'All yours then,' said Henry Davidson. 'Sprinkle your fairy dust. Wave your magic wand. Cast your spell. Let me know when it is done.'

Vicki handed the phone to the man with glasses. 'No idea how to switch this off.'

The man laughing, tapped the screen.

'Why are you here?' said Linda Nchaba.

'Good question,' said Vicki, sitting on the couch beside her.

'They want me to go back.' Linda Nchaba looking down at her hands. Long-fingered, slender hands Vicki noted. 'That's right, isn't it? They want me to go back. The videos on the flash drive weren't enough.'

'We haven't seen them, they're protected.'

'So what? Passwords can be cracked. You haven't done that yet?'

'No, actually, I haven't. That's not my line.'

Linda Nchaba held out her hand, waggled her fingers. 'Give. Come on. Give. Let me have your netbook.'

Vicki obliged. Looking hard at the pretty face of Linda Nchaba as she conjured out first the computer, then the flash drive. Watched the long fingers click through to video clips of men she recognised.

'You know who these men are?' said Linda Nchaba. Derision in her voice.

'Some of them.'

'Bastards,' said Linda Nchaba. 'All of them. Bastards.' Closed the computer top, pulled free the stick. 'All yours.' Handed them to Vicki. 'Satisfied?'

'Not quite,' said Vicki, getting no further.

'They want me. Don't they? They want me to go back.' Linda Nchaba raising her eyes to Vicki's. 'I'm right? They want me? He wants me to come back.'

In Linda Nchaba's eyes Vicki saw a dullness. An inevitability. Even resignation. Believed she could maybe change the odds to five to three in favour.

'Tea first,' said Vicki. 'And I need some biscuits.'

The short man brought round a plate with the Maria biscuits. A mug with the chamomile bag in it. 'You'll make someone a good wife,' said Vicki, squeezing the bag between her fingers. Ignoring the sting of the hot water. Plopped the bag in the palm of the man's hand.

'You feel no pain?' he said.

Vicki grinned at him. Bit into a biscuit. Shifted herself into the corner of the couch.

Linda Nchaba said, 'My God! How can you do this?'

'Has its perks. International travel for one.' Vicki brushed crumbs from her jeans. 'Just can't do without these biscuits. Have one?' Offering the plate.

Linda Nchaba shook her head. 'They assaulted me.'

Vicki frowned. 'What? Who? Who assaulted you? Assaulted you how?'

'Undressed me.'

Vicki looking from the short man to the one with glasses. Both of them not meeting her eyes. Uncomfortable.

'Not these men. The ones that took me at the airport. These ones knew it happened.'

'These two men?'

'You can ask them.'

Vicki moved forward, stuck cushions behind her back. 'Wait. Wait. Slowly. Let me catch up. What's going on here?' Sipped tea. Swallowed the biscuit mush. Said to Linda Nchaba, 'You start.'

Heard out her story about being stripped naked. Photographs taken of her.

'You know this?'

'Someone undressed me. Left me naked. No bra, no panties. Of course they took photographs.' Linda Nchaba not emotional, keeping it together, her voice hard.

Vicki thinking, a fair deduction. Turned to the men. Heard out the men's story, the man with glasses doing the talking.

A silence in the room. Long minutes. Vicki wondering, shit, what to do with this? Decided, okay, move on. Not strictly the problem at hand. Finished her tea. The short man coming from behind the counter to take the empty mug.

'We're going to have to talk about that later, okay? There's something else we have to talk about first. You know why I'm here?' she said to Linda Nchaba.

Linda Nchaba nodding. 'You don't have to say anything. I'll go. I've decided what to do. He can't go on. They can't go on doing it. So I'll do what you want.'

'Come home?'

'Yes.'

'And what about him, you know who I mean?'

Again the silence. The long minutes. To Vicki the nagging doubt: this'd come too easily.

'Because of him.'

Vicki not convinced. Why? Why this sudden change of heart? 'Why?' Watching every gesture.

'Because.' The word sighed out. 'Because.' Linda Nchaba raising slow eyes to meet her gaze. 'When you see what he does, you'll understand. When you see more of the videos.'

Fair enough. Vicki not looking away. 'You don't want to hear our plans?'

'They don't matter.'

'You will be safe. Protected. I can assure you.'

Linda Nchaba shrugged. 'It doesn't matter. This thing must end.' She held up a finger. 'One condition.'

'What's that?' Vicki waited. Looking beyond the finger to the woman's unblinking eyes. Could see Linda Nchaba was exhausted. Had run out of options.

'They free my grandmother.'

She came in quickly. 'That can be done. Can be done immediately.' Asked for a call to Henry Davidson. Was given the phone, said to her handler, 'It's agreed.'

'That was fast. Well done, Ms Kahn.' The tick, tick, tick of Henry Davidson clicking his tongue in thought. 'Or something we're missing here?'

'I don't think so. She wants her grandmother freed. Now. A Skype call'd do it. Would convince her.'

'Skype?'

'Come on, Henry, kidnappers carry smart phones. Get them to call me.'

Twenty minutes later on the phone's screen is a woman in a print dress, adjusting her headscarf. An elegant woman. No recognisable background. No one else in the frame. The woman took off her glasses, wiped them. Leant forward, peering.

'Gogo,' said Linda Nchaba.

PART TWO

TWO WARNING SHOTS TO THE HEART

The girls came from the coast, from the river plains, from the mountains. From villages in the outer provinces. From Maputo, Beira, Matola. Some were brought by their fathers, others by relatives. Some were the bounty of traders. All were there to be sold.

A raggedy group in thin dresses, tracksuits, old T-shirts.

They sat beneath a large tree, huddled together. On this hot morning, a group of thirteen. The youngest six, the oldest twelve. They watched those who had brought them with anxious eyes.

Occasionally one would call for her father. One would whimper.

They were given no water, no fruit. Some had been travelling for days.

About them stood guards with Kalashnikovs. Young men in camouflage fatigues, their guns pointed at the ground. Playing Angry Birds on their cellphones.

Those who'd brought the girls lined up at a double-cab to be paid. They averted their eyes, held out their hands. Received rolled wads fastened with elastic bands. These men hurried off. Did not look back.

They heard the girls cry out for them. They walked on faster.

The girls sat fearful on the red earth. One keened, rocked, hugging her knees. Only went quiet when a guard hit her.

In the afternoon came an eighteen-wheeler from the north, circled the clearing in a rise of dust. Like a beast wheezing, throbbing, hissing.

'Olá. Ninjani.' The truck driver waved, flashed his teeth in a smile. 'Greetings, my friends.'

A woman climbed out the passenger side, went to the children, spoke to them in broken Portuguese. A beautiful woman, impala eyes, red lipstick. Long legs in skinny jeans. High heels. Her voice gentle. She held out her hands, touched them, brushed their cheeks. Told them not to worry. Used the Portuguese word for fear. Medo. Não medo. Shook her head. No fear.

The guards put away their phones, cradled their rifles. Alert.

'You are late. We've been waiting for many hours.' The man from the double-cab tapped his watch. 'This is not the time we agreed.'

'It's a long way. A slow way.' The truck driver jumped down, wiped his hands on his shorts. 'We're here now.' Looked over at the girls beneath the tree. 'That's all of them?'

'We said thirteen. We said there would be thirteen.'

'Okay. Fine. Fine.' Reached into the truck for a plastic bag, flung it at the man leaning on his double-cab. 'You want to count it?'

'Of course.'

They waited. The girls clustered in the shade, watching the woman and the men.

'Pee-pee,' the truck driver said to the woman. 'Get them to piss.' Pointing at the girls, going, 'Pss, psss, psss, pisss. Now. Pee-pee. We have a long way to go. They must pee now. Tell them in Portuguese.'

One of the men spoke in Portuguese. The girls shook their heads, the younger ones crying.

The guards laughed. The girls cowered away.

'Shut up,' said the young woman, 'I'll deal with it. You sort him out' – gesturing at the man counting the money. 'I'll look after them.'

The girls stared at her. Her caressing fingers brought tears.

She spoke to them in English, asked if anyone understood her. No one did. The girls gazing at her, big eyes, open mouths.

'Go,' said the man from the double-cab. 'Go. We've been here too long.' He shouted at his men to move the children.

The men prodded with their rifles at the girls, herded them into a container on the flatbed. Pushing them inside. Swearing. Shouting.

The young woman screaming at the men, telling them not to hurt the girls, telling them they were animals. Savages.

The girls big-eyed, frightened. Staring out as the steel door slammed closed.

***

The girls were kept in a warehouse. Thirteen of them.

The warehouse part of an industrial estate on the outskirts of a small town. Most of the premises vacant. Abandoned, vandalised. Once a siding for freight trains. A while since freight trains shunted in these yards. Rails ripped up for scrap metal. Sleepers sold to garden nurseries. Weeds grew where tracks had been.

This warehouse well maintained. High tin roof, iron girders, fluorescent tubes humming day and night. Beneath the girders skylight windows hazed with red dust. On the cement-block walls the patterns of tools, empty racks, empty shelves. Dry oil stains on the concrete floor.

One drive-in entrance closed by two doors: an inner grille padlocked top and bottom, an outer roller shutter with a walk-in doorway.

At first the girls cried, begged the young woman not to leave them. She told them to shush, be quiet, that she would come back to see them soon.

Hours later the girls beat their fists on the metal shutter, shook the grille. A vagrant heard them. Had heard girls before. Knew to stay away. Kept hunched over his fire, a dog at his feet. Knew the girls would tire.

Their warehouse fitted out: showers, toilets, hand basins; a dormitory of twenty beds, the beds with sponge mattresses, heavy grey Pep Stores blankets. Pillows without cases.

A scattering of plastic chairs. Flattened cardboard boxes as carpets. In a corner, a kitchen sink for washing mugs, plates, spoons. Opposite, a wall-mounted television played a cartoon channel, the sound muted.

In the morning the young woman came with two men, brought pots of food, bottles of water. Made the girls undress, collected their clothing in plastic bags.

Pointed over their heads at the washroom. Said, 'Wash, lavar.' Raised her left arm, used her right to rub her armpit.

'Yes? Understand? Sim. Compreender.' Had the men give them towels.

'New clothes,' she said in Portuguese. Dumped a pile of jeans, T-shirts with pussy-cat designs, red Crocs, on the floor. The two men watching the girls clean themselves. The woman helping the younger ones.

When the girls were dressed, she went off. Blew kisses from the doorway, laughing. The girls in their new clothes listened to them drive away.

In the evening the woman returned alone. From a plastic bag she gave them hamburgers and chips, jelly babies, Bar Ones, Crunchies. Fruit drinks. Had the girls sit on the floor, told them in English that everything would be alright. Smiled at them.

Told them to eat: comer. As she always did, used her right hand to indicate eating.

The girls nodded. The older ones smiling.

'Tomorrow,' she said, 'amanhã. School. Escola. Sim. Sim. You go to school.' She walked her fingers through the air. Yes. Alright. You will be alright. No fear. Não medo. Compreender.'

The girls staring at her, this kind mama with the gentle voice who touched them, dried their tears, comforted them. They ate their burgers, the chips, left only crumbs. The woman watching them.

'Eat your sweets,' she said. 'Comer, Bar One.' Herself tearing open the wrapping, taking a bite. Offering the chocolate bar to a child at her feet. The child stroking her high heels. She raised the child's face. Said, 'It will be alright. Tudo bem. Promise. Promessa. I promise you.'

The girls beginning to chatter. Relaxed. Eating their sweets.

At the door a man appeared, said in Zulu it was time to go. The girls went quiet at his voice.

The beautiful woman stood, said, 'Tomorrow, amanhã, escola. Yes? Sim?' She nodded.

The girls smiled, nodded back at her.

Watched her walk on her high heels across the concrete floor.

1

They took a 21 Squadron Falcon 50 out of Waterkloof Air Force Base before dawn. Two men dressed casually, light jackets, open-necked shirts, Italian slip-ons, wheeling overnight bags across the apron. Not hurrying through April's early chill to the plane. Confident men. Men at the top of their game.

The flight plan over Zimbabwe, Zambia, Congo, landing at Bangui, Central African Republic. First night the five-star Ledger Plaza Hotel.

Welcome back, Monsieur Zama, Major Vula. Enjoy your stay.

They did. An hour in the fitness centre, treadmill work. Massage. Saunas. Then dinner, French wine. Hostesses, young hostesses.

Next morning the hop to Berbérati, from Berbérati by helicopter to the mine. An aerial survey before touchdown to get the scene: this red slash in the jungle. The mine at maximum capacity. Up and running for a week, as Kaiser Vula had left it.

'Impressive,' said Zama. 'Like magic. We have done a good job. Would you not say so, Major?'

The buildings repaired, mechanical diggers in the opencast cuttings. Men working lesser seams by hand. New troops guarding the site. A cleared break around the operation.

'What did I tell you? Only military men can do this.'

Kaiser Vula thinking possibly more the work of one military man than two.

'The president will be pleased. What am I saying, he is pleased. There will be rewards, Kaiser. Plentiful rewards.' Zama flashed whites in a big laugh. 'You are sure she will meet us?'

'It is arranged. She said she will be here.' Kaiser Vula looked down. No entourage of 4×4s parked outside the office buildings. No dust of approaching convoys. In this country nothing was sure. You made arrangements, hoped they would take place.

'Yes, Major, she will be here.' Zama snorted. 'If she is not imprisoned, or shot dead, or forced to flee. They call our country a failed state. What is this place, then? We are a strong democracy. Here are only bandits.'

They came down on the helipad beside the barracks. Armed security patrolling the perimeter. Zama fast out the chopper, striding through the dust towards the welcoming party. Hand out, shaking, slapping shoulders. Kaiser Vula followed into the sudden heat, shielded his face against the swirl. The rotors winding down, the engines shutting off.

At his ear the commanding officer shouted, 'She has radioed, Major. They are not far.'

'On the ground?'

'That is what we were told.'

'There were no vehicles approaching. Nothing we could see.'

Hooting. The crackle of the radio.

'They are at the gates,' said the operator.

'So quickly.' The CO frowning at Kaiser Vula. 'Do you think they have been outside, watching us?'

Kaiser Vula wiped sweat from his face. That would be just like her. Cautious. Check out the scene.

Was also like her to pitch not in a convoy but a 1970s-model Jeep, a driver, one man riding shotgun. The Jeep stopping under a shade-cloth awning. Out stepped a woman wearing dark glasses, a beret, dressed in camo fatigues, toting a briefcase.

'You don't recognise me, Major?' she said.

Major Kaiser Vula snapped his heels. 'Ma'am,' he said. 'You took us by surprise.'

'Caution, Major. There must always be caution.' She smiled quickly without humour. 'I have learnt that. To my cost. Pleased to see you again, Major Vula. In my own country for a change. My troubled country. Now, where is Mr Zama. It is time we met.'

'Please.' Kaiser Vula led her into the building. 'Inside it is air-conditioned.'

'You don't like our heat, Major?'

'It is not what I am used to.'

In the common room, a spread laid out there on a trestle table. Sandwiches, crusts cut off, strips of lettuce garnish. Cocktail sausages on sticks. Bacon curled round prunes. Bowls of diced fruit. Fresh orange juice. An aroma of coffee. Two waiters in bow ties, hovering. Zama stood beside the table, relaxed, twirling a toothpick between his fingers.

'Welcome. Welcome.'

Kaiser Vula made the introductions. 'Her Honour Cynthia Kolingba.'

'Mrs is good enough, Major.'

'One day president,' said Zama, shaking her hand.

'We'll see. When there are elections, we will see what the people want.'

Kaiser Vula stepped back, watched Zama introduce her to the mine captain, the co, other senior staff. Bring her back to the table. A dignified woman even in a uniform. The uniform a political statement. Her support of the coup.

'Your husband, how is he doing?' Zama offered her a plate, serviette.

Cynthia Kolingba paused. 'I'm sure you know, Mr Zama.' The two of equal height, assessing one another. 'He is still in a coma. Two months it has been now.' She took the plate.

'Of course. I know that. I am sorry.' Zama breaking eye contact. Glancing down at the table, still holding the serviette.

Kaiser Vula loaded up a plate with sausages, the round tasty bacon prunes, thought, this is one tough lady, my friend. Step carefully.

Zama saying, 'I mean, you are satisfied with his treatment?'

'Naturally. You have provided the best. Your government has been very generous. Your father very attentive.' She selected a bowl of mixed fruit. 'But at least my husband is still alive. My daughter is not. That is the trouble with assassination attempts, Mr Zama, the innocent who are killed. What our friends, the Americans, call the collateral damage.' She reached out for the serviette. 'Is that for me?'

Zama released it. 'Yes. Please.' He picked up a sandwich, shaking off the lettuce shavings. 'We are sorry for your loss.'

'You see, Mr Zama, grief for a child is not like other grief. A mother, a father, you know they will die. Even a husband, there is this possibility. But not a child. You do not expect to grieve for your child. It is a painful grief. A long grief. Sometimes I think it is a pity the man who killed her was not caught. I would like to have talked to him.'

Zama bit into his sandwich. 'Your husband had many enemies. We think they left the country the same day. The assassins.'

'That is the story I heard, yes.'

'You don't think so?'

'I don't know. There are so many possibilities. My husband was … is … an important man.'

'Now you are important. You are their leader.'

'And I can be shot. That is why I am cautious.'

'In an old Jeep with one guard.'

'Ha hah.' No humour in Cynthia Kolingba's laugh. 'You think a blue-light brigade will help? All they do is tell the bandits where you are.'

'We find them useful. Especially my father.'

'Yes. I have seen him flashing by.'

'It is a stupid thing but he likes it.'

'The men do.'

'And ladies. We have lady ministers. They want the blue lights.'

Cynthia Kolingba moved to stand at the window. 'Your ladies, Mr Zama, they look like men. They behave like men.' Spooned fruit into her mouth. 'It is a pity. Then I think it is difficult for ladies to behave in a different way in this world we have. Look at how I must dress.'

Kaiser Vula did. Thought Cynthia Kolingba in fatigues more striking than his wife in a negligee. Almost as good as Nandi. The hurt of Nandi's memory striking across his chest.

'But you do not come here to talk about these things, Mr Zama. We have other matters to discuss. This, for example.' She pointed out towards plumes of dust, the signals of distant mining. 'It is good to see.'

'We must thank you,' said Zama. He finished his sandwich. Picked another. Joined her at the window.

'You must thank the coup,' said Cynthia Kolingba. 'You must thank whoever shot my husband, whoever killed my daughter. Without that the mad man, our former president-dictator, would still be the president. Your mine would be still in ruins.'

'We appreciate your protection, madam.'

'Quid pro quo. You know this expression?'

Kaiser Vula watched Zama nod. Could see puzzlement in his eyes.

'I have an agreement with the major.' She turned towards Kaiser Vula. 'That is in order?'

'Of course,' said Zama. 'Of course. Whatever you want. Whatever you need. We can supply. That is our agreement. Men, weapons. Because of you we can work our mine. It is safe here again. What can I say? Thank you. We support your democracy.'

'It is not a democracy yet, Mr Zama. As you know. We who were rebels are now the rulers. Those who were rulers are now the rebels. And there are other rebel groupings. It is a complex situation. We play musical chairs. Men like this game.' She put down her bowl of fruit, half-finished. Opened her briefcase. 'I have a photograph for you. A memento for your father.' With long fingers drew out an envelope, handed it to Zama. 'Have a look.'

Kaiser Vula stepped closer. Saw a colour photograph of two men in bathing costumes in a gazebo. Bare-chested men. Women leaning over them. Women wearing kikoys, skimpy bras. The two men drinking cocktails, Manhattan-style, olives in the glasses. The photograph taken across the swimming pool with a zoom lens. The men in clear focus.

'I am sure you recognise your father and our former president-dictator. Enjoying the good times. You might not realise, this was taken at our presidential palace. You cannot see them but there are guards not far off with hyenas on chains.'

Zama flicked his fingers across the image. 'The past is the past.'

'They were friends, Mr Zama. Maybe they are still friends. Maybe you have given our ex-president refuge too? No one knows where he is. Perhaps he is sitting beside your father's swimming pool. Maybe someone will take a photo like this.'

'He is not there. I can tell you … I can swear to you, he is not there.'

Cynthia Kolingba smiled at Zama, eyebrows raised, included Kaiser Vula in her disbelief. 'Good. Then our understanding, our agreement is safe.'

'You are saying … threatening …'

'I'm saying nothing, Mr Zama. It is not even a threat. One Sunday a man is shot, a child is killed. The world changes. It can change so easily again.' She held out her hand to Zama. 'I

must go. I have rebels to execute. It is not easy being a leader.'
Again the smile, charming, disarming.

Kaiser Vula wondering if she meant what she said. Expected she did.

They walked with her to the Jeep. As they approached, the driver and the guard crushed out their cigarettes.

Kaiser Vula felt the humidity prickling sweat down his back. A heaviness dragging at his legs. Reminded him again why this was no country for comfort.

'Goodbye, gentlemen,' said Cynthia Kolingba. 'Let us hope the world continues as it is. For the benefit of your mining venture. We need the taxes.' No smile, the blankness of her dark glasses.

Zama reassured her. Mentioned again the weapons, ammunitions, support equipment. Stabilising forces.

'I shall rely on you, Mr Zama,' she said.

Kaiser Vula and Zama watched the Jeep drive off, stop as the gates were opened, turn onto the track through the jungle.

'Tsho, tsho, tsho.' Zama shook his head. 'That is one lady. What the English call a ball-crusher, nè. Colonel Kolingba can be glad he is in a coma.'

2

Fish thought, bullshit. Sat on his barge on the backline in a decent swell. For Surfer's Corner as hot as it got. The promise of good-time winter waves in coming months.

Thought, bullshit this stand-off with Vicki. What in the hell was her case? Like she'd just drifted away.

'I can't tell you, Fish. Trust me, please.'

Bullshit.

'I'm out of town again for a while.'

Bullshit.

And again.

And again.

And again.

Bullshit.

'This will come to an end, I promise. It's just really difficult right now.'

Bullshit.

Put his calls on voicemail. Didn't respond to SMSes. Had closed her Skype account. Hadn't been out to see him in weeks. Probably more like over a month.

Still some of her clothes in his cupboard. Shoes. Toiletries. CDs. Magazines.

Didn't seem she wanted to end things. Just that she couldn't fit him into her life.

Maybe it was her job. The secrecy thing. What'd they tell you in the spy novels? There would be secrets. Secrets, like sharks, came out of nowhere, took off your leg. Maybe. Maybe it was that, the secrets of her job. Also, maybe she was back at the cards. The tables. Whatever it was she gambled on.

Fish paddled the board round to face the shore. The car park filling up. Happy surfers heading for the glassy waves. Hadn't been anything like this for weeks. Surf reports would be full of it, mid-morning you'd be hustling for waves. Not that Fish had any thoughts about staying longer. He'd had the best of it. The dawn shift. Just him and a couple of locals strung out along the backline. Enough water between them to prevent any chit-chat. The way Fish preferred it.

He waited for a swell.

Glanced up at the mountain, the twin peaks hot, yellow, Peck's Valley in between. Last time he'd been up there was with Vicki. In the spring. Flower season, patches of colour among the sandstone. They'd sat on a high rock looking down:

the beach scything eastwards to the barrier mountains. A blue haze over False Bay.

She'd said, 'It might not be easy for us, my new job.'

A warning he'd ignored.

'Come'n, Vics, what'll be so different? Lawyers drive desks. So do spooks these days. Not going to be a quantum of solace.'

'I don't know. I'm just saying. I might have to travel.' Turning to face him. Her hair pulled back in a short pigtail. Brown eyes, serious, ancient. A tension in her cheeks, tightening her mouth.

'This's Henry Davidson giving you the rah-rah spiel. The agent in foreign capitals.'

A quick sadness that she blinked away. She'd reached out to stroke his face. Then the Vics he knew, bright, smiling.

'Henry? Where'd Henry come from?'

'Henry's all I hear about these days.'

'Stuff and nonsense, said Alice.' And she was on her feet. Pulling him up. 'Can't sit here all afternoon. You've got supper to make.'

There'd been nothing about Henry after that. Like he'd ceased to exist. She'd been a desk-jockey, as he'd said. But the office chatter dried up. No more: this prick the minister, that arsehole the DG. No more I'm working on this ... What do you know about that? There had been the odd bit of farm-out. Mundane research work that an intern could've handled. Like the Linda Nchaba titbits. Then that went away fast. After the Berlin trip everything went away fast.

There'd been a flare-up: 'Leave it, Fish. Just forget it. Subject gone. Over. Time to move on, okay?'

How weird she'd been. Given him the minimum about Berlin. Dropped out of his life bit by bit over the weeks. Like the disappearing Cheshire cat she'd mentioned.

Thing was, he hadn't paid enough attention to the slippage. Been too focused on other things: getting background for his mother's Chinese on the politician and one-time gangster Rings Saturen for one. Making some serious bucks from a corporate client for another. Had let things slip with Vicki.

Except it wasn't him. It was her. She didn't return calls, messages, emails. She didn't leave voicemails. Didn't send emails. No SMS traffic. She'd let things drift away.

Why? Why'd she done that? Let it go this far.

It was bullshit. Least he deserved was a straight fuck off. Nothing like the present for sorting that out.

Fish glanced over his shoulder, a set sliding towards him. Nice, neat little boogers that held up for a decent ride. He paddled over the first one, came round, went with the second swell. Felt the wave take the board. Got to his feet. Bit like riding an escalator. You could stand there, roll a joint, it would be that exciting.

Let the wave take him into the shallows. Resolved now: he'd go into town, to her apartment, wouldn't leave until he'd talked to her. Sometimes, you had to hustle to get what you wanted.

Fish wanted Vicki.

When the wave power gave up, stepped off the board, ripped the leash from his ankle. He'd get the Perana out of the garage, settle into the black leather, let the v6 rock 'n roll. Pitching in the mean machine'd show her that it wasn't over. Not by a long chalk. Also. Could probably do a few drops along the way.

3

Melissa Etheridge sang of the scratches on her soul. Of having to choose. Of untold lies. Of the shadow of a black crow.

Vicki Kahn thought of Fish. The song always made her think of Fish. The fish she'd let go.

Stood at the window of her apartment, waiting for a call from Linda Nchaba. Gazed out at the city. The city bright in the early sun. An April sun losing its heat. Her thoughts on Fish.

There were times Vicki Kahn ached for Fish.

It would be so easy to stop the ache. Pick up the phone. Talk to him. Drive to his house. Let him make lasagne. Sit there watching him prepare the meal. Sit there with a glass of white, candles fluttering on the table, her sentimental lover's idea of a romantic dinner. Nothing wrong with that.

'Got to have candles, Vics. For the atmosphere.'

More like to disappear the chaos of his kitchen.

She smiled.

Could picture it: her attentive surfer boy chatting about his weird clients, rolling a joint, the sweet smell of grass permeating. The back and forth of the doobie. Their chatter dying.

He'd be playing who? Alison Krauss. Laurie Levine. Jesse Sykes. Some sad heart-breaker.

That was okay. Her heart was breaking. Because Fish couldn't be her lover, her surfer boy, anymore.

Didn't stop the longing for the feel of his fingers as he took the roach. That electric touch.

She'd take his hand, lead him to the bedroom. Pull off his T-shirt. Reveal those pecs, the ripple of his stomach. Make him strip her. Place his hand on her breast. Looking at him all the time. Fixed on his eyes. Make him kneel. Pull his face into her. Wait for his tongue.

Enough.

It'd been too long.

Vicki moved away from the window, thought, come on, Linda, ring, for heaven's sake. Linda's idea of time sometimes too flexible. Every morning the anxiety of the check-in.

At her desk, tapped her laptop's keys, brought up a photo of a wetsuited Fish coming out of the water, surfboard under his arm. Walking up the beach towards her. Blue sky, white water roiling behind him. Blond hair plastered down. Broad smile.

In the next pic she had him stripped to the waist, those bronze pecs gleaming.

All you had to do was phone, explain why you hadn't returned SMSes, answered Skype calls, responded to voicemail. Why you let things drift.

Tell him …

All you had to do.

Vicki clicked through more photographs. Pictures of the two of them. Selfies mostly. Mostly outdoors at surfing spots. One at a braai, not a selfie. A posed shot: standing arm in arm. Her hair pulled back. Both in jeans and T-shirts, bare feet. Fish with the inevitable stout bottle dangling from his fingers. He was into stout then. That'd been about six months after she'd been shot. A couple of months before she joined the Agency. A while before the names of Linda Nchaba, Zama, the president, Detlef Schroeder altered her world.

'Thing is here, Vicki,' Henry Davidson had said, 'sometimes the personal gets in the way. When that happens, you have to let go. Or get out of the Agency. Your decision.'

Hadn't been any quips from Alice that time.

Henry again. 'Look, I prefer not to interfere, but this operation is high priority. You know that. You know how important it is. And for that I need you on it. Focused. Totally focused.' The pause, the sniff. The pat of the toupee. 'You're going to have to sacrifice. We all do sooner or later.'

Subtext: end it with Fish. Henry Davidson not exactly a fan of private detectives. Terminate your relationship.

Terminate. The medical profession's word.

So much she'd had to terminate. Sometimes she thought about it; mostly she didn't. When she did, it got her in the chest. She took a deep breath, moved on as best she could. With Fish always on the backline of her thoughts. Could come surfing in at any moment. Pop out of a pipeline, flick back his hair. Be there. The smell of him: sea and wax, salt and sweetness.

Jesus.

Sliding towards her the shadow of the black crow.

Vicki Kahn circled her sitting room, waiting for the call, trying to push Fish away. Thinking, phone me, Linda. Phone me now. Circling the room.

A comfortable room. A place she could be herself. Old Persian she'd inherited, three-seater couch facing a flat-screen, glass-topped coffee table scattered with magazines: *Economist*, *Financial Mail*, yesterday's newspaper.

At the wall unit ran her hand over the cherry wood, warm, soft beneath her palm. Scandinavian-style wall unit. Straight lines, simple, beautiful. Custom-made by a German cabinet-maker Fish'd recommended. Another surfer dude. Guy had fitted out her kitchen, made her bookcases, her desk.

Her hand stopped at two photographs in silver standing frames: her parents; Amina Kahn.

Her parents posed outside the street window of their Athlone law office sometime in the 1980s. Smart couple: her mother in a skirt and jacket, her father in a suit. Neither of them smiling. She liked that – the severity. Behind them, reflected in the glass, a street of hawkers, cars, people. Late 1993, they were dead in a car accident.

The Amina Kahn photograph a new addition. Taken on some windy beach with a brown choppy sea, Amina arms out wide like she wanted to fly. Probably also in the 1980s. Part of the surprise from Detlef Schroeder.

She lifted it, looked closer, as she'd done many times. You

could read anything in Amina's face. Happiness. A moment of freedom. Desire for a bright future. A few months later she was dead. Stabbed in a Sunday crush of people getting onto a Metro train in Paris. What had Detlef Schroeder called it? 'A useful assassination.'

She put the photograph back on the unit. How to deal with that one? That was a long game, that one.

Heard Melissa sing of being rocked and rolled all night long. Again brought up her ache for Fish. Thing was, she might've ended it but it wasn't over.

Plopped down on the couch, her gaze shifting round the room. The blank television screen, the crowded bookshelves, through the doorway to her unmade bed. Which reminded her of Fish.

Just phone him.

Her cellphone rang: Linda Nchaba.

About bloody time. Vicki got up, turned down Melissa, took a breath.

'What's happening?'

'You won't believe this.'

'Try me.'

'He's taking another wife.'

'Who?'

'The president. Big party at the palace coming up.'

'We've not heard anything.'

'It's hush-hush. Not the party. The engagement. The party's one of the things he does.'

'I've heard about them.'

A pause. Vicki waited.

'You alright?' The handled handling the handler.

'Of course.'

Another moment's silence. Vicki looked down into the square. Gym people in tracksuits at the coffee shops. A young family eating breakfast. Keep control. Keep it solid. Said, 'Everything okay?'

'Yes. Yes. Still waiting.'

The operation had been running two weeks. Linda in it from the get-go. Had been in Mozambique for the collection, the cross-border journey, the holding arrangements. Had kept the girls quiet, gaining their trust, getting them used to her. In their new harsh world, not a difficult task.

Since she'd come back from Europe, there'd been no contact from Zama. She'd expected it. Part of his game: unsettle her, let her understand he was angry, hurt by her running away. She'd been part of the run from the start, met with the other traffickers, been in on the planning, but no sight or sound of Zama throughout.

Couldn't go on much longer. He'd have to auction the girls soon, disperse them. Each day he kept them, he risked discovery, someone chancing on them.

'It's okay,' she said now to Vicki. 'This's how he does it. Cautiously. Chooses his time.'

Vicki thinking Linda was holding up well. Not easy, what she was doing. The long gaps in between her time with the girls. Not knowing when Zama would make contact. Said, 'The hotel still bearable?'

'Not exactly five star.' A splutter of a laugh. 'I'm watching a lot of YouTube. Series. Movies. It's just …'

'Just?'

'Each day …'

Each empty day that passes, the anxiety ratchets up. You are dealing with a fearful agent, you are dealing with a problem. The wisdom of Henry Davidson.

She should be there. To hell with the old-school way of things, she should be there. Because you had to give it to him, the man they'd codenamed Walrus. Henry's choice of name.

You had to give it to him, he was one cool player. One very cool player. Didn't go rushing into things. Checked out the scene.

He's got the pepper, the vinegar, the loaf of bread, was Henry Davidson's way of looking at things. The Walrus'd pitch eventually.

'Hang in there, Linda,' Vicki said. 'Things are moving. We know that.'

Linda's 'I know' barely audible. Then: 'Sometimes I get scared.'

Vicki came in quickly: 'You have to phone me. When the fear comes, you've got to phone me. We can talk through it.'

'I need you here.'

'I can't be there. You know that.'

A silence lengthening. It didn't surface much, Linda's fear, but it was there. Lurking in the endless hours. In the waiting. Nibbling away at her motivation.

Vicki moved off the subject. 'Tell me, where'd you hear the engagement gossip? I can't believe we don't know.'

'It's everywhere. It's no secret round here.'

'When did you hear?'

'Yesterday afternoon.'

'Who told you?'

'The cleaning lady told me. Her son's a gardener in the palace. Says this one's young. Says she's got him with muti.'

'What? Like cast a spell?'

'It happens. You can get all kinds of stuff for that. I got powder in the market to rub on my shoes. Keeps anyone from following me.'

Vicki didn't respond. Changed tack again. 'That party'll be interesting. The sort of party we need to be at.'

'Maybe I'll be there.'

Which took Vicki by surprise. That the thought had occurred to Linda already.

'You never know, I could be.'

'You could. That'd make your life really exciting.'

'If the Walrus comes knocking.'

'Oh he will, Linda. Guaranteed. Then you phone me, okay, let me know immediately. The moment he appears. Right?'

A hesitation. The pause of doubt.

'Linda?'

'Alright. Alright.'

Vicki disconnected soon afterwards. Thought of Linda in some hotel room, in some desperate town, waiting. Spending time grooming the girls, then going back to her hotel room. Not easy. 'You mean I'm the live bait,' was the way she'd phrased it. Vicki hadn't disagreed. Hadn't said anything. Had thought of the Walrus, of his reputation.

She came away from the window, wound up the sound system. Went through to shower. Even under the deluge could hear Melissa fancy-free, raising a cup, falling or flying, falling up.

Fish came back into her thoughts.

All you have to do is phone.

Or get some muti powders to cast a spell.

4

'You's had a delivery, Mister Fish. From a darkie.' Janet waving an A4 envelope.

Fish came around his bakkie, hauled his wetsuit from the back, hung it over the washing line. Hosed it down. 'From the postman.'

'No, man, I told you from a darkie. Very nice darkie, this one. Very smart clothes. Got a jersey over his shoulders like the rich men wear it. Soft pink jersey. I could see it was soft. Said to me he was a friend, that I must put this in your hand. I must wait for you. I said to him but, Mr Man, Mister Fish could be surfing anywhere. Maybe he's not gonna be back all day. What must I do then? He gives me fifty rand, Mister Fish. One whole pinkie. To wait here give this to you personally. You got a very nice friend, Mister Fish. Is he maybe from another country?'

Fish held up his hand. 'Whoa, Janet. Whokaai. Slowly. Let me finish this.' Switched off the water, coiled the hose on its wall bracket. Held out his hand to Janet. 'Well, give it to me.'

'It cost you. Ten rand, toast 'n tea.'

'Yeah, yeah. Give it to me.'

Janet holding it against her chest. 'Where's Miss Vicki? Why's she not here? I never see her anymore. You made a problem with her, Mister Fish. I said to you treat her proper. You can't be like a surfer dude with Miss Vicki. Miss Vicki's got class 'n style.'

Fish reached out, gripped a corner of the envelope. 'Hannah, hannah, hannah. You're worse than my old lady.' Tugged at the envelope, tearing off the corner. 'Come on, give it to me.'

'Whooo, holly, holly. Look what you done now, Mister Fish. You mos torn it. Shame on you.' Janet holding it above her head. 'Shame on you.' Running behind the *Maryjane*.

Fish chased her. Grabbed her, the two of them falling on the thin grass that was his back lawn. Not so much grass as patches of kweek scrubgrass that took hold in sand. Janet giggling. Fish on top of her stretching for the envelope, his face close to hers. She lifted her head, kissed him on the mouth. Let go of the envelope at the same time.

Fish pushed up on his elbows, looked down at her face. Janet winked. He levered himself onto his knees, his haunches, stood. 'You're a piece of work, Janet. You know that.'

She held up her hand. 'Give me a rise up, man, please, help a lady.'

Fish pulled her to her feet. She dusted off her dress.

'What about the ten rand, toast 'n tea. For keeping it safe.' She pointed at the envelope in his hand.

'You'll get your tea and toast. First things first.' Tore open the envelope, eased out two colour prints. Janet jigging at his shoulder. Fish blocked her view.

'Let me see, man, Mister Fish, what's it?'

'Nothing you need to know about.' Fish headed for the kitchen. 'You take a seat, I'll get you something.'

'Just like inna restaurant, hey. Very larney.'

On the kitchen table Fish put the prints side by side: one a long shot of a man at the wheel of a car, stopped at a traffic light. The zoom close in on the man's face. Impossible to tell what sort of car. Impossible to tell the intersection. Some stonework above the car roof, could be any city building. The man's face in profile. A face Fish thought he recognised. A face grimacing, mouth open, teeth showing. Like he was looking at something bad.

The other photograph of the same man sitting on a couch. His face in harsh light, fluorescent light, relaxed this time, bored even. Staring straight ahead. Could be he was in a waiting room, pastel pictures on the walls, bland beige wallpaper. Bland beige couch. A blue carpet. The man dressed in summer gear: green golf shirt, fawn chinos, trainers.

Fish thought, bloody hell! Could be a hospital waiting room. Could be the hospital waiting room on the Kolingba guy's ward. Could be where he'd last met Cynthia Kolingba.

'Thank you for your services, Mr Pescado,' she'd said then, giving him an advice of electronic payment. Very smart in a black suit. Young female bodyguard standing to one side. She was new. 'Our situation has changed.' A quick smile.

'What's changed?' he'd said. Thinking, your daughter's still dead. Your husband's still out of it.

'Politics. In my country. And in yours.'

Took the payment advice she held out, glanced at it. His fee for a month's work.

'I didn't put in that many hours.' Had flicked at the page.

'Please,' she'd said. 'I must go.' Again the brief sad smile. 'We all have our lives, Mr Pescado.' With that had turned to the bodyguard, followed her out of the waiting room, down the stairs. Fish'd wondered, why're you brushing me off?

What the heck? Was her money. Still niggled at him over the weeks, this change of heart she'd had. Ending his services before he'd really got anywhere.

Now the photographs. Spy pix. Telephoto jobs. The one in the car was interesting. Interesting angle downwards. More angle than a person's height. As if the cameraman was a step or two up. And slightly behind. Not a chance photo. Someone had been anticipating the moment. Whatever the moment was. Whatever the man was watching.

'Mister Fish, man, where's something for a poor lady?' Janet at the door, scanning the kitchen. 'Sho, Mister Fish, you need some cleaning done. You can see Miss Vicki's not making you vacuum. Yous need a cleaning lady, I'll be your woman. Fix this place up nice 'n tidy, quick sticks.'

'Maybe,' said Fish, focused on the pictures. 'What was the guy like who delivered these.'

'I told you.'

'Tell me again.'

'Ah, man, Mister Fish …'

'You didn't tell me how tall, you know, his size. Fat, thin, muscles.'

'A fris man like you Mister Fish. A gym man. Nice shoulders, no stomach boep. No beard. Shiny top like the darkies like it. I couldn't see his legs. But I can tell you he motors. You know, walks fast. One minute he's standing next to me, then he's gone. Poof. Like a ghost.'

Mart Velaze.

The name strobing in Fish's thoughts.

Brought up a set of questions. Such as: Who was the dude in the pictures? What was he watching? Why was he in the hospital? Let alone who took the pix? Mart Velaze? If not, where'd he got them from? Why'd he wait till now? Seemed timing was the critical thing.

Janet said, 'Mr Fish, come back, man. We got the real world here. Help a poor lady with a little toast 'n tea.'

Fish held up a finger. 'First a phone call. Your stomach can wait a couple of minutes.' Used the number in the telephone book. Asked for Mart Velaze.

'We don't have a Mr Velaze working here,' the receptionist said.

'Sure you don't.' Fish waved Janet back to her chair outside. 'Just tell him we need to speak.' He left his name. The woman insisting they didn't have a Mart Velaze.

By the time he'd cut two slices of bread, his cell was ringing.

'Thought you didn't want any more contact,' Fish said to Mart Velaze.

'Thought you were a private detective. How much help do you need?'

'More than a couple of photographs.'

'No, my friend, it's all there.'

'So why'd you ring me back?'

'To tell you your mate Vicki Kahn's deep in the shit, like she doesn't even know how deep.'

'Why're you telling me?'

'Cos she's not going to listen to me.'

'You're SSA. So's she.'

'Doesn't mean anything. Warn her, okay? I'm doing you a favour here. Seriously.'

End of conversation.

Fish saying, 'Wait, wait, wait. The photographs.'

Janet at the door looking in. 'Can you put the bread in the toaster now, Mister Fish? Please, man.'

His cell rang. The corporate client. 'We need you, Fish, now.' Kind of wiped out his good intentions. All he had time for was an SMS to Vicki: Call me. Urgent.

As before, it went unanswered.

5

They took the helicopter back to Berbérati in the afternoon. Hopped the Falcon to Bangui. At the Ledger ran the treadmills, showered, met at seven for dinner.

In bad French Zama ordered wine, a crisp sancerre. 'For the heat.' Said, 'Why don't they get waiters that know English? You're an international hotel, you've got to speak an international language. In Europe you can speak English everywhere.'

His phone rang. Zama looked at the screen. 'I told them, don't phone me until I am home. What do they do? They phone.' Connected with a huff. Changed his tone, lowered his voice. Major Vula caught the word 'auction'. The insistent: 'This Sunday, okay, this Sunday, my brother. It has been long enough. I do not want stories. The auction is this Sunday, after the party, you tell people.'

Kaiser Vula listened, looked round the restaurant. Couple of European white men, some Chinese, Arabs, seven Africans with their women. Wondered what auction, the first time he'd heard of any auction. The mysterious Zama with his mysterious life. Even after these months, he didn't know the man.

Zama saying to him, 'Sometimes people make you mad. They can't organise a simple thing.' Put his phone on the table.

'But now, Kaiser, other things. You see I have been thinking of the esteemed leader, Mrs Kolingba. She thinks we shot them, her husband and daughter. That it's a story we've invented about these rebel hitmen.'

'She thinks so,' said Kaiser Vula. 'Yes. She went to a private investigator.'

'Ah ha. You see. She is devious, this one. What did he find?'

'I don't know.'

'No, no, Kaiser.' Zama wagging his finger. 'You know about him, so you must know more.'

'He got nowhere. Then she stopped him.'

'Joh! Let me see. Let me guess. Because you talked to her. Because things had changed.'

'Yes.'

Kaiser Vula indicated the waiter, poised beside Zama, holding out the bottle of wine.

Zama put a hand on the bottle. 'It is cold. Fine. This is a good start.'

'Oui, monsieur.' The waiter poured a taster.

Kaiser Vula watched. Zama performed as always. Always the swirl, the tilt, the colour-check against the light, then the sniff, his sharp nose deep in the glass, the comments about plums, apricots, mown grass. The raised finger to the waiter. 'We can drink this.'

'Oui, monsieur.' The waiter poured, plunged the bottle into an ice bucket. 'You make order?'

Zama scanned the menu. 'Fish. Grilled fish. No starter.'

Kaiser Vula went with that. Ordered for them both. Using his basic French.

'I am impressed, Major Vula. You are an international spy. Very sophisticated. Now, a toast. To our mine and Madame Kolingba.' They clinked glasses.

Kaiser Vula tasted the wine, felt it fill his mouth. Heard Zama ask, 'Did she accuse us?' Swallowed.

'Accuse us? No.'

'Not directly?'

'No. She is diplomatic.'

'She has a nice voice. That Afro-French accent. Very sexy. I like it.' Zama came forward. 'Did we shoot him?'

Kaiser Vula shrugged. 'I don't know.' Didn't lower his eyes from Zama's gaze.

Zama chuckled. Sat back in his chair. 'Kaiser, Kaiser, Kaiser. The secret agent with all his secrets. You are ssa, Kaiser. You must know.'

'I don't.'

'Alright, let us say you don't. Here is what I think. I think when the rebels shot up the mine, my father ordered Kolingba's assassination.'

'He can't do that. He doesn't do that. We have a constitution, we acknowledge human rights. No one can do that.'

Zama sipped wine. 'It is a good wine, don't you think? Very clean in this dirty city.'

Kaiser Vula nodded. Wondered where Zama was going with this.

Zama saying, 'In Botswana, he did that. In those days. When the president was number one in intelligence. I heard the stories, growing up there. He could order hits.'

'Those were different days. There were bombs. There were infiltrators. It was dangerous for those in exile.'

'That is the story, yes.'

'You don't believe it?'

'I believe it. What I am saying is this is like it was before. In apartheid times. When we talked of the Boere's third force. There were no orders to the security police, what did they call it, the Civil Cooperation Bureau. No phone calls to their farm where they murdered people. Instead there was a culture, an understanding, you could say. Today we have another culture.

The president's culture. We sense what the president wants, we see the president is upset, we must do something so he feels better.' Zama set down his glass. 'I am right, yes?'

Again Kaiser Vula raised his shoulders. Blank-eyed. His lips damp with wine. 'It was probably the CAR.'

'Of course. Of course. You would say that. Because that is what it looks like. Because two weeks after the colonel is shot, there is a coup. A palace coup. How amazing. Such coincidence. One thing happens in one place and then something else happens in another place. We read novels like this. Another thing from the novels ...' Zama paused, glanced quickly at Kaiser Vula. 'You have heard of a threat to my father's life?'

'Yes.' Kaiser Vula seeing no reason to deny it. Thinking of the list of names he'd received. Those suspected of plotting against the president.

'You are concerned?'

'Of course.' Yet in a month there'd been nothing to confirm the conspiracy. 'We are alert but it doesn't seem likely.'

'Those are my thoughts.'

'And the president's.' A lie. Major Kaiser Vula had seen no cause to alarm the president, not until he'd done the background checks.

'There have been many before, you know. All empty noise. No one will take the final step. For that they are too scared.'

Maybe, thought Kaiser Vula, but had there been a list of conspirators before? A list of comrades, communist comrades? Probably not. But this time should you take these old men seriously? These grandfathers. Struggle heroes a step from the grave. Major Kaiser Vula didn't think so. Major Kaiser Vula thought it hot air. On top of that, didn't trust unsourced drops, never knew what agenda was being pushed.

Said, 'The president is too well loved.'

Zama laughed, raised his glass. 'Another toast. We cannot

know how the world works. What happened outside the cathedral doesn't matter. The mine is in operation. We have our soldiers to protect it. We have Mrs Kolingba on our side. We must toast to money and the president.'

'To money and the president.'

The thing about Zama Kaiser Vula didn't get was his skin colour. Light. That was strange. The president was dark. Then you looked at Zama's nose, the shape of it. Middle Eastern. Arab. Indian. Could also be Italian. You wondered about Zama's mother. Not one of the current wives. You wondered about the life story of the president.

'Something else,' Zama said, leaning forward, 'that might come to your ears. A girlfriend, Linda Nchaba, is soon to be back in my life.'

'Why should I hear about it?'

Zama grinned. 'I know about your types, Major. I know what you do.'

'A girlfriend is your private life.'

'Ha. Come, Major, come, you know I do not have a private life.'

Vula wasn't convinced, held his counsel. For a man without a private life, Zama had plenty secrets.

'What I'm saying is, you hear whispers about her, you let me know.' Zama drained his glass. Stood. 'Now there are the night's attractions.'

6

Mart Velaze thought as dead-drops went you could do a lot worse than a community notice board in a shopping centre. Had heard of computer chips sewn into dead rats, pouches

260

replacing the stomachs of deceased cats when you needed more space. The bodies no doubt placed in dark alleyways.

This drop was in plain sight: a notice asking for a Saturday char. Always assuming it was a drop. Mart Velaze believed it was. If Henry Davidson really needed a char, a better bet would be Marvellous Maids. You could set that up by phone. You didn't need to pin an index card on a corkboard in a shopping centre.

Thing was, who was Henry Davidson handling? Who was going to pop by to read his message? Let alone the when question.

Mart Velaze phoned the Voice. Told her what Henry Davidson had done. Told her Henry was shopping at Woolies.

'You see, Chief, something's going down that Henry's in the middle of,' the Voice said. 'He's the postman. Just need to give him a bicycle and a bag. Has to be this commie plot against the president, maybe has more intent than we credit.'

Mart Velaze realising the Voice had an inside track on Henry Davidson. Had probably bugged his office. The Voice getting her little listeners in everywhere.

'Now, all you've got to do is see who comes to look at the notice board, nè. Could be a long night. Coffee shops're all going to close soon. Thing I remember about fieldwork, Chief, how exciting it was.' The Voice giving a low chuckle. 'Got to salute the old spies, hey, they're full of tricks.'

Mart Velaze didn't respond, no ways he was going to waste time playing watchman. Had already seen half a dozen people give the board a scan. Could've been any one of them picking up whatever it was: info for a meet; operational intel.

The Voice saying to him, 'What other news've you got for me? What juicy gossip from our beloved Mother City? See you're right up there on the statistics: most violent city in the country. All those coloureds, Chief. Beware of coloureds. Even the pretty ones.'

Mart Velaze wondering was she getting at his girlfriend, Krista Bishop? How the hell'd she know about her, anyhow? Deciding to keep schtum on the Zama trafficking front. At least for the moment, no point in telling her. Would maybe keep that secret from her for maximum return when the pay-off was right. Did put into play that he'd got Fish Pescado chasing Prosper Mtethu for the Kolingba hit.

'Funny name, Fish,' said the Voice. 'Whiteys love that nickname nonsense. Like Blackie Swart or Nobby Clarke. How'd the English work that one? Nobby? I asked my MI6 people. They said it's after a hat, the famous bowler hat. Who wants to get named for a stiff little black hat?' Gave her chuckle. Mart Velaze unable to work out if she was serious. With the Voice it was possible she'd done just that. Might even have MI6 people. A pause, then she zeroed in: 'Get me more on Prosper, Chief, he's an unknown. Used to work for the major that's in with the president and son. You know what gets me? What really gets me? It's the alliances. You don't know who's connected to who. Or's that whom? Bloody English language.'

Mart Velaze said he would.

'Good man, Chief. Listen. Listen, there's a big gedoente, really big occasion, big party-party at the president's palace on the calendar. Upcoming this Saturday to be precise. Could be useful to have you in the vicinity. Just in case. Don't need to get onto any guest list. Half of the Aviary's flying in as it is. So're all the bigshot movers and takers. Couldn't think of a better moment to pull a wet job, if you were going to, of course. Best to have you nearby. Observer status only, okay. Strictly, strictly. If there's action, you're not in it. Not our remit, Chief. You got me? BWO. Bear witness only.'

Mart Velaze said he understood.

'Pack your bags for Saturday.' The Voice wished him safe travels. Assured him the ancestors would have oversight on the project.

7

Was on Fish's mind all day: what to do about Vicki? He'd woken with it. At unexpected moments it caught him, this nag: to take Mart Velaze at his word or not? Thing was, Mart Velaze came across as a serious dude. Not one to arse about.

So Fish'd left voicemails, twice: 'I don't know what this means but you're not safe. Call me.' 'This is no joke, Vicki. You're in danger. We must talk.'

sMSes: You are not safe. Serious. Call me.

A couple of hours on: I'll come round tonight if I don't hear from you.

Email: I'm not joking about this, Vicki. The warning comes from Mart Velaze. Please be careful. Please phone me. I need to know you're okay.

No response.

Late in the afternoon Estelle rang. Fish in the Canal Walk shopping mall tracking a smart woman into Mugg & Bean, wishing he could use a long lens. Cellphone cameras didn't crack it on some jobs. So much easier snapping clandestine meetings in car parks from a distance. Saw his mother's name on the screen, thought to press her off. Then: No, this's good cover.

Said, 'I'm on a job, Mom, but we can talk.'

'Oh, very kind of you. What sort of job? One of those cheating husband larks?'

Fish went with it. 'Something like that, yeah.'

'It's sordid, Bartolomeu. Unworthy of you. That sort of behaviour, people cheating on those who love them, leaves a bad odour on all it touches. I keep telling you. You should get a job. A real job. Join the decent world.'

'Didn't know there was one,' said Fish, turning his back on

the coffee shop. Watching the reflection of another woman approaching.

'Don't be clever with me, Barto. It doesn't suit you. Now, I've got a favour to ask.'

Surprise, surprise. 'Sure,' said Fish, 'what's it?'

'Research. Paid at your hourly rate. Your normal hourly rate.'

'Since when do I overcharge you?' The second woman, corporate mover, blonde hair short, carefully styled, walking up to the first, arm outstretched. The women shaking hands.

A turn-up for the books. The first time in a week his target had made a contact. Usually her lunchtimes were shopping expeditions. Ms Public Works getting down to business at last. Would please his client. And cause him grief. Want the good news first or the bad? Fish headed for the Mugg & Bean. Lousy coffee but what could you do?

Heard his mother saying, 'It's for my Chinese principals.'

When was it not?

'You see we've been invited to the palace.' A silence. 'You do know what I'm talking about don't you?'

Fish sat down a few tables away from the women. Took out a voice recorder. Good directional mic would pick up their chatter.

'I'm talking about the president's residence. Bambatha Palace, no less. Apparently – this much I have found out – he holds parties there, well, not so much parties, call them events, from time to time. You know, meet and greets. Ooze and schmooze occasions. For all the high rollers who make the world go round. It's an honour getting onto that list, Bartolomeu. It's the equivalent of an invitation from the Queen. The English Queen, obviously. Now.'

Fish ordered an apple juice, waved away a menu. Smiled at the waitress. Got a whiff of BO in return.

'Now, what I need to know is who else is on that list? I need to brief my clients.'

'Hell, Mom,' said Fish.

'Can do?'

'What, like phone the president's secretary, ask who's on the list?'

'Don't be facetious. You're an information analyst, or that's what you tell me. For an information analyst this should be easy-peasy.'

Fish watched Ms Corporate take an envelope out of her bag, letter size, put it on the table. Leave it there. 'Doesn't require me to phone the secretary, Mom.'

'Estelle. When are you going to call me Estelle? You're thirty-four now, Barto. I'm so over being mom.'

Fish ignored her. As the women ignored the envelope, talking quietly. You glanced at them, you'd say they knew one another. Maybe not friends but easy colleagues. 'You can do it. Phone the secretary. You're going to be there, you'll be on the list. They'll tell you chop-chop. No harm in asking.'

'I don't want them to know, Bartolomeu. Don't you get it?'

'Nothing I'd worry about.'

A sigh. 'It's called being discreet. My gentlemen are very particular about this. They like to be prepared and unobtrusive.'

Ms Corporate tapping her finger on the envelope. A polished nail. Varnished. Slid the envelope closer to Ms Public Works. 'When's the great occasion?'

'On Saturday. I've still got to decide on something appropriate. We stay there, you know. We've been invited to overnight. Not an invitation that's extended to just anybody. My principals are important men. More important than the Dalai Lama, I'd say. Mr Yan and Mr Lijan thought it a wise decision, withholding the Lama's visa. You learn that from history, Barto, there are always meddlesome priests.'

Ms Corporate standing. The women shaking hands. The envelope still on the table. Fish took the phone from his ear, muted his mother, selected the camera. Wondered how long it'd be before his mother realised he wasn't listening. She was into a history lesson, could be a while. Ms Corporate offered a fifty note for their coffees. Left it lying on the envelope. A final ciao.

A Samsung moment: the envelope going into Ms Public Works' handbag.

He keyed back to his mother. Dead air.

Sat there watching the woman finish her coffee, pay the bill. Thought of Vicki. What'd happened to them just such bullshit. Keyed the second sms to her into his phone.

8

'Hello, Linda,' said the voice.

A voice Linda Nchaba recognised. The oily tone. Like his mouth was awash with saliva.

'Long time.'

Her pulse up. Her throat constricted. Her mouth dry.

She clutched hard on the phone. Managed: 'What d'you want, Zama?' Took a quick drink of tea. Knowing the answer.

'To see you.'

'Why?'

'You came back.'

'I didn't have an option. Remember.'

'Why not? You can go anywhere in the world.'

Linda Nchaba stood at the first-floor window, staring into the street. Typical Zama, the snappy reply. Deflect the issue.

'You kidnapped my grandmother. You had me kidnapped.'

'No, no, no. That wasn't me. Not my style. Not at all. No, no. Man, what you think I am? I didn't kidnap you.'

Liar. Lying one of Zama's stock-in-trade responses. His world a mix of fact and fiction. Of omission. Linda relaxed her grip on the phone. Kept tense, alert, watching the street. Down there a man leading a donkey cart, a woman and child walking behind. A clutter of scrap iron on the back of the cart. The man singing out a constant refrain.

Heard Zama going on: 'Why'm I likely to do that? Why? I can phone you any time, baby, ask you personally, like now. Why would I do that? Look, we had a problem. I know. I was, what you say, out of line. My bad, okay, my bad.'

'You hit me.'

'Baby. My bad. I'm saying sorry. That's why I'm phoning. To say sorry. I want to see you.'

'My grandmother's dead.'

That dropped heavily. Left a silence. Linda kept her watch on the street. No pedestrians. A knot of people outside the bottle store. A man perched on his bicycle, talking on a cellphone. With Zama you never knew. He could be outside in the street. Watching.

'Yes. Sorry. I know that. Sorry for your loss. This was a sad thing.'

'You killed her, Zama.'

'No. She was fine. No one hurt her. I know. I know, every day I checked up. I made sure. Personally.'

'It wasn't enough. She was old. With a bad heart. Why, Zama? Why do that to an old lady? Why take her away from her home? Lock her up.'

'You made me mad, baby. You made me mad, running away. I had to bring you back ...' A pause. Linda silently finishing his sentence: ... because you knew too much. The real reason he wanted her back. 'All you had to do was come back.'

She could hear the distant hubbub from the taxi rank. Hooting. Whistles. 'I came back a while ago. I've been out on a collection. As you would know.'

Imagined Zama in his air-conned SUV, the smell of new leather. Could be parked round the corner. Mr Cool: blue shirt, chinos, slip-ons, no socks. Planning to surprise her. Zama's way.

'You see, when you came back, we took your gogo to her home. No problem. We always treated her nicely, with respect. We bought flowers for her home. Food, meat from the palace, chocolates. Every day with us she had chocolates. We didn't lock her up. She could walk around the house, sit in the garden. Sometimes she made food for everyone. It was a holiday for her.'

'She was a hostage.'

'It was a holiday for her. Top class.'

'You kept her where she didn't want to be. She was my gogo, Zama. Why do that to my grandmother?'

'To bring you back. We only did it until you came back.' A silence, Linda listened for background noises. Nothing obvious. 'I'm sorry she passed. She was a very nice person. Always kind, always smart. Always smiling.'

'She was an old woman.'

'I am sorry. I have said this. I am saying this. How many more times?'

Linda Nchaba heard her gogo. 'You must promise me you will not go back to him, Linda. Promise me.' The old woman's hand in hers. The thin skin, the bones almost visible, still a strength in the grip. She'd faded so quickly. Gone within a few weeks of Linda's return. 'Promise me, child. He is not a good man. When I am dead, you must go. Leave this place of weeping.'

She'd wept for her grandmother.

At the graveside said, I can't leave, there are the girls. I can't let him do that anymore.

Heard Zama saying, 'I want to see you. I mean this. We can have lunch. The Cape Grace is my favourite. You will like it there.'

'Where? I don't know it.'

'The Waterfront.'

'In Cape Town?'

'Yes. Why not? By plane it is two hours only.'

Once she would've laughed at crazy Zama, the crazy playboy. Gone along for the ride. The extravagance. Hopped his jet, tooted French champagne on the flight. Enjoyed the lunch. The buzz. The whirl. Nestled against the window on the return, nursing a Johnnie Walker Black. Watched the white strip of coastline spool past. Thinking, this is my life.

Now she hesitated. 'I'm scared of you.'

A laugh from Zama. 'You came back. That is not a woman afraid of me. That is not Linda Nchaba. I know you, baby. You're strong. All the times you've been to get the girls, you're strong. That's why I need you. One lunch. I'm asking nicely. One lunch. We can talk.'

That feeling again of Zama playing with her. About to surprise her. See, you cannot escape me.

Linda stepped back from the window into the shadow of the room. Could still see the street. The man on his bicycle peddling away. 'Where are you, Zama?'

'Close. We can eat now if you are hungry. Kentucky Fried Chicken.' Again the laugh. 'It's not the Grace, but it's food.'

There, the black Fortuner, tinted windows, driving slowly down the street. The driver's window sliding down. An arm, a hand waving. The spooky bastard. Very smart. Very cheeky.

She heard Vicki Kahn, 'Don't make it too easy for him. Resist. Just don't lose him.'

'Isn't there somewhere else?'

'Haibo, there speaks my expensive Linda Nchaba.' A pause. 'We have many things to talk about. Not only about you and me, there is also the auction on Sunday. You must be ready for this.'

'This Sunday?'

'We have waited too long already. This weekend we must be finished. Everyone is prepared. We can do it, then you can leave that hotel. I'm sure you won't be sad to go.'

Linda looked down on the car stopped opposite her window. Needed to talk to Vicki, to tell her.

'Tomorrow, baby, we have a lunch date.' The Fortuner accelerating away, the hand withdrawn. 'Somewhere to please you, I can promise.'

End of conversation. Linda keyed him off, put down the phone on the coffee table, her hands trembling, a pain in her stomach. She finished the tea. Too milky now.

Paced the room, keeping an eye on the street. The moment she'd wanted, the moment she'd dreaded. Dreaded more than wanted. Picked up her phone, keyed through to Vicki Kahn.

Said, 'He's phoned.'

'The Walrus?'

Such a childish codename. 'Yes, the big man himself. It's what you wanted, isn't it? It's why you made me come here.' The anxiety rising fast.

'We, Linda. We. It's what we agreed. Remember. It's what you wanted to do.'

'To get my grandmother released.'

'To stop Zama. We've been over this.'

'I'm frightened.'

'I know.'

Heard Vicki Kahn telling her to stop, breathe deeply, asking what happened. Told her. 'He phoned just now, ten minutes ago.' Gave her the gist. Adding, 'He's going to get rid of the girls.'

Heard Vicki Kahn say, 'When?'

'On the weekend. Sunday.'

'Good. Okay. Good.'

'Good? It's not good Vicki. They're girls, little girls.'

'It's good that things're moving, Linda. That's what I meant. We can get this over with. Look, you did the right thing, stringing him along. Phone him tomorrow, confirm the lunch, find out where he's taking you. You'll do that? You'll phone him?'

'I can't do this.'

'It's just a phone call, Linda. Just a lunch.'

Just a lunch! 'Nothing is just a lunch with him.' Down in the street, the man with the donkey cart returning. The woman and child behind. The child limping. 'Can't you come here?'

'You know I can't.'

Operational reasons.

The rules of that prick Henry Davidson with the funny hair. 'Look at it this way, Linda,' he'd said to her, 'if something goes wrong, you need a handler who has the whole picture. How can you have the whole picture if you're sitting in the middle of a mess? As the queen said, "Jam tomorrow and jam yesterday – but never jam today."' Whatever that meant.

'Look, Linda,' said Vicki now, 'it'll be alright. Confirm the lunch date. Don't let him pick you up. Go in your own car, come back in your own car. Don't go anywhere with him afterwards. Keep your phone on. We'll be watching.'

Yes, like that was comforting. Watching from sixteen hundred kilometres away.

'I'm going now,' she said to Vicki. 'I want to be sick.' Didn't hear Vicki's last words as she headed for the toilet.

9

There'd been a time, in the early days debriefing Linda, Vicki'd said to her, 'Why? I just don't get it. Why'd you do it?'

Vicki was just off the 'termination', as the white-coats phrased it. A bit raw emotionally, a bit all over the place, trying to keep it together. Trying to keep it hidden from Fish.

Aware she was the last person who could ask the question of Linda. Asking it anyhow.

The two of them at a pavement café away from the centre of the city. At the other tables three office workers peering at a laptop, a couple of kids tapping at their phones.

One of those warm days without humidity. Still put a sheen of perspiration on your face. Vicki could see it on Linda, a dampness to her skin. They sat in a tree's shade, the sun sliding towards noon, the shadow disappearing beneath their feet.

'I don't know,' Linda said. 'He asked me to go there, I went. The money was a lot more than any modelling job I'd ever had.'

'You did it for money?'

A nod. Her face turned away. A soft, 'Yes.'

Vicki didn't respond. Thought, okay, at least that was honest. Across the street, a woman parked her car on the slope, came over to the café, took an inside table. A young woman, pretty, her face familiar.

'And after the first trip?'

'There's no way out. Not from him.'

A silence between them. The murmur of the laptop trio.

'You think I'm awful.'

Still no eye contact. Both of them looking up at the mountain behind the roofs. Its solidity in the air.

'It's awful what you did. I can't say anything else. Truth: I don't know how you could've done that.'

Linda finished her latte. Glanced at Vicki. 'I don't either.'

A face in a magazine. *Heat* magazine. There'd been photographs of a party at the president's palace. Had to be she was one of the trendoids about town. Her name on the tip of Vicki's tongue.

'Zama helped me, you know. I got modelling jobs I wouldn't have got without him. Big contracts. Brand signings. He makes things happen. Zama takes you up, you fly. Parties, cruises, he's the scene.' She paused. Played with her empty mug. 'He asks you to do something, you do it. Once he's got you, he doesn't have to threaten. You know there's no out.'

'But you got out. You left.' Vicki coming in quickly, seeing Linda raise her face again, this time her gaze steady. Something like anger in those eyes.

'And what happened?'

Vicki nodded. 'There're always consequences.'

'But that's my problem, right?'

'No one's judging you, Linda.'

'You just did.'

'Look, you had your reasons. That's history. The thing is now you want to stop it. That's why I'm here. We're helping you.'

Nandi something. That was her name. Had to be a hot spot if she was here.

'I'll be there alone. By myself. That's not help.'

Vicki wanted to shake her head. Sit back. Marvel at this woman playing the victim. A money-grubbing child-trafficker, she wants you to pity her! See her as the victim here. Empathise. Even like her. Vicki kept poker-faced. Heard the diatribe coming.

'Why should I trust you people? I hardly know you. I don't know you. You could be going to drop me, use me as your bait, throw me away afterwards. Hamba wena, Linda, piss off, goodbye. Enjoy your life. That's what you people do. That's all you think about. Not me. Not the children.'

No tears. A flash in her eyes but no tears.

'You're doing this for some political game. I don't know. Some bigshot politician's pulling these strings.' The pitch of her voice raised. Linda pushing her chair back, standing up.

Vicki saw the laptop group had looked up. Nandi in the window of the café watching. Said, 'Sit down, Linda.'

Linda glaring at her.

'Sit down.'

The Noon Gun on Signal Hill going off then, loudly. Louder than Vicki could remember hearing it. A boom. Linda jumped. Sat down. From the tree, the clap of pigeons beating up. Vicki watched them turn in the light, glide towards the rooftops.

'That bloody gun.'

'You get used to it.'

'I'm not going to be here long enough, am I?'

Vicki let it go. Noticed Nandi on her cellphone, talking, staring at them. Disinterested. The gaze of the distracted. 'We should go.' Drained the dregs from her cup.

'You satisfied? Now you know I'm a bitch.' Linda challenging her with hard eyes. 'The evil queen.'

'Don't push it,' said Vicki, standing. Paid the waiter, hurried to catch up with Linda striding down the street.

Now, in her office, Vicki put down the phone, thought, you brought it on yourself, Linda Nchaba. No one else to blame. Then again, she was making good, that took guts. No question about it. Going through what Linda Nchaba was living ranked high up the courage charts. You had to give her that.

10

On his way home Fish stopped at the professor's.

'What're you doing here, Fish?' The man looking out of it, dishevelled, like he'd just smoked a large doobie. Rheumy-eyed, a smear of food on his upper lip. That cat-piss smell oozing from the house. 'It's not delivery day. I've still got what you'd call a stash. You can't come pushing your drugs, Sugarman. I'm not some street-corner punter.'

'Whoa, Prof. Chill, my china, chill.' Fish took a step back.

Professor Summers glaring at him. 'Mr Pescado, what the hell d'you want? I'm busy. I have students.'

Fish thinking, here? A student's come here? Brave person. Or desperate. Said, 'Okay, okay, I just want to ask you something, okay. Then I'm outta here.'

'What?'

Fish pulled out the photographs. Gave a quick explanation of the shooting.

'Very dramatic.' Summers handed them back. 'I'm always intrigued by your interesting life, Fish. And so, what's your question?'

'Why're we protecting this guy, this Colonel Kolingba?'

'My living Mary!' Prof Summers hamming it up, smacked his forehead, 'Don't you know anything, Fish? Don't you read the papers? Watch the news? Even Google the news? You've got too much water sloshing around in your skull.'

Fish caught a waft of underarm. Maybe deodorant needed more advertising.

'Firstly, your president has substantial interests in a little gold mine in the CAR. But you knew that, didn't you? Tell me you knew that. We all know that. It's even in the newspapers. Secondly, your president's looking after his friends because he's a troubled man. Why else the bunker at his magnificent palace? Why else the underground tunnels? The helipad? The huge goon squad we employ to protect him? The man's worried he's going to need them. I can't believe you didn't know this, that you hadn't put two and two together. There're plots and plans and conspiracies to take him out, Fish. If he doesn't run away first. Now be a good Capey, go surfing. Let the world proceed with its affairs.'

'How d'you know this? About wiping him out?'

'Ah, the surfing metaphor, how it doth colour our speech.' Professor Summers put his finger to his lips. 'Shhh. I have my sources.' Lifted his finger, tapped his nose. 'We hear things. Even in the Ivory Towers, we hear things. Of course I don't know for certain. But I've heard the whisperings. It's the communists, Fish, the communists.' Summers laughing.

Fish thought, yeah, gossip, rumours, theories, wishful thinking. Communist conspiracies. Like the communists in government were going to take out the president. How Cold War. How quaint.

Said, 'Okay, thanks.' Walking backwards to the gate. 'A great help.'

'Remember my order on Friday, Fish. I'll need it then. Good-bye, Mr Sugarman.' The professor tapping a stubby finger against his own nose again.

Later, Fish staked out Vicki's apartment. Sat in his Perana, in Solan Street, miserable, cold. Life in the apartment block going on all around him. Couples drinking on the balconies. Couples heading for the restaurants, hand in hand. Laughing. Emphasised his aching heart.

Fish stared up at her dark windows, checked the time, half eight. Thought, hell, Vicki, where are you? Tried her cell again, voicemail. Didn't leave a message this time. Did consider going up, letting himself in, waiting, except that would freak her. Not a good idea.

An hour later Fish decided, to hell with it, he'd come back in the morning, get it sorted with her then.

11

Vicki Kahn got home late. Collapsed on the couch, kicked her shoes off. Realised no ways she could sleep yet. Opened her laptop, powered through to 888poker, got quickly into a game. Hour after hour of it. Finally holding a pair of kings, a pair of aces. Proved a winning combo. The payout brought her loss down by a couple of thousand. Some consolation. A new game on the screen. She hesitated. Rubbed her eyes. Was strung out. Worried. Worried about Linda Nchaba. Also there was this stuff from Fish: the warnings that she was in danger. She couldn't see it, but not like Fish to be anxious.

Long gone midnight, too late to phone him. She'd delayed it all evening and Fish wasn't a night man. Any rate, what serious shit could she be in? Wasn't like she was in the field.

Clicked out of the game, closed the laptop.

Looked across the lighted city, up at Lion's Head, two cars driving slowly along the rump. At this hour, up there, not a place you'd want to be.

The call came on her cellphone while she was making a mint tea.

Linda Nchaba.

'I can't do this. I can't do this, Vicki. You get me? I can't do this anymore.' Linda uncontrolled. Unusual for Linda to drink. Except that's what it sounded like. 'Please. Not again. I can't do it again.'

A new one on Vicki. Earlier she'd been fine. A little nervous, but fine. Although Henry Davidson had warned her. 'As Alice found out, Vicki, things are not always what they seem. When you're out there, the world's a different place. You are alone. You are caught up in what's happening. You can't see beyond that.'

As she'd discovered in Berlin, those many weeks ago. Like another lifetime.

'Get me out, Vicki. Get me out.'

'We're going to. You know that.'

'Now.'

'There's a plan, Linda. Stick to the plan.'

'I don't want to go back there, to the warehouse. I can't lie to those girls anymore.'

Vicki switched off the gas. Mint tea would have to wait. 'We're so close to finishing this, Linda. So close. We mustn't stop now.' Putting herself into the frame.

'You're not here. You haven't seen them. You don't know what it's like to see them every day. I can't be with them again. I can't. It tears my heart out.'

'This's the last time, Linda. Remember that. If you don't go, that's the end of it for them. For lots of other girls. If you don't go, the whole scene just carries on. Don't give up now, not so close to the auction. You can stop these traffickers, Linda. For good.'

No response. Vicki went into the obvious one.

'You had anything to drink, Linda?'

'No. Yes.'

'Stop now. It doesn't help. Just phone the Walrus in the morning, as agreed.'

'Yes.'

'Everything's normal.'

A silence.

'I'm scared.'

Vicki thinking, okay, this is more like it. Except, how were you supposed to handle someone sixteen hundred kilometres away? 'Because that's how we do it, Vicki.' From the case officer's book of rules according to Henry Davidson. 'Look at it this way, if something goes wrong it's best to be miles from the mess. If an agent is lost, then an agent is lost. Bloody terrible. Might get awkward for the case officer but what's a case officer? Just a telephone number. Easy to get rid of a telephone number. Like the queen, it can just vanish before Alice's very eyes.'

The drollery of bloody Henry Davidson.

'He scares me.'

'You'll be alright.' Vicki not convinced. Keeping her voice strong. She needed to be there. With the Walrus around, she needed to be there. Frowned at her reflection in the window. Her straggly hair. The dark sockets of her eyes. Ran fingers through her hair.

'He can't hurt you.'

It's paranoia. You've got to talk them through that, Vicki. It's what happens out there. You've got the full story, you've got to keep them calm.

Vicki going over old ground. 'It's just a lunch, Linda. You can handle it. You can handle him. String him along. Play Miss Nice. I don't know. Give him something to hope for. You know … That you'll think about it, about whatever he wants, maybe. Just keep him relaxed. We don't want Mr Zama jumpy. We want him thinking life's sweet as your smile.' Vicki waited. 'Alright?'

Heard a whispered alright.

12

The president woke, found his genitals covered in a grey powder. Dusty powder, you rubbed it, it disappeared beneath your fingers. You blew at it, the powder vanished. He sat up, stared at his groin. Not the first time he'd woken like this. After Nandi, there was always this ash across his thighs.

He'd asked her, what's this?

She'd told him, muti, to make you strong. Would dangle her breasts in his face, make him strong.

'This is mumbo-jumbo,' he'd tell her. 'Superstitious nonsense.'

'But it works.' She'd smile at him.

That beguiling, bewitching smile. He'd take her hands. 'Those sangomas are witchdoctors. They prey on people's fears, their traditional beliefs.'

Back she'd come without fear or favour. He liked that, her abrupt, sometimes even abrasive retorts. 'And who is the man with three wives? The traditional man?'

'I do it to fulfil custom. To uphold my people's expectations. I am Zulu,' he would respond.

He lay now thoughtful. Perturbed by Nandi. Puzzled by her dark imaginings. Let his thoughts drift to the talk that came from his advisors. Rumours of discontent. Dissent. Stories of late-night meetings. Secret gatherings of his comrades.

Amid these dark obsessions became aware of Nandi in the bathroom singing softly. She would be soaking in a bath beneath her bubbles. Shaving her legs, her armpits, her pube. Even though he told her not to.

'You cannot tell me that,' she'd replied. 'It is my body.'

Another point he'd had to concede. At heart, pleased by her candidness. This was a woman who knew her mind.

He sat up, reached for his cellphone on the bedside table, dialled Kaiser Vula.

'Where are you, Major?'

'I am here, Mr President,' Kaiser Vula replied.

'In the bunker?'

'With your secretary.'

'You have your file for me?'

'Yes.'

'All the names?'

'Those that we know.'

He paused. 'Good. Good. I will be down. Let me talk to my secretary.' To his assistant said, 'You have served the major coffee, breakfast?' Was told it had been ordered. 'He can sit inside. Give him the document we prepared. For his eyes only.'

'Of course, Mr President,' said the secretary. 'Even with …?'

'Yes.'

The president disconnected, swung his legs off the bed. Brushed a hand at the powder in his pubic hairs. Shook his head. The contradictions of the girl sometimes beyond understanding.

A gripe of pain ziggered across his stomach. Made him bend over, gasp at this sudden stabbing. They were becoming more frequent, more intense, these bolts of fire. He'd even had to call off a tennis practice the previous day. There were occasions he had to smother a cry.

When the spasm eased, he straightened, lifted a white dressing gown from a chair, shrugged into it, fastened the cord. In the bathroom said to Nandi, 'You have been to the sangomas again.'

'Of course.' Her face turned up to him. Those wide eyes sparking.

'Enough, please. We've been through this.'

'You must trust me, Baba,' she said, reaching up.

He took her soft hand in both of his. Had told her not to call him baba. 'I am not your father,' he'd said. 'For me you can use the name husband.' But still she called him baba.

Said now, 'I am not asking, my dear.'

Not a flicker of doubt crossed her face. 'I have powers. The sangomas tell me I have powers.'

The president sighed. 'You must stop.' He released her hand.

'Baba,' said Nandi. 'I have organised the party. Everything is ready. You can make the announcement.'

The president turned to the mirror. Peered closely at his image. There seemed to be a grey tinge in the whites of his eyes. He needed honey. A spoonful of honey would sort out his problems.

13

Her buzzer went. Vicki about to leave for the Aviary, update the Linda file, do some legwork on the palace party, get background on the president's new piece. Would be news to Henry Davidson. Which would piss him off. She liked that. Anticipated Henry pouting, his lips pursed in sour resentment that she was one-up.

She frowned at the buzzer box: on the display, Fish staring at her. Blond surfer hair awry, pleading look in his eyes.

The last thing she wanted. The first thing she wanted.

Her pulse up.

His lips moved. Please. Was he saying please? Pleading? Fish pleading?

Not the moment. Not right now. She couldn't handle it on the fly, not without some psyching.

He'd brought his hands into view. Holding them up to her, palms out.

Don't, Fish, don't. Not now.

She got out of the apartment fast. Could hear the buzzer going again and again as she closed the door. Could imagine his face on the screen, begging.

She couldn't be ambushed. Could only do it on her own terms.

Vicki took the stairs, went out the opposite side of the building. The mountain above her, the ancient god Adamastor looming down, disapproving. Went left up the street, the pavement damp with night dew, the sun on the old cottages opposite. Had decided to skirt round the top of Wembley Square. Chances were Fish would've parked in the underground. When he gave up he'd go back to his car and by then she'd be down Glynn Street behind the Archives to the crumbling homes of Harrington Street. Easy to keep out of sight.

The feeling kicked in halfway along Glynn. The sense of being followed.

When you get the feeling, don't stop. Go with your instinct. Best not to let on that you're aware. Wait for an opportunity. Wait for a rabbit hole, to use Henry Davidson's term. None such here. She was exposed. The stone wall of what had once been the hanging prison one side, on the other cars parked at the kerb.

Should have known Fish wouldn't be an easy dodge. Vicki crossed Solan Road, waiting for the call of her name, the sound of his running. Her phone rang. She stopped beside a window, an arty media house, enough reflection in the glass of the street behind her. Fish not mirrored. His name on her phone screen. Pressed him to voicemail, walked on.

The rabbit hole came at the Book Lounge. She'd jay-walked

Roeland Street between hooting cars, continued on Harrington past the charity hall, jinxed left into Commercial. In Buitenkant, with no sign of Fish, slipped into the bookshop's side entrance, taking the stairs down in leaps. Neat, short man wearing a bow tie coming out of an office said, 'Whatever it is, it's not sold out, no need for you to rush.'

Gave him the wither stare.

He held up his hands, said, 'Oh, dear.' Clucked his tongue.

In a corner chair Vicki phoned Fish.

'What're you doing, stalking me? You don't have to do that.'

'I'm not stalking you. It's …'

'Look, give it up, okay. I've got stuff going on, Fish. Just give it up. We can talk when this's over.'

'You're being followed.'

'Being stalked, you mean.'

'Listen, Vics. Listen to me.'

The Vics catching her. When he called her that, he could still do it. Flutter her heart.

'There's a guy on you.'

'What?'

'Stay where you are. I'll call on another line. We can't talk on this one.'

'It's my phone.'

'Exactly.'

The call dropped. Vicki sat looking at her phone. Fish could be the limit. Thought about someone stalking her. A watcher. Who'd have her under bloody surveillance?

The bow-tie shortarse returned holding out a mobile handset. 'There's a call for you on our landline, madam. If your name's Vicki. It sounds very mysterious.'

Vicki took the phone.

'A thank you would be nice.' Mr Bow Tie, pouting, spinning on his heel.

'Listen, Vics,' said Fish in her ear. 'I got a call earlier. You're in shit street.'

'What're you talking about, you got a call? Who from?'

'Doesn't matter.'

'It does.'

'Okay, how's this: I'm looking at him, your watcher. The dude's about my height, dressed like a bergie, bit fat for a bergie. Does a lot of dustbin work. Mutters to himself. Not far from the Book Lounge, actually across the road at the shop that sells Gatsbys, that's where he's standing. Probably he eats too many Gatsbys, all that bread and chips, that's why he's fat.'

'Don't be a prick, Fish.'

'I'm not shitting you. I mean this. Look out the window, you'll see him.'

One thing she'd been sure of was being clean going into the bookshop. Did a quick scout up the stairs, Mr Bow Tie calling out, 'Don't walk off with our phone, madam.'

There was the vagrant, pawing in a bin.

'Where're you?'

'Up the road a bit. I'm not gonna wave. Believe me now?'

She went back to her chair. The neat man standing in his office doorway, stroking his moustache, keeping her under surveillance. Everyone at it.

'He was onto you from Wembley Street. About the same time I was.'

'Oh, very smart.'

'It happens, Vics. To the best of us. Problem is also whatever this other thing is you're doing.'

'And you got this from?'

'An old friend. Well, not a friend as such. What do you call them? An informer. A low-level informer.'

Vicki knew who that meant. Could be only one person: Mart Velaze. She closed her eyes, leant back in the leather. In all her time at the Aviary she'd never seen him. Not once. Not so much as glimpsed a fleeting shadow of Mart Velaze. Wasn't a record anywhere he worked for the Agency.

'He's full of nonsense.'

'I don't know. I'm telling you what he said. If you're under surveillance, maybe he's right. You need to watch it, that's all.'

'For heaven's sake! I'm only going to the office, not as if I'll be meeting covert operators.'

Vicki saw Mr Bow Tie coming towards her. 'Can we have our phone back, please? This is a business, you know. Not a telephone café.' Holding out his hand, his fingers going give, give, give.

'Wait,' she said to Fish. To the shortarse said, 'Don't do that.'

The vehemence stopped him, had him back-pedalling. 'Oh, my dearie me.'

'We got to talk,' Fish was saying. 'About us. About why the fuck you won't return my calls. About why you just let us unravel.'

'You mean it's my fault?'

'I mean we've got to talk.'

Vicki bent forward, looked down at her neat feet, her shoes, black slip-ons, a scuff on the left toecap. He was right. They needed to talk. 'Okay,' she said. 'I'll call you.'

'Tonight.'

'Tonight.'

A silence. Then: 'You want me to sort out the bergie?'

She nodded to herself. Said, 'Yes.'

'Tonight,' said Fish. 'You better do it.'

Vicki pressed off the connection, stood. 'Here,' she said to the bow-tie guy, 'catch' – lobbing the handset. He missed. Dropped it.

'You're very rude,' he said, picking up the instrument.

'And you're no cricketer.'

She left the bookshop through the main entrance, closing the security gate behind her. Glimpsed Fish talking to the bergie, the bergie struggling to get out of his grip.

Her phone beeped a message: 'Walrus lunch tomorrow. Phone me tonight.'

14

Kaiser Vula sat at the long table in the bunker. The flat-screen showed CNN news, the sound muted. Problems in Gaza. Putin holding forth. Obama hurrying with his aides across a lawn. Kaiser Vula didn't watch it, sat at attention, his hand on a thin manila file, his eyes on the secretary entering.

The secretary brought a cafetière of coffee. Three slices of lightly buttered toast. A pot of jam. A bowl of grated cheese. An apple. He had not asked for the jam, the cheese, the apple. Breakfast on a silver platter.

'Major,' said the secretary. 'The president says he will be fifteen minutes. I have a document I must give you.' The secretary unlocked a cabinet door, lifted out a folder. 'These are names the president wrote down. He prepared it. You must not show anyone.'

Kaiser Vula glanced round the empty room. 'I won't.'

'Perhaps you should remember the names.'

'I will.'

'You know there must be no paper trail.'

Kaiser Vula reached out, slowly depressed the cafetière's plunger. Kept his eyes on the secretary. A gay man, he suspected. Not like some, not flamboyant, this one discreet. But you could hear it in his voice, the soft lilt. You could feel it in the small handshake. The president joked about them, yet had this one in his office? Puzzling.

'When you're finished, I must shred it.'

'Alright.'

Kaiser Vula stared at the file.

'Yes,' said the secretary. 'Well, enjoy. I'm the other side of the door if you need me.'

Kaiser Vula flexed the corner of his mouth, a stiff smile, left his hand on the plunger until the secretary had gone. Then relaxed, pulled the file closer, opened it. A single sheet inside, a handwritten list of names. All the names from the party's national executive committee. All who were not communists.

The president was a communist. A member of long standing.

Kaiser Vula poured himself coffee, black, no sugar. Bit into a slice of toast, crumbs spraying over his suit. Thought: This will not be easy. There had not been a worse time in his life. The humiliation by Nandi, the taunting thrusts of his wife, the grasp of the president, the business of the son. He brushed the crumbs from his lap, clucking in irritation.

How quickly it had got like this. How quickly he had been sucked in.

Become the confidant.

To Zama who revealed nothing, who lived nowhere, who was running the Sydney Sun Run or the Tel Aviv marathon. Or had stopped at this beach hotel in Bazaruto, or that golf resort in Guyana. Or was hunting with American senators in the forests of Michigan. Or fishing with Russian oligarchs in the Caspian Sea. Who might phone from New York, London, Shanghai, Cairo, Mumbai.

'Yes, Kaiser, we must visit the mine.'

'Yes, Kaiser, we must be in touch with Madame Kolingba.'

'Yes, Kaiser, we must meet with the president.'

'Yes, Kaiser, we must have a drink. The One&Only. Tonight.'

Where Zama'd said, 'You've heard about my father's plans? No?' A laugh. 'You won't believe it. This man, he is seventy something, he has three wives. Now he wants another one. Which will mean a child, of course. Without a child can it be a marriage? Not in our culture. The old gogos will whisper about him. The old gogos think already there are too many children. Enough, old man. No, he must marry again.' A pause, a sip of whisky. A tap on Kaiser Vula's knee. 'Actually, Major, you know her, his intended.' A snort of derision. 'Very beautiful. Very smart. Very young. Yes? Yes, the woman who left you. Nandi. I forget her family name.'

Nandi.

Who would not tell him what had happened that night of the party. Who had stayed in their room until it was time to go. Who had said on the flight back to Cape Town, 'I hate that man. I really hate him.' Who had told him later, 'We are finished, Kaiser. I am leaving the city.'

Next thing he learns, she has been seen at the palace, a regular visitor there. She's moved in, become the president's favourite.

'I hate that man. I really hate him.'

Kaiser Vula heard her vehemence. Low. Intense. Angry.

'So your little lovebird is screwing the president,' his wife had said when gossip became news. 'You groomed her well, Major.'

'She is not my lovebird.'

'Sorry. Was. Was your little lovebird.' His wife holding up the magazine spread. Nandi and the president in full colour.

'If you want a divorce, then it is easy to arrange.'

'Snatched off by your president.'

'Give me a divorce.'

'Are you mad? How am I to live without your money? I am your prisoner, Kaiser Vula. And you are mine.'

The truth. He drank off the coffee. Poured another cup. Never more than now, a prisoner. Through the door, heard the president's voice, cheerful, booming.

'Major. Good morning. You have been looked after? More coffee? More toast?' Formal in his suit and tie, sat opposite Kaiser Vula at the long table. Stared at him. Kaiser Vula lowered his eyes. Thought he could smell Nandi's scent ghosting. 'You have done some investigations?'

'I have.' Kaiser Vula slid his file across the table.

The president left it lying there. 'No, no. I don't want to see it. What about the names on my list? Do they match?'

Kaiser Vula shook his head. 'They are not the same.'

'No?' A frown. 'You are sure of this?'

'We are. I am. Yes. You have been given a decoy list.'

'The minister of security would do this to me?'

Major Kaiser Vula kept silent. No emotion on his face, his eyes steady on the president. A perfect servant.

The president sucked at his lips. Silence in the room, except the soft plosive of the president's breath.

'Who are they? Give me their names.'

'It is the communists.'

The president didn't respond. Shifted in his chair, staring at the major. 'Which communists?'

'The leadership.' Kaiser Vula cleared his throat, named the comrades.

'You are sure?'

'It is our information.'

'You have someone in the committee?'

Again the major had to clear his throat. 'We have someone.'

The president leant forward, nodding. 'Of course. There is always someone. Always someone who is not what you think. That is how it was in exile. In government I thought it would be better. That the plotting would stop. But it is how we are.

There is always the spy. In those days, we took the traitors to the Quatro camp. It was easy. The camp was far away in Angola. Far away anything can happen. Now we cannot do that anymore. What can we do now?'

'We can raid them with the Hawks.'

'Pah.' He waved a hand. 'The Hawks. The Hawks are a joke in the police service. We have no laws for traitors now.' The president got up, walked the length of the bunker. 'We must do nothing, Major. We must listen. Wait. You are sure of these names? You are one hundred per cent? These are my friends, these people. They have benefited. Look at where they live: the garden suburbs, safe behind their walls. In their big houses, driving their smart cars. They have international holidays. They are the rich. In twenty years, they have all this. More than they could have if they worked for a lifetime.' He came back. Stabbed his finger on the manila file. 'That is what I have allowed them. Now what do they want? What is their plan? To kill me?'

'That is what we heard.'

'What?' The president sat down. 'You mean this? You are serious? These comrades think they can do that? What? They will shoot me? They think I am a dog, they can shoot me? How can they do this? Where will they do this? Will they have a coup? Like the CAR?'

'There are no details.'

'But they have talked of this?'

Kaiser Vula nodded slowly. Sucked in his breath. 'They have talked about it.'

'My comrades. My friends.' The president stared at the table, the manila file lying there.

'Other ways can be used.'

'Other ways?' A pause. 'No, no. No. We wait.' Pushed the file back to Kaiser Vula. 'Destroy this.' Raised his eyes, Kaiser

Vula seeing no fear there. Only the president's shark stare. 'They will not dare. They know me. I am president-for-life. For communists, if they are not planning something secret, their lives are empty.' He placed his hands together. 'Now tell me, how is Zama, my marathon-running son?'

'He is fine. Very fine. Since CAR, he has been travelling.'

'So much travelling? What for, I cannot think. He is never here.' The president broke off a piece of toast. 'He has not taken you into his business?'

'Only the mine.'

'That is a pity. But you have found out what he does, his business?' Chewed on the toast.

'Only the mine. Of course also he is a director on many companies.'

'You like dry toast?'

Kaiser Vula watched the bobbing of the president's epiglottis. Sharp, hard against the skin.

'You know which ones?'

'Some here. Some in America. China.'

'America? How? Tell me, Major. How does this happen to a Zulu boy?'

Kaiser Vula held up his palms. 'You are the president. He is your son. There is black empowerment.'

The president smiled. 'Where would they be without black empowerment?' Toyed with another piece of toast. 'You have seen his bank account?'

Kaiser Vula shifted his eyes to the flat-screen. A refugee camp in Syria, a young girl, four, five years old staring at the camera. 'Yes, we have seen his bank account.'

'Don't worry, Major. It is what I asked of you. You can tell me about it.'

'Everything is in order.'

'In this country. But we do not know offshore. There could be a different story.'

'It is possible.'

'It is likely.' The president crunched into another slice of toast. 'You know his mother died, Zama's mother. I have told you that story? You see there is his problem, he had no mother. Only gogos to bring him up. A grandmother is not the same as a mother. Even me, I didn't see him grow up. It was too difficult in those years of the Struggle. For the children of the Struggle, nothing was easy. No mothers. No fathers. They are the lost ones.'

The president swallowed.

'Zama doesn't come on your list?'

Why would he, thought Kaiser Vula. The last thing Zama wanted was a change in the presidency.

'No,' he said, 'your son supports you.'

'This is good, Major. Without me he has no lifestyle.' A pause. 'I hear one of his girlfriends is back in favour. Linda Nchaba. A most beautiful woman. Have you met her?'

Major Vula said he hadn't.

'A strange type of girl. A woman of moral conscience. Perhaps you should flag her, Major. It can do no harm.' The president stood, walked to the door. 'We must always be alert. For all things. We must watch. We must wait. But there is no reason to be anxious.' At the door, held out his hand. 'You will be here for the party?'

Kaiser Vula picked up the manila file, walked quickly towards the president. 'Of course.' Shook the outstretched hand.

'A last thing.' The president keeping hold of his hand. 'It is time we said goodbye to Colonel Kolingba. You understand me? Today, it is important, today. I have my friends to think about. We cannot allow this nonsense. My friend is suffering in the CAR because of that woman troublemaker.'

That woman, thought Kaiser Vula, his hand still firmly grasped, saved your investments.

'I mean you,' said the president. 'You must do it.'

Kaiser Vula noted a twitch of what looked like pain tighten the president's face.

15

'Hey, my china, you want one of those?' Fish took the bergie by the elbow, pointed at the shop selling Gatsbys. Strange thing about the bergie, he didn't smell like a bergie. Not like Janet. Janet ponged. That sour sweat and smoke BO. This one had dirty fingernails, old clothes that hadn't been washed, lacked the intense smell. Had to be SSA. Only the Agency would be this casual.

'What sort?' Fish steering him into the shop. The bergie didn't resist, kept in character, but twisted to look back at the street. 'Check here, you get your roll with vinegar chips, then you got a choice: polony or hake or calamari. And a chilli sauce. Which one, hey? Which one you gonna go for on your lucky day.'

'The best one in the city, I tell you.' The shopkeeper getting in on the sale. 'Fresh rolls this morning.'

'Calamari,' said the bergie. 'The calamari one.'

'The gourmand man's taste,' said the shopkeeper. 'Top calamari, I tell you.' He picked out a bread roll, cut open a mouth to push in the chips.

Fish kept his hold of the bergie, but looser now. Not a bad job they'd done on the disguise. But smell was the thing. They always forgot the smell.

'We have one calamari Gatsby in one moment's time,' said the shopkeeper, squirting chilli sauce from a plastic bottle into the stuffed roll. To Fish said, 'This is most kind of you, my good sir.' He named the price.

As Fish dug for notes in his pockets, the bergie pulled free, dashed into the street.

'Hey, my friend, my friend, don't run away. This is fine food for you. A most nourishing meal. You are one fortunate fellow on this beaming day,' the shopkeeper shouted. Turned to Fish. 'You try to help these people, that's what you get, I tell you. There is no appreciation. Every day they come in here, please give me food, please give me a bread. They think I am a charity. That I am here to feed all the rubbish of Cape Town.' Held up the Gatsby. 'So, now it is all for you.' Repeated the price.

'I don't want it.' Fish shook his head. 'It was for him.'

'I have made it. You must pay for it.'

'Someone else will buy it.'

'You must buy it. You are the customer.'

Fish looked at the shopkeeper, his baggy eyes, his stumpy teeth. His face set, determined. Thought, what I do for you, Vicki. Said, 'Sorry, okay. I don't want it.' Got out of the shop, the man swearing at him, shouting, What did he think this was, Gift of the Giver? Good Samaritans? Red Cross? Seaman's Mission? Nelson Mandela day? The Gatsby man coming round the counter with a cricket bat.

Fish jogged away up Roeland Street, glanced back once at the Gatsby man yelling from the corner, his cricket bat raised. Couldn't resist a toodle-oo wave, as his mother would call it. Then headed back to Wembley Square through quiet streets, office workers smoking on the pavements, young suits making for the deli for their morning croissants. Followed them up the steps into the square. At the lift to the apartments, keyed in Vicki's security code. At the apartment door used the key she'd given him months back.

Could smell her instantly. Stood there just breathing her in. The scent of her hair, her deodorant, the hint of perfume. Felt the loss of her in his chest. She'd better bloody ring. She didn't, he would. Took the GSM bugs from his jacket pocket, wondered where'd be the best spots. The apartment so Vicki. Neat. Everything in its place. You didn't know who lived here, you might wonder, obsessive-compulsive tidiness.

First, did a sweep of her apartment, found a bug beneath the couch, another really sexy little thing behind the bed's headboard, a third in the bathroom. Whoever had installed them really wanted aural on Vicki Kahn. A relief: no cameras.

Thought, Vicki, Vicki, Vicki, you need to do some house cleaning. Of course, could be she knew, didn't want them to know she knew. Either way, Fish left the gizmos.

Stuck one of his own beneath the corner desk, the other under her bedside table. Thinking, might be a complete waste of time. Except you never knew what you'd pick up. Felt a shit for doing this. Then again a man had to do what a man had to do, but he wasn't a snoop, not in the jealous sense. Wished he could test them, but he said a word, whoever else was out there listening to the private life of Vicki Kahn would prick up their ears. No other option: trust to the gods of electronics. Took a last look round, wondering if or when he'd be here again. Not a thought he wanted to think. Got out of her apartment before the morbs attacked.

Fish's next call: the comatose colonel. Recalled something Cynthia Kolingba had told him about the colonel being close to home. Close to home was Constantiaberg. He knew that hospital. You went in with a bunch of flowers, you could get more or less anywhere. Duly went in with a bunch of flowers. At reception asked for the colonel. Was told second floor, ICU, no visitors except family. Could leave the flowers, a messenger would take them up.

No bother, Shereen, said Fish, reading her name tag, he'd do it, drop them at the nurse's station. Quick as a flash.

'You can't, sir,' said Shereen. Buzzed a security guard, told him to take the flowers. 'Please, sir, respect our regulations.' Shereen a large lady of wobbling fat.

'No problem,' said Fish, walked with the guard to the lifts. Pulled out the photographs, plus a blue hundred bucks. 'You seen this guy?'

The guard nodded. 'I seen him.'

'Here?'

'Every day. Upstairs.'

'Can you give him a message?'

'What message?'

'Give him these.' Handed the photographs to the guard. 'Tell him I'm in the foyer.'

'You?'

'In the foyer.'

The lift doors opened, Fish stepped aside for attendants pushing wheelchairs. People in the wheelchairs looked like zombies.

Before the doors closed, said to the guard, 'What's his name?'

'We call him Prosper.'

Prosper! There was a name to conjure with.

Fish ambled back past Shereen. Smiled at her. Said, 'You see, obeying your regulations. Get you something from the canteen? Custard slice, maybe? Chocolate cupcake?'

Shereen glowered at him.

'Lighten up,' said Fish.

He didn't wait long for the man called Prosper. Saw the security guard step out of the lift, point a man in his direction. The man holding the envelope with the photographs.

Came up. 'Eh, who are you?' Deep voice. Stepped right up to Fish, crowding him.

Fish held his ground, told him, friend of the Kolingba family. Stretched it a bit that he was working for Cynthia Kolingba. The man glaring at him, his brow furrowed.

'I don't know you. Where'd you get these?' Tapping the envelope against Fish's chest.

Fish took hold of the envelope. 'Doesn't matter where I got them.' Took out the one of Prosper in the car. Decided to up the ante. 'I know what's going on here.'

The man grinned. Two teeth missing from his lower jaw. The others yellow stubs. 'You think, eh? You think you know. You a clever? Such a clever.' Snatched back the photographs.

Fish smelling the cigarette smoke on the man's breath.

'You, blond man!' The words spat out. 'I am the colonel's security. Go.' Shoved Fish towards the door. 'Go.'

Fish stumbled, regained his balance. Saw over Prosper's shoulder, Shereen smiling. Felt the hard jab of a gun muzzle below his ribs. The man pushing him out of the foyer.

'You think you know what is going on? You come with your photographs, you think you know what is going on? You know nothing. Nothing, my friend. You are dog shit.'

Fish being frogmarched through the ranks of cars to the back of the parking lot. Being patted down, glad he didn't have the Ruger in his belt.

'ID? ID? Who are you?'

Fish brushed the gun aside, took a pace back. 'Cool it, okay? What the fuck you think you're doing, man? I'm working for Cynthia Kolingba.'

'Mrs Kolingba's in CAR. I am the colonel's security.'

'You are SSA.'

'Where's your ID?' The man still holding his gun, his arm lowered. 'Show me.' Clicking his fingers. 'Show me. Quick. Quick.'

'Look, screw you,' said Fish. Opted for another flyer. 'You know Joey Curtains?'

Prosper squinted at him. 'Joey Curtains is dead.' Paused. 'How'd you know Joey Curtains?'

'I didn't,' said Fish. 'We didn't get the chance.'

'Maybe you're lucky, blondie.' Prosper putting the gun muzzle against Fish's breastbone. 'You think you know lots of things. You think because you got pictures, you a clever. Let me tell you, you know fokal.' Jabbed the muzzle, pushed Fish up against a concrete fence. 'You go away, blondie. You go away from the colonel. You go away from Mrs Kolingba. You go away and stay away. No more funny blondie business.' The man tucked his pistol into his belt, pulled out a cellphone, took a few quick snaps of Fish. 'For my Facebook.' Laughed, shook his head.

Fish watched him walk away, a limp in his gait as if he swivelled from the hips. His life catching up with him. One thing about Prosper, he could get excited. Fish massaged his breastbone.

Shouted, 'You want me, Prosper, my card's in the envelope.'

The man didn't even turn round.

Had to make you curious, too, thought Fish, why Mart Velaze was pulling your strings?

16

Vicki reckoned she was clean. Had headed along the empty pavement, past the dingy shops, paused at the car lot, ensured there was no one following. Could see all the way back. Other side of the street, two women talking outside the Kimberley Hotel; her side, a man stepped from the bottle store, his daily bread in a paper bag, went off in the other direction. No sign of the bergie. Good for Fish. The thought of him brought back the pain of longing. Made her feel worse that he'd been watching out for her. After the way she'd treated him. Considered SMSing him thanks. But didn't.

Later. Later they could deal with it. She hurried on.

At the Aviary went straight to Henry Davidson.

'Tell me,' she said, standing over his desk, 'what's going on, what's happening?'

Henry Davidson glanced up from his screen. 'Have you seen this? Have you ever actually Googled the palace?' Jabbed a finger at the screen. 'It's amazing. Like Sun City. Like a fantasy. Those fabulous buildings. The whole place. A present to him from we the people. Extraordinary. And in what we like to call a democracy. One-party democracy. Or have we had a silent coup d'état that no one noticed?' He squinted at Vicki. 'You're looking peaked. Sit down. Tell Humpty all about it.'

Vicki removed files from a chair, perched on the seat. 'You tell me.'

'Ooo, bit aggressive for this time of the morning, I do believe.'

'I'm under surveillance. Again. First in Berlin. Now here.'

Vicki watched his face. No change to his expression. No sudden glint of interest in his eyes. No twitch at his mouth. Not the first time she wondered if he played poker. Never dared ask. Never dared broach the G-subject. He'd be on it afterwards, exploiting the angle.

'Are you now? Interesting.' Drawing out the four syllables. 'Who's doing it? Why're they doing it?'

Henry Davidson leant back in his chair. 'Good question.' Came forward, stood up. 'Much better to talk about it over coffee in the Gardens. Such a nice day. Pity to be cooped up in here, don't you think?'

On the walk down Plein Street, along Spin, round the back of the Slave Lodge, Henry Davidson nattered about one day in Paris.

'There I was, strolling beside the medieval Seine, Sunday morning, lovely morning, September, sunny, clear, bright blue sky, song in my heart, all is right with the world. I am dawdling, taking it all in: sights, sounds, aromas. Parisians at their cafés, enjoying the last of the summer sun. Then I get this feeling, you know, that there is someone following. I stop. Lean on the wall, looking at the river. Look up at the sky, turn round, look up at the buildings, your general tourist behaviour. Ah, what it is to be in this great city! Look back. There I see this Frenchman about twenty metres away: coiffed hair, summer jacket, smart shoes. Short man. Shorter than me by a good three or four inches. Got his hands cupped round a cigarette. Slightly turned away as if he is shielding the match from the wind.' Henry Davidson paused. 'Is that your watcher scratching in the bin up ahead?'

Vicki'd seen him already. Wondered how he'd known where they'd be. 'Uh-huh. How? How'd ...'

'Bug in my office,' said Henry Davidson. 'Leave him be. He's happy in his work. Anyhow, back to Paris. I realised I had seen this chappie before, on the Metro. Had to be DCRI, whatever they were before that, RG, DST, one of the French counter-espionage agencies. So I thought, best not to let on. Best to let him do his job. Lovely day like that, the last thing you want to do is spoil it.'

'Why're you telling me this?'

'For a reason, my dear Vicki, for a reason. Come.' Took her arm, guided her off Government Avenue towards the café. 'You see this was, let me see, this was 1988. Different place the world was in 1988. Dangerous place. All sorts of chatter coming from all sorts of quarters. Nervous Ruskies, paranoid Yankees, foolish Brits pretending they knew it all. Mossad knocking off whomever they pleased. The French jittery because they had big money involved. Nuclear contracts. Dangerous times. Full of menace. All very exciting. Now the reason I was in Paris was because of your aunt.'

'Amina?'

'The very same.'

'Why? What were you doing there? You were part …?' Vicki pulled herself free.

'No, of course not. Of course not. For heaven's sake, Vicki. What do you think I am? I wasn't a field agent. I was never an agent. I wasn't there to kill her.'

'You were BOSS, the Security Branch.'

'Well, not exactly, no, not part of them at all, actually. National Intelligence Service as it was then. Very different. Very different type of people. Very different spectrum of operations. More about keeping things together than blowing them apart. Reason I was in Paris was because of what I had heard. You see I had had word from Detlef …'

'Detlef? Detlef Schroeder?' Vicki stopped. 'What's this about, Henry? What's this got to do with my being followed? With the bloody bergie behind us?'

Henry Davidson took her arm again. 'Our bloody bergie is watching. Best to go on and have that coffee. Advisable not to get him all excited.'

Vicki allowed the pressure at her elbow to propel her forward, thinking, now what? Bloody Henry and his damn stories. Where was he going with this one? Always some twisted fable, some Alice in Wonderland quotation.

'I've got a letter for you from Detlef,' he was saying. Pointed at an outside table, towards the back. 'That should do nicely.' No early breakfasters anyhow. 'We can keep an eye on our friend. And even if he has some listening device, we're going to be out of range, I would imagine.'

Vicki about to say, Detlef Schroeder's dead. I saw his body, remember. Instead ordered a double espresso. Henry a latte.

'Yes, Detlef's letter. It came a few days ago. Not sure why it has taken so long, but it has. Sorry, I should have given it to you earlier, I should have. Slipped my mind what with the goings-on.'

Like hell, thought Vicki. You wanted the right time to put it into play.

'It came to you? For me?'

'Yes. Nothing mysterious in that. An old network of Detlef's that we used now and again, in the dangerous times. I don't know. This occasion you cannot say it was very efficient, took a while. Rusty cogs in the old machinery.'

'Well? Where is it? I want to read it.'

'Not that simple, Vicki.' He dug in his trouser pocket, took out a key. 'This is for a post-office box. At the central post office. A facility I have had for years, for documents I would rather no one else knew about.'

She held out her hand, closed the key into her palm.

'Look, another thing you need to know is this.' Henry Davidson patted his hair, cleared his throat. 'Confession time. Mea culpa. Actually, I was not only working for the NIS. I had other, shall we call them, irons in some fires.'

Vicki laughed. 'Wouldn't have doubted it for a moment.' Then got serious: 'What sort of irons? Which fires?'

'Sealed lips. Cannot spill the beans,' said Henry Davidson. Pursed his lips, put a finger to them. 'Top secret. Fifty-year embargo.'

Vicki shook her head. 'Jesus, Henry, just stop giving me half the story.' Sat back, feeling the plastic chair hard against her shoulder blades. 'I mean what have you told me? You were in Paris when my aunt was killed. Why, I don't know. You might have been a double agent, for whom, I don't know. You and Detlef Schroeder had a secret network, why, I don't know. It doesn't faze you that I'm under surveillance, probably by our own people. But you're not going to tell me who. Or why.'

'Ah.' Henry Davidson wagged a finger. 'I did not say I would not tell you who.'

'Who then?'

'Coffee first.' Beamed at the waitress. 'How kind. You wouldn't have a currant bun you could butter for me, would you?'

The waitress bit her lower lip. 'No, sir. Sorries.'

'Pity. There was something satisfying about a currant bun in the middle of the morning.'

'We have the cupcakes. Vanilla. Chocolate. Strawberry.' The waitress smiled hopefully.

'Too sweet. Much, much, much too sweet.' Henry Davidson pointed at the coffees. 'This will do. Thank you.' Waiting while she backed away. 'Such a shame about the demise of the currant bun. Nobody appreciates those sorts of buns anymore, I have to say. Where can you get a currant bun in a café these days? You have to wait until Easter. For the rest of the year there are only these damned sweet things. No wonder we wobble around like a nation of blobs.'

Vicki tasted the coffee. Not French roast but you could drink it. 'You going to tell me now?'

'I am. First another confession. In Schiphol, those SMSes to Linda Nchaba's cellphone, that was me.'

'You? You bastard!'

'Wanting to hurry things along, Vicki. Make things easier for you. Looking after your welfare, you know. Anyhow, as things go, not a big intervention. Nothing like taking her away on a stretcher. That was not my doing.'

'Whose then?'

'I have an idea, as I was told soon enough where she was.'

'Well who told you?'

'Above your pay grade for the moment.'

Vicki holding hard to her temper, feeling an anger flushing heat through her body. Heard him saying, 'Probably a chap called Kaiser Vula behind our bergie. Major Kaiser Vula to give him his rank. From our very own Agency, indeed. Formerly military intelligence. Which is another story all of its own.'

'Probably? You don't know for sure?'

'Nothing is for sure in this business, Vicki. I'm assuming he is watching me. If that is so, then he is also watching you to see what I might be up to.'

'Why? Why's he watching you?'

'It is what we do. We are in opposing camps, so to speak. From what I hear the good major is as tight as a remora with the president and the president's number-one son, Zama. The son without a mother. I drop that in as a titbit. Probably the major is the mastermind behind the botched assassination of Colonel Kolingba of the Central African Republic. Whose wife, Cynthia Kolingba is now, to all intents and purposes, as we speak, running that vicious little country. Where, another titbit, the president has considerable mining interests. Where our soldiers are playing war games to keep his mining interests safe. The pieces all fitting together now, ummm?'

Everywhere the Zama connections. Vicki finished off her espresso in a mouthful. Tasted burnt. The kickback harsh. Said, 'You were going to tell me this?'

'Naturally. Of course. But until now it has not exactly been necessary.'

'Like it hasn't exactly been necessary to show me the rest of the videos on the flash drive.'

'You should not even have seen the ones you did.'

'But I did. With Linda in Amsterdam. She showed me. There're important people involved, aren't there? Important European people. Politicians I recognised. Probably also businessmen. The cosseted rich. And what else's on the other clips? More about the trafficking?'

'Again, need-to-know rule. Sorry about that. No, not sorry. You do not want to know any more than you do. Believe me.

You do not want to know what certain people are getting up to. Fingers in pies. As Alice noticed, "Every single thing's crooked."' Henry Davidson giving a mirthless grin. 'Back to the situation in hand: Linda. Linda is still our little secret.'

'We've got to get her out this weekend.'

'That is the plan, is it not? Just got to fly with it until the right moment. Timing, Vicki. Timing is everything.'

Vicki let that settle. Could come back to it. Went with: 'Why were you in Paris?'

'Excellent question. Flick back to confuse the interviewee.' A forced grin. 'Following up on our, on my, intelligence.'

'Much good it did.'

'That was the surprising thing, Vicki. There I am on the banks of the Seine on this beautiful day with a French secret-service fellow lighting a cigarette not half a dozen paces away, when, voila, he disappears. Like the Cheshire cat leaving only his smile. Well, metaphorically speaking, you understand. I have no clear idea what happened. Maybe he had a pager. If he did I do not believe I heard it go off, did not see him look at it. Thing is right then and there, a couple of moments after I had spotted him, he walked away. Disappeared among the Sunday strollers. Never saw him again. Never had anybody following me afterwards. Couple of hours later I heard about your aunt being killed in the Metro. I worked out that it must have happened while I was walking beside the river. Once it was done no one needed to follow me anymore. That is why my French companion took off. Could now go to the park for a game of boules.' Henry Davidson raised his eyebrows, took a sip at the latte.

Vicki looked off over the foliage. No sign of the bergie. Said, 'I'm confused. You're telling me you knew she was to be killed, that the French were in on it. You didn't think to warn her?'

'We had no confirmed intelligence. Nothing was certain.

That was the thing, you see. It could have been our very own dogs or some township special from uMkhonto we Sizwe or a French poodle even. Or maybe it was all bow-wow, the intelligence that we had.'

'But it wasn't.'

'No, in the end, it was not, unfortunately. Your aunt was a target. It seems she knew too much that was disturbing to too many people. If you wanted me to guess who did it, I would say the French. But I could be wrong.' Henry Davidson drank half his latte. 'Never put quite enough coffee in these things, do they?' Patted his lips with a paper serviette. 'History, Vicki, history. Nothing we can do about history.'

'Except it haunts us.'

'It does. In strange and unexpected ways.' He reached across, patted her arm.

Avuncular Henry. The wise man about the world. Sometimes, Vicki thought, he could be such a prick.

'Enough of that matter, shall we leave it until you have read Detlef's letter? Alright? Let us move on. Let us consider now, as they say, our options. Tell me what is new on the Linda front. Or in the modern idiom, talk to me about Linda.'

'Zama's been in touch.'

Henry Davidson leant back, his toupee shifting with the sudden movement. 'But that is marvellous. Exactly what we wanted. Exactly what we expected would happen.' Smoothed a hand over his hair.

'He's after taking her for lunch.'

'Charming. Nothing wrong with that. Lovers trying to rekindle old flames. Very touching.'

Vicki caught movement out the corner of her eye: the bergie being shooed off by the waitress. 'She's scared of him.'

'Yes. Yes, I could see she would be. He has taken his time getting in touch with her. I was beginning to wonder ...' Henry

Davidson smiled at the protesting bergie. 'You would think he really was a vagrant, would you not? Good for him, getting into the act.'

'Also he's going to do the auction on Sunday. I think I should be there. When we get her out.'

His eyes flicking back to her, assessing her. Vicki held his gaze. 'Do you now? You don't say.' A pause. He signalled the waitress for the bill. 'Ummm. I wonder. Put you in the field again. I wonder.' Then a sudden: 'Alright. If that is what you want. Alright, then why not try it? But you do not get her out until I say so.'

'What about my watchers?'

'What about them? Poor chappies.'

'Henry! Be serious.'

'They are doing a job, Vicki. Let them be. Better to know where they are. So much easier to get rid of them when you really need to. Who knows, they might even come in useful.' Smiled at her, that fleeting all-knowing irritating smile. Made Vicki grind her teeth.

17

Prosper Mtethu phoned Cynthia Kolingba. As arranged.

'Every night you go off duty, you call me,' she'd ordered. 'If I don't answer, you leave a message. I want to know his condition.'

Every evening, same time, Prosper Mtethu sat at a table in the hospital café, made the call.

'Quickly, Prosper,' she said.

Prosper heard engine noise, voices on a two-way radio.

'He is fine.' Said it every evening. He is fine.

'No change?'

'They say a stable condition.'

'Good. How's your lovely granddaughter?' A question she'd asked every evening from the time he'd first told her about his home life. 'You're proud of her,' she'd said then. 'I like that, Prosper. You're a good man.'

Every evening he would smile as he replied: 'Fine. She is fine thank you.'

'Look after her. She is lucky she has you, Tata.' Using the colloquial. Then the polite goodbye.

Prosper wondered what she felt, half a continent away, fighting a bush war? Not an easy one. Her sons in a safehouse somewhere, her man a vegetable, her daughter dead. Because of what he Agent Prosper Mtethu had been ordered to do. A stain on his conscience. A stain he would wipe away.

Every evening Prosper ordered a toasted cheese sandwich, a can of iced rooibos tea. Sat at a back table eating.

This evening his thoughts on the blond man. Who was the guy? How'd he got the photographs? Why now? Took the photographs from the envelope. Day of the hit: fuzzy but good enough, Prosper Mtethu behind the wheel of the white Honda. This shot a zoom-in. You pulled back, you'd see the field men, the colonel going down, the little girl collapsing.

The other photograph more recent, six weeks ago, after he'd left the Agency. Someone keeping track.

Had to be SSA. Had to be expected. Question: Why leak it to some mlungu surfer-type?

The blondie'd said he worked for Cynthia Kolingba, knew of Joey Curtains. Prosper upended the envelope, out slid Fish Pescado's business card. Time for another talk.

On his phone the blondie's picture: straw hair, tanned skin. Prosper about to finish his toasted sandwich, he saw Major Kaiser Vula walk across the foyer to the lifts.

Prosper Mtethu put away the photographs, pocketed his phone, sat there with the last of his iced tea, waiting. Not a long wait. Four, five minutes, give or take. Reckoned the major must have gone to ICU, checked on the patient, come right back out again. Hadn't happened in months. Why the sudden interest? Why the same day blondie comes round?

Prosper watched his former boss step from the lifts, leave the building. Decided wouldn't be a bad idea to check on the colonel.

All well in ICU.

The nurses telling him, 'Go home, Prosper. You got your men here. Relax. The colonel's fine.'

He was: the monitors beeping; the IV lines feeding him.

Prosper Mtethu called it a day. Sat in his car, pondering. Took out Fish Pescado's card, tapped it against the steering wheel. Decided, if you don't phone, you don't know shit.

When Fish Pescado answered, said, 'We need to talk.'

Fish Pescado coming back, 'Hallelujah, Joseph and Mary. Has to be Mr Muscle. Guess what? That's why I came to see you.'

Prosper biting down on the sarcasm. 'We can meet now.'

'We can. Only supper time. But what the hell. What's that in a life of action and derring-do? I can nuke a lasagne as well later as now.'

'You know some place?'

'I'm guessing you're knocking off. Still at the hospital.' A pause. Prosper waited it out. 'How about the Toad on the Road?'

'Fifteen minutes,' said Prosper Mtethu. 'You better be there.'

Phoned his granddaughter.

'Khulu, I'm at home. Don't worry.' Her voice easing the tension in his shoulders. As she could do. The only woman who'd ever brought him comfort.

'I will be late,' he said.

'That's cool. No probs.' Sounding more like a TV star than his Nolitha, the teenager he'd raised for ten years. Seen her through the grief of her parents' deaths.

'There's food ...' he started to say.

'Eaten already.' Her chatter taking off into her school day, the results of a test, her tennis practice. Prosper listened as he always did to this world he couldn't imagine. Her enthusiasm for it. Eventually broke in.

'Don't stay awake for me, sisi.'

'You've got a date? Oh wow! What's she like?'

Prosper laughed. 'A blondie,' he said.

18

Fish's cellphone rang: the patch through to Vicki's apartment. Vicki's voice saying, 'Linda, I'm flying in tomorrow. Yes, really.'

Linda? Fish thinking, Linda? Linda? Linda? Could be the Linda he'd tracked down those weeks ago. The model? Never had got to hear the rest of that story from Vicki. The only time he'd raised it, she'd ducked and dived. Then the curtains'd come down.

Fish paused, about to head out for the Toad. Prosper could wait a few minutes.

Flying in?

That Linda had been Durban-based.

Vicki saying, 'What? The Walrus? That's okay.'

The Walrus? Who, what was the Walrus?

'You're at lunch that's fine. What'd he say? Mm-hmm. Mm. Play it cool. Don't turn him off.'

Play the Walrus cool? Fish thinking, who else was hearing

this? Mart Velaze's warning coming to mind, 'Your mate Vicki Kahn's deep in the shit, like she doesn't even know how deep.' Case in point the bergie doing surveillance, had to be one of the lurgies from the dark side. Vicki kept on talking to Linda most of the Agency would know her plans. Then the thought: Maybe that's what she wanted? Keep everyone watching her happy.

'I'm not going to get there till the afternoon, anyhow.'

Fish thought, me too, Vics. Gonna be your guardian angel on this one.

Vicki said, 'I'm hiring a car. The drive up's what? An hour, hour and a half?'

Fish reckoning, chances were he could get the first flight out, be ahead of her. Tag in behind as she left the hire-car zone. Hour and a half's drive put the destination somewhere in the Midlands or up the North Coast.

Vicki now doing the rev. 'It's going to be alright, Linda. It's going to be fine.' Listening.

Fish thinking, the last thing it sounded like was alright. Sounded like a beach break. Fast, hollow, closed out with a bonecrusher.

'No contact, okay. No contact. You don't call me, I call you. Promise me. No, you got to promise me.'

Fish shut the back door, locked it. Walked quickly to the Isuzu.

'Linda. Linda. Stop. We're watching, okay. Just keep your phone on. We've got this covered.'

Got what covered? The Agency'd got it covered? The Agency couldn't cover its arse at a baby shower.

Fish fired up the Isuzu.

'This weekend it'll be all over. That's the idea. Just hang in there. I know, Linda, I know. The girls too, sure, of course.'

The girls?

Fish thinking, what sort of girls? Models? Had to be, in Linda's line of work.

'I'm going now, okay. I'm going to ring off.'

Fish heard the goodbyes, the last, 'Yes, I'll be at the party.'

The party?

Estelle had mentioned a party at the palace. Hour and a half from the airport you'd be somewhere near the palace. Could be. Could be.

Vicki heading for the Bambatha party as part of a spook brigade? Official SSA security. Made sense.

Fish thought, phone Estelle. Contract his services as a bodyguard. Businessmen like the Chinese had to have bodyguards.

Heard Vicki saying, 'Jesus, Linda, just keep it together.' Feeling certain Vicki was talking to herself.

Only then thought, bit tacky stalking her.

Her phone again.

'Henry. You've read the letter, I assume.'

Fish thinking: China, you're in the kak. Wished he could hear this one out. But no time. Didn't want to leave Prosper having second thoughts.

19

'Henry. You've read the letter, I assume.'

'What do you think, Vicki? Of course I read it. A letter comes for you from a dead Detlef Schroeder, I am going to read it. Obliged to read it, you know.'

'I don't know. How can I know? You didn't tell me. I don't get why you didn't tell me earlier. It's my letter. A personal letter.' Vicki walked about her apartment, touching surfaces, avoiding the letter from Detlef lying on the coffee table. Avoiding it, but her eyes drawn to the flimsy paper. The neat blue handwriting, sloping right. Nothing weak or shaky in the form of the letters. Nothing to presage his death.

'Well, hardly.'

'Concerning my family.'

'I would have thought it was more than that.'

'My aunt.'

'I would have thought otherwise. Given the people who are involved. I would have thought there were concerning issues here.'

'Concerning issues. That's nice. Concerning issues. Like the killing of my aunt. Her possible rape by the man now our president. The fact that she might have had his child.'

'Conjecture, Vicki.'

'Which part?'

'You know which part.'

'It adds up.'

'In the mind of an old Cold War spy, a paranoid old Cold War spy miffed that his lover might have had a one-night stand.'

'And was then mysteriously redeployed.' Vicki stood in front of the photograph of Amina Kahn. The wind in her hair. Her arms open wide. A carefree moment in a harsh time.

'For which there were probably very good reasons.'

'Pregnancy being one of them.'

'Supposition. Remember that the pigeon thought Alice was a serpent.'

'What? Jesus, Henry. I don't know what you're talking about.'

'Supposition. I am talking about making assumptions. Deducing one thing from another. Incorrectly.'

'Whatever. I can find out, you know. There will be records.'

'In Botswana? Going back thirty years! Good luck to you. Leave it, Vicki. There is nothing to be gained.'

'In learning that our target is my relative, you mean?' A silence. Vicki waited. Wondered what Henry Davidson was doing. Where was he? Probably in his chair, a discarded supper tray at his feet. A glass of whisky on the chair arm. Inevitably. She tried the oblique.

'Why was he killed? Detlef?'

Imagined a slow shake of his head. 'I am too old for that one, Vicki. Very sad, though. Very sad.'

She ignored this. Said, 'Was it us?'

'Oh, God, no. We wouldn't do a thing like that. What for, for heaven's sake? No, no, it wasn't us. I don't know who it was. Or why. Detlef was an international man of mystery, a man with many secrets. Perhaps he was finding them difficult to contain. Trust me. We were not involved.'

'Then why didn't you give me the letter earlier?' Vicki wondering, if Detlef wasn't connected with the videos of European men on the Nchaba flash drive, why hold back the letter?

'No particular reasons.'

'So connection: Detlef and the flash-drive videos?'

'No connection. Coincidence. Separate stories. Look, I could take you off this operation.'

'You could. But then why reveal all these things?'

'Because you have a right to know.'

'At this time. A little too coincidental, wouldn't you say?'

'I would not say anything, Vicki. It is not coincidental. It is the way things happen. There are causes, there are effects. Actions and consequences. That is what we are dealing with: consequences. Now. You are off tomorrow. Sparrows, I hope?'

'Yes.'

'Good. Should be an interesting little operation. Mixing

with the great and the powerful. Watching the beautiful people at play. Get some sleep, Vicki. Keep in touch. I need reports. I need to know what is going on. And please, please stay lead-free. Things might get a little ... what is the buzzword?'

'Hectic.'

'Exactly. Hectic.'

Vicki disconnected. Sat on the arm of the couch, leant down, picked up the letter from Detlef Schroeder.

My Dear Vicki,

I have not much time so I have to tell you quickly straight away. I have told you that Amina went very suddenly to Botswana. There she was for six months when we did not have any physical contact. I have told you that afterwards she did not tell me much about her months in Gaborone. She would tell me only about her work there, about the MK soldiers and people escaping from South Africa. I have told you that it was not a happy time for her.

Yesterday I told you that after we were together in Paris at the Tuileries it was a month before we were together again in Berlin. Then some months later she goes suddenly to Botswana for some half a year. When I see her again, I said she was my same Amina. This is true but it is also not true. She was hiding some things from me. Maybe she was more quiet, more thoughtful. When I think of it now I must write that Amina was different when we met in Paris. She was not the same laughing person. In those days I did not know why.

There are some things I have found out that I did not know in those days. What I have discovered is that in Botswana Amina had a baby. This baby was a boy.

Afterwards the baby was taken to a safe place and Amina must return to Paris. In Paris when we met she is like the old Amina again but there is something not right with her. That is what I think. Of course she is joking, and happy and we are having a good time. But now I think she was acting for me, hiding her sadness. All the time she was pretending when inside there was a deep hurt. Two painful things she could not tell me.

I think the baby she had in Gaborone is the baby of the man who is now the president of your country. I think he has raped her. I have no proof of these things. But I do know she met with this man in Paris some months before she went to Gaborone. He was her boss in those days, and we know what this man's reputation is with the ladies. What I do know for certain is that Amina was pregnant and that she had a child. Of this I have proof. I have photographs. I have the documentation papers. The child was not my child. The opportunities do not match.

Then in Paris before Amina was killed I told you she met with this man Dr Gold from the old South African nationalist government who had gold bullion in Switzerland. Some of that money went to your president and his men before they were even the new government. This is not the only thing.

Amina also found out that there was other nuclear trade between the French and South Africa. Moreover there were contracts for armaments: some navy ships, some weapon systems, and maybe even some jet fighters. This was a lot of money. I know Amina knew this because she told me. I also know that Amina told this to the ANC top men. She wanted them to make this information public because of the arms embargo against

South Africa in those years of the late 1980s. She threatened if they did not go to the newspapers then she would do it.

What I write now I cannot prove. What I think happened is an arrangement between the African National Congress and the apartheid government hit squad to kill Amina. She was too dangerous to them all when she was alive. The nationalist government told the top people in the African National Congress that there was lots of money in the arms deals. They told them when they were the new government the leaders could make so much money from these deals. The man they talked to is now the president. Only your aunt Amina was in their way. It was easy in those days to sort out this type of problem. The apartheid people could make it happen.

I am sorry I have to write this for you. It would have been better if I could tell you this story in the way we were talking yesterday. Unfortunately other things in my life make this impossible.

It would be nice if we could meet again but I do not think this will happen.

Thank you for coming to visit here with me yesterday. You brought comfort to an old man, and you stirred up memories. You are so much like Amina. You remember I told you yesterday, you are the spitting image.

So much like Amina.

Dead Amina. Assassinated Amina. Amina who'd abandoned a child. Though it would have been better had he, too, been aborted.

Vicki stood, a sudden pounding in her chest. Flashed back to the gynaecologist leaning over her. 'You can go now, Ms Kahn, that's sorted.' *That. Sorted.*

Now she grabbed her car keys, rushed out. In the basement parking fired up the red Alfa MiTo, headed into the night. Took De Waal Drive, going too fast through the corners, hearing tyre squeal even above Melissa Etheridge. Melissa singing about it being too dark to see. About falling up. About flying or dying. About the darkness in front. The MiTo's headlights cutting into the night down the highway, the mountains coming at her. End of the highway, Vicki thought, what am I doing here? Like she was on autopilot headed for Fish.

Melissa sang about having a heavy heart.

She could go to him. Be there in five minutes. Confess all. Her body wanted to. Wanted to press Fish against her, wanted to hold him, have him hold her. Skin to skin.

Her mind said, no. You are an agent of the state. You have commitments. Obligations. Responsibilities. You have put your life aside. There are the girls. Fish would have to wait.

At the end of the highway she turned round, drove back to town.

Melissa sang about falling off the edge.

In the quiet of her apartment, Vicki opened her laptop, logged onto 888poker. Just for an hour, to wind down.

20

Cape Town International Airport, 19:30

Kaiser Vula watched the queue shuffle past the boarding desks, the airline staff telling passengers to have a good flight. The passengers rumpled businesspeople at the end of a long day. The major stood aside to make the call. Spoke softly into the phone.

'We can meet at Majuba whenever it is convenient.'

'Tomorrow. Tomorrow for lunch would be suitable. I will make a reservation.'

No hint of gratitude. No note of relief. Just the agreed code. 'Very good,' said Kaiser Vula. 'I hope the weather is fine.'

'The forecast is promising.'

'Until we meet.'

Kaiser Vula about to disconnect.

'Have you heard of a Vicki Kahn?'

'No.'

'From what I have been informed she works in your Cape Town office. We have also found out she makes a lot of phone calls to a certain person. And she gets a lot of phone calls from that person.'

Kaiser Vula thinking, Zama had other sources in the Agency. The cunning jackal. Everyone spying on everyone else. Trouble with Zama he had to go off-script. Could be anyone listening in. How often hadn't he warned about it? Cleared his throat now, wanting to close down the conversation. 'You would like to change the arrangements?'

'No. We can discuss this at lunch. Everything is in order, my friend. She is coming to us. But I have an auction on Sunday. I do not want her causing problems.'

The line went dead.

Kaiser Vula keyed off, noticed one missed call: Cynthia Kolingba. There would be time for Cynthia Kolingba, but not now. Switched off his phone, headed for the boarding gate.

Thinking, was it possible, someone in the Agency running Linda Nchaba? This Vicki Kahn running Nchaba. What for? To get close to Zama? To get another line into the presidency? That was the trouble with the Agency, too many hidden agendas.

At cruising altitude, Kaiser Vula ordered a whisky and soda. Pushed his seat back. Zama had said, 'I have been informed …' Meant he had another source in the Agency. Or someone in the Agency passing on information. This the more likely scenario. Some shit-stirrer with maybe no higher motive than making quick bucks. Trouble was there was always something to sell. Always someone willing to buy.

He finished the whisky, closed his eyes. Not a weekend he looked forward to. A too-confident president. The so-called communist threat. The call back to Cynthia Kolingba. The lovely Nandi parading her sweet body.

21

Fish Pescado said to Prosper Mtethu, 'You were SSA?'

The two of them in the Toad on the Road: the pub jumping, a rugby match on the widescreen. The pub's team chalked high to win. Sighs and yells with every breath.

Fish focused on Prosper. Not a twitch of his lips. No movement in his face. Thinking maybe he should've chosen a quieter place. People bumping past their table to get to the loos. Laughing, joking people stoked on the moment. Fish shook off apologies, pulled his chair into the table. 'You're Agency?'

Prosper didn't say yes or no. Sipped his beer.

'That's a question.' Fish leant forward, watched Prosper wipe a hand over his mouth.

'It doesn't matter.'

'It bloody does.'

'Now I'm not.'

'Ah, so that means once you were. Like when this picture was taken you were.' Fish stabbed his finger at the close-up of Prosper in the car.

'Already I have told you, what does it matter?' Prosper's mumble inaudible under the roar of the pub.

'What? What're you saying?'

Prosper waved a hand. 'It does not matter. This is not important.'

'It bloody is, my china. Who took this picture, Prosper? Why? Why was it taken? Why do I even have these pictures?'

'That is the question I must ask you.'

Fair enough. Fish gave it some thought. 'A trade?'

'That is why we are here?' The man not even looking at him. Gazing at the enraptured drinkers.

'You phoned me. You first.'

'No, my friend. It was you who found me. We must start from there.'

Fish ran his fingers through the damp ring on the table. Decided, what the hell. Break the impasse. Decided to give up Mart Velaze. 'You know the name Mart Velaze?'

Again the slow response from Prosper. The drink. The hand over the lips. 'I can say maybe.'

'I'll take that as a yes.'

'Is it from him, these pictures?'

Fish laughed. 'We're trading here, bru. I need something first. You understand me? I need something. Like where was this taken?'

With his head down, Prosper said, 'I was the driver.'

Fish caught the word driver. 'I can see that. I'm not a complete stupid moegoe. I can see you're sitting behind the steering wheel. But where's this? What's happening here? Actually, really happening. Is it what I think?'

'Kolingba.'

Fish heard that. Clearly heard that. Sat up. 'Faaaack. You're kidding me?' Impressed that he'd got it right.

A shake of the head from Prosper.

'And now you're working for her. Protecting him. No. No. That's fucked up, my bru. That's radical. Way too radical.' Fish laughed again. 'I don't bloody believe it.' He took a large draw on his beer. 'You're telling me you were there on an Agency operation. Couple of weeks later they let you go'n become hired security for their target? You want me to credit that? You're still working for SSA. You have to be.'

'I have told you the truth.'

Fish stared at him. Nothing in those eyes: no open window to the soul there. Perhaps a sadness in the sag of his face. That sort of Labrador look. 'Okay, let's go with that. So why'd Mart Velaze give these to me to out you? What's all that about?'

'The president.'

'The president? He ordered this? You're telling me he ordered the hit?'

Prosper drained his beer, stood. 'My friend, finish your drink, we can have a short drive in my car. It will be easier to talk then.'

They drove up Boyes Drive, Fish waiting for Prosper to break the silence. Looked out at the blaze of lights strung down the peninsula, thinking, come on, dude, what's it about?

At the Shark Spotters lookout Prosper drove onto the pavement. A couple in the opposite lay-by sucking face. Just asking for it, someone to come tapping on the window with a gun.

Prosper switched off the ignition, pointed at the sea way below. 'You go surfing down there, with the sharks?'

'Yeah,' said Fish.

'You seen sharks?'

'Yeah,' said Fish.

'You not worried about them?'

'No hassles,' said Fish.

'Wena, my friend, you abelungu.' He tapped his head. 'Crazy white people.'

Fish left it at that, didn't feel the need of a response. Heard Prosper sigh.

'Okay. I will tell you. This thing is about money. Always it is about money. You understand, in the Struggle days, there was never money. Our friends, Mugabe, Kaunda, Qaddafi, they have to help us with so many things. Some give weapons. Some give refuge. Some give money. Some give us investments in mining. In diamonds, gold, other minerals. Now our president has those investments in the CAR. Colonel Kolingba is a threat for him. His rebels can make a coup in the CAR that can make a big problem. Our president does not want this. Also the president wants to help his old friend the president in the CAR.'

'By shooting the colonel.'

Too dark for Fish to see any reaction on Prosper's face.

'Then there is a coup in the CAR, everything is upside down.'

'This is Africa. Shit happens.'

'But the man Colonel Kolingba, he is a good man.'

Fish came in. 'You reckon, hey?'

'It is why I work for him.'

'Doesn't tell me why Mart Velaze hooked us up.'

'We are not hooked up. He is pushing me against the president, this Velaze.'

'I'm lost here, Prosper. Help me out. Why'd he do that?'

Prosper left a long gap. Fish waiting. Three cars came past, headlights sweeping over them. In the dark again, said, 'There are people against the president. They don't want him to be there anymore.'

'People in SSA?'

'SSA. Even in the cabinet. In the movement. Many are communists.'

'They want a coup? Here. In our democracy.'

'A coup? A coup? What is a coup? We call it a redeployment. For this occasion they want someone for the job.'

Fish wondered if he was on the right wave here. Reckoning Prosper was talking about a hit. 'You. They want you for the job, a triggerman?'

'Me.' Another exhalation of breath.

'Why?'

Prosper laughed. 'That is a story from a long time ago.'

'I'm in no hurry.'

'No. It is not a story for you.'

'Okay. Then will you take the job?'

Prosper's phone rang. 'My friend, you think I will tell you?'

Fish watched him squirm about to get the phone out of a pocket. 'Leaves one more question, why'm I the messenger boy?'

Prosper squinted at the phone's screen. Shook his head. 'For that answer you must ask Mart Velaze.' Swore. Clicked on the phone. Said, 'Ma'am.'

Fish could hear the voice of Cynthia Kolingba.

Heard Prosper say, 'You can phone me later. At any time.' He disconnected, stared into the darkness. Said, 'The colonel, he is dead.'

22

Cape Town International Airport, 20:45

'Interesting, Chief,' said the Voice. 'Nice bit of initiative on your part.'

Mart Velaze gritting his teeth at the sarcasm.

'Going to cause some … what do the Yanks call it? They've got that sexy word. You'd think they had someone at Langley making up the lingo to keep them hip. Blow something, isn't it?'

'Blowback.'

The Voice clucked her tongue. 'That's it. I was thinking of blowjob. Blowback. Good one, Chief. Nice. Going to be some consequences to this demise I would say. Yes, yes …' The Voice drifting off.

Mart Velaze waited. Nothing else to do anyhow, Mart Velaze sitting in the holding pen at gate nine. Had been there long enough to see Major Vula take an earlier Durban plane. Both of them heading to the same destination. The birds were flocking.

The Voice said, 'Sometimes it makes you wonder what sort of intervention we're talking: divine or secular. What's your leaning, Chief? You favour the colonel was ushered out of the building? Or're we talking natural causes? Organ failure? Not as if the colonel wasn't on a waiting list. Hadn't been toeing the precipice for some weeks now. Don't answer that.'

Mart Velaze wasn't going to.

'Rather keep me in the loop as and when. Be starting my own thread soon enough, to mix in some more metaphors.'

Mart Velaze said he would.

'Moving on to our man Prosper. Clearly your well-connected type of gent. What's it you know about him?'

Mart Velaze rattled off the basics: MK vet; tortured in the hellish Quatro camp because he was thought to be an apartheid spy; held there for many years, seems that might have been at the now-president's pleasure; no evidence that he was an impimpi; after the dawn of democracy was with the National Intelligence Agency, mostly a fieldworker, reliable, was the driver on the Kolingba job. Left the Aviary unexpectedly on a week's notice to guard the colonel. No history with his immediate boss, Major Vula. Nowadays on Mrs Kolingba's payroll. Political leanings more communist than Africanist. Wife deceased. Daughter deceased. Takes care of his teenage granddaughter.

'How touching,' said the Voice. 'Our Prosper gets more and more interesting.' Her voice easing off again.

Mart Velaze heard his flight called. Everyone already in a queue at the gate counter. What was it with people? Like they enjoyed standing in queues. Wasn't as if their seats weren't booked. Wasn't as if the plane would leave without them.

'Any more activity on our Prosper's phone you let me know asap. Doesn't matter what time of the night.' The Voice suddenly brightening. 'Enjoy your little weekend break in the country, Chief. Should be very interesting. But like I said, we're not active on this one. Watching only. Non-intervention. Even if the commies get their act together, you stay out of it. Don't want to hear that you saved the president, Chief. That would displease me.'

Not much chance of that, Mart Velaze could've said. But didn't.

'Be in touch tomorrow, Chief. Until then, go with the ancestors.'

Mart Velaze disconnected. Joined the queue.

23

Cape Town International Airport, 09:45

Vicki in the terminal building waiting to board, phoned Linda. Was worried Linda'd back out. That during the night she'd change her mind. Maybe even do a runner.

Stared out over the planes, across the apron to the mountain ridge. The blue Hottentots Holland mountains buttressed against the sky. This morning the colour of riesling. The sort of day you didn't want to leave the city.

She counted the rings. Five, six, seven.

A sleepy voice. 'What time is it?'

'Late. I'm on my way. Be there in two hours. We need to meet this afternoon.'

The sound of Linda yawning. 'I've got lunch. Remember. With the Walrus.'

'I hadn't forgotten. It's not something I could forget. Afterwards is fine.'

Another yawn. 'Oh, God, why'm I yawning? I've slept for seven hours. I can put him off if you want.'

Vicki heard her flight called, saw the airline staff open the gates, passengers crowding forward. 'No you can't. You know you can't. We've got to keep everything as it is. Stay with this, Linda. Stay with it please.'

'You don't know what it's like. What he's like.'

'No, I don't, which is why I'm going to be there.' Vicki angled away from the passengers, leant against the glass. Chiding herself. She should have gone earlier. Days ago. It was wrong to leave her alone. Henry'd screwed up. Not like Linda was a trained agent. Trading on her guilt, her shame, her commitment to the girls, to keep them safe, stop the trafficking wasn't enough. Not with Zama now working the fear factor. The other thing that worried Vicki: that Zama was onto Linda. He'd been quiet for so long, had to've been watching her in that time. Checking her out, making sure she wasn't a trap. In that time could have picked up a link between Linda and herself, tracked her back to the Agency. Which might be another reason for the surveillance.

'When you know where you're meeting for lunch, SMS me.'

'What if he just pitches?'

'You tell him you'll go in your own car. Come'n, Linda,

we've been through this: you go in your own car. Don't let him drive you. How many times? Your own car.'

'It's not that easy.'

'It is. You give him grief, give him some of your sharp tongue.' Vicki joined the tail end of the queue. 'I've got to go now. Remember, you SMS me, let me know what's going on. We'll meet this afternoon.'

'Where?'

'That's my worry. I'll organise something.' Vicki wishing her good luck, disconnected. Smiled at the flight attendant scanning her boarding pass.

At cruising altitude Vicki thumbed listlessly through the in-flight magazine. Decided four of a kind with a kicker to a straight flush this thing would go badly. Linda wouldn't hold up. Zama was playing good cards. Then again there was always the final twist. You could come through on the final twist. Brought a dryness to Vicki's mouth. An increase in her heart rate. An anticipation.

24

'You know who did it?'

Prosper Mtethu on the hands-free hunched forward over the steering wheel, said, yes, he did. A long silence. No background noises. As if they'd been disconnected. He waited. Then could hear her breathing, a tapping of a fingernail against wood.

'You are sure?'

'I am.'

'Your people, not mine?'

Prosper nodding to himself. His 'Ja' more a grunt than a word.

All night, he had expected her call. As he drove into the dark between towns, knew she would phone. Knew what she would ask. Knew that he would not say no. Why else was he on the road if not for this purpose?

'It is the same people?'

He told her, yes. The same people who killed her child.

'Why have they done it?'

To that had an answer. But no answer for her.

'It is never enough. Always there is something else these people want. More money. More power. More women. More of everything.' He heard her sigh. 'Do you think we are like them, Prosper?' Again a silence. 'Do you think I am like them? That I am killing for power?'

Prosper kept his eyes on the narrow road. Burning, tired eyes. He should pull over, sleep. Twenty minutes would be enough.

He'd expected her to phone earlier, not wait until the morning. Would rather have spoken to her in the dark. Conspirators conspiring. Would rather not have had this conversation in the banal light of midday.

Prosper Mtethu shifted up his sunglasses, pinched the bridge of his nose, felt a grittiness in the corners of his eyes. Just twenty minutes. Maybe he should stop.

Here the traffic was occasional. Goats, cattle that strayed onto the road a greater hazard. You lost concentration, you ended up in a cow's stomach.

All through the night he'd thought of men who'd killed in this terrain. Of the men who'd died among the aloes. For what? For this empty frontier. These game farms. These hunting lodges. These safari parks.

Land. Always blood for land.

The colonel had died for land. Now his wife was killing for it. For the power to rule those who lived upon it.

'I could walk away, Prosper,' she was saying. 'Leave here, be in exile with my sons. Watch them grow up. One day play with my grandchildren. I could forget this country. I could live another life. Have a successful career in science. Attend conferences. Write papers. Live without fear. United States. United Kingdom. Europe.'

You could not, thought Prosper. We cannot live other lives. We have no options. There is no choice. There is only the life we get. Why else was he here now, in this car, on this road? In his bag a gun.

'But it is not to be, is it Prosper? You and I are not those sorts of people. We have surrendered our lives.'

Prosper slowed at a widening in the road, pulled off the tar onto the verge, the dirt crunching beneath the tyres. Here was the top of the world. The hill sloped away, dropped into a gorge. In that, he knew, there'd be a river. Women washing clothes. Laughing. Their constant chatter. Children playing in the pools. Scenes from his early life. The way things had ever been. Until it was not like that anymore.

Until policemen with dogs came for him.

Hunted him. Forced him to flee.

Until he returned, a soldier. A killer.

'You do not have to do this for me, Prosper,' she said. 'You know that? You understand that?'

'I know that.'

'But you are going to do it?'

'Yes. There are others …' Left it there.

She said, 'I see.'

Others. The other. Who'd given him the order. Paid him a fee. Supplied the weapon, the ammunition. Told him it had to be done now. This weekend. That there was no alternative. That the man had become a dictator. His family out of control.

She said, 'That does not change our arrangement. What we have agreed is between us.'

Prosper switched off the ignition. A quiet flooding in. Didn't respond to her. Could not say thank you.

Heard her say, 'I am going to take over their holdings. The mines, the businesses, all the assets. They have stolen enough.'

Again a silence.

'We should not talk anymore, Prosper. Goodbye. Au revoir, my friend. You are a good man. A man of conscience. Your granddaughter will be proud of you. I will ensure.' Disconnected before he could reply.

Prosper got out of the car. Stood beside it, gazing across the valleys. Drew air into his lungs, roared it out: 'Yakhal'inkomo!' The bellow of the ox before slaughter. The sound echoing, becoming muted, distant.

25

Fish waited three hours in King Shaka International Airport. Some of the time at a coffee shop, some of the time strolling around the terminal, an activity you could do in twenty minutes. Not much happening in King Shaka International Airport this time of a Saturday morning. Did allow him to check out the scene. No welcoming committee, unless they were cleaners. Only drawback, he was on a lot of video footage.

A Joburg flight landed. Fish saw faces he recognised: MPS, DGS, business people. Smiling faces. People in a happy mood. Party people.

Among them his mother. Everything-under-control Estelle. Meeting the security muscle. Gathering the baggage. Shepherding her Chinese businessmen towards a black Benz at the entrance. Estelle, playing the organiser in a cotton summer dress, bold green-and-gold flower pattern, mid-length hem, a deep v-neck. Trust his mother to put her boobs out there. Hard to tell her age, given the blonde bob, the way she moved. No underarm sag noticeable. Even her face, people thought she'd done a Botox. 'This's me,' she'd say. 'Original me' – putting the back of her fingers under her chin, on show. Now glancing around, her cellphone to her ear.

His phone rang: Estelle.

'Where are you, Bartolomeu? I thought you would be at the airport. If you're supposed to be part of my security, you should have been at the airport.'

'Catch you later, Mom,' he said. 'At the palace. Can't talk now.' Hoping there'd be no tannoy announcement to give him away.

'You're being very irritating. Very mysterious, Bartolomeu. We had an arrangement. At least, I thought we had an arrangement. You should stick to your commitments.'

'Something unexpected. Cheers, okay?' Watched her open the Merc's passenger door, put one elegant foot inside, scanning the surrounds as if she felt his presence. Uncanny. Her free hand shading her eyes.

'You'd better be there. I've put you on the security list. They're expecting you. Four o'clock all security're supposed to be on site. Signed in. Kosher. Don't disappoint me, Barto. Don't make things difficult. You know what security's like at these affairs. Everyone gets jumpy if there's a hitch.'

'Don't worry, I'll be there.' No reason he shouldn't if Vicki stayed on point. All depended on her, really. Heard his mother's goodbye as she slid onto the leather seat. The door closed, the car pulled slowly away. Over the tannoy, the arrival of the Cape Town flight announced.

Fish grinned. Lucky escape. Time to rock 'n roll.

For the next forty-five minutes sat in a white vw Polo in the hire-car lot. The humidity higher than comfortable for April:

caused a sogginess in his armpits, put a sheen on his face. Five rows ahead, the Toyota Corolla that'd been reserved for Vicki Kahn. Amazing the sort of info you could charm out of the dispatchers.

What he wanted was to see Vicki drive away, know she was in the right car. Spooks could pull funny moves: change hotel rooms; change flights; change hire cars. Almost like it was a rule. Tradecraft 101: be paranoid, change your plans. Don't go with what's given you.

Fish banked on it.

Then there she was. Gorgeous, gorgeous Vicki Kahn. Brought a pressure to his chest. This woman with the long legs in skinny jeans, linen jacket over a dark T-shirt, wheeling her suitcase through the cars. You looked at her you saw a career woman right on her game. Confident. Relaxed. Coming to the Dolphin Coast for a bit of R&R. Maybe to see old friends, family. Catch up with the life she'd left behind.

Fish slid down in the seat. Thought not much chance she'd spot him anyhow. Saw her stop at a Chevrolet Cruze, pop her bag in the boot. Thought, just as well he'd waited. Vics being ultra careful. Thought, the old Vics wouldn't have dreamt of pulling such a sneaky move.

Watched her take off her jacket, lay it along the back seat. Then straighten, apply a gloss stick to her lips. Fish's eyes on her, her proximity raised a rasp in his throat. What the hell had happened that she'd drifted away from him?

He followed her out of the airport onto the highway. Enough traffic for it not to be a problem. Fish aware that if the new Vics was that careful, she'd be onto any followers soon enough. He'd worked out the route she'd take, just wanted a positive that they were both headed in the same direction. Twenty minutes later could relax. Everything going as he'd foreseen. Slotted Laurie Levine into the CD player. Hoped whatever serious shit Vicki'd got into wasn't going to play out on the motorway. Laurie hadn't sung through her first number, he saw them: two dudes in a black BM.

Realised he'd seen them way back. Twice. First time stopped on the side of the road outside the airport. Next they'd overtaken him going balls-out. Here they were, two cars ahead. Should have been halfway to paradise the speed they were doing. Fish wondering if Vicki had noticed them. Chances were. Chances were the next exit, she'd take it. Fish closed on the BM.

The next two exits Vicki sat tight, the Beemer behind her, Fish a few cars behind it. Upcoming a One Stop garage, Vicki's flicker on, the BM not indicating. Glued to her nonetheless. Put Fish in a quandary: following them in too risky, best to leave Vicki to pull her own moves.

Fifteen minutes later, at the next exit, Fish came off the highway, found the slip road back on. Waited there within sight of the motorway, hoping there'd be no traffic patrol to move him on. Fifteen minutes passed. Twenty, Fish thinking, now what? They'd got her? Take him an hour to get back there. If they had her, they had to come this way. Drummed his fingers on the steering wheel. Why were they in this shit, the two of them? Why hadn't she stayed a lawyer?

Saw then a white Chev Cruze, recognised the number plate. Fish fired the Polo, took off in a spray of gravel. The Cruze five cars ahead. No sign of the dudes in the BMW. Continued that way for ten, fifteen kilometres, Fish wondering what'd happened back at the filling station. How'd she get away? Next thing Vicki's pulling over to the side of the highway. Clever move. Would give her an opportunity to check out any followers.

Fish put foot, shifted into the fast lane, drove parallel to an old Merc towing a caravan, hid him from Vicki's sight. Trouble was, being ahead of her wasn't his plan. He slowed, went onto the hard shoulder when he no longer had sight of her in the rear-view. Stopped. Checked the map. If she was heading for Trekkersburg, he could go on, take a chance. Except Fish was no gambler. Had already got one call wrong today.

Instead slid down in the seat, angled the mirror to give him the rear view. Didn't have long to wait, Vicki in the Cruze came past at speed. Fish gave her the count of sixty, jumped out, took off the front number plate. No need to give her any advantages.

Ten kays later had her in sight, doing the speed limit. About six cars between them. Stayed that way, the speed slowing. Most of the cars overtook the Cruze. Fish dropped back. Noticed a small white car, probably a Fiat, stuck to Vicki. She'd be aware of it too.

26

The president in the bunker at the long table. Nandi on his left, her hand on his thigh. His first wife to his right, her hands in her lap, her head bowed. Major Vula standing.

Major Vula saying, 'We think this occasion must be reconsidered, Mr President.' Major Vula thinking the little bitch looked ripe for patta-patta. Always looked ready when he saw her. Her words again, 'I hate that man. I really hate him.' Wondered what had happened to that hate.

'Oh, no, impossible. You can't do that.' Nandi turning to the president. 'Please, Baba, it is all organised. This morning everybody is coming. From Joburg. Cape Town. They are flying right now. In a few hours they're here. All your people.'

'I think you must listen to the major,' said the first wife. Still she didn't look up.

'You hear them, Major. They talk different things into my ears.' The president enjoying this to Kaiser Vula's way of thinking.

Nandi talking over him, not letting up. 'No, Mama, no. This time is important. How can we tell people they must go home? Why? Why, Kaiser?'

Major Kaiser Vula thrilled at the use of his name. Kaisy, she used to call him. Darl, too. Come to me, darl. He glanced down at her. Lovelier than ever in a silky shift. The lure of her bare arms, the sheen on her skin. He could feel the velvet beneath his palm.

'You are a child,' said the first wife. 'You do not know about these things.'

'I know Major Vula. He has no reasons.'

Kaiser Vula's face flushed with embarrassment. The little bitch. These things she said.

'Also the president is ill.' The first wife saying this implacably. No love, no concern on her face.

'Baba?' Nandi caressing the president's arm.

'Mr President?' Kaiser Vula said.

A grimace passed over the president's face. 'It is nothing. Some stomach cramps. It is nothing.'

'It is a witch,' said the first wife. 'It is a witch has done this. We will find the witch.'

'Wait. Wait.' The president stood. 'Enough. I am fine. This problem is indigestion. Let me talk to the major alone.' Spoke in Zulu to his first wife. To Nandi said, 'Give me some time.'

'You promised,' she said. 'You promised me this.'

Kaiser Vula waited while the two women left the room, the first wife sweeping out ahead of Nandi.

The president sat down. 'One wife should be enough. Why do I have more?' Gestured at an opposite chair. 'Sit down, Major, tell me what the problem is.'

The major pulled out the chair, hitched his trousers as he sat. Was about to ask how serious was the president's stomach pain. Did he need a doctor?

The president held up a hand. 'Tell me first, where is Zama?'

'He is here. He has come to the palace. At the moment he is training, running in the forest.'

'With bodyguards. He is safe?'

'He is protected. We have people everywhere.'

'You are sure it is still my comrades?'

'I am sure.'

'But will they act, Major? Will they act? It is not possible to think so. They are conspirators, they like to plot and plan, they have no balls to be assassins.' He sniffed. 'We will not catch them with a smoking gun.'

'We have intelligence.'

'What is intelligence but rumours? It is what your agents want you to know. What they think you expect.'

'We cannot take risks.'

The president shrugged. 'There is security. We must trust the security. I will wear a bulletproof. What do they say in the townships? Two warning shots to the heart.' He laughed again, put a hand over his chest. 'They won't be able to do that.' Seemed to go rigid, then sighed. 'You worry too much, Major. You think, what about his head? But a head shot is difficult.' He jigged his torso from side to side, gasped again. 'See, too much movement. They will want to be sure. They will want my chest.' The president drew in a deep breath, puffed out his chest. 'Maybe we could paint a target for them?' He let the air out in a whoosh. No humour in his face. Pushed back his chair. 'Don't worry, Major. It will be okay. We are ready. I am ready. The bull doesn't hide from the jackal. There is only one way to stop this. We must catch them after the party.' Walked to the door, turned to Major Vula. 'You hear what Nandi says. This is a woman who doesn't understand no.'

'I hear,' said Major Kaiser Vula. More quietly, 'I know.'

Saw the president bend over, groan at a spasm of pain.

'Mr President. Please. Let me fetch a doctor.'

The president straightened. Massaged the side of his stomach. 'No. No. I will be alright. I am sure Nandi has medicine, sangoma's muti, for stomach problems. You know she has many powders. Without her, the witchdoctors would have no business.'

27

'Miss Nchaba, I have come to fetch you.' Again a knock. Tentative. Light. 'Miss Nchaba, Miss Nchaba. Please, Miss Nchaba.'

Linda Nchaba fixed her earrings, discreet silver studs with azure drops, frowned at herself in the mirror. A once-upon-a-time present from Zama. Wore a red dress, short on her thighs, a scoop neck that would keep his eyes off her breasts, her feet in black pointy pumps. Those shoes made men look at her legs. She could handle that. Most of the time her legs would be under a table.

'Please, I have come to fetch you.'

'I don't need fetching,' she called out. 'I told Zama I'd get there by myself. Wherever there is.' Turned from the mirror, stepped to the door, slotted the security chain into place. Only hotel room she'd ever been in there was a chain on the door. 'Who are you?'

'I am from Mr Zama. He has sent me to bring you to lunch.'

Exactly what she'd feared. Zama taking control. Precisely what Vicki had warned against. 'There's no need, thank you. I've got a car. I can drive there myself.'

'He is worried about drinking. The traffic cops are very strict.'

She laughed. 'He doesn't have to worry. I only drink mineral water. Where is the restaurant?'

'The palace, ma'am. There are no restaurants anywhere in Trekkersburg. It will be easier for me to drive you. You can relax in the car.'

Typical Zama. Would have some smooth-tongue working for him. 'I'll follow you. Wait for me outside the hotel.' She opened the door the length of the chain.

A man stood there, good-looking, fit, military stature. Wore a blazer, white shirt and tie, dark trousers. 'Please ma'am,' he said. 'It will be more convenient for me to take you. There is all the security at the palace. It is too much trouble.'

'I am sure you can get me through. We won't have any problems.' She smiled. 'Who are you?'

'Me.' He tapped his chest. 'I am Mr Zama's assistant.'

'Sure. But your name? What's your name?'

'Major Vula.'

'Alright then, Major Vula, I will see you outside the hotel in five minutes.'

'But ma'am, this is not …'

'It's the way it is going to be,' said Linda Nchaba.

Five minutes later she stopped her hired Tazz alongside a black Merc. The major standing on the pavement. He walked round her car to the side window. 'There is no need for this, ma'am,' he said. 'You can be driven.'

'This way is fine, Major.' She gave him a glossy smile, a hint of teeth. 'I'll tell Mr Zama it was my insistence.'

He nodded. 'It will take about forty-five minutes.'

'No problem.'

Again a curt nod.

She followed the Mercedes out of Trekkersburg onto a new

road. Wide shoulders, no potholes. A surface of smooth tar. A road of little traffic. A road that went only to the palace. Farmlands either side, cattle ranches of grasslands, acacia plains. Occasional groups of people walking, women with bundles on their heads. There were always people walking, Linda thought. No matter where you were in the country, there were always people walking. From where, to where, you couldn't imagine. An unsettled nation.

She considered SMSing Vicki, telling her the destination. Would make sense, give her a heads-up. But Vicki had said no contact until she was back at the hotel. Vicki had said, we've got you covered. We're watching. Like, oh yes, they were watching! No watchers that she could see. No car behind her. She sent it, one word: palace. Vicki would put it together. Relief relaxing the tension in her shoulders. It was just a lunch.

She hadn't expected the grandeur of the palace. Came over a rise, there it was on the opposite slope: a compound of buildings, a fantasy of architectural styles, large houses, gardens, lawns, tennis courts, a swimming pool bright as a jewel, a helipad, roads for electric golf carts, closer to her, pastures of cattle, some antelope. All of it behind an electric fence. This flamboyant mirage in the savannah.

At the gates, she had to leave the Tazz. The guard adamant: 'No unauthorised inside, sisi.'

She'd swung her legs out of the car, stood. 'So authorise me.'

The guard not giving anything. Eyes behind shades, lips tight.

'You expect me to walk? In these shoes?'

The guard's eyes going to her shoes, coming back up her legs. 'It is security, my sister.'

When Major Vula intervened. 'Please, Miss Nchaba, let me drive you. It is a short distance only. Better than walking under this sun.' His hand at her elbow.

She'd allowed him to usher her into the cool of the Merc's air-conditioning.

They'd driven through the gates, gone left to a grand building, parked. The car driven off by a uniformed woman, who'd opened her door, hadn't looked at her. The major led her up through Doric columns, held open a glass door. Inside, a cool hush.

'Come, please,' he said. 'It is better if you follow me.' Showing her across wide floors thrown with Persians, her heels ticking against the travertine, down stairs into a reception room. Photographic portraits on the walls of cabinet ministers.

Major Vula stopped at an antique door. The architrave, carved, ornate, a history of battles. Swept a hand at the photographs. 'The president calls this his rogues' gallery, Miss Nchaba. It is his joke.' Pushed through the doors.

Inside the light was azure, shot with ziggers of sun dazzle. Linda blinked rapidly, trying to adjust to the gloom.

'We are underground, Miss Nchaba.' The major tapped on the glass wall. 'You are looking into the swimming pool. The president likes to watch people swimming. At night especially. The pool has underwater lights.'

Linda Nchaba looked from the swimming pool to the shelves of booze to the cool room of wine. This had to be one of the rooms in the famous bunker complex. Not exactly the concrete hideout she'd imagined.

'You would like mineral water? Still or sparkling? Or some champagne maybe?' The major held up a white bottle. 'Lanson. The suppliers of Wimbledon. You see the president is a tennis fan, each year he tries to be there. When he cannot be there he has television. Television and Lanson.'

Linda smiled. 'I see why you are friends with Zama. You talk like him.' Watched the major twist off the cork, pour the bubbly into a flute.

'We can have someone drive back your car. This is no problem. You can relax, Miss Nchaba.'

She took the glass he held out. One drink. What was the harm in one drink? He filled another glass.

Linda raised the wine to her lips, tasted, the bubbles rich in her mouth. Let a mouthful lie on her tongue. Swallowed. She raised the glass again. 'Cheers.'

'Akubekuhle,' said a voice behind her. 'Your good health.'

'Zama!' Linda caught his reflection in the glass wall. Turned slowly. Her hands suddenly sweating. Her heart rate up. A flutter in her stomach. 'Always the man in the shadows.' Smiled at him. 'Impilontle, Mr Zama. Cheers.' Clinked her glass with the one the major gave Zama. 'I did not expect this.'

'I thought it would be better than KFC. Or the Trekkersburg Country Club. Of course, there are shebeens in Peacehaven township. But Linda Nchaba would not like those places.' He smiled at her. 'Would she?' Reached out to stroke her cheek.

Linda pulled back. The man's touch like branding on her skin.

Again his smile, mocking. 'You have forgotten my fingers,' he said. 'It has been too long. Too long for lovers to be apart. I'm pleased you came back, Miss Nchaba. The lovely Linda.' He sat down at the table. Indicated the other chair. 'Relax. Please. We have missed you.'

Linda sat, aware that somewhere behind her stood Major Vula. Would Zama have him wait on them?

'You came back. This is the important thing. For me it is the important thing. Is it important for you too?'

'I'm here.'

'You are. Here with me.' He gestured with an expansive arm. 'You like this room? Kaiser has told you my father sits down here when the girls are swimming.' He pointed at a leather armchair. 'That is the chair he sits in, sipping champagne

343

and orange juice.' Zama shook his head, chuckling. 'What a strange man he has become.' He looked down, his voice lowered. 'The president. Our father.' Glanced up again, the reflective moment passed. His face alive. 'But he is our president. We must love him, respect him. We have him, our constitution, our democracy. We are the rainbow nation of God. At least according to the archbishop. Yet the lords of hell are here. Do you think so, Linda? Lovely Linda.'

Linda frowned, unsure what he was talking about. Went with, 'I'm sorry? I don't …'

'Understand,' he supplied for her. 'No reason you should. Just saying. Just talking politics.' He drained his glass. Held it up. 'But we don't want to talk politics, do we?' Major Vula came over with the bottle. Topped up Linda's glass, filled Zama's. Retreated into the shadows. Zama leant towards her, reached out, put his hand on her wrist. A loose hand, that began caressing her.

Linda let him. Didn't like what he was doing. Remembered Vicki's 'Play it cool. Don't turn him off.' Left her hand for him to play with.

'It was good, Linda, the time we had. You think we can have that again?'

His eyes coming up to meet hers. Linda didn't look away. Saw a hardness set in his face. Held his stare until his smile returned. The spidery movements of his fingers continuing on her arm.

'Those crazy lunches, hey? Flying all the way to Cape Town, Maputo, Vic Falls. What were we thinking? Doesn't matter, it was fun. Not so, my jet-set model? Straight off the catwalks of Europe, the States. Live fast, die young, be a good-looking corpse. Ja, my honey. Wonderful times, wonderful times.'

'I thought so,' said Linda. Sipped at her champagne, wondered where Zama was going with this.

'You should've stayed. That was a bad thing running away.'
Once more the shake of his head, the tightening lips.

'I came back.'

He let go her wrist, relaxed on the chair. 'You've said. That's the important thing. You came back. You still wear my earrings. That says something. It says much.' A pause. Those dark eyes on her. 'You know, since you came back it is easier. With the girls, I mean. The girls like you.' He kept focused on her. 'They feel you are their friend, their mother. They ask where you are, when you are coming to them. This time your help has made it much better. There was one lot, joh!' He looked back over his shoulder at Kaiser Vula. 'I have told the major. Joh! That lot. So much trouble. If you had been there it would have been alright. Nothing would have happened to them. Instead …' He left it hanging, shook his head.

Linda ran her fingers up the flute through the condensation. Play it cool. 'What happened?'

'You don't want to know. It was nasty.'

Saw the quick stretching of his lips. His face hard. To the side, the major's low cough. Felt a cramp seize her stomach, almost cried out.

'No, really, you don't want to know. It was a carnage, a terrible business. Such unnecessary waste. But now I have you back again. Also I have the major now, so this time it is easy, everything according to plan.'

He came forward, reached out for her hand. Held it. His fingers warm, their pressure closing. 'Why did you come back, my beautiful one?'

'You had my grandmother hostage.'

'That! That was a joke. I told you, she had a holiday.' His grip fiercer. 'No, why did you come back to me? For love?'

'Maybe.' Linda trying for a lightness. A flippant toss of her long curls.

'Maybe. Ah, my playful Linda. Then tell me, my playful Linda, who is Vicki Kahn?'

28

Vicki got wise to the man in the Fiat soon enough. On the national road had decided odds were he was a tail, but discreet. Not like the BM buffoons. They were an embarrassment! After all the training.

But this guy was smart. Small car, kept himself to himself, way back. He'd absorbed the lessons. Vicki wondered how he'd handle her ducking and diving.

Took the Trekkersburg turn-off, stopped at the first picnic lay-by. The place a mess. Like people came out here specially to throw away their rubbish. Beer tins, Coke tins, plastic bags, fast-food wrappers littered in the veld grass. Wet-wipes thrown down beside turd piles. Vicki shuddered. Two pied crows hopped off the concrete table onto the fence. Perched there, looking at her.

Talk about being followed by crows.

Vicki kept the engine running, waited. One minute, a bit longer, the Fiat buzzed past. The driver wearing shades, eyes on the road. Must have pissed him off that she'd pulled this move. Vicki grinned. Followed him into Trekkersburg, wondering, who jerked his strings? Someone at the Aviary? Someone close to Zama? Irritated her, this constant watching.

Saw the Fiat man stop at a petrol station at the town entrance, drove on with a flick of her hair. As Henry said, better to let them do their job.

29

Prosper Mtethu had to get loud entering the palace precinct. Parked among a dozen delivery vehicles, approached security, briefcase in hand. Flashed his Agency credentials at the service entrance, said he needed to inspect access and exits. The guards nodded, glanced at papers in his briefcase, shrugged, went back to their conversations. One waved a magic wand over him, it screeched going down his back.

'My weapon,' said Prosper. Took it out of his belt, placed it on the table.

The guard wanted his ID again, the other guards clustering round. The men hesitant, the corporal telling him he should go in the main gate. Be properly registered.

When Prosper got loud. Swore in Zulu. Told them, look, they had his name, Wiseman Dlamini, his number, his contact details. He was SSA. What more? Brought out his cellphone, wanted the number of their sergeant.

The men stared at him, at the gun he now stuck in his belt behind his back. Movie-style.

Prosper Mtethu, hands on hips, stared them out. Challenging: your move, soldier. Watched the corporal's dilemma. Knew how this would pan out; in the end the click of the tongue, the dismissive wave. Kept his smile to himself when it did.

Prosper walked through storerooms, kitchens, cloakrooms, left the briefcase with a receptionist.

'It will be safe here, sir. You can fetch it any time.' The receptionist giving a numbered receipt. Showed him a plan of the lounges, the banquet hall. Refreshments at the poolside bars. 'Enjoy your afternoon, sir.'

Prosper said he would, stepped out of reception onto a

wide patio beside the swimming pool. Scattered groups chatting beside the bars. Swimmers in the pool. Loungers asleep in the sun. A band making music.

He circulated. Got people used to seeing him so that they wouldn't notice him later. Seeing him and not seeing him. A man in beige. A quiet man. Always on the side of the groups, wary of the long shadow of Major Kaiser Vula. Needed to stay hidden from Major Kaiser Vula. His time would come.

What he needed first was a quiet place to pass the afternoon hours. Somewhere he could sleep, make up for the time on the road. Found it among the servants' quarters: a room empty, bar a bed, behind the guest cottages. Prosper Mtethu lay down, thought of Nolitha alone at home. She'd manage. She was a good girl. He was doing this for her, so she had a future. Had to keep reminding himself of that. 'Khulu, when'll you be home?' she'd asked in that larney accent of hers. He'd not answered. Didn't trust that his voice wouldn't seize up. 'I don't know, I'll see you when I see you.' Her hamba kahle, take care, Khulu, in his head long after they'd disconnected. Could hear her voice now, see her, smell the lavender scent of her soap that drifted through the room after she'd showered. Prosper Mtethu wiped the wet blur from his eyes, slept to the distant beat of marimba with an ache in his chest.

30

Linda Nchaba lay on the floor, dress hiked over her waist, white panties exposed. Curled on herself, gasping. One shoe off. His sudden violence astounding. The punch to her stomach.

Zama stood over her. 'I have asked you nicely, sisi.' His voice coming softly behind the hollow pain. 'For all this time

I've asked you nicely. You sit here, all you tell me is she is a friend.'

Zama crouched, patted her thigh. 'Talk. I want to know.'

Linda felt the burn of his hand on her skin. 'Leave me. Don't touch me.' Hit out, struck at his arm.

'Hau, sisi. This is how you treat me. You won't eat with me. You won't taste my food. What is wrong with my food? This is the food the president eats. It is the meat of our cattle. Every plate the major brings, you push away. I raise my glass, I toast, you won't drink my wine. You won't talk to me. You won't tell me this one small thing: What sort of friend is Vicki Kahn?'

Linda heard the scrape of a chair pulled close to her. Through blurred eyes, saw him sit, reach out a brogued foot to stroke her shin. 'I ask you nicely, is she another model? Maybe you were at the same school? Or maybe the same university?' A pause. The rasp of his shoe against her leg. 'I tell you about what has happened in my life since you ...' Left it unfinished. 'About my mine in the CAR, about the people I meet. The princess of Monaco, Beyoncé, the sheik of Qatar, Barack and Michelle. I am open with you. Friendly. But you won't say anything about your friend Vicki Kahn.'

Linda thinking of her grandmother, of the girls, the pain subsiding, her breath less ragged.

Sensed he had turned away from her. Heard the major say, 'Enough.'

Zama softly, 'You should go, Major. This is my business.'

The major asking, 'What business?'

The sharp retort: 'Personal business.'

The major asking, 'Who is this Vicki Kahn?'

Zama's irritated, 'I told you. Yesterday I told you. You should listen to me. She is one of your colleagues, Major Vula. Someone in your office you didn't even know about. Someone who talks to the lovely Linda. Someone the lovely Linda likes to talk to. About what, Major? About what?'

The shoe against her ankle.

Linda pushed herself into a sitting position, gasped at the bruising to her stomach. 'Take me back to the hotel.'

'No, that can't happen.' Zama not looking at her, still focused on the major, pointing at the door. 'Go, Major.'

'I want to leave.' Her eyes on Major Vula, not pleading, demanding. You got me here. Take me away.

'Out, Major. Out. Lock the door.'

Heard his disapproving grunt, the whisper of his movement to the door, the wheeze of the door opening, the click as it shut. The finality.

'Now, you can tell me.' His hand before her face. 'Come, stand up.'

'I don't need your help.' Linda stood, bent over with the hurt, breathing loudly. Eased off her other shoe, moved it aside.

'Some water?' Zama held out a glass. 'I'm sorry. It is bad to hit a woman. I apologise.' Linda knowing he wouldn't leave it there. 'You make me angry, that is the problem.'

She took the water, drank some, a cold relief in her stomach. Looked at him then, venom in her eyes, seeing how he knew it, her hate. In a quick movement dashed the remains of the water in his face. 'I want to go.'

Zama blinked, wiped the back of his hand across his eyes. Damp patches blossomed on his shirt. 'You are a woman that likes to fight. The only woman who does this to me. You know that, the only woman.'

Linda threw the glass, hit him in the face. Watched Zama stagger back, his mouth a grimace, fingers probing at his forehead. This man staring at her, frowning. Staring at her for long minutes. Said, his voice low, 'Fuck you, Miss Nchaba. Fuck you for that.'

Linda knowing the rest, the Zama of old. Lifted a knife from the table. A wooden-handled steak knife. The one she should've used to cut her beef. Gripped it, ready to lunge.

Zama snorted. 'You hold it like a tsotsi. You fight like a tsotsi? Linda Nchaba the gangster.'

'Try me?'

'Of course. Why not? You have the knife. Now we are equal.' Zama feinted, arms up across his face.

Linda came forward, slashing down.

Zama ducked away. 'You see, you are a tsotsi fighter. Me, I don't fight like that.'

'Why'd you wait, Zama?' Linda on the balls of her feet, circling. 'Why'd you wait so long?'

'To see what you would do. To see if you were a problem. Were you still my Linda? Also you were doing a good job with the girls. I liked that. But then too much yannah-yannah with Vicki Kahn. I didn't like that.'

Linda keeping on the move after him, forcing him backwards round the room. Went in again, low. Zama danced away, fast on his feet.

'You must be quicker, Linda Nchaba.'

She was. Brought the knife up, the blade catching his arm.

Zama swore. 'Bitch. Little bitch.'

Linda saw the blood, jerked at him. Zama turned away, a slice opening across his thigh.

'You have first blood, my sisi. But that is all. Now we are finished with the games.' Picked up a chair, raised it, his shirt pulling free, his stomach exposed. 'You want to stick it to me, baby? Come on, stick it to me. Your last chance.'

Linda thinking, stomach, rip the stomach. Throw it at him, dash for the door. Kept her eyes on Zama. The big man standing there, chair above his head. Blood oozing.

'The door is locked. You see, I can read your mind. We are here, you and me, Linda Nchaba, alone. But you can tell me: Who is Vicki Kahn?'

'She knows everything. She will finish you, Zama.'

'You think. I don't think so. In a short while your Vicki Kahn will be here too. Then we can all talk.' Threw the chair.

31

Trekkersburg. One of those arse-end–of-the-world towns. No wonder Linda was strung out. Men standing around, packs of kids, women resting under trees. A main street of junk dealers, second-hand clothing shops, Ellerines furniture, Protea Electronics, Abdul's supermarket. Some old, gabled buildings, some art deco, some fascist face brick. A boarded-up Tudor Tavern. You spent too long here, you'd slit your wrists.

Vicki drove past the Commercial Hotel, turned down Buchan Street, through the taxi rank on Biddulph into the parking lot of a KFC, took out her phone. Linda's SMS: palace. Jesus, Linda! Why'd you do it? What'd I say, no contact. What d'you do? Fire off an SMS. Handling Linda like coaxing a cat. No telling which way she'd jump. Thank Christ, not the end of the world in the greater scheme, except why let everyone in on the arrangements?

Vicki put a call through to Linda on a pay-as-you-go. Three o'clock, her lunch should be well over. The call went to voicemail. She left a bright message. 'Hey, girlfriend, this's Gita. Where've you been forever? Long, long time. We gotta chill again, sister. Catch up. What's up. You call me, sisi. We can hang whenever.' Disconnected. Waited a minute. Phoned again. Hoping this time Linda'd pick up. Voicemail. Went with: 'Meant to ask: where're you these days? Jozi? Durbs? You outta the country? We gotta do facetime. Call me, hey. Ciaowee.' Repeated the exercise. Voicemail once more. 'Forgot to say, I'm in Durbs, homie. Be here three days. Let's party.'

Vicki not happy about this. Staring across the lot at the KFC counter, two young men there collecting large tubs. The men pulling out chicken pieces even before they'd got their change. The food people ate! She swallowed hard. Came back to Linda. Linda should be answering. Should be at the hotel. Nothing she could do but wait it out. Head off to the palace, sign herself in. Linda would phone when she could. Except one thing she could do: take a look through Linda's hotel room. She had the room number, wouldn't be too difficult getting in.

The pay-as-you-go rang, Linda's number on the screen. Vicki connected. Said a bland hello.

'You are Vicki Kahn?' said the voice.

Male voice, strong, pleasant. No aggro in the tone. 'Who's this?' she said.

'A friend of Linda's. My name's Zama.' A pause. 'She's not well.'

Vicki played the part. 'Oh no. What's wrong? What's the matter?'

'She asked me to phone you.'

'Where's she? What's wrong with her? I want to speak to her. Let me speak to Linda.'

'She'll be okay,' said Zama. 'She's resting. It was a bit of food poisoning. Vomiting.'

Zama still reasonable, chatty. Acting his role, too, Vicki realised.

'Please give her the phone. I want to talk to her.'

'No, you can't right now. She's resting. Asleep. The doctor gave her something.'

'The doctor? What doctor?'

'She was bad. We had to call a doctor.'

'Where is she, Zama? Where are you? I'll fetch her.'

No response. No sound. The call disconnected.

An SMS pinged: We will meet later. The text from Linda's phone.

32

The force of the chair took Linda down. Caught her head, her shoulders, her arms coming up too late to shield her. She collapsed, hit the floor hard, lost hold of the knife. Sprawled on her back, exposed. Zama at her, kicking. Her thighs, her stomach, the brogue toes unrelenting, battered her kidneys. Electric pain sparking behind her eyes.

Then an intermission. Far off, her phone ringing.

She lay expecting more. Could hear his fast panting.

'Get up, bitch.'

Lay unmoving. Hurting.

'Get up, bitch.'

Tasted blood in her mouth. Saw the stickiness of it running down her arm.

'You going to get up?' The thump, thump, thump of his Monmart shoe against her head. 'We haven't started yet, bitch. You want me to be a gentleman, help you?'

Again her phone's ringtone. Had to be Vicki. If she could reach her handbag, answer her phone ... Looked over at where her bag hung from a chair.

'Don't even think it at all.' Zama found her phone, held it up. 'You want to hear the messages?' The phone rang in his hand. 'Popular girl, Ms Nchaba. We better listen to what's up.' Played back the messages. 'Your homie, hey? Gita? I'd say more like Vicki Kahn. What d'you think, we phone her back, tell her where the party is?'

She had to move. Knew she had to move to distract him. Heard him say, 'You are Vicki Kahn?' Tried then to shout. 'Help. Help me.' Her voice a whisper. Zama looking at her, shaking his head. Chatted to Vicki, ended with, 'She was bad. We had to call a doctor.'

Linda got onto her hands and knees, head hanging down, vision blurred. A dizziness, a loud shrill in her ears. Not knowing if she had the strength to stand. Willing herself, moving like a dog away from him. Slowly on all fours towards the knife. The glint of it on the green carpet.

Zama kicked her. Kicked hard under her arm, a straight slam to the breast.

Linda screamed, howled, the agony scything through her. Collapsed again onto the carpet, her fists clenched, the gorge at the back of her throat, choking her. The throb in her chest, sharp, blinding. Behind the sear, Zama's voice.

'Up. Up, up. Come on, tough Linda Nchaba. On your feet, sisi.' His fists bunched into her dress, pulling her erect.

The scald in her breast unbearable. She moaned.

'You think this is sore? Na, no, my honey, we haven't got there yet.' Slapped her face lightly, flick-flack, flick-flack. 'Come. Talk to me. Talk to me.'

Linda without thoughts, without words, seeing his face melt and shape. His open mouth, the yellowness of his teeth, the threads of saliva between them. Groaned.

'What? You're saying what? Please, lovely Linda, tell me about Vicki Kahn. What've you told her?'

Linda spat blood, the spray flecking Zama's shirt. Swayed before him, couldn't focus through the hurt.

'Ah, fuck you, bitch, fuck you.' Zama released her. Wiped at his shirt with the back of his hand. 'This is Saint Laurent. What'd you do that for? You know what this cost? I'll tell you: seven hundred Brit pounds.'

'Fuck you,' said Linda. Hearing the words in her head. Not knowing if she said them. Repeating them, her tongue thick in her mouth.

Zama hit her, punched her in the face, broke her nose.

33

Fish had come past the filling station, seen the Fiat on the forecourt, a petrol jockey in attendance. The driver on his phone to one side, his face hidden, his shoulders hunched, back to the street. Like he didn't want his conversation overheard. All Fish could do not to hoot and wave.

No sign of Vicki's Cruze. No great matter to Fish. He knew where she was headed, what happened in between not of that much concern.

Going down the Trekkersburg main street past the Commercial Hotel, the shabby shops, Fish thought, you went into one of these dorps, you went into them all. Came to the end of the town the road forked: one north to Johannesburg, the other west to Bambatha.

'Go west, young man.' The pop song coming to mind, something about evil going east, except perhaps not this time. Ten minutes down this stretch, his phone had rung: Estelle.

'Bartolomeu, I want to know that you're here. I don't need any hassles at security.'

'Almost,' Fish'd said, cresting the rolling hills, on the farther slope the whole magnificent presidential spread. 'I see it.' Whistled. 'Wowie. This's some place. Looks like the little hotel guy, what's his name ...'

'Sol Kerzner.'

'Yeah, him, looks like he built it.'

'Yes, well. Extravagant is a word that comes to mind. Still, nothing like you'll see inside. No expense spared. Just don't gawp, Barto. Don't gawp. Show some sophistication. God knows you should be able to manage that.'

Fish heard the tinkle of glass.

'You're drinking?'

'Champagne, Barto. The real thing. Why not? Should we expect anything less here?' A pause. 'Ummmm, very nice. Lots of tiny bubbles. I'm relieved you've made it. And almost on time. Security will tell you where to find me. Mr Yan and Mr Lijan are taking a swim. I'm relaxing under an umbrella. It seems most of the cabinet is here. Hurry along now, Barto, won't you?'

Fish disconnected. Two kilometres farther, turned off the road at the palace gate, a guard in shades, AK across his chest, waved him into a parking lot. Half an hour later was accredited: a card-carrying, gun-carrying member of the security staff. Stowed his overnight bag in a small bedroom in the security quarters, doubted he'd be sleeping there. Checked the gun: a RAP-401. On the heavy side but easy to conceal. A niner with eight up. Mild recoil, solid reliability. Useful on both counts. Tucked the pistol under his belt in the small of his back and set off to get the lay of the land. Skirted the main buildings, the compound of houses, this suburb of the guest accommodation. Saw his mother stretched out on a lounger, her Chinese businessmen talking with faces he recognised but couldn't name. In the swimming pool, people cooling off after their travels. No sign of Vicki.

Found a vantage point in deep shadow among the shrubbery. Could wait there unseen, check the comings and goings of guests, security, the spooks obvious in their quiet circulations. No signs of untoward security, no crackle of radioed anxieties. Everyone chilled in the dying light.

Then saw Prosper Mtethu. Couldn't believe his eyes, but the man there cucumber cool in a beige jacket, beige golf shirt, beige slacks like he'd come in from eighteen holes. A long blue drink in his hand had a paper parasol in it. Prosper standing beside a group as if part of it. Except he was scoping the scene, taking in every person, all the muscle, waiters, the position of every table and chair. Made Fish grin looking at these parallel worlds. Made him wonder when these realities would intersect, what sparks would fly. The thought even crossing his mind that he wasn't doing anything to stop it.

Then saw Vicki. Saw a man approach her.

34

'You are Vicki Kahn?' the man said.

Vicki had seen him come out of the building with the Doric columns, pause there on the steps looking over the gathered guests. The light going fast now, the braziers become flickering beacons taking hold across the patio. A chill in the air. Had watched him scan the area. Got a feeling he was her man. Had stepped away from a group, walked into plain sight.

He'd noticed her instantly. Clipped down the steps towards her. Athletic, purposeful.

'You are Vicki Kahn?'

'I am,' she said. 'How ever did you guess?' Knowing full well how he knew. After all, didn't he have her under surveillance?

'We've been expecting you.' He waved in the direction of the gate into the palace. 'Security at the entrance ...' His face bland, unsmiling.

'They're very efficient.' Vicki looked him over. Couldn't recall ever seeing him at the Aviary. Then again, if he was from the military ss, he could have an office in the outer reaches of the nest. A compact man. Something rigid in his face, disappointment perhaps. A man disillusioned with his life. Something to work on, Vicki reckoned. If it came to that.

'And you are?'

'Major Vula.'

No extended hand. No make-believe politeness. Vicki kept her arms at her sides, could also play hardarse if he wanted to. 'It is Mr Zama I want.'

'I know.' The major gestured back up the steps. 'He is waiting for you. Please follow after me.'

She did. Into the marble reception hall, up a flight of stairs, down a long passageway to a door at the end. The major running his knuckles against the wood, more a warning than a knock. Opened the door on a twilight room. Standing framed by the window, the black shape of Mr Zama. Not subtle, Vicki thought. A man who liked to work his status.

'Joh, at last! The mysterious Agent Vicki Kahn. The lady of the messages.'

'I can't see you,' said Vicki, squinting. 'How about some lights?'

'You don't like the effect? My advantage.'

'I don't like playing games.'

The man said something in Zulu to the major, forced a laugh. Said, 'I said to him you're a tough cookie. That's what we've heard.' Spoke again in Zulu. 'You don't know Zulu, Agent Kahn? You should. You would understand some things.'

Vicki walked up to him, moved to his right, forcing him to turn his head. 'I was going to learn a language, I'd learn an international one.'

'Ah ha. She bites, Major. She bites.' Zama flicked his fingers, feigning a nip. 'Such as?'

'French, Chinese, Spanish. Something useful.'

He pushed away from the window. Spoke in vernacular to the major. 'You would find it useful now, Agent Kahn. For example, if you knew Zulu you'd know I'd just called you an Indian whore.'

'You can call me anything you like, Mr Zama. I have come to fetch Linda Nchaba.'

'Your secret agent.'

'Where is she?'

'As I told you, she is sick. But a doctor has seen her, there is nothing to worry about. She is lying down, asleep in dreamland. She is looked after, Agent Kahn. She will be fine.' Zama began circling the room, switching on table lamps. Easy in his movements, graceful. 'There? This is better for you? You can see me now. Come.' He indicated a couch and chairs. 'Let's talk. A little chat. You see, at this moment I am more interested in you than Linda. I am more interested in why our glorious State Security Agency is spying on me. What would you say, Agent Kahn, to that charge?'

Vicki didn't move, noticed the bruise on his forehead, the plasters on his knuckles. His clothes were fresh, his shirt uncreased, unmarked. The bulk of a sidearm under his jacket. 'I would say I want to see her first.'

'You don't believe me?' Zama turned to the major. 'Please convince her, Major.'

'I will bring her through soon,' said Kaiser Vula. 'First I must do some duties, then I will bring Linda Nchaba.'

'There, Agent Kahn. You have the major's word. Do we have a deal?'

Vicki glanced at the major. No reason at all to trust him. Every reason not to. But what options? Perhaps best to play along. There was the letter. In the interim the letter would give Zama pause. Something to think about.

'Okay. Deal. In half an hour I want to see her, though.'

'Fine.' Zama touched the spot on his forehead. Winced. 'The major will be back in thirty minutes. Until then you can explain things to me. Please sit.'

Vicki sat on the couch, relaxed into the leather. The image of cool, calm, collected. Watched the major exit quietly, the door snapping closed behind him. 'Actually, Mr Zama,' she said, fishing a letter from her jacket pocket, 'before we get onto other matters you might like to read this.' She waved the folded paper.

'Why?' Zama perched on a chair opposite her. 'What is that, that it is so important?'

'A message from the dead.'

35

Fish watched Vicki and the man: the formality of their meeting, the way he led her up the steps into the building, expecting her to follow. A man of authority. Held the door open for her, though.

Wondered, should he get into the building? Or wait? Stayed in the shadows, hesitant. Two minutes. Three minutes. Five minutes later lights came on in a first-floor room. There was Vicki, clearly visible. A man passed across the windows. Not the man who had met her. A man too briefly seen, too far off for Fish to ID.

Best to get closer.

He came out of the darkness, slipped among the partygoers. Their mood excited, cheerful, waiters circulating among them with drinks. Beside the pool, a new band went into their routine: funky, upbeat with a tune from Freshlyground he recognised.

His phone vibrated: Estelle.

She opened with, 'Don't think in this half-light I can't see you over there, Bartolomeu. Beside that brazier, next to that dolly bird in the short dress. Don't tell me you didn't notice. And don't go creeping away. You need to check in, show my principals I've got them covered.'

'Later,' Fish said. 'I can't do this now.'

'When then?'

'Now-now.'

'Now-now's the same as never, Mr Clever Dick. What're you doing that's so important? Except for perving the talent.'

Fish spotted his mother now on the outskirts of the crowd, the two short Chinese men beside her. He didn't move quickly, she'd be starting towards him.

Heard her say, 'Actually, I saw your Indian friend go into the building. You're after her still, aren't you? You can tell me, Barto, I'm your mother.' A pause. Fish declined a champagne flute, smiled at the waitress. 'She's giving you a merry run for it, isn't she? I can tell, you know. I can tell. Didn't you see she's with another man? Really, Barto, don't make a fool of yourself. Your girlfriend's multi-tasking. Best thing you can do is forget about her. Completely. You can't tell with Indians. It's that Karma Suture stuff in their culture, believe me.'

Fish disconnected, decided, best if he got into the building. Got out of his mother's sightline, got closer to Vicki. Found out what was going on there. Could be she was attending a briefing for spooks. Though he doubted it.

Fish angled away from the crowd towards the side of the main building. Had to be other doors round the back. Kitchen doors, scullery doors. The servants' way in.

Realised as he moved through the groups, Prosper had been invisible for a while.

Fish's phone rang twice as he hurried along a gravel path away from the laughter and the music, guided by solar lights on stalks. Both calls he let go to voicemail, both calls he reckoned were Estelle. Sometimes she didn't know when to let things be.

The path took a right angle to the back of the building, voices ahead, a drift of cigarette smoke. Fish pushed through a half-open door into a courtyard, three people in aprons and hairnets standing there, smoking. Moved to crush out their cigarettes.

'Hang five,' said Fish, flashed his credentials. 'Relax. Just a security check.' Kept his face impassive, asked for their IDs.

The three digging under their shirts for name tags. Fish glanced at them, nodded, went on into the kitchen. The place a maelstrom. People shouting. The sizzle and flare of cooking food. Nobody even noticed the man with the blond hair, the bronzed face, the sturdy shoulders, passing quietly among them, lifting a sausage roll off a platter.

Fish now followed the passageways Prosper had taken a few hours earlier through the building. Cloakrooms, anterooms with their bored attendants, coming to the empty reception area. Could see through the glass doors the outside party lit only by braziers, candles, a myriad of garden uplighters. The swell of music and voices rising in volume. On a paved area beside the pool, people already dancing. The president's people knew how to throw a party.

36

Major Kaiser Vula stood hesitant in the president's bedroom. A slow rise of smoke from burning herbs acrid in his nostrils. The room stuffy, uncomfortably warm.

'He cannot go outside,' said the first wife. The woman behind him, sitting on a chair at the door.

Kaiser Vula looked at the president, prostrate on the large bed, grey-faced, eyes closed, perspiration oozing from his brow. The man's collar loosened, his shirt creased. Nandi beside him stroking his hand. Nandi in a short white dress, stiletto pumps. Ready for her party appearance.

'You can see he is a sick man. The witch's power is strong.' The voice of the first wife at his back, insistent. 'There is a sangoma we have called to protect him.'

No doubt the president was a sick man. Major Kaiser Vula considered the options. Unlikely there was an assassin among the crowd, he couldn't see it. With the precautions there was low risk. And the president needed to show himself. Convince them he was their leader.

'Perhaps, Mr President ...' he began.

'Exactly, Major.' The president opened his eyes. Hooded eyes. Eyes on fire. 'I cannot believe they have sent anyone, my comrades, the cowards. They will not go against me, they are too weak. They have always been too weak. He sat up, held out a hand. 'Where is the bulletproof? Come, come. I must go out. People must see me. I am their president.'

Kaiser Vula caught Nandi's triumphant glance: you see, he is my man.

Thought, the man must have a fever. But he was right, he needed to be seen. He was the man of the people. Major Kaiser Vula snapped to. 'I will secure downstairs. You will be safe.' Alerted the head of security: the president is coming out. Maximum presence. Maximum vigilance. Maximum response.

The first wife let out a wail, her lamentation echoed by the other wives waiting in the passageway. 'Ai, ai, ai, this is the wrong thing. This is the wrong thing. Wait. Wait. You must wait for the witchdoctor.' A man in a suit carrying a bucket of brown liquid in one hand, a wildebeest's tail in the other entered. Greeted the president by his clan name, sang his praises.

The president acknowledged the greeting with a raised hand.

Muttering, the sangoma dipped the tail in the liquid, flicked it about the room, damp stains appearing on the floor, the bedspread, the curtaining. Dip, flick. Dip, flick. Dip, flick. Until the room had been purified, strengthened.

At the door he stood mumbling, drew a wet line across the entrance. Was led away by one of the wives.

The president changed his shirt, slipped on the bulletproof vest. Nandi helping him into a light jacket. 'We are ready, Major.' The stern face, the upright posture. He drank from a glass Nandi handed him. 'We can join the party people.'

Major Kaiser Vula brushed at the wet spots on his trousers, the globules on his shoes. If the president believed such nonsense he couldn't say. The president looked a very sick man. Unlike the radiant Nandi walking beside him.

37

'A message from the dead! Very dramatic, Agent Kahn.'

Vicki held out the letter. 'Go on. Read it.'

'What can be so vital in a letter?' Zama settled back in the chair, crossed his legs. Made no effort to take the letter. 'Later.'

'Now would be better.'

'Later. After the party. Now I think it is more important to talk about you.'

Vicki ignored him, flicked open the pages. 'We've got thirty minutes. Let me read you a small bit. A taster, so to speak.' Read the section about her aunt going to Botswana to have a baby. A son.

'You,' she said, her eyes on Zama, alert for any tell: fingers touching his nose, a squirm.

'Of course.' Zama laughed. A quick, hard snort. Threw open his arms. 'This all fits together. I am the right age. I am born in Gaborone. No one knows what happened to my mother. Everyone knows my father cannot leave women alone. There are his babies everywhere. Of course, why not believe this person Amina, your aunt, why not believe she must be my mother? Why not? It is a good story. You can say we are family.'

Vicki watched him, the ease with which he brushed off her charge, as if he'd been confronted with it many times. Unless Zama was a poker player, this was not a man surprised. This was a man confident, untouchable. Caught her by surprise, though, his attitude. She took the killshot.

'There's more.'

Again the blasé gesture, the languid hand. 'There is always more, Agent Kahn. But let me tell you the rest of the story. Yes? You can see if it matches with your secret message from the dead.'

Vicki glanced down at Detlef Schroeder's letter: *I think the baby she had in Gaborone is the baby of the man who is now the president of your country. I think he has raped her.* Back at Zama: no embarrassment in his face, but a mocking glint in his eyes. He was playing with her.

'You want to hear it?'

Vicki shrugged, go ahead.

He grinned, uncrossed his legs, sat forward, elbows on knees, hands either side of his cheeks. Stared at her. 'You want to hear this, Agent Kahn? Really, you want to hear it?'

You cocky bastard, Vicki thought. Be a whole lot less cocky when she'd finished with him. 'I'm waiting.' Her tone abrupt.

That took the smirk off Zama's lips. 'Remember where you are, Agent Kahn. Remember who you are talking to.'

Vicki kept up the eyeball until he said, 'Fine. It goes like this: one night these two people made love, your aunt, my father. But, Agent Kahn, that is what happened in the Struggle. All the time this happened. You can understand it: people are lonely. They are in foreign countries, sometimes half a world away from home, they can't go back, so where must they find love and comfort except from their comrades? People need it. We all need love. All you need is love. In the long dark night people need it. Maybe this is what happened to your aunt. She is with my father in Paris, in Zurich, Berlin, London, Moscow, any city, I don't know, and they have this one moment. One moment.' He held up a finger. 'But one moment makes her pregnant. So my father says, come to Gaborone, have the baby, he is my child. So this is what your aunt does. Why not? Maternity leave. Get away from the grey skies of Europe to the sunshine. Be among her own people. But afterwards there is still the Struggle. She must go back to fight the white devils, she cannot be a mother.'

Zama held up his hands. 'Yes. This is the story in your letter? I can tell you there are ten, fifteen stories like this with my father. Now that he is president, a rich man, there are even more stories like this. All the time people come: I am your son. I am your daughter. I am one of your Struggle babies. It's an old story, Agent Kahn. We have heard it before. Many, many times.'

Zama sitting there before her, smug. In control. Thinking himself untouchable.

'There is something else,' said Vicki. 'About my aunt and your father.'

'I'm sure you are going to tell me.'

Vicki took her time. Kept her face averted, eyes cast down. He wore good shoes did Zama. Expensive shoes. Brown brogues with a white sole. Very cool. Not her favourite shoe style, too self-congratulatory. Too arriviste. His feet solid on the carpet, unmoving, undaunted.

'Your father was head of intelligence in exile?'

'This is history.' The feet moving: the right on its side behind the left.

Vicki looked up. 'My aunt ran the Paris desk. Reported to your father. She was there for a couple of years.'

'If you say so. They had their structures for sure.'

'She found out something. Something serious.'

'What can that be?' Zama amused, not taking her seriously. Vicki wanting to slap the mockery from his eyes. 'A top secret.'

'Two things, actually.'

'Two secrets. Your story gets better.'

'The first that your father was given gold bullion. Gold held in Switzerland by the old apartheid government.'

'A bribe! Oh no. Never. Not my father. Never. The president is an honourable man. How can you say such things, Agent Kahn? You slander his reputation.'

'I'm serious.' Vicki unsure of Zama's tone.

'I'm not. You have no proof.' He frowned. 'This is nonsense. Stories dreamt up by bitter people. Nothing we haven't heard before.'

'The second is about arms contracts with the French. And nuclear trade.'

'Agent Kahn, this is ancient history. Things that happened a quarter of a century ago. Time to move on. You know, we all know, there have been commissions looking into these things. We even have commissions looking into the commissions. We are a nation of commissions. But we find nothing wrong.'

'My aunt was assassinated.'

'I'm sorry. I didn't know that.'

'Stabbed in the Metro because of what she knew.'

'But Agent Kahn, many comrades were killed. Disappeared. Blown up by parcel bombs. It was a hard struggle. The Boer hit squads were everywhere. They used all the dirty tricks.' He paused, clicked his fingers. 'Maybe the French killed your aunt. Have you thought of that possibility? You are a spy, you know how the spies work. The CIA, Mossad, MI6, the KGB, whatever they call themselves today, they all do these things. The French must do these things too.' He laughed. 'I know. I've seen the movies.'

'Maybe your father didn't mind that she was killed.'

'Pah! Nonsense.' Let out a run of Zulu. Came back: 'Why? Why do you even think this?'

'Why? Because she knew too much. She was in the way. An inconvenience.'

'Kak, Agent Kahn. Rubbish. What the Afrikaners call kak-stories.' Zama stood. 'You want to ask my father? You want me to call him?' Took out his cellphone. 'Let the president tell you what happened? Put your mind at rest.' Keyed to his contacts.

'Good idea.' Vicki stood. Arms loose, wary. 'We can talk about the girls you traffic at the same time. Let Linda Nchaba tell him about his son.'

Zama held up a hand, phone against his cheek, said, 'Major, we need to sort this situation.'

38

Prosper Mtethu noticed movement among the security. A drift imperceptible to those not looking for it. A securing of the flanks, a concentration along the walk the president would take towards his guests. A greater presence of men in black at the centre.

Told him the president was expected.

Prosper Mtethu put down the blue cocktail on a table. He'd only sipped it, his kind of drink, that sweetness. Had kept it in hand merely to ward off the persistent waiters bearing trays of champagne. Oysters, caviar, tapenade, canapés. Not the moment for Blue Lagoons.

Inserted an earpiece, fed the wire inside his jacket collar, clipped it to a receiver. Heard Kaiser Vula say, 'Twenty minutes. The president will be down in twenty minutes.' Slipped the receiver into his shirt pocket.

Moved now with the spooks towards the centre. They would think he was one of them. They'd seen him around long enough to be unconcerned.

To Prosper Mtethu, the only problem was the major. The major'd be scanning the crowd, picking up on shapes, movements, any sudden shifts. Anyone pushing closer. Wouldn't be able to see faces in the dark. At least not until it was too late.

Prosper stood behind two Chinese businessmen, both on tiptoes to see over the heads. Their chaperone, a woman in a black pencil dress, too tight for her age, saying, 'We have been promised five minutes. We're on the schedule, I'm told. We won't meet him here, we'll meet him later.'

Prosper thinking, sorry to disappoint you, lady. There will not be later for him.

His cellphone rang: a private number. He answered. Moved to the side of the chaperone.

A voice said, 'The deposit has been made to the account you specified.' A voice he'd not heard before. This one Cape Town English. White. Older.

Prosper said nothing; thought, it better be.

'Don't let us down, Prosper. As the queen said, "Sentence first, verdict afterwards."'

He disconnected.

The chaperone glanced at him. Curious. Tapped at her ear, smiled. Said, 'Could you tell me when the president's expected?'

Prosper stared at her, his face a mask.

The woman became flustered. Flushing. 'Of course, I'm sorry. You're working.' Turned away from him.

In his ear Major Vula said, 'Confirm positions.'

Heard the roster of confirmations. A tight band across the crowd. Which left him little room to manoeuvre. He'd realised it would be a close shot. Escape would be difficult. But Prosper Mtethu did not think of escape. He thought of the job. Of moving in close. Drawing the gun, lifting it to fire. Once, twice. Easing onto Kaiser Vula. Firing: once, twice. He would have to be quick. No shifting of his feet. Nothing to disturb his balance. Merely a slight pivoting of his torso. A short realignment of the gun.

Bam, bam. Refocus. Bam, bam.

There'd be security around him. He'd have to trigger the bomb before they took him down. He could do that, there was an outside chance he could escape. Slip away in the turmoil. He had the phone in his hand. The number ready.

Prosper Mtethu took up a position facing the doors the president would come through. People in front of him laughing, joking, waiting for their leader. Their president.

Major Vula said, 'Hold positions. Coming out in fifteen minutes.'

39

Fish'd gone upstairs, headed down the passageway towards the room where he'd seen Vicki and the man. Not intending to bust in on them. Not sure of his intentions. Just wanting to be there, in case she needed help. Have her back. Be the cavalry, the white knight, the prince.

At each door he listened. Every room quiet, most doors locked. Those rooms he could peer into seemed offices, the only lights the red glow of computers on standby.

As he neared the last room, heard the man's voice, 'It's an old story, Agent Kahn.'

Heard, too, a moan, 'Help me. Help me.'

Fish paused.

Again, a groan.

Opened a door onto a dark room. Gagged at the stench of vomit, blood. Could make out the shape of a body on the floor. A woman's hand raised towards him. Fish entered quickly, closed the door. Shone the light from his cellphone on the woman's face. Bloodied, gashed. Her eyes swollen closed. Something familiar about her all the same. Not someone he'd met. Someone he knew from photographs. Shone the light over her body: her clothing stained, torn. Bruises on her limbs, open wounds. Her feet bare.

'Help me.' The plea weak. The woman's lips a mash of flesh. Her hand wavering.

He crouched, gently took her hand, felt its stickiness. Said, 'You're going to be alright. I'll get medics.'

'Zama,' she said.

'Zama?' Fish frowned. 'The president's son, what's he ...?' Left the question unfinished.

The woman's grip on his fingers tightened. Tried to pull him closer. He bent in near enough to smell stomach acid on her breath. She moaned with pain. The sound becoming a rattle in her throat.

Her ribs, thought Fish. Might be broken ribs, a punctured lung. A helluva beating she'd taken. He shone his light around the room. Everything neat, orderly. No sign of a fight. She'd been dumped here.

'Zama,' the woman said again.

'I'll get help.' Fish prised loose her grip of his hand. 'You're going to be okay.' Made to stand up. She grabbed at him.

'Vicki.'

He heard that clearly.

'Vicki. What's ...?' Realising this had to be Linda Nchaba.

The model he'd researched. The woman he'd overheard Vicki talking to. 'We're watching. We've got this covered.' What a joke. What'd they got covered? Hadn't helped Linda here. Seemed the agents had cocked up big time. What'd Mart Velaze warned about serious shit? Serious shit in the country's number-one national keypoint: Bambatha.

Christ! The guy Prosper down there aiming to shoot the president. Up here the president's son beating women: right now across the passageway with Vicki.

The woman Linda pointing behind him. 'Go.'

Not without you, Fish thought. He walked in on Vicki without obvious reason wouldn't be a good thing. Especially as she didn't know he was here.

'Can you stand?'

The woman nodded.

'You're Linda?' he said. 'Linda Nchaba?'

A faint yes. The woman squinting at him through her swollen eyes. 'Who're …? Who're you?'

'Fish,' he said. 'I'm Fish. With Vicki.' Was as good as, for the purposes of the moment. 'Can you walk?'

Helped the woman onto all fours. On his haunches in front of her, slid his arms beneath her armpits, clasped her. Said, 'On three I'll straighten up.' Counted. On three raised her. She fell against him, breathing hard, moaning.

'You okay?' Her head against his face. Fish let her rest there, gather her strength. Could smell a linger of perfume on her skin. Felt her body tensing against his, taking its own weight. The woman had guts.

'I'm going to move,' he said. 'Take your weight on my left side.' Wanted a free right hand to pull the RAP, if necessary. Felt her head nod.

They shifted through a slow shuffle until she stood beside him, leaning heavily. Her breath still coming in a loud hiss.

'Right,' he said. 'Here's how it goes: we walk to the door, cross the passage, go into where Vicki's with this Zama dude. That sound okay?'

A low yes.

'Anything you can tell me about him? Like is he armed?'

A nod.

'A gun?'

A nod.

'Fair enough.' Fish reached round, whipped out the pistol, chambered a round. Vicki'd be packing too, some SSA issue plus her little .32. Two against one was fair odds. Would suit a gambler like Vicki. Stuck the pistol in his belt. No need to cause chaos and mayhem. Said to Linda Nchaba, 'Should we do this?' Felt the tightening of her fist in his jacket.

They hobbled to the door, Fish reaching out to open it. His movement hampered by the injured woman. A swell of music coming at them, people calling for their leader. Arselickers, thought Fish, they'd tear Prosper apart. Adjusted his grip on Linda.

Said, 'If I have to drop you, I'm going to. If things get rough. No offence, hey.'

Linda Nchaba didn't respond. Except to say, 'Shoot him.' The words a whisper, soft as the brush of clothes against skin. Fish unsure he'd heard right.

'Say again?'

'Shoot him.'

'Yeah, well, let's see how the wave builds.'

They crossed the passage slowly, Linda favouring her left leg. At the door Fish paused. Could hear Vicki say: 'We can talk about the girls you traffic at the same time. Let Linda Nchaba tell him about his son.'

'You ready?' Fish said, felt her lurch forward as an answer. 'Here we go' – opened the door, hustled them inside.

40

Mart Velaze didn't like Trekkersburg. One of those old-style white dorps that'd gone to ruin with democracy. More Nigerian hairdo joints than food stores. The must-have Chinese junk shop among them. Funny how the locals never shot up the Chinese. Shoot the Somali traders for selling single cigarettes, airtime, cans of Fanta Grape but never the Chinese with their plastic crap.

Trekkersburg desperate enough to darken your soul.

Mart Velaze didn't want to contemplate spending too many hours there.

Thought he'd take a ride out to the palace anyhow, escape the depressing town. No reason why he shouldn't. Came under the tradecraft rubric of scoping the terrain. Also wanted to see what it looked like. Given all the money the president had spent, had to be quite something.

He did. At sundown pulled over on the approach hill, sat in the little Fiat marvelling. Some spread the president had put together.

Phoned the Voice. Her first words, 'It's going down, Chief, at his party. Our Prosper's in the lead role.'

Could have told her that. Mentioned the two calls he'd listened in on: Cynthia Kolingba; an unknown male.

'That'd be Henry Davidson,' said the Voice. 'Told you he was the postman. Seems he's also the bagman. Where're you, Chief, as of now?'

'Outside Trekkersburg,' said Mart Velaze. Not exactly a lie.

'You keep away from the palace. We're letting whatever happens happen. No interference. If our Prosper gets lucky, so be it. Seems to me he's on a suicide mission, like those jihadi types. Except Prosper doesn't profile as the bomb sort. Doesn't have the cowardly streak. Not given what he's been through. Makes you feel sorry for the granddaughter, though. But then as they say, we are but players, strutting and fretting.' Paused. 'There is another insert, I've gathered, another one of our own.'

This was new to Mart Velaze. Waited for the revelation.

'I believe her name is Nandi. Know anything of her?'

'Nothing.'

'So. You see, there are still surprises in the world.'

The Voice went quiet. Mart Velaze looked at the palace: all the cars parked at the entrance gates. Two ten-seater minibuses among them. Still the odd partygoer zipping past him. You sat there looking at it, you got the sense that you were missing out. This major situation going to occur, you were on the outside, missing all the action.

Weighed up if this was the time to drop the Zama trafficking gig. Cleared his throat. Did so.

Silence, like he'd been talking to dead air.

Then: 'Wondered when you were going to tell me, Chief.'

Mart Velaze stayed shut up. Should've known she'd be on it. Not much she didn't know about.

'Here we need your intervention,' said the Voice. 'Give you something to do in Trekkersburg. Attractive dorpie, I'm told. Has an interesting history of murders, if you like that sort of thing. Probably you're not going to have the time for sightseeing. Because as of now, I'm designating you the cleaner, Chief. See what you can do to get that all sorted.'

'Any pointers?' Mart Velaze bringing the Fiat to life. Did a u-turn, headed back to Trekkersburg.

'Sorry, Chief. Can only wish you the help of the ancestors. Except you might start looking in the industrial area. Can't be very big, can it? A small town like that. That's probably where they've got the girls.'

41

Major Vula went ahead of the presidential party onto the patio. As the expectant faces turned towards him, eager to greet their leader, he scoped the buildings to his left. The lighted reception hall, the upstairs in darkness except the room where Zama was holding his tête-à-tête. Damn Zama, the problems he brought.

Raised his gaze to the roof line. Any assassin would be up there, take a sniper's long shot. No movement he could discern. Got the all-clear from his roof detail.

Looked again at the crowd: such happy smiling people, jiving to the music, bubbling with champagne. Waiting to adore their president. The most important person in their country. Who made everything possible. Gave them wealth beyond dreams. Big houses, new cars, the five-star lifestyle.

A chant going up: Mr President, Mr President, Mr President. The band joining the rhythm. Women ululating.

'Coming out,' he said into his radio, held open the door for the president.

Saw clearly how ill the man was. His pallor grey, his face tight against the pain. So slowly he moved, kept his arms rigid at his sides. This wasn't the striding president, the athletic figure.

You are a dying man, Kaiser Vula thought. The communists had no need of hitmen or sniper assassins. In a few months the vultures would be tapping on the balcony windows.

What then for Nandi? All smiles now, arm in arm before the adoring hordes. Radiant. Young. Healthy. How she had changed. From hate to love. Could someone go from hate to love? From love to hate was all too easy. Once he'd loved his wife. Still loved Nandi. Or lusted for her. Her smooth skin, her firm body, the dirty phone talk. Did she talk dirty to the president? An image of her floated up, Nandi with the phone tucked between her shoulder and her ear telling the president where she had her hands. Sending a photo. Asking for intimate shots. She'd done that. He'd done that. What Nandi must have in her phone beyond troubling. Kaiser Vula shook away the thought. Refocused. Moved into the press of people, opening a path for the president.

Hands reached out to touch the leader, women showering petals, their ululation shrill in his ears.

And the president responding. Even raising his hands, smiling. The strong head of state in charge. Whistles, shrieks as he stood before them; Nandi at his side with her soft body shimmer. The beloved hosts, the adoring guests.

When Major Kaiser Vula saw Prosper Mtethu.

Glimpsed his face, lost it in the swaying mass.

Wasn't even sure he could trust his eyes. No ways Prosper Mtethu could be here, could even enter the palace grounds.

Then saw him again. Moving closer to the president. No doubt this time. No doubt in the mind of Major Kaiser Vula what Prosper Mtethu intended.

Yelled the man's name. Shoved to get through the dense throng. Screamed into his radio: Bambatha, the lockdown code.

When he heard the first retort. To his left, dull, too dull for an outside firing. Glanced at the palace, saw a blue flash in the lighted window, the second shot.

42

Vicki swung round at the door banging open, banging closed. Fish stood there holding up Linda Nchaba, a battered, bloodied

Linda Nchaba. Her first thoughts: What the fuck'd happened to Linda? Where the fuck'd Fish come from?

Saw Linda raise her head, her face mashed.

Jesus!

Heard Zama shout, 'Who're you? What're you doing here?'

That grin Fish had in times of trouble. His comeback, 'I'm the white knight, dude.'

Said, 'What happened to her, Zama? What the hell've you done to her?' Moving round the couch, seeing Zama pull a gun from under his jacket. Shouted, 'No, no.'

Saw Linda stagger away from Fish, a gun in her hand, waving wildly. Her first shot going wide of Zama into the wall. The second punching through the leather couch.

Vicki smelt cordite. Saw Fish charge Zama. Bloody surfer boy had to always be in on the action. Reached for the .32 at her ankle. Came up with the Guardian as Zama fired: the blood-splatter from a hollowpoint writ across the wall.

Linda went down, Vicki catching the movement out the corner of her eye.

Saw Zama focus on Fish.

Fired.

43

Prosper kept to the centre of the crowd, let the president come to him. Was bumped, elbowed, pushed by happy partygoers. Felt a coldness wet his back. A young voice shout in his ear, 'Sorry, Baba, sorry, hey. I spilt on you.' Ignored her.

About him women ululating. Everyone jiving: become a great beast in motion.

Could see between the bobbing heads the tall Major Vula,

beside him the shorter president's dome, gleaming like peeled garlic. Worked the pistol free, held it low beneath his jacket. Needed the target to move closer. Gripped the cellphone in his other hand.

Slowly through the jostle forced a way to the major's right, thinking to come on the target from the side or back. No problem with rear shots on them both. The mission here to make the kill.

In the mill and bunch met the eyes of Kaiser Vula across the heads. The man seeing him, recognising him. Prosper ducked down, squeezed between people at a crouch. Heard the shots in the palace.

Felt the crowd stiffen.

Brought the pistol up, thrust his way towards the president. Stared at the face of his target, the man looking back at him, frowning. Watched the president lurch forward, vomit a black spray on the feet of a howling woman. Did two things: pressed speed dial on his cellphone, went for a body shot. Bring the man down, finish him on the ground. Saw the impact low in the president's gut. Adjusted his aim, fired again.

Major Kaiser Vula leapt forward, took Prosper Mtethu's second shot in the chest. Staggered him back, didn't drop him. His hand grabbing for the gun in his shoulder holster. Took the third shot in the stomach. Went down with that, the pain shutting out his vision. He blinked, pulled the gun free.

About them the chaos of screaming people. People fleeing, trampling over him. The sound of glass breaking, more gunshots from the palace. Through it all the clear pitch of Nandi's howl. He couldn't see her or the president. Looked down at the spread of blood across his chest, the rose blooming over his stomach.

The pistol a weight in his hand. Too heavy to raise. He

squeezed the trigger, shredded the ankle of the man who stood over him.

Prosper Mtethu dropped. Did not hear the explosion. Felt the first of the kicks to his kidneys, his stomach, his crotch. Felt a boot stamped hard on his gun hand shatter his finger bones. Surrendered, as he'd known he would have to. Was beaten to death there amid the broken bottles, the discarded shoes, the remains of the canapés, by men in black suits.

44

Vicki saw the spit of flame from Zama's gun. Heard Fish cry out, collapse behind the couch. Squeezed the trigger, felt the tug of the .32 in her hand, saw the bullet open a hole in Zama's cheek. Fired again. The bullet smacking higher at the soft bone of the eye socket. Zama dropped, a finger snagged in the trigger ricocheting a wild round off the walls.

From outside gunshots, the screams of terrified people. One thought: Fish.

Found him writhing on the floor, his hand to his head, blood flowing between his fingers. Vicki bent over him.

'Let me look. Take your hand away. Heaven's sake, Fish, I need to see the wound.'

The wound a shallow furrow through his blond hair above the ear. The blood leaking out fast as head wounds did. Vicki tore a strip of lining from her jacket, tied it round his head.

'You'll live.' Pushed back a quick desire to kiss his lips. Instead gripped his hand, helped him up. 'Come'n, we've got to go. Chop-chop.'

Fish complaining, 'Hey, slow down.' Holding onto her arm.

'Gimme a break. I'm dizzy. I could've been dead.' Stopping her. 'You shot him. Killed him.'

'Yes,' said Vicki, surprising herself. No feeling for what she'd done. 'He won't be missed.'

When the bomb exploded somewhere downstairs, the reverberation thrumming in Vicki's ears. The lights flickered, went out. Sirens starting in the building, an overhead sprinkler system raining down a fine mist.

'Great, like we need this.' Used her cellphone as a light to lead them to the door.

'The dude was serious,' said Fish. 'About whacking the prez. Didn't think he had much chance.'

'Who? Which guy?' Vicki coming round on him. Recanting. 'Doesn't matter. Later.' Paused over the body of Linda Nchaba. Laid a gentle hand on the dead woman's head. Too jigged now for remorse. Or sorrow.

'She was strong,' said Fish. Retrieved his weapon, prying it from the slack fingers. 'Never thought she'd pull that one.'

Vicki didn't respond. Opened the door onto a dark passageway. The stench of smoke. Voices shouting. The high wail of a woman in agony.

'Here's the plan,' she said. 'We're going to the main gate. Give me your security tags. You don't say a word. Okay?' Squeezed Fish's arm. 'Okay?'

'Yes ma'am, okay,' said Fish, handing her the lanyard with its security card.

She held up the light to his face. His hair damp. The make-shift bandage soaked. Runnels of watery blood on the side of his head. Fish grinned.

Vicki thought, long time since she'd seen that grin. Had missed it. Said, 'You're bloody crazy.'

Fish coming back, 'And you're not?'

She let it go, kept her smile to herself.

They edged along the corridor, the smoke thickening. Down the staircase into the wrecked reception: the cloakroom on fire, flames licking at the panelling. Two men, beating at the burn with their jackets. Went through the shattered glass doors onto the entrance steps. Before them, a chaos of toppled tables, discarded clothing, spilt braziers, their coals scattered, glowing. About the patio people sat, heads in hands, stunned. Men in shock, women crying. Security personnel picking themselves up. Two bodies on the slasto paving. Men in black on their radios, others carrying a figure between them.

Vicki took it in, pointed down the stairs to their left. 'Let's go. That way.'

They hurried on. Fish complaining his head hurt, he was dizzy, he wanted to puke.

'Don't be a wuss,' said Vicki. 'The quicker we're outta here the better.' Gripped hold of Fish's arm like she was medevacing a damaged man. Emergency services coming past them now. A nurse in a blue jumpsuit asking, 'He okay? You need help? He's bleeding bad.' Vicki going, 'I'm okay.' Waving an arm back the way they'd come. 'There's more. More wounded. There's been gunshots. A bomb.' The nurse nodding, shouting, 'There's ambulances coming.' Not for my walking wounded, thought Vicki.

Got Fish to the gate, flashed her security pass. The guard taking one look at Fish's bloody head, waving them through.

'I've got a hire car here,' said Fish.

'Yeah, sure,' said Vicki. 'Like you're okay to drive?'

'My bag's in the quarters.'

'You want to go back'n fetch it? Don't think so, babe.' The babe coming out before she could stop it. Catching the look in Fish's eyes. His cheesy grin. Said, 'Oh, what the …' Beeped open the Cruze. 'Just get in and shut up, okay. Let me think.'

'There's a couple of other things,' said Fish, fastening the seat belt. 'My mother's inside somewhere. You shot the president's son.'

'You could phone her,' said Vicki. 'There's always that option. The president's son I wouldn't worry about too much. Not troubling my conscience.' She switched on the ignition, headed down the road towards Trekkersburg.

Half-heard Fish phone his mother, her thoughts on the girls. Like how to find them. She didn't, they'd die. Starve to death wherever Zama'd been holding them. That'd be on her conscience. That she'd failed them. Had failed Linda, come to that. Didn't want to think too much about Linda. Linda was going to be one of the question marks. One of the ghosts that'd rise in her life from time to time: had she got what she deserved? Or had she deserved redemption? To be remembered for trying to right her wrongs? Enough.

Heard Fish say, 'You'll be alright. I'm …' Had to smile at the guy's backtracking, excuses. Remembered it was ever thus with Fish and Estelle. The mothering he got. Glanced at him in the dark, glad to have him beside her. Fish disconnected the call.

Said, 'She's okay then?'

'In her element.'

The two of them laughing. Fish saying, 'Where've you been, Vics? What happened?'

Vicki came back quickly. 'Not now. Okay, not now. Now we've got to find the girls.'

'The girls?'

'The girls Zama was trafficking. It's why I'm here.' Then pulled a spook-trick, changed tack. 'Tell me about the hitman.'

Fish did. In ten minutes laid out chapter and verse. The loyalty of Prosper Mtethu. Also the Agency agreement, the Kolingba kill, the CAR connection, the communist conspiracy. And Mart Velaze.

Mart Velaze. Vicki kept both hands on the wheel, eyes on

the blaze of road in the headlights. That name again. 'Talk to me about Mart Velaze. Who's he?'

'Not much I can tell you I haven't already. He's one of yours.'

'He came to you?'

'You could say.'

'Jesus, Fish, do I have to dig it out?'

'He sent me some photographs.'

'Of what?'

'Hey, hang on. I'm getting there, alright? Hell, Vicki, gimme a break. You got water in here?'

Vicki told him on the back seat. Fish found a bottle, took a guzzle.

Said, 'One was of Prosper at the Kolingba hit. The other of him in a hospital. Turned out to be the hospital that had Kolingba as a patient.'

'So why'd Velaze give you …?'

'Dunno, Vicki. You spooks have insane reasons.'

Vicki held a hand out for the water bottle. Drank. 'You were talking how to Velaze?' Drank again. Gave the bottle back to Fish.

'On the phone.'

'You didn't meet?'

'Not that time. The first time, ja, at the *Athens* wreck car park, the second time he phoned me. To tell me to warn you. Nice of the guy, don't you think?'

'What'd he say?'

'Ah, heck, how'm I supposed to remember? Hell, Vics, it was something like to tell my mate she was in deep shit. Quote unquote.'

Vicki let the my mate slide. 'That's all he said? Didn't tell you anything more?'

'That's all I know.'

'More than me.'

'Which is why you've gotta talk to me about us.'

'You reckon?'

'I do. What's happened to us, Vics, since you got back from that Berlin trip?' Fish reaching out his hand, his fingers going through her hair to massage the nape of her neck.

She wanted to push back against his fingers, tell him, don't stop. Said, 'Fish, please.'

'You used to like it.'

'I'm driving. There's things we've got to do.'

'Like talk.'

Vicki didn't answer, let the kilometres pass in silence. Her thoughts on what she'd never know: the true story of her aunt Amina for one thing. She'd reached the end of that history. No one left to say yes or no to an old man's letter. An old man she probably couldn't trust anyhow. Whatever'd happened to Amina in Botswana, whatever it was she'd found out about stolen bullion or nuclear trades or armament kickbacks, the secrets'd died with her in that Metro station in Paris. Same with Zama, if he'd had secrets to tell, which she doubted. Zama was rubbish. His life a legend concocted by the grand spymaster, his father. The truth long ago forgotten, brushed under the palace's Persian carpets. No ways she could see him as blood family. No resemblance for starters. Just one of the president's peccadillo kiddies. End of that game.

At Trekkersburg phoned Henry Davidson. Said, 'You know what's happened?'

Was told, 'We're getting some reports.'

'You're getting some reports? That's all? Jesus, Henry, there was shooting. A bomb. It's the presidential palace. What about the president?'

'The situation's unclear at this time.' A pause. 'You're not still there, obviously.'

'Trekkersburg,' said Vicki.

'Good,' said Henry Davidson. 'Good. Drive home. Don't take the flight. There'll be too many complications at check-in. Police, that sort of thing. Drive home. Better if you're what they call in the wind for a while.'

'What're you saying, Henry? What's going on?'

'Internecine, my dear. Sharp knives and stealthy killers. We hit everything within reach whether we can see it or not, to misquote Tweedledum. You get my meaning?'

'And the girls?'

'Let the SAPS find them. They're looking already. I've told them.'

'The cops? What use have the cops ever been?'

She heard Henry Davidson mock gasp. 'I'm shocked and horrified, Vicki. How could you say such a thing? They're an integral part of our justice system. Now get out of Trekkersburg. Hole up in some small town for the night.'

45

Vicki drove north out of Trekkersburg, told Fish the gist of Davidson's warning.

They talked then in the long dark hours on the road. Vicki staying away from the one subject she'd buried. The secret she couldn't share.

'I had things on my plate, Fish.'

'What? That you couldn't tell me?'

'Yes. That I couldn't tell you. It's that sort of job.'

'Then give it up. Please. Go back to law.'

'I might,' she said. There, had voiced it. The realisation that'd come with Linda's shooting. This wasn't her life. Nor the life she wanted, the secrets and lies. Didn't want to work for a corrupt state. Didn't want to be part of the looting, the civil war.

'You might?' Fish's fingers at the back of her neck, massaging.

'I might.' Flashing him a smile in the dark. This time not telling him to stop. An ache in her body she'd long suppressed. Wanted the feel of Fish's skin beneath her palms. Wanted to scream: Gimme skin, babes, give me skin.

Drove off the dark plains into a Free State town, stopped at a small hotel, the Delerey. The rush on Vicki now, like she was gambling. Playing a bluff hand to high stakes.

'We're stopping here?' said Fish.

'It'll have a room, Fish, a bed, that's all I want.' Purposefully not looking at him, close to the point she'd drag him out of the car.

The hotel foyer smelt of mothballs. Prints on the walls of beach scenes. The only light a standing lamp on the reception desk. Its shade burnt brown near the globe.

'You don't have the baggage?' asked the night porter. Had his knobkerrie on the counter. A blackwood stick with a beaded hilt. Stroked his grey beard, glancing from Vicki to Fish.

Vicki signing them in, shook her head, didn't look up. 'They were stolen.' The lie coming easily. 'They mugged my partner.'

The old man's rheumy eyes on Fish. 'Hoh! You are strong. You must fight. You must protect your woman. Your beautiful woman.'

'Ja, indoda,' said Fish, 'it's not easy, hey.' Touched a quick hand to the bloody strip round his head.

Vicki put down the pen, picked up the room key. Took Fish's arm, feeling the muscles flex beneath her fingers, responding to her touch. Put the buzz on her, the anticipation of the surfer's body hard against her: skin on skin. Flicked her hair, said, 'He does his best, Tata. What else can a man do?'

In the quiet night the girls heard a car stop outside the warehouse. They were hungry. Scared. The little ones cried. Lay on the mattresses, curled on themselves. In a corner, an older girl rocked on her haunches, keening. During the long hours since they'd last seen the woman, a few had banged on the metal door with their fists. Had shouted. Until their voices died, their fists hurt. After that all had ached for their homes. For the mothers who had washed them; for the fathers who had held their hands. Had woken with the smell of woodsmoke, woken to the sultry heat, the smell of the toilets, their hunger, the pain of longing.

Then they heard the car. Heard it stop, a door bang closed. The whisper of footsteps approaching. The click of the lock opening. They cowered at the back of the warehouse, bunched together. The door opened, a man stood silhouetted against the light. A man they had not seen before. He stepped towards them, stopped. With his finger counted them. Looked at each one for a long time. An older girl said, 'Mister, mister.' The only English words she knew. In Portuguese she said they were hungry.

The man spoke, his voice soft. Took a step towards them. The girls pulled back. Again he spoke, held up his hands. Then he turned, went back into the dark.

The man brought them sandwiches, cooldrinks, water. Apples, bananas, chocolates, packets of sweets. Left these on the concrete floor. Spoke to them again in his soft voice. The girls stayed together, holding one another. Watched him wave at them, step through the door. Watched him drive away. At first they waited. When the man did not come back, they rushed for the food. There was enough for them all. When they had eaten, an older girl approached the door. Looked out. She turned to them, said there was no one in the street. No cars. The high mast lights casting shadows. Three of the older *girls left first. Took sandwiches, fruit, cans of Coke, walked into the hot night. The others watched them go, unsure. More left in the faint light of dawn. The youngest were the last to leave. They waited into the morning, dreaming of their other lives. Then ate again, and carried whatever they could into the day.*